RECORD OF REGRET

D1224689

CHINESE LITERATURE TODAY BOOK SERIES

RECORD OF REGRET

A Novel

DONG XI

Translated by DYLAN LEVI KING

UNIVERSITY OF OKLAHOMA PRESS : NORMAN

This book is published with the generous assistance of China's National Office for Teaching Chinese as a Foreign Language, Beijing Normal University's College of Chinese Language and Literature, the University of Oklahoma's College of Arts and Sciences, and *World Literature Today* magazine.

This book is a work of fiction. Names, characters, places, and incidents are either the product of the author's imagination or are used fictitiously, and any resemblance to actual events, locales, or persons, living or dead, is entirely coincidental.

Library of Congress Cataloging-in-Publication Data
Names: Dong, Xi, 1966– author. | King, Dylan Levi, translator.
　Title: Record of regret : a novel / Dong Xi ; translated by Dylan Levi King.
　Other titles: Hou hui lu. English
　Description: Norman : University of Oklahoma Press, [2018] | Series: Chinese
　　literature today book series ; Volume 7
　Identifiers: LCCN 2017038785 | ISBN 978-0-8061-6000-9 (pbk. : alk. paper)
　Subjects: LCSH: Regret—Fiction.
　Classification: LCC PL2914.N538 H6813 2018 | DDC 895.13/5—dc23
　LC record available at https://lccn.loc.gov/2017038785

Record of Regret: A Novel is Volume 7 in the Chinese Literature Today Book Series.

The paper in this book meets the guidelines for permanence and durability of the Committee on Production Guidelines for Book Longevity of the Council on Library Resources, Inc. ∞

1 2 3 4 5 6 7 8 9 10

TRANSLATOR'S NOTE

Dong Xi (b. 1966) began his literary career at an interesting time: a turning point in the 1980s when new ideas and literary theories were being introduced into Chinese academia. In addition to translations from the West, scholars within China were helping to feed the hunger for knowledge through book series like Translations of Academic Masterpieces, which has been published by Commercial Press since 1982. At the same time, writers were rediscovering ethnic and folk traditions (*xungen*, or "roots-seeking" literature). Literary journals popped up to serve this new generation of readers and writers, and Dong Xi began submitting work to southern Chinese magazines while still in his teens. By the late 1980s, at a small college in his native Guangxi, he was reading the important works of China's pre-Liberation time, including Shen Congwen and Lu Xun, and was also exposed to the Western literary canon, as well as recent work by writers like Mo Yan, Wang Anyi, and Can Xue.

It was after taking a post as a teacher in the remote Tian'e County of Guangxi in 1985 that Dong Xi began to find an outlet for his work, publishing a handful of stories under his original name, Tian Dailin, in small literary journals. In the early and mid-1990s, he finally broke into larger journals such as *Flower City* and *Chinese Writer*. Like the work of many of the writers in what Chinese literary critic Chen Xiaoming calls the "belated generation" (those who came of age in the 1990s), his prose is minimalist and severe, vacillating between sincerity and irony. Upon finding further literary success, Dong Xi resigned his rural post and published a string of well-received novels and novellas, including *A Slap to the Face* and *Belly's Memory*, and worked on several adaptations of his work to film and television, including *Sky Lovers* (adapted from *Life without Language*) and *Our Father*.

Dong Xi's book-length works take a form somewhere between critical realism, long-form jokes, and existentialist fables. His novels are indebted to the modes and concerns of Chinese realism. In fluid prose, he aptly describes certain conditions of existence that are usually overlooked in the Chinese novel, such as disability, depression, and male sexuality. *Record of Regret* reads at times like an elaborate joke told at the expense of its protagonist, Ceng Guangxian. Dong Xi is often described as a satirist, and *Record of Regret* can be read as satirical, even if the punchlines are buried deeper, the content is darker, and the concerns of the novel are more existentialist than political. In this and his other book-length works, he sinks his teeth in deeper than other Chinese satirical novelists of the same generation.

Dong Xi's fiction is unique, and difficult to define. Much of the Chinese literature that makes its way into English translation and is well received by Western readers tends to tread a line between vernacular and literary. Two traits that are particularly praised by Chinese critics are prose that is florid and full of allusions to classical literature, and prose that contains earthy dialogue that suggests authenticity. Some of the great works of Chinese literature that have made it into English translation fit this mold, such as Jia Pingwa's *Ruined City*. *Record of Regret*, in contrast, abandons flowery language, and although it is bleak and grimy, the scenes of everyday life ring true.

In translating *Record of Regret* into English, I have attempted to preserve the tightness and brevity of the language of the original, while maintaining the spirit of the work.

LIST OF CHARACTERS

Primary characters, listed in alphabetical order. Names are provided family name first, followed by given name.

Ceng Changfeng — father of Ceng Guangxian and Ceng Fang, husband of Wu Sheng; formerly the privileged son of a wealthy family who used the warehouse where his family now lives

Ceng Fang — younger sister of Ceng Guangxian

Ceng Guangxian — the main character in the novel; son of Ceng Changfeng and Wu Sheng

Chen Baixiu — wife of Zhao Laoshi; mother of Zhao Shanhe

Chi Fengxian, aka Xiao Chi — a classmate of Ceng Guangxian at the Number Five Middle School; daughter of a relatively wealthy family; later becomes an artist

Director He — director of the zoo where Ceng Guangxian's mother and then Guangxian himself work

Director Liang — aunt of Zhang Nao

Fan Laidi, aka Mimi — supervisor of the female employees at Yu Baijia's sauna

He Caixia — a gossipy woman with designs on Ceng Guangxian; daughter of Director He

Hou Zhi — a prisoner at the Beishan "Reform through Labor" Tractor Plant; a serial rapist

Hu Kaihui — coworker of Ceng Guangxian at the zoo

Jia Wenping — warden at the Beishan "Reform through Labor" Tractor Plant

Li Dapao — prisoner at the Beishan "Reform through Labor" Tractor Plant; convicted of rape

Liu Canghai	coworker of Ceng Changfeng at the Number Three Loudspeaker Factory
Lu Xiaoyan	coworker of Ceng Guangxian at the zoo
Luo Xiaoyun	Li Dapao's victim and later his wife
Rong Guangming	student and class monitor at the Number Five Middle School
Wu Sheng	mother of Ceng Guangxian and Ceng Fang, wife of Ceng Changfeng; employed at the zoo
Yu Baijia	student at the Number Five Middle School; friend of Ceng Guangxian
Zhang Du	professor at Lingnan University and attorney for Zhang Nao (although Zhang Nao and Zhang Du later marry, the shared surname is coincidental)
Zhang Nao	performer with the provincial propaganda team; head of the Dongfang Construction Materials Corporation
Zhao Jingdong	coworker of Ceng Guangxian at the zoo; cousin of Zhang Nao
Zhao Laoshi	father of Zhao Shanhe and Zhao Wannian; former servant of the Ceng family; lives with his wife, Chen Baixiu, in the warehouse
Zhao Shanhe	daughter of Zhao Laoshi and Chen Baixiu; begins a relationship with Ceng Changfeng that continues until her middle age
Zhao Wannian	principal at the Number Five Middle School, and leader of a Red Guard faction; later becomes director of the Tiema District Revolutionary Committee

RECORD OF REGRET

‹ 1 ›

If you don't mind, I'll get started.

Now, when this story began, I still had curly hair and my voice had just changed. I wasn't even shaving yet. I remember my dad always said that you can't trust anyone with smooth cheeks.

Like I said, this was a long time ago, when things were very different than they are now. You know, nowadays there are a million things to do to kill time. We didn't have TV, and of course we didn't have the internet. The streets were pretty empty because there was nowhere to go: the teahouses had all been shut down, and there weren't any coffee shops like there are now. You can forget about dance halls. And don't even think about asking about saunas or massage joints. Basically, we went to school and we went to the struggle sessions, where they'd criticize class enemies or just common criminals. Sometimes our teachers would organize us to sing the Communist Party anthems that were popular back then. There wasn't a lot going on. Even our school was a lot different from the schools kids go to now. We didn't learn much, I'm saying. Nowadays, kids get sexual education class, right? But my first sex ed class was taught by two dogs.

The two dogs were in front of the warehouse. I saw them before anybody else did. They were mounting each other at first, but then they became stuck. They were stuck ass-to-ass. When I went over, they panted and looked up at me, as if asking for a hand with getting unstuck. My dad eventually came out and held one of the dogs still. He reached over and grabbed one of the bamboo mats that were drying in front of the warehouse. Yu Baijia came over with another mat, and they formed a wall around the dogs so they couldn't make a break for it. Yu Baijia started calling people out of the warehouse: "Come one, come all! Five cents a ticket!" Yu Baijia's parents came first. Their names were Yu Fare and Fang Haitang. The next two to come out were Uncle Zhao and his wife, Chen Baixiu. Everyone was pointing at the dogs trapped behind the mats. I remember the sounds of their laughter, all those distinct laughs that I knew so well. I remember their mouths, too, mouths open in howls of laughter, white and yellow and black teeth slick with spit. I will never forget Uncle Zhao's rotten black teeth as he roared with laughter, or the way Auntie Chen's eyes creased up when she laughed, or the way my dad seemed to soak everyone around him with spittle when he tipped his head back to laugh. The dogs were scared and looked up pathetically. The female dog started to go around in a circle, the male dog bumping along behind her.

You might not know this, but back then it was hard to find anything to laugh about. Nowadays, people want to make money. A full bank account or a bunch of cash under your mattress is what you want. But what everyone was looking for in those days was something to laugh at, something to make them happy. This was like a lottery win, I guess, those dogs bumping along, stuck together. Everyone was filling their bank accounts. The laughter ended abruptly when Zhao Shanhe came out through the warehouse door. She pointed at my father: "Who do those mats belong to?" Uncle Zhao and Auntie Chen tried to hide their smiles, but they burst into laughter.

Zhao Shanhe was Uncle Zhao and Auntie Chen's daughter. At the time, she was working at a munitions factory in the suburbs. She was shaped like a particularly lumpy rubber ball. Especially up top! Even at the big department store downtown, she hadn't been able to find a bra that fit her.

My dad said, sternly: "Shanhe, we're dying here. Give us a break. Let's have a little show tonight, then, eh? We can put up a stage."

"Where did those mats come from? How about you go inside and get your own mats and set up a stage?"

"How do you know these aren't my mats? And maybe this is my dog, too."

Zhao Shanhe looked down at the dogs, frowning. Finally, she laughed, too, harder than anyone else. Her older brother, Zhao Wannian, who was just arriving home on his bike, saw his sister and the others overcome with laughter. When he saw the object of their amusement, he went around tapping them on their foreheads. Zhao Wannian said: "You've got to be careful. This isn't something you should be laughing about. You're going to get yourselves in trouble."

Zhao Wannian was the principal at the Number Five Middle School. It's not that he was particularly well-read. He wasn't an intellectual, by any means. Some recalled him stumbling over a not particularly difficult couplet in one of the Chairman's poems, the one that goes: "The mountains dance like silver snakes / And the highlands charge like wax-hued elephants." But he was given the position primarily because of his unimpeachable working-class credentials. When Zhao Wannian arrived, the fun was over. Silence fell; faces paled. The mats were hung back up. Zhao

Wannian called: "Bring me a big stick." I rushed into the warehouse and came back with a wooden rod. Zhao Wannian took the rod and advanced on the dogs. He raised the rod and brought it down with a fierce chop on the lump of flesh connecting them. The dogs yelped. They ran for the street as fast as they could, marching in step as if somebody were calling rhythm for them. As the dogs crossed the middle of the road, a bus roared into view. The next thing I heard was a sound like a fist striking a gong as the dogs were smacked by the bull bars of the bus. The sound was still echoing in the street as the tires of the bus rolled over the dogs and spread their blood and guts in the road. Even flattened in the dust, I could see that they were still stuck together.

Tears came to my eyes. My father put the dogs on a mat and dragged them back to the front of the warehouse. Yu Baijia got another wooden rod and helped Zhao Wannian hang them up in the tree in front of the warehouse. The dogs hung from the lump of flesh that still connected them. I felt like I was seeing double. It looked like a dog looking at itself in the mirror.

Zhao Wannian pointed at the dogs: "Don't think this is their fault. Who was behind all this? Let them hang there as a message: spreading sexual depravity is even more serious than passing around pornography. Spread that message."

My father hung his head and walked back into the warehouse. The group stood motionless. The gap in the crowd was filled by my mother, who had just come back from work. When Zhao Wannian saw my mother, I noticed his eyes flick over her. My mother's name was Wu Sheng. She was from a good family. She understood things like calligraphy, and she could play instruments and had learned embroidery, things like that. But her reputation was more for being beautiful than it was for writing calligraphy or embroidering flowers. After Liberation, my mother had changed her worldview and joined the cause. She took a job at the zoo and worked hard, taking care of the animals. Zhao Wannian looked at my mother and said: "Let everyone who witnessed this scene of animals copulating write a report and self-criticism. I want it in my hands in three days."

People began to drift away. Uncle Zhao walked away, too, spitting one last time in the dirt. Finally, Zhao Wannian was left standing under the tree looking at four of his students from the Number Five Middle School. It was me, Yu Baijia, Xiao Chi, and Rong Guangming. As we walked away, he called after us, repurposing a bit of martial doggerel: "When danger confronts us, we must have our sworn brothers by our side! Going into battle, there is only the teacher and his pupils!" He said to us: "Listen, maybe they won't write it, but I know you will. I want you to show them how it's done. I will choose the best essay to read during the school's morning announcements."

I should say a few things about the warehouse, I guess. My grandfather was a capitalist. It was his warehouse. His business was medicine—the new Western medicine, not traditional Chinese medicine. In 1949, the warehouse, along with the rest of my grandfather's property, was taken over by the new government led by the Chinese Communist Party. He decided that it was probably best to get out of town, so he packed a few things into an old suitcase and went to the train station. He was planning to go back to the village where he was born. When the new mayor heard about my grandfather skipping town, he sent two of his officials down to the train station. The mayor intervened and got hold of the confiscation order. He decided to give the warehouse back to my grandfather. It sounds better than it really was, because his beautiful home was already occupied by the municipal government. At least he had a place to live, though. But some grumbled when they pictured the old capitalist still holding on to his massive warehouse. Two other families were sent to live in the warehouse as well. Uncle Zhu's family moved in, and so did Yu Fare's family. Back before Liberation, the Yu family had worked as housekeepers and accountants for my grandfather. The Zhao family had been his servants, working in the warehouse. I wasn't even born yet, though, and I heard all of this while eavesdropping on conversations between adults. My grandfather died before I was born. I'm not really sure exactly what happened back then. But it stayed with me somehow, that legacy. It was like the curls in my hair or the mole on my sister's hand. No matter how hard I brushed or how hard she scraped, there was nothing we could do. That mark, the mark of capitalist ancestry, it was like a hat set on your head, and the hat was as tall as a ten-story building. No one could stand up straight with that kind of weight on your skull. Have you ever seen *Prime Minister Hunchback Liu?* It was like that. You'd always have your head forced down. You'd be staring down at your feet all the time because you couldn't lift your head up.

Hey!

I was supposed to be talking about the warehouse. Let me get back on track.

The warehouse was divided into three homes by walls made of red brick. Each home had bedrooms and a living room and bathrooms and whatnot. The only things that were shared were the toilets and the ceiling. The toilets were out back. There were five pits: three for men and two for women. The ceiling was shared, too, because the walls that were used to divide the warehouse were only about ten feet tall. All the sounds of the families in the warehouse floated up and met and mixed under the eaves and tiles.

The day the dogs got hung up in the tree, we had sweet potato and pumpkin for dinner. My father ate a few bites and then set down his chopsticks. He picked up the cleaver and said: "I should go skin that dog. Braised dog sounds really good."

I shouted back: "I won't eat dog!"

He flicked the cleaver and said: "What are you worried about? It's good for you."

"It's all your fault," I said. "If you hadn't put the mat around them, the dogs wouldn't have died."

"Hey, those dogs ran in front of a bus. How is that my fault?"

"It's your fault! You could have let them go. Principal Zhao wouldn't have seen them. If Principal Zhao hadn't seen them, he wouldn't have hit them with a stick. And if he hadn't hit them with a stick, they wouldn't have run in front of the bus."

"All right, then. Let me ask you: who gave the wooden rod to Zhao Wannian?"

That shut me up. I was the one who had handed him the stick, right? Why did I run over to get it for him? Maybe if I had just stood there, the dogs would still be alive.

"Be careful trying to place blame, or it might come back to you," my father said, and then went out the front door. My mother smacked her chopsticks down on the table. She shouted after him: "You always want to place the blame on somebody else, too. It's never your fault! If you eat that filthy thing, I'm getting a divorce." My father shouted something back at her, and I listened to them argue back and forth about eating the meat that was hanging in the tree. My father sat back down and took up his chopsticks. He swallowed a mouthful of pumpkin and chewed. He sat silent while my mother babbled on: "You know, the zoo just got a tiger. That tiger, it is one of the fiercest tigers you could imagine. They just caught it a little while ago, right out of the jungle. Anyways, the head zookeeper decided to give it a really feminine name. I forget what it was, something like Lan Lan, but—"

She was cut off by another voice echoing down from the ceiling of the warehouse: "If you don't wash, don't ever look at me again. I'm worried you'll pass that filth to me." It was Zhao Wannian's voice. I jumped up from the table and ran to the door of the Zhao family's part of the warehouse. Yu Baijia met me there. There was a basin of water on the Zhao family's dinner table. Zhao Wannian was telling Zhao Shanhe to wash her eyes.

Zhao Shanhe said: "I've never heard of anyone washing their eyes before they eat!" Zhao Wannian grabbed her by her hair and forced her toward the basin of water. She twisted away from him, splashing water on his pants. "What the hell are you trying to do? You want to practice what you're going to do in your struggle sessions?"

"How dare you talk to me that way! You were right there with them, watching those dogs." Zhao Wannian tried to brush his legs dry.

"Dad saw it. Mom saw it. Auntie Fang saw it. All those kids saw it. Why wouldn't I have seen it? I saw what they were doing." Zhao Shanhe ranted and sobbed, loud enough to shake the tiles on the warehouse roof.

"You know they're nothing but the descendants of capitalists. I expect it of them, but what about you? You are pure working class—and you're a girl!"

"That doesn't mean I'm not human, does it?"

"A girl is like a sheet of clean white paper. It's very easy to stain that paper with dirty things."

"I like dirty things. I don't want to be a sheet of white paper. I really, really want to be stained. What are you going to do about it?" Zhao Shanhe spun on her heel and walked into her bedroom, slamming the door behind her.

Zhao Wannian had never heard anything so shocking in his life. This was supposed to be the dictatorship of the proletariat, and the loyal comrade hadn't expected that kind of ideological struggle from his own sister. He fell back, clutching at the wall. He grabbed for a picture frame and knocked it to the floor while trying to stand up. The glass in the frame was shattered. Under the threads of cracked glass was a picture of his sister. He looked down at the picture, and a thought came to him: I have to lead a powerful struggle session, the most powerful yet, and attack the depraved thoughts stirred up by those dogs. He went to his father to discuss the proposed struggle session. Uncle Zhao spat in the dust and said: "Ah, my esteemed principal, who seems to think only of new ways of stringing people up, I wish you had something else to do. Whatever you do, keep it away from the warehouse. Out of sight, out of mind." Zhao Wannian mumbled something about the evils of the capitalists and their descendants. He vowed never to ask his father for advice again. He'd never give his father advice again, either. He'd let his father run into a wall before he said anything! Let him fall on his face.

That night, I heard my father tossing and turning. When I looked over, his ass had slipped out from under his blanket, and he was scratching furiously at it. Maybe it was hemorrhoids. I don't know. I heard him speaking to my mother in a voice like you'd use to ask for a loan: "Just one time, Comrade Wu Sheng. Come on."

"You're worse than those dogs."

"Just one time. I can't sleep with these thoughts going through my head. I knew you were awake. I promise, just one time."

"I'd rather you just put a knife in my chest. I want to be clean. Imagine a pair of brand-new white tennis shoes. I'm that clean. If you're my comrade and you really believe in the revolution, you'll keep your muddy paws off me."

My father sighed, got out of bed, and went out the front door of the warehouse. He sat by the door until morning brought the first slivers of sunrise to his red eyes. He shook himself, sneezed, and pinched a few ants that had climbed his calf. The first broadcast of the morning came over the PA. The broadcast brought some life back to him. It wasn't the revolutionary fervor of the announcement but the technical marvel of the PA. He had installed it himself, actually. I guess he felt like he was still of some use to the world. I probably forgot to mention my dad's job. He worked in a workshop at the Number Three Loudspeaker Factory. He had installed the loudspeaker in the warehouse. As he sat there, the sky brightened, and the street came alive with the sound of street sweepers and the bells and brakes of tricycles going back and forth. The gray shape in the yard resolved into a tree, and then he could see the branches in the tree and the leaves on the branches. When the sun was almost up, he could finally see the dead dogs hanging in the tree.

My dad thought maybe he'd take the day off and wait for my mom to go to work. He wanted to get those dogs down from the tree and cook up lunch for himself. He was going to braise the choice cuts in a broth of soy sauce with cane sugar and star anise. But my mom wasn't dumb. She saw him sitting in front of the warehouse staring up at the dogs. She cut the dogs down herself and wrapped them in a burlap sack. She said: "I'm going to take them to the zoo. We'll feed them to the tiger. Maybe they'll give me some money for the meat." She tossed the burlap sack across her bike and went down the road with the dogs bouncing on the handlebars. My father watched her go and then went back inside the house and washed his face. He said: "If I can't eat those dogs, I might as well go to work."

That day when my mom came home, she was carrying a paper box. The first person she saw was Fang Haitang. My mom went over to where Fang Haitang was pulling clothes down from the line. She told her about feeding the dogs to the tiger. Fang Haitang sneezed. "I think I'm getting a cold," she said. Uncle Zhao walked out of the warehouse, and my mom told him the story, too. He puffed at his pipe and brushed past her, headed to the store on the road.

Nobody seemed very interested in the story, and she couldn't figure out why. She felt a bit disappointed and stood for a while in front of the warehouse, holding the paper box. It was Zhao Wannian who finally offered some praise. When he came home and heard the story, he patted her shoulder and said: "Good job, comrade." As Zhao Wannian went inside, my mother felt the weight of the box in her hand. The box was full of soap.

I mean, you know she wasn't just going to tell the story a few times and shut up about it, right? The story of the tiger eating the dogs was told countless times. She never got tired of it, even if other people did. That night when we sat down around the dinner table, she started telling us about how the tiger pounced on the dead dogs. The tiger tore into the dogs and then tossed them up into the air. She said when the dogs tumbled back down, it was like she was watching it in slow motion. It was only when the dogs hit the ground again that they finally came apart. I don't really remember much of the actual story, but I remember how she told it. She took pleasure in it, cutting the air with her hands while she spoke. The story seemed to burn somewhere deep inside her. I remember that first time she told it, my dad asked her: "What about the money? You could have gotten us some pork. That would have made it all worth it." That shut her up right away. It seemed like the fire that had burned in her went out. For a while she didn't say anything, and then she told us about the soap. My father said: "What the hell did you buy so much soap for? I wanted to eat some meat!"

"Look at how dirty everything is. Look at these kids. Look at your collar. The mosquito nets are filthy. I don't even know if this is enough soap. I might need to buy more. You can't worry about meat when everything is so dirty. Everything! Every part of you: your earlobes are dirty, your fingernails are dirty. You can't be clean inside if you're dirty outside."

When I came home from school, I started soaping up my hair. I would lather the soap and spread the frothy bubbles over my head. After the soap was worked in, I'd run my fingers through my hair, trying to pull it straight. Sometimes I'd pull at my hair until my fingers hurt, and I'd get Ceng Fang to help me. I worked at it until my scalp felt like it was going to come right off. After I was done pulling, I'd let the soap dry on my hair. The soap left my hair straight. It was like women use hairspray. I wanted to straighten my hair, but Ceng Fang mostly wanted to wash her hands. She scraped the soap off my head and put it back in the basin and whipped it into a big, cottony mess. Her hands were white, but she could never wash the mole off her palm. She asked me why she couldn't wash her hands clean.

"That's your own skin. You can't wash it off."

She wouldn't believe me. It was like we were in a competition to waste soap. She wasted it on the mole on her palm, and I wasted it on my hair. After a while, I gave up and got a haircut, and there wasn't enough hair to really curl.

In preparation for the struggle session, I got my essay about the dogs ready. My mom helped me. I really threw myself into it. Every word of it was like an artillery shell—I could have launched an attack on Taiwan with all those rockets ready to lift off the page. I used phrases like "guilty of the most heinous crimes," "corrupting public morals," "evil beyond redemption," and stuff like that. It was all the phrases I saw on the public bulletin boards, attacking class criminals and rapists. But Zhao Wannian seemed to be too busy to collect the essays. He didn't even come back to the warehouse that week and spent his nights at his simple apartment connected to the school. At school I noticed him skulking about, but I never got a chance to talk to him.

That weekend, my mom had me and Ceng Fang wash the mosquito nets that we hung over our beds. We rinsed them with soap and then spread them out to dry. The water dripping down into the dirt made wet rectangles in the dust beneath them. It was a hot day, and when the water stopped dripping into the dust, the netting seemed to steam in the sunlight. I thought I could hear a sound like water in a hot pan. Ceng Fang shook the mosquito nets and splashed water in every direction, ruining the muddy rectangles under them. I looked up from the nets and saw that Zhao Wannian was coming up the road, his forehead dripping with sweat and his face frozen in a grimace.

Zhao Wannian entered the house. There was silence from inside. That wasn't like the Zhao house. It wasn't long before a sound from within broke the silence: "Give me that!" It was Zhao Shanhe. It was followed by the sound of someone kicking a piece of furniture.

"So, this is what you had under the covers with you every night. You know, I actually thought you were memorizing Marx, maybe Lenin, whatever. But this—this I can't even look at without blushing. Every sentence is perverted! You're wasting your time with this shit, and you plan on becoming a workshop director?"

We heard the sound of brother and sister fighting over something and Zhao Shanhe shouting: "Give it back!"

"Sure, I'll give it back. I'll give it back right after you tell me who gave you this piece of filth."

We heard the sound of struggle again. There was a sudden crash of broken glass. We heard running back and forth. Doors were slammed and shoes were flung. We heard Zhao Wannian cry out: "Why did you bite me?" We heard a sound that could only be a hard slap to the face. We heard Zhao Shanhe sobbing.

Zhao Wannian walked out of the warehouse shielding his face with a letter. He stood in the shade of the mosquito nets and began to skim the contents. The nets were dry now and fluttered in the midafternoon breeze. We stood beside the warehouse door and watched him. After scanning the letter for a few minutes, he waved us over and motioned for us to come behind the shade of the netting. The breeze strengthened, and the mosquito nets hid us in a gauzy dusk. The people who had come to the warehouse door to look into the yard could barely see us. He held the letter out to me and asked me: "Have a look. Looks like your father's handwriting, huh?" I looked; I shook my head.

"Maybe it's Yu Fare's."

"I don't know."

He held the letter up to his nose and furrowed his brow. "Then who the hell wrote it? They had balls, I'll give them that. Have your mom and dad been fighting?"

I nodded.

"About what?"

"My dad wants to do something with my mom—just one time! But she won't do it."

"That sounds about right. Could you get your dad to write a few characters with his left hand?"

"You want him to write some of the characters from the letter, right?"

He nodded. He scanned the letter.

"Should I get him to write 'Beloved Shanhe'?"

"Hell no. Just get him to write . . . 'Thinking of the Motherland,' that's it. And remember, he has to use his left hand. Don't tell anyone about this, either. You want to get a red armband, don't you?"

I nodded and took from my pocket the essay I had written about the dogs. He looked down at it and said: "What's wrong with you? I was just trying to scare them. I didn't think anyone would actually write an essay." He crumpled the paper and tossed it. I picked it back up. It was a shame, I thought. It was a hell of an essay, and he'd barely even looked it. He was the one who had told me he was going to read the best essay over the school's PA.

I started watching my father's hands after that. The left hand wasn't much different from the right hand, I realized. They looked about the same size, and they had the same network of veins straining the thin skin of their backs. The knuckles had the same black hairs across them, and the nails had the same black dirt under them. The left hand did a lot, but I never saw him write with it. He'd stuff it down his pants or scratch his armpit with it. When he ate, he'd hold his bowl with his left hand. He'd hold pieces of fruit while shaving the peels off them. He did a lot with his left hand, but I sure never saw him write with it.

Looking at my father's left hand all the time caused some strange sensation to come over me, and I started using my own left hand a lot more. I'd use it to hold my spoon when I was eating soup. One day I ate my lunch with my chopsticks in my left hand. I hung my backpack on my left shoulder instead of my right. Somehow, in a few days, I figured out how to do just about everything with my left hand. Actually, I'm still left-handed even now. My dad noticed first, and he took a pen out of my left hand and said: "Since when are you a leftist?" I took the pen back and tried to write with my right hand, but I couldn't do it. I was writing the same phrase over and over again with my left hand, four characters: "Thinking of the Motherland." My dad looked at my handwriting and grabbed the pen from me. "Your left hand is too weak. Watch this." With his left hand, he wrote the same phrase: "Thinking of the Motherland."

I used a knife to cut out the section of paper my dad had written on, and I put it inside an envelope. I thought maybe that wasn't safe enough, so I wrapped the envelope in a plastic bag, and then I put the plastic bag inside a book and put the book in my schoolbag and hid the schoolbag, too. And then I got into bed and hid under the covers.

I tried to sleep, but the sound of my father snoring would jolt me wide awake. I crept over to where I had hidden the schoolbag and carried it back to my bed. I slid it under my pillow. I felt like I could feel the piece of paper through the pillow and through the schoolbag and through the plastic bag and through the envelope. That was the only way I could get to sleep. It was like taking a sleeping pill. I was out in minutes.

The next day, I went to Zhao Wannian's office. I set the strip of paper down on his desk. His eyes flashed as he picked it up. He pulled the letter out of the front pocket of his jacket. He took a pair of scissors and cut the strip of paper in half, so that "Thinking of" was separated from "the

Motherland." Those were the characters he needed. He held the scrap with "Thinking of" up to the letter. I saw his eyes darting from side to side. He looked up at me: "Altogether, there are nine 'thinking of's in the letter. Four of them match your father's writing. Have a look." I looked down at the letter. "Am I right?"

"Maybe a bit. I'm not sure."

"I can't decide, either. This will require an expert analysis. Your job will be to watch your father. If you notice anything different about him, I want you to tell me right away."

My dad slept through most of the night, but he'd always wake up early in the morning and go into the kitchen and drink water. He'd drink cold water from a jug that was on the kitchen table. He said he was overheating. He said his body felt like it was on fire. Uncle Yu from next door would sometimes tell me how many jugs he heard my father drinking. He was that loud! You could hear the water gurgling down his throat. That wouldn't wake me up, but one time I heard him shout at somebody: "Can you keep it down? How do you expect me to live with that noise?"

I listened for the sound, too. It seemed to echo through the entire warehouse. I sat up and tried to hear better. It was the sound of Auntie Fang. It sounded like she was in pain or something. It was like the pain was really intense sometimes, and then the thing that was hurting her moved away and her moans softened. Sometimes she whimpered, "Ai ya, ai ya," and sometimes she just grunted. Auntie Fang's bed creaked along with her in a sympathetic chorus. I'd only heard a bed creak like that when somebody was sick or in pain or something like that and they were rolling around. I heard my dad go to my mom and shake her and say: "You hear that? Listen. Listen to what they're doing." My mom kept sleeping. My dad patted her on the thigh one last time and then went out the door.

Most nights, my father would go outside to the cistern in the yard and drench himself in cold water. He would let the water run down his body for a long time, trying to quench the fire inside him. After he was done, he'd sit down on a stone bench and let himself dry in the night air. He started to measure time in cigarettes. He smoked Jingji-brand cigarettes, one after another. He told me one time that smoking couldn't get rid of the black thoughts, but you could chase away the light gray ones, at least, the annoying thoughts that hovered like mosquitoes around your ears. Uncle Yu would come out like clockwork for a piss. Most nights he'd go out the back door of the warehouse to the shared toilets. But sometimes he'd go out the front door and piss under the big tree. It saved a few steps.

When he saw my father sucking on a glowing red butt, he'd never say anything and would slink past like a stray dog.

But one night my father saw Uncle Yu pissing under the tree and called out to him: "Cang Shan." Uncle Yu seemed unable to keep the stream going. He looked back at my father and stammered: "M-master?" That was what they would have called each other before Liberation. Before the revolution, Uncle Yu was my grandfather's accountant, and my father was the young master of the household. Cang Shan had changed his name after Liberation. He thought he needed a name with a bit more revolutionary spirit, so he chose Fare, which meant to give off heat. Uncle Yu pulled up his shorts and went over to my father.

"It's been so long," my father sighed. "Can't you be a bit quieter? Tell Haitang not to be so loud. That sound is like the smell of roasting meat to a vegetarian. It's torture. I don't think I can handle it."

"That fuckin' bitch can't shut her trap. I put a pillow over her face the last time."

"I mean, don't suffocate her."

"That's the way it is, living here. Nobody has any secrets. If we all lived apart, you could say whatever you wanted. I could put a megaphone right up to her mouth."

They talked for a while, and then Uncle Yu turned to go. My father called him back: "Cang Shan . . ."

"What is it now?"

My father started to speak and then hesitated and said: "Forget it. Go on to bed."

"What is it? You're a little short this month? You're going to ask for a loan?"

"It's not that. It's . . . something else. But—I don't know how to say it."

"So you don't want to borrow money or what?"

"This is something worse. It's like I have a scar and I'm ripping open my shirt to show somebody. It's just, since Wu Sheng joined the study sessions, she's changed. She thinks I'm dirty somehow. It's been about ten years now. Hearing you and Haitang, I realize it's been a long time since we . . . I feel like if I hear it again, I won't be able to take it."

"I've heard you and Wu Sheng fighting, but I wasn't sure what it was about. How did she end up like this?"

"She just thinks it's dirty. Or at least it's dirty according to whoever teaches those study sessions. She thinks it's below her. She hasn't listened to a thing I've said. All this time, and I don't think I ever got through to her. But whoever teaches these fucking study sessions, she'll do whatever they say."

"Maybe there's some kind of medicine or something you could give her."

"I've tried everything. Sometimes I wonder if it's even worth living. Help me, Cang Shan."

"How the hell am I supposed to help you? It's not like you're asking for help sweeping the yard or something."

My father got on his knees in front of Uncle Yu. "I'm begging you. You're the only one who can help me."

"I know what you're thinking, and I can't do it."

"Just one time! Talk to Haitang for me. I'll do anything to repay you, right into my next life."

Uncle Yu turned and walked so fast that he sent gravel flying. My father stayed on his knees for a long time.

A few days later, Uncle Yu came to my father with a paper box: "I had somebody get this for you from an old doctor who works on Sanhe Road. It's traditional medicine, might let you get some rest. You only need to take it twice a month." My father took a whiff of the box and then threw it against the windowsill. Uncle Yu bent and began sweeping the spilled herbs into the crushed box.

"If you don't want to help me, that's fine. Don't give me this junk, though. You could kill me."

"Come on. You can't be sitting awake all night. That can't be good for you."

"Thank you for thinking about me. I'm sorry."

"If there's anything else you need, I'll do my best. But I can't help you with that. That's a favor I can't do for you. "

"Our family used to help everyone who came to them. Even the beggars who came to the door, we'd never let them go away empty-handed. There are good people in the world. Not everybody is like you."

Over the following week, my father began to get some color in his cheeks again. He began to sleep through the night. I could hear his snores loud and clear. He stopped getting out of bed in the early morning. He took to humming folk songs to himself when he made dinner. I wondered if he'd taken the traditional medicine that Yu Fare had brought, but it seemed he hadn't.

If it hadn't been for the sparrow, my father would probably have stayed like that, happily humming over the steam from the rice pot. But that sparrow kept chirping at me from the tiles of the warehouse. It must have been a female sparrow. That's how women treat you, taunting you from just out of your reach. I didn't think that way then. I just wanted to catch that damn sparrow. When it came down to the lower levels of the warehouse, I tried catching it, sneaking along behind it and trying to snatch it with my hands. It would hop away, taunting me again. I held my breath and moved as slowly as I could toward the sparrow. I leapt at it and missed, smacking my nose on the ground. Finally, I picked up a rock and threw it hard at the little bird. The sparrow looked back once and then flapped up to a nest somewhere in the eaves.

‹ 3 ›

I went up after the sparrow, getting myself up onto the wall that separated our rooms in the warehouse. I shimmied up one of the wooden posts that held up the warehouse and reached the eaves. I put my hand into the sparrow's nest. The two birds in the mud nest flapped wildly and shot out between my fingers. I grabbed back onto the post and tried to steady myself. Like I said, the warehouse was divided into rooms occupied by three families, but they were only separated by walls. From up on the post, I could look down into all the rooms. I was right above the Yu family's rooms and the mosquito net over the bed, the cabinets in the bedroom. I could see Uncle Zhao in his living room, pulling on a pipe. When he exhaled, the smoke wrapped around his face and neck like a scarf.

When I looked over to Zhao Shanhe's room, I saw my father. He was asleep, right on top of her! I shivered, and the hairs on the back of my neck stood up. It felt like the warehouse was shaking, and I reached up for a tile to steady myself. The tile slipped from its place in the eaves and crashed down right in front of Uncle Zhao. It smashed into a thousand pieces, and Uncle Zhao looked up. "Who's there?" I saw my father roll off of Zhao Shanhe and grab for something to cover himself. He looked up, too. They might not have been able to see my face up against the eaves, but I could see them.

Uncle Zhao ran out of his house and looked up the post. "It's you, huh? You little bastard. I'm going to deal with you."

My father came out next and stood there, waving a bamboo switch menacingly. "Come down from there!"

I stood in the eaves, shaking like a leaf. Uncle Zhao took the switch out of my dad's hand. He snapped it in half and tossed it on the ground. "Don't scare the boy."

I went back to the post and wrapped my hands around it. I was going to slide down, but my hands were numb. I couldn't get a grip on the post. Uncle Zhao saw me shaking and called up: "Guangxian! Just hold on. Don't be afraid. Just hold on and slide down. That's right. Both hands. Yep, yep. Hold on with your legs, too. Don't worry. Your Uncle Zhao used to climb up there, too, when I was a kid. I used to catch sparrows to give to your grandpa. We used to roast them, and he'd have them with his liquor. Sometimes he'd let us have a few cups with him. Yep, keep coming."

I followed Uncle Zhao's instructions and slid down the post. My feet hadn't even touched the ground before my dad grabbed me by the ear. "What did you see?"

"I saw you naked."

He twisted my ear hard between his fingers: "Tell me exactly what you saw."

I reached up to my ear with both hands. I started to cry.

"Tell me! Stop crying and tell me. Tell me exactly what you saw."

"I didn't see anything!"

"Exactly. You didn't see anything. Remember that, or I'll knock out your teeth."

My father relaxed his pinch on my ear. The side of my head felt like it was on fire. Uncle Zhao brought me back to his living room. He poured salve on a cotton ball and wiped it on my ear. He said: "You're an adult now. As of today. When I was your age, I had already almost starved to death twice. I was out on the street. The last time, I ended up at your grandfather's door, and he took me in. I take that very seriously. I remember what your grandfather did for me. Nowadays, things are different. My class background is good. I was a poor worker. But I'm not going to go looking for revenge. If somebody feeds me, I'll pay them back when I can. I did it for your family and for your father's health. He can't take it anymore. If he can't go on living, if he tosses himself into the river, what would you and your mother do? I can't explain what I owe your father and his family. I hope you can understand. I need you to keep this secret. Don't tell anybody what you saw today."

Uncle Zhao pressed hard with the cotton ball, sending a tingle of pain through my body. I looked up and saw that somebody was watching us. It was Zhao Shanhe. She was leaning in the doorway, cracking sunflower seeds. She spat the shells toward me, and they accumulated on the floor of the living room. Her face was calm. She was wearing a new dress. You'd have thought she'd just wandered in from outside and nothing had happened. One of the shells hit Uncle Zhao, and he turned back to her: "Get out of here. Lounging around like the emperor's concubine . . ." She turned and went out the front door.

When you know somebody's secret, it changes you. When you look at them, you feel your heart beating faster. It's like the secret is a drumbeat in your chest, and you're always worried somebody is going to hear it. I started drinking water like my father used to. I could drink two big jugs full, pour them right down my throat. Back then, I really thought my father was a cruel man. I couldn't understand how he could do something like that. How could he put that kind of burden on me? I was fifteen years old.

My father started not coming home some nights. He'd always have an excuse: a meeting at his factory or an extra night shift, or they were working on a new type of PA loudspeaker that would be louder and clearer than the ones they'd made before. He became a member of the strategic planning group at the factory, which gave him even more reason to be out of the house. But my mother didn't seem to mind. She was always in a better mood when he wasn't there. One night, she sent me and Ceng Fang to take a bath and made sure we scrubbed ourselves even cleaner than usual. When we came back into the living room, she had put out new underclothes for us to wear. The shirts and shorts were pearly white, and we didn't even want to sit down. My mother said: "Come on. Have a seat. I just scrubbed those benches." We sat down, and she examined us. "I want to show you something."

She went into the bathroom and came out wearing her white pajamas. The pajamas weren't new; there were a few stray threads around the collar, but they were even whiter than our new shirts and shorts. We looked up expectantly. "Are you ready?" We sat with our hands on our knees. A mosquito bit my cheek, and I didn't even smack it away.

My mother produced a wooden box that held a single bottle of perfume. "Not a word," she said. She took the bottle from the box and put a drop of perfume on each of us.

"It smells so good," Ceng Fang said.

My mother sighed with pleasure. It was the first time I had ever smelled perfume. She put a few drops of it on herself. "Every time I smell this, it reminds me of being young." We pressed close to our mother, sucking in the smell. We didn't want to waste a single drop.

"This is petty bourgeois thinking. If you say anything about it, you'll be criticized. But I made an exception today. Do you know why?"

We shook our heads.

"Because Guangxian turns sixteen today."

I didn't even realize it was my birthday. My bottom lip started to tremble. My eyes watered. I wanted to blurt it out. I wanted to let the secret out. I felt it moving around my guts and coming up into the back of my throat like bile. But something inside me forced it back down. I felt a chill run down my spine. I clapped my hands over my mouth. I looked up at my mother, whose eyes were closed. Her face was pale. Her eyelashes were fine and dark. Her nostrils were sniffing for the scent of the perfume. I couldn't do it, and I couldn't imagine how any man could cheat on a woman like her. But the more peaceful she looked, the more I wanted to blurt it out. My mouth seemed to be trying to force itself open. It was like it was under siege from within. The citizens were trying to force open the city gates and escape. Her eyelids fluttered, and she looked down at me. I turned away from her, my hands over my mouth. "Don't be silly. You can't hold it in your mouth." She opened the bottle again and wet the tip of her finger with perfume. She wiped her finger down my neck. What a waste, I thought.

My hands stayed over my mouth. She giggled in her feminine, dignified way. "Mom. Somebody's lying to you." I forced my hands back over my treacherous mouth. She opened her eyes a bit wider.

"Who's lying to me?"

"Dad." I couldn't cover my mouth anymore.

"He's not working the late shift?"

"It's not that."

"Then what's he lying about?"

"I saw him sleeping on top of Zhao Shanhe. He told me not to tell you."

My mom stumbled back and found a bench to sit on. "I knew it would happen," she said. "If it weren't Zhao Shanhe, it would be some other girl like her. I knew it would happen." She put the stopper back in the perfume bottle and placed it back in the box. It seemed like she wasn't exactly shocked, but I saw that her fingers were shaking as she struggled with the box's fastener.

When I heard my father arrive back home, I started to shake. I was worried that my mom and dad would argue. They might tear up the house. I had seen broken glass on the floor before in the morning. My mother had swept it up, and we'd all tried to forget it. We lived in a fantasy world, I guess. I imagined that everything was fine, and once the glass was swept up, there had never been a fight. After a fight like that, we went about our daily affairs as if nothing had happened. Our imaginations were strong, but so was my mother's ability to hold things together. She never showed that she was upset. The only time I saw any sign was when she'd wipe the table after dinner. The rag would be pressed down a bit harder, rubbed a bit faster. And sometimes she'd pause while drinking her tea and seem to be lost in her thoughts.

I didn't want to say anything else, but it was hard to stop myself. I couldn't shut my mouth. It's like when you're drunk and everything just comes out. You can't stop yourself from talking. I told Yu Baijia first. He's two years older than me. He looks like one of those hardened revolutionaries, the kind who falls into enemy hands and never gives up his comrades, even if they stretch him on a rack. I made him promise not to tell anyone, though. He held up his hand: "If I ever tell, may my lips rot and fall off." I don't think anybody put him on the rack, but he lasted two days before he told his dad. "Shut up about that. Don't get our family involved in that shit."

I realized that I couldn't tell anyone. If even Yu Baijia had sold me out, there was nobody I could trust. When I met Chen Baixiu, I didn't say anything. Fang Haitang, too, I didn't tell her a thing. One night when Zhao Wannian came home and found me sitting outside, he patted me on the head and said: "It turns out your father didn't write that letter. I got an expert to look it over."

"Who cares? They already slept together."

"What! Say that again."

Zhao Wannian grabbed me by my collar, but I squirmed away and ran toward the road. I put my hands over my mouth. I didn't want anything else to come out.

I had told three people already, and nothing had really happened. I had actually prayed that things would keep going as they were and that Zhao Wannian wouldn't fight with my dad. Things seemed the same as they'd always been. Uncle Zhao's cough was getting a little worse, but that was about it.

That Wednesday, my mother told me: "You're not going to school today, Guangxian. We're going to your father's factory."

"I think he's working overtime."

"He hasn't been home in three days. You don't think that's a little strange?"

I went with my mother to my father's workshop at the Number Three Loudspeaker Factory. The workers at the gate said: "Ceng Changfeng? You're too late. He got taken away two days ago. Some Red Guards came and got him." My hand was over my mouth again. My mother stared down at me. Her eyes were steely.

"Zhao Wannian must be behind this. Did you tell him anything?"

I ran from her, and she followed. I heard her puffing after me, her feet hitting the dust. I knew she was mad. She wasn't just mad, though—this was something different. I hit the drill ground near the factory and ducked into a public toilet. I heard my mom's heavy breathing outside. "Come out of there, Ceng Guangxian!" She was silent for a moment. "You know what this means? You know what could happen? They might come to get us, too. We're going to be up on the stage at a struggle session. Your mother is going to be a widow. Your big mouth got us into this. You thought that was something you should go around telling people? And you had to tell Zhao Wannian. Get the hell out here. I'm going to cut your lips off."

I broke down suddenly and sobbed. I cursed my big, stupid mouth. Rubbing my eyes, I walked out of the bathroom. I was ready to take my punishment. There was a small crowd outside the bathroom now. I went to my mother, and she pinched my lips lightly and took me into her arms. I hid my face in her arms and she hid her face in my arms, and we both cried. She didn't wipe away her tears, even with so many people watching. She held me in her arms, and she held me until I stopped shaking. My mouth was in one piece for the moment.

We went to the Number Five Middle School and stood at the gate. My mom said: "I don't want to see that guy, but you need to talk to him. Go find out where your dad is." I went into the school. Zhao Wannian was in his office. I rushed in the door.

"Why are you all sweaty? Wipe yourself off." He handed me a towel.

"Where's my dad?"

"Why didn't your mother come herself?"

I looked behind me.

"She's at the gate?"

I shook my head no.

"I know your mom's mad at me. That's the anger of the capitalist class when they get what's coming to them. Your father committed a crime. What can I do? Nobody else is going to be punished except for him. I'll sit down with her if she wants to talk. If she doesn't want to talk, let your father rot in his cell. The Ceng family has to pay the price, just like everyone else. Go get her. I'll sit down with her."

I tried to ask him where my father was, but he waved me off. I went out to the gates. My mother asked me: "Where's your father?"

"Zhao Wannian wants to talk to you."

"How did he know I was here?"

"He figured it out. I looked back."

My mom turned on me: "Why the hell did you look back? You're going to be the death of your father. Go tell him I already left. Tell him to take you to see your father." She pushed me back through the gate. I steeled myself and walked forward. I was going to do it this time: I would be strong, and I wouldn't let my mouth get ahead of me.

Zhao Wannian looked out of his office. "She's not coming?"

"She left."

"Then you're the only one who can save him."

"What did you do with him?"

"It seems his memory is a little rusty—he doesn't remember raping Zhao Shanhe. Perhaps you can tell us what you saw that day, jog his memory. If he admits what he did, there might be something I can do for him."

"I didn't see anything."

"You're only going to hurt your father if you keep lying. He's in the hands of some very capable men. It's best not to be stubborn. They'll break his right leg. If he keeps it up, they'll break his left leg. Maybe he'll keep his mouth shut even after that. But they'll break both his hands next. You'll be the one sitting there feeding him. Is that what you want?"

I shook my head no.

"Then you'd better tell them what you saw."

Zhao Wannian slammed the window shut. He came out of his office door and grabbed for me. I shook him off and ran to the tree in the schoolyard. He grabbed me by the shoulders of my jacket and pulled, but I held fast to the trunk. "Stubborn little bastard," he said, trying to drag me off the tree. He went for my right hand, trying to peel it from the trunk. I wanted to cry, but I held back. I had to hold on. The trouble with my father was all my fault.

I looked over my shoulder and saw my mother coming into the schoolyard with Uncle Zhao. He strode over to Zhao Wannian and knocked the bowl of his pipe on his forehead. "Dad! This is the school. Please, we have rules."

"Rules for how I should speak to my own son? Let Guangxian's father go."

"He's still not telling us the truth."

"The truth about what? He slept with your sister? You might not have any shame, but I still do. In the old days, he could have taken her as one of his wives. He would have been your brother-in-law."

"This is all your fault. I don't care if you're my father. We'll see what happens to you at the struggle session."

"I wasn't scared of starving to death. What do I have to fear from your struggle session? Release the man."

"It's not my decision anymore."

"If you don't release him, I'm going to tear this tree out."

The tree in the schoolyard was thick enough that I couldn't even get my arms around it. If it came down to Uncle Zhao and the tree, I thought the tree would probably win. Zhao Wannian saw the veins in his father's neck pulsing and the whiskers on his chin trembling. "Get out of here. He'll be free tomorrow," Zhao Wannian said.

"If he's not free by tomorrow, there'll be hell to pay. If he's not free by tomorrow, you are no longer my son."

The next morning when I opened the door of the warehouse, I saw my father lying on a stretcher beside the door. He was asleep, or at least his eyes were shut. His hands were filthy and clenched so hard that he had drawn blood. I knew he must have been tortured.

We carried him inside. His face was unmarked. There were no wounds on his chest or his back. His arms and his legs were unbroken. How did they torture him? Why did he look like he was on the verge of death? Uncle Zhao came in, carrying a concoction of herbal medicine. "Take down his pants. I know my son well enough to guess what happened."

Uncle Yu started to unbutton my dad's pants and then stopped when my dad cried out: "Don't do it." My mom came over. "No, no, don't do it," he cried again. Uncle Zhao came closer, and my father cried out again.

"Master, there's nothing to be ashamed of. I watched you grow up. I've seen everything. I know your body better than you do."

My father gaped like a dying fish. He said: "Let Guangxian give me the medicine. Guangxian? Where are you? Where is my son?" I'd been the one to betray him. But he still called for me. He wanted me to give him the medicine. I couldn't believe I'd treated him like I had.

The room emptied, and I was left alone with my father and Uncle Zhao. I unbuttoned my father's pants. His dick was stuck to his pants with blood. There was blood everywhere. When I tried to pull his pants down farther, I saw pain on his face. I tried to work as slowly and gently as I could. When his pants were off, I heard Uncle Zhao breathe a curse. "Evil," he said. He began to apply the herbal medicine.

I finally saw what had been done to my father. If I hadn't seen it myself, I wouldn't have believed it. His genitals were swollen beyond recognition; they were two or three times their normal size, shiny and red. There was only a round, red mass between my father's legs now. As Uncle Zhao applied the medicine, my own body began to shake. My hands went to my mouth. I wished I could scrape those words up and stuff them back down into myself.

"Guangxian," my father croaked. "This might be the last thing I say. I don't know if I'll make it through this. I'm sorry. I'm sorry that I put you through this. I don't have much to give you, but I want to tell you something . . ." There was a long pause. "In the future, I want you to do whatever you want to do, but never do what I did. Don't be a man like your father was. I tried to hold on. Ten years, I thought I could hold on.

But I wasn't strong enough. Guangxian, will you remember what I told you?"

"Yes."

"Master," said Uncle Zhao through his tears, "please don't worry. This is your father's own secret recipe. This is the best medicine possible. You'll be fine in a few days. I knew my son was cruel, but I didn't expect this of him."

My father had said what he wanted to say. He didn't speak again. I wish I could have kept my mouth shut, like my father. If I had kept my mouth shut, none of this would have happened. I made a silent promise to myself: I would never sleep with a woman. Even at gunpoint, I wouldn't do it. I looked at my father, my father who would never piss through his dick again, let alone sleep with a woman who was not his wife. I knew that as good as it might feel, this was where it would end. I thought about it over the days after that morning when we found my father. My resolve strengthened.

In the days after my father returned, my mother entered the hospital with a swollen appendix. One day when I went to the hospital, I fed her her lunch. She could feed herself, but I thought I could maybe show her my love by doing it for her. She pushed the spoon away and said: "Guangxian, I want to die. This world is a mess. I've had enough." She stopped and looked up at me: "I don't want you to tell anyone what I said."

"Of course. Except maybe Dad. I have to tell him. If he knew, he wouldn't let you die."

My mother's face darkened, and she was silent for a moment. When she spoke again, there was a new light behind her eyes. She pulled off her blankets. "That mouth is going to be the death of you. Do you understand? I can't even die peacefully." She dragged me toward the door. She told me she was taking me somewhere. She didn't look like a person who had been lying in a hospital bed a few moments before.

I followed my mother to Six Alley, off of Sanhe Road, and into a dark doorway. It was already dark outside when we got to the alley, and it was even darker in that room. My mother called out: "Auntie Nine!" The light from a bare bulb pricked the dark. The face of an old woman emerged from the shadows.

"It's been a long time, Miss Wu."

"I want you to seal the mouth of my Guangxian. This mouth of his is going to get him into trouble."

My mom handed some money to Auntie Nine. The room went dark again. Auntie Nine struck a match and lit three sticks of incense. She handed the incense to me. "Close your eyes," the old woman said. She put a rough old hand on the top of my head and dragged her fingers down over my forehead, my eyes, and my nose, resting them firmly on my mouth. Her hands left a string of pain down my face.

"After your mouth is sealed, Guangxian . . . you will only speak what needs to be spoken."

I nodded my head. She put a scrap of paper over my mouth. The scrap of paper was red, about two fingers wide. She stuck it on vertically, connecting my upper and lower lips. Auntie Nine told me to leave the paper on there for at least half an hour. When my mother and I took the bus home, I noticed people looking at the red paper on my lips. On the walk home, it fell off a few times, and I picked it up off the ground and put it back on my mouth. I didn't know how the paper was supposed to work, but it felt like a certificate, a merit badge attesting to my new reticence.

Zhao Shanhe didn't come home much anymore. My father was around, and I guess neither wanted to run into the other. When my father did run into her, his lips would start to tremble. It seemed like there was something he wanted to say, but he was always worried that somebody was listening. Zhao Shanhe kept her chin in the air, never making eye contact Whenever he came near, she walked away as if she didn't recognize him.

Uncle Zhao knew that they couldn't live under the same roof. He found her a husband, a railway engineer who stood almost six feet tall. Their courtship moved as fast as the building of the New China.

One Sunday, the engineer rolled up to the warehouse in a truck. He and his comrades from the railway jumped down in their dress uniforms. They grabbed Zhao Shanhe and five boxes of shells from her munitions factory, then sped off in the truck. The truck was covered in banners and flags, and a loudspeaker blared out slogans like "The Great Proletarian Cultural Revolution is great!" Except for my dad and Zhao Wannian, all the families in the warehouse stood at the front door and watched the truck drive off to the sound of singing and chanted slogans. Everyone stood there for a long time, as if they could still hear the sound of the loudspeaker.

Afterward, my dad admitted to me that had been watching the truck from an alley up the road. As it passed, he saw Zhao Shanhe standing in the back with her hair whipping in the wind. She had a peaceful look, he thought. She had no regret on her face. There was no pain. He followed the truck down through the center of town, past the department store and the Zhaoyang Hotel, chasing after it until he couldn't keep up any longer. He began to cry, and he cried all afternoon.

He came home very late that day, so I believed his story. His eyes were swollen and bloodshot, too. He seemed to be in a daze when he sat down to eat. He stared into space for a while and then picked up his bowl and his chopsticks. Pieces of rice fell from his mouth as he chewed. He reached for a plate of fried pork, but his chopsticks hit the table instead. He fumbled through the meal, reaching for things and returning his empty chopsticks to his mouth, chewing mechanically as if he were grinding cardboard between his teeth. He didn't seem to be in his body. Maybe this is how he thought Zhao Shanhe had treated him.

My father was silent that night; the warehouse was silent that night. When he went to bed, he tossed and turned and fell asleep sometime around dawn. He did not snore as he usually did but ground his teeth. When I drifted off to sleep, I felt his hands suddenly tight around my body. He moaned: "Shanhe. Shanhe!" When I looked up, I saw that he seemed to be frozen in place. Maybe he realized what name he had called in his sleepy haze. My mother called to him from her bed and went to his side. He returned to bed as we were getting ready to start the day. The warehouse was alive with its normal sounds: people going out the back door to the bathroom, Uncle Zhao spitting and coughing. My father was the last one in bed.

I forgave my father for his mistake—I mean calling her name. I think my mother could have forgiven him, too. But it wasn't the only time. For the next several nights, I would be awakened by my father moaning her name. It gave me goose bumps on top of goose bumps. If I wasn't there for him to grab onto, it would be his pillow that he would mistake for that girl. When my mother had finally had enough, she smashed a glass on his head and screamed: "You're sick in the head. Get the hell out of here."

My father did just that. He wrapped himself in some old clothes and went out the door. That was when he started going down to the railway tracks. He'd sit there and watch the trains go by. The whole town was asleep. This was late at night, of course. But the trains would still be running. You're probably wondering why he went to watch the trains, right? At first he'd thought about going to the munitions factory where Zhao Shanhe had worked. But he remembered that her coworkers had told him that she'd left the factory. Zhao Shanhe had transferred to a job in the railways, working on the same line as her husband. Her coworkers had said with admiration that she was going all over the country.

One day, we came home to find a note written by my father on our kitchen table: "I'm going to be gone for five days. I'm off to Beijing."

My mother held the letter with trembling hands. She asked: "Do you know why he went to Beijing?"

Ceng Fang said: "To see Chairman Mao!"

"I doubt it. He's going to Beijing by train. He wants to see Zhao Shanhe." My mother ripped up the note and let the scraps of paper fall to the floor. She ground them into the floor with her feet and said: "Your father is a pervert. I'm so sick of that man. If it weren't for you two, I would have left him a long time ago. What does that girl have that I don't? I can recite poetry. I can play the guqin. Can she write calligraphy? All she knows how to do is shake her ass. They deserve each other. They're both sick in the head."

After dinner, my mother began to pack. She put her and my sister's things in an old suitcase, along with the half bottle of perfume. I asked: "What about my stuff?"

"We can't all go. You have to stay here. It's strategic."

My mother packed and repacked. She would come home from work and remember something else, a book or a photo album or one of her combs, and she'd cram it into the suitcase. When the suitcase was full, she got a net bag and started to fill that, too. When the net bag was full, she unpacked everything and repacked it. The process was repeated until my father came home one night. She pointed at the suitcase. "We have two children," she said. "I will be responsible for one child, and you will be responsible for the other." My father asked her where she was going.

"I'd rather live at the zoo. An animal would be a better companion than you. When you figure it out, let me know, and we'll do the necessary paperwork."

My dad dropped to his knees and covered his face with his hands. My mother took her bags and Ceng Fang and left. I kicked a bench. "You deserve this," I said.

"What do I deserve?"

"You still don't get it? You'll never change."

My dad stood up. "This is love," he shouted. "Do you understand?"

"You should love your wife. What you're doing is sick."

"You'll never get it. It's like I was starving and she gave me a plate of food—meat! How can I forget that?"

"My mom cooked you plenty of food. How can you just let her go?"

"You don't know shit. She didn't cook for me for ten years. If you don't believe me, go ask her. I wanted meat and she gave me a bit of lard. You aren't a man yet, but someday you'll understand. I wanted it so bad, so bad that I didn't want to live if I couldn't have it."

"Remember that day you came home and told me to make you that promise? Do you even remember that?"

My dad sighed: "One day you'll understand."

"Even if I live to be a hundred, I won't understand. You're sick."

‹ 5 ›

After my mom left, I found the photo albums that she'd left behind. She had taken the most important ones, but there were a few that she hadn't been able to take with her. Most of the images were in black and white, but some of the family photos were in color. I took out all of the pictures that had my father in them. I laid them out and used a pair of scissors to cut him out of each photo. With some of them, I had to cut away parts of me and my mother or my sister. In the oldest album, I found a picture of my father holding me when I was a baby. I cut him out and was left with an image of my father holding a blank space. The way his arms looked, the arms that had been holding me—I shivered. I cut away his arms.

I could cut my father out of the pictures, but I couldn't cut him out of my life. When I was done, I felt clean. But my father still wasn't clean. There was no amount of soap that could bleach his sins from him. I started to ignore him when he came home. I'd just sit there, neglecting all the things I used to do around the house. I sat cross-legged reading the newspapers that he brought home. When he came in, he'd drop a new paper in front of me, and I'd pick it up and read it while he went to make our dinner. He'd have to ask me, "Are you going to eat?" It was pathetic. I'd drop the newspaper and go to the table and eat without saying a word. I noticed him glancing at me, and I knew he must be hoping I'd break the silence. I'd read the fiery editorials in the paper, the ones about freezing out the enemy. The enemy should be treated as if they didn't even exist.

My dad talked tough, but I knew he'd grown up pampered, the son of a capitalist. He wasn't used to this kind of treatment. After a while, he started pleading with me: "Back in the old days, it was normal! Your father, I could have had four or five wives. Who cares about Zhao Shanhe? What does it even matter? Your mother doesn't understand. That's just how my family was. I don't care if you understand, but can't you at least sympathize? You're my son." I could tell he was still thinking about Zhao Shanhe. She wasn't just some girl to him. He hadn't changed at all. But I had changed. I wasn't the old Ceng Guangxian anymore. I'd learned a lot from all those editorials in the paper. I knew how to protect my mind.

One night, I discovered another of my father's secrets. He had hidden a book in the waistband of his pants. The book was wrapped in old newspapers, but there were no fiery editorials contained within the volume—the book dropped from his pants and fell open on the floor, revealing the bare ass of a girl. I was stunned. He took the book back, and I saw him take it down behind the cistern in the yard. I watched him from a distance, his hands working in front of him, his hair wild, his undershirt rumpled. I knew that he was on a downward spiral. I'd learned: it would start with this and end with him groping women and then becoming a rapist. I couldn't let that happen.

You probably don't understand, right? I was political, first of all. I was precocious when it came to politics. Nowadays young people don't really bother with political stuff, but it was a big deal to me. There was somebody else who was political, too: Zhao Wannian. There weren't many people he admired. He was arrogant. He had his nose up in the air even while taking a piss. But anyways, he liked me. When I saw the road my father was going down, I knew I had to go to Zhao Wannian for help.

Zhao Wannian told me to give it up: "You can get him up onstage at a struggle session, but what are you going to criticize him for? He's in love with her. It's not worth it."

"But," I said, "there's something else. There's something there." Zhao Wannian looked at me closer. "Like this stuff about marrying three or four wives. Uncle Zhao is always saying the same thing. Isn't that a hold-over from feudalism? In the old days, your family were like his servants, so he thinks he had a right to sleep with Zhao Shanhe. The capitalist class still believe in their superiority." As I spoke, I heard Zhao Wannian smacking his lips. "And he's looking at dirty books. That's even worse than the thing with the dogs. That's a hundred times worse."

I saw his eyes flash. He patted my head, his face full of admiration: "You really fucking know politics, huh?"

The Red Guards came and took away my father and his dirty book. He was hustled out between two big men in green uniforms, followed by other men in green uniforms. The men were rough with him, dragging him headfirst toward the truck that they'd parked in front of the warehouse. My father was tossed into the back of the truck. He called down to me: "Guangxian, I won't be home for dinner. The ration tickets are under the mat. The money is behind the brick in the cabinet. Don't go out at night. Bolt the door. If you get scared, go to the Bais." The truck was moving down the road, and I could barely hear him now. "If I don't come back, go to your mother, live with her, make her forgive me. You hear me? Guangxian?"

I didn't want to cry. I told myself that they were just going to fix him. They were going to scrub his brain like you'd wipe off a chalkboard. But the tears came anyway. Zhao Wannian patted me on the head. He told me that lots of revolutionaries had sacrificed their loved ones for the sake of the greater good. I didn't look much like a revolutionary with tears in my eyes watching my father go. Zhao Wannian got in his Jeep and drove off.

A few days later, the truck came back. The men on the truck kicked my father to the ground in front of the warehouse. Uncle Zhao and Uncle Yu helped me carry him inside. He was completely covered in blood. His face and his chest and his arms were dyed scarlet. When we got him onto his bed, he rolled over and retched, bringing up blood and broken teeth. He said: "One book. I brought it from Hong Kong, so they said I was 'having illicit relations with a foreign state.' Idiots don't even know you can buy that at a bookstore in Hong Kong. They've never seen any art. They don't know that the human body is art. They called me a spy. They're dumber than any of the animals at your mother's zoo."

That night I heard my father sigh deeply, and he called me to turn off the light. In the dark, he said: "If they come again, if they come back for me, I'd rather die than go through that again." Now both my mom and my dad had said they didn't want to live anymore. It's like they were in a competition or something, some kind of championship of suffering. My father said: "Come here, Guangxian." I didn't move. "There's something I want to tell you. Come here. Your father has a problem. I'm obsessed with women. I'm going to teach you something, though. It's something I realized too late. Maybe I wouldn't have had to go through all of this if I'd realized it sooner. With things the way they are, I might not have another chance to tell you. Come here and I'll tell you." His voice got lower. "If you really can't stop thinking about women, just push it to the side and take care of yourself: use your hand. You know what I mean? Just use your hand. It's your own body, so you should be able to look after it as you please. See, I always thought I needed a woman to do it for me. But I finally realized, just do it yourself." He sighed. "If we can do it ourselves, what the hell do we even need women for?"

I didn't realize the extent of my father's perversion until it was too late. They hadn't wiped it clean at all. I ran from the house, slamming the door so that it echoed through the warehouse like a gunshot.

My father was the type of person I hated the most, the perverts, the sick-minded. When another group of Red Guards came and grabbed him and hustled them to their truck, I didn't even go outside. I drowned out the sound outside by singing a song from a patriotic opera about a woman who goes to the execution ground instead of confessing. The song went: "A red plum on a red cliff blossoms / Ice and snow and the cold wind blows / Even through the bitterest winter / She still looks up to the sun and smiles / She still looks up to the sun . . ." Suddenly the window beside me shattered. At first I thought my voice had done it. But then I saw the rock lying on the floor. Another rock flew through the other window. I saw the rocks and kept singing. I knew it must have been Yu Baijia and Rong Guangming who threw them. I sang louder and longer. It was the middle of winter, with the windows broken, but I was drenched in sweat.

The day after they took my father, two trucks rolled up to the front of the warehouse. They weren't there to return him. Two gangs of men jumped down from the trucks and went inside. They trashed the Zhao and Yu families' homes and carried what they could to the trucks. Uncle Yu ran out with his toothbrush still in his mouth: "What the hell are you doing?"

The leader of the men shouted back: "This warehouse is being confiscated. You're moving out."

Uncle Yu spat toothpaste froth: "How can you do that? You can't just tell us to move. You won't even discuss it?"

The leader said: "Shut your mouth before you end up in more trouble."

Uncle Yu said: "My wife isn't even dressed!"

The leader said: "You filthy capitalists are really fucking something. Out sunbathing, huh? Why isn't she wearing any clothes?"

Uncle Zhao sprawled across the doorway to the warehouse, but the men stepped over him, carrying out trunks and boxes and bed frames. He finally stood up and shouted: "What the hell are you doing? Don't you know I'm the father of Principal Zhao?"

"He's the one who told us to move you out," one of the men called back, laughing.

When the warehouse was empty, Uncle Zhao was left holding on to the frame of the door, refusing to leave. He was eventually carried off by some of his neighbors, as if he were another piece of furniture. He squirmed in their arms like a chicken going to the chopping block. "Where the hell are you sending us, Zhao Wannian? What the fuck are you doing? I've lived here half my life. If you take me out of here, I'd rather die. I'd rather die in this warehouse than be dragged out. I can't live anywhere else. You can do what you want now, but there will come a day when you get what's coming to you." Uncle Zhao kept shouting until he was dragged past me. He went quiet and looked at me hard: "This is all because of you, you and your fucking mouth."

It wasn't only Uncle Zhao who had realized what had happened. Yu Fare and Fang Haitang and Zhao Baixiu spat hard into the dirt beside me, splashing my shoes with saliva.

When the truck pulled away, Yu Baijia was the only one left in the warehouse. I didn't think he'd be angry at me. We were friends, after all. The sound of the truck leaving brought him running out of the warehouse. His dusty slippers stopped in front of me. He looked me up and down and then spat in my face twice. I lunged for his neck, and he stepped out of his slippers and knocked my hands away, putting up his fists. How could they treat me like that! I was ideologically healthy, unlike them. I wondered if there was something I had missed when I'd read all those editorials in the newspaper brought home by my father.

I ran to the zoo and went into the workers' dormitory. The door to my mother's room was unlocked. As I pushed it open, I heard a voice: "No, please no." I stopped and listened. It was Director He! When I peered inside, I saw him running his hands over her, trying to pull her shirt off. I kicked the door open, and the director put his hands behind his back and walked around me and out of the room. My mother's neck was covered in puffy red scratches. I spat in her face. I spat in her face as many times as those people had spat on me. She protested: "I can explain. Please let me explain."

"I don't want to hear it!"

"He made me do it. He threatened me and said that if I didn't testify against your father . . . I wouldn't do it, so he forced me. Think about it: would I just jump into bed with somebody like that? That's shameless. But he's my boss, so what could I say? I didn't want to back him into a corner, or it could have been even worse for me. Look at what I've become. From a proud woman to this . . ." Her face was flushed a deep red.

"Something happened at the warehouse."

"From the way you look, I'm guessing it's not good."

From its cage deeper inside the zoo came the roar of the tiger. A drop of cold sweat ran down my back. I followed my mother out of the zoo, and we took a bus toward the warehouse. On the bus, she fell into her old habit and repeated again and again the story of Director He taking liberties with her, just as she'd repeated the story about the tiger eating the dead dogs. She stopped only when the warehouse came into view. Her mouth froze. She was the first off the bus. I ran behind her and stopped in the doorway. The warehouse was enveloped in a haze of dust as the Red Guard men swung sledgehammers at the walls that had divided the building into homes. The wall around our home toppled with a crash, and the men stomped into the already-looted bedroom.

Thick dust swirled against the ceiling of the warehouse. From the rubble, my mother picked up a brick. Crushed underneath it was a photograph that had been taken the year she had come to live there. On the back was written "1950." She seized the photograph and rushed out of the warehouse, tears running down her cheeks. There was blood on her hands from searching in the rubble. The clothes that she worked so hard to keep clean were filthy with dust. But she returned to the incident with Director He, pleading with me: "You have to believe me, Guangxian. I would never, ever do anything like that. It's shameless!"

I used to think my mother must have died of shame. I still think that, actually. I think back to what she was like when I was a kid. She was a clean woman. She had pride. She hated perverts and people with sick thoughts, just like I did. So when I saw her being harassed by a man like Director He, it was like that all went out the window. The type of woman who would be groped by a man like that was the opposite of my mother. It must have been shame that killed her.

The day after she took the photograph from the warehouse, she went back to the dormitory at the zoo and sent Ceng Fang off somewhere. She went to the tiger cage. This was the tiger named Lan Lan that had eaten the two dogs. She walked along the front of the cage and then went through the door into the tiger's viewing area, where there were a few trees and fake rocks. She usually tossed meat down to the tiger, but this time she went inside. She wasn't carrying any meat. Instead of meat, she offered herself to the tiger. The tiger took half and left the rest for her comrades from the zoo to wrap in a white blanket. They stood around her, the workers from the zoo and Director He. I remembered her face that day, blushing as she tried to explain that Director He had forced her . . . I remembered her face, streaked with dust, as she held the photograph from the warehouse. I knew it must have been shame that killed her. My father had no idea what had happened, and I had no idea where Ceng Fang was. I was alone in the world at that moment, with nobody to rely on. Standing on the street, standing in that city—I was alone in the world.

I went back to the warehouse and stood in the doorway. A cold wind bit at my ears and rushed through the open door and back out again, carrying the smell of broken bricks and smashed concrete. I stood there, sniffing the cold wind, and I began to smell the warehouse's old smells, too: the stink of the bathrooms out back, Uncle Zhao's pipe, my dad's sweaty undershirt, the perfume in the secret bottle . . . I coughed. I stayed in the doorway until early morning. The streets were quiet. Suddenly I remembered my father. I couldn't stop myself from thinking about him. He was sick—I didn't want to remember him! But the thoughts piled up like the rubble in the warehouse. I realized I'd been lied to, but I wasn't even sure who it was that had lied to me or what they'd lied about.

In the morning, I went to find Zhao Wannian. I asked him about my father. He told me: "It seems your father is very popular. I can't even get hold of him now. A real specimen of the exploiting class is a rare find for the Red Guards—and he's an unrepentant pervert, which makes him even more attractive. They might as well pickle him and put him in a jar so that everyone can study him. It's going to be hard to locate him. I wouldn't even where to look. He's being passed around from group to group now. They're finding many uses for him."

The streets were full of people selling New Year's decorations. I wandered among the sellers and into the side streets of the city, going from school to school, searching the assembly halls and parade grounds. The day was cold, and my nose dribbled snot as I walked. On Sanhe Road, I saw a group of uniformed boys standing around an old man. His arms were pulled up behind him at an unnatural angle, and his face was pointed at the ground. I kept walking and saw another group leading a middle-aged man across a schoolyard. His arms were bound at his sides, and his glasses had been smashed, cutting his eyes. Blood ran down his face. On West Tiema Road, men in green uniforms were standing around some boys who had been stripped of their coats and were being forced to lie face-up on the cold asphalt of the road. The boys stared up at the sky without speaking. I did not find my father. It began to snow.

Maybe he had already been taken somewhere else, I thought. Maybe he was dead. I didn't want to consider that, but when night came and I returned to the warehouse and climbed up into the eaves to sleep, I had lost hope. When morning came, I sat in the doorway of the warehouse. Uncle Zhao found me there and told me to come live with him at the family's new home. I didn't want to go. Uncle Yu tried to get me to leave the warehouse, too. I had to stay. I told them: "I'm going to wait for my father to come back." The New Year was approaching, and my dad still hadn't returned. I thought that he must have died.

The days grew colder. The next morning would be the start of the Spring Festival. From the doorways on the road around the warehouse came warmth and the smell of stewed pork. The snow came harder that day, and within a few hours everything was covered in a layer of white. The streets emptied. The branches of the tree in the yard bent under the weight of snow. I noticed a group of men dragging something through

the snow. I knew what they were dragging. I shouted: "Dad!" He seemed
not to hear. The men dumped my father in the snow beside me, and
he began to crawl away. His ragged beard was gathering snow, and his
face was covered in cuts scabbed over and fresh cuts oozing blood. His
head had been shaved in the yin-yang haircut that the Red Guards gave
their victims. I put his head in my lap. My father jerked away from me,
shouting: "Get away from me, you son of a bitch!" I looked down at him,
stunned. He tried to rise. He fell into the snow, and it covered him like
a clean cotton blanket. He crawled toward the warehouse, dragging his
right leg behind him. He looked like a reptile. He left a track as he went,
a deep path through the snow, deeper than the tire tracks left by the cars
in the snowy road.

‹ 6 ›

I knelt down beside my father. He pushed me away with all the strength he had left and shouted: "Get away from me! Don't ever come near me again. When I found out it was you, I couldn't believe it. I thought it had to have been somebody else. You told Zhao Wannian everything." My father kept crawling forward. "Whose son are you? Fuck off. I never want to see you again." He kept crawling, not realizing that his home had been wrecked. There were only smashed bricks where his bed had been. He didn't know that Ceng Fang was missing and his wife was dead. I wanted to tell him everything. But for once I held back. I put my hands over my mouth. I began to weep bitterly.

I knelt and smacked my forehead against the snowy ground. I wanted to crack my head open in the snow and die.

I'm sorry. I don't know how to tell this part of the story. What are you crying about? Take this. Wipe your eyes. I guess you sympathize with me, right? It's fine to have sympathy for me now, but back then . . .

Nobody wanted to hear my story. I tried talking to Yu Baijia and Rong Guangming. They avoided me as best they could. Zhang Nao was even worse. She went to the phone company and had them install a thing on her phone so that if I called, the ring would play out the folk song "Jasmine Flowers." That way she'd know not to pick up the phone. When she got tired of "Jasmine Flowers," she'd change the tune to "Honghu Waters, Wave upon Wave" or "Memory of My Comrade in Arms."

Anyways, one time I went to her place and rang the doorbell. A kid came to the door and peered through the crack and told me: "My mom says she's not home."

I'm off topic again. Let me tell you about Xiao Chi.

I was at my lowest point, with my mom dead and my sister missing and my dad staying in the ruins of the warehouse. I'd lost my family, and my home was destroyed. I didn't even have a place to sleep. I went to the Zhao family and the Yu family and took the little food they could give me back to the warehouse to eat. I tried to feed my father, but he wouldn't take anything I had brought for him. He would lift the food up, sniff it, and then toss it to the floor, as if I were trying to poison him. When Uncle Zhao and Uncle Yu brought him something, he would eat sparingly. They brought him stuffed buns and steamed bread along with weak tea.

My father wrapped himself in old newspapers and wrecked bamboo mats. He had nowhere to go and was resigned to staying at the warehouse. That building was going to be his tomb. He lay in the warehouse, wrapped in bamboo mats, tossing and turning on the broken bricks, trying to get some comfort on his rough bed. When I went to his side, he pushed me away, shouting, the veins in his neck glowing blue. I watched him through the window until the winter wind froze me. I wished I could freeze to death. Let the wind blow. Let the north wind kill me right there. The cold would heal my heart, I thought. The pain would wipe away my sins.

One afternoon, a team of workers arrived at the warehouse. They came in with their tools and set up levels and string lines. They began to go through the piles of bricks, lifting them and checking them for cracks and for good weight. I had an image of a bureaucrat checking the political background of a model worker candidate. They began mixing cement and setting the bricks, building walls inside the warehouse. The final pile of bricks was the pile that my father was sleeping on. They began to pick through it, selecting bricks to put in the new walls. My father slumped down, and his head knocked against a jug of water, spilling it over the steamed bread beside his brick bed. He was left lying on a few broken bricks and one of the bamboo mats. That mat was actually Zhao Shanhe's. It was one of the mats that they'd used to block the dogs from escaping. The workers left him there and went to smoke a cigarette. When they exhaled, the smoke floated up to the ceiling of the warehouse, where shafts of sunlight lit up the mix of cigarette smoke and brick dust. One of the workers said: "Are we just going to throw him out or what?"

The workers tossed their cigarettes down and clapped the cement dust off their fingers. They lifted the old bamboo mat and carried my father out on it. He wriggled on the mat, kicking his feet, trying to reach the ground. He shouted at the workers: "Don't! Don't take me out. I want to die here. Give me a few days. I won't last much longer. You'll see. Just let me die here. Toss a rope up over the beams and hang me. If you have any heart, you'll let me die."

The workers looked like they were carting a dead dog. One of the men pointed at me: "Get your dad out of here. Take him over to Number Three." My dad continued shouting up at them. Wrapped in his old mat, he began to shiver in the cold. His lips froze so stiff, he could no longer shout at the workers. After a while, he closed his eyes and looked as if he had fallen asleep. I took off my jacket and wrapped it around him. I put him in a wheelbarrow and pushed it toward the Number Three Factory.

The streets were busy, but to me there were only shadows moving around me. The ground was strewn with yellow leaves, some freshly fallen and crisp and some wet and moldering. The buses passing on the road moved silently, but under the wheels of the wheelbarrow, the leaves crackled. The wind blew hard and cold on my face. I pushed the wheelbarrow until I grew tired. My hands on the handle ached. The wheelbarrow pulled me downhill. I pulled it uphill, standing in front of it. As I neared the top of one of the hills, I was about to give up. I couldn't go any farther. But the wheelbarrow suddenly felt light. I thought I was going downhill again. I looked back, prepared to get behind the wheelbarrow. I saw Xiao Chi behind me, pushing the wheelbarrow with all of her strength.

Xiao Chi's full name was Chi Fengxian, but everyone called her Xiao Chi. She was the fattest girl in our whole grade. Her dad worked as the head of a food distribution center, so she got to eat meat and all kinds of other stuff. But "fat" didn't mean the same thing then that it means now. If you were fat back then, it just meant that your ribs weren't showing. She looked more mature than most of the kids our age, too. She had color in her cheeks. She looked healthy, basically.

When we arrived at the Number Three Factory, a crowd formed around us. My father looked up at them blearily: "Where am I? Who are you? Can't you wait for my legs to get better? I'm not ready for more torture."

"Changfeng, it's me, Hu Zhipeng."

"It's Xie Jinchuan," somebody else said.

Another said: "It's Liu Canghai."

As his comrades gave their names, my father opened his red eyes. Xiao Chi and I were squeezed out of the crowd. She took out her handkerchief and wiped the sweat from my forehead. She didn't even ask; she just started wiping. I came to my senses and jerked back from her. She said: "You have to wipe yourself off. You're all sweaty." I shook my head and slipped away from her. She asked me: "Guangxian, what production team are you going to join?" She covered her face with the handkerchief.

"I don't know. If they give me the choice, maybe I'll go to Tianle."

"You aren't sure?"

"There's not really anywhere else I'd want to go."

A few days after that, she came to me and said: "I know why you want to go to Tianle."

"Why?"

"I read that article in the paper, too. It was really good."

The article about Tianle had been in one of the provincial papers. Back then, people paid attention to the slogans and editorials in the paper, but essays like the one about Tianle were mostly just filler. The handkerchief was over her nose again. She said: "The essay was good, but there are three other good things about Tianle." I actually had never heard of Tianle before reading the article. Even after reading it, I didn't really know exactly where Tianle was. She said: "First, the average temperature in Tianle is sixteen point three degrees. If you go to join a production team there, you won't need any winter clothes. Second, Tianle is on a railway line. If you go to work in Tianle, you can take a train to get there. Third, there's Wuse Lake, way up in the mountains. You've got Xiangya Mountain, too, which is high, but probably not as high as Mount Everest. But nobody's ever climbed it. So if I go there, I can be the first to climb it."

Xiao Chi chose to join a production team in Tianle. There were five other kids in our class who signed up to join the Down to the Countryside Movement, including Yu Baijia and our class monitor, Rong Guangming. I used my father as an excuse not to join. I told Xiao Chi about it while we were in the schoolyard, near the big tree that Uncle Zhao had threatened to pull out. I told her I would have to stay in the city to look after him. Xiao Chi pressed me: "He doesn't need you to look after him. His leg is better now. He has a place to stay. What are you going to do?"

"Just be there with him. He needs somebody to talk to."

"I heard he won't talk to you. He doesn't even want to see you. "

"So what? Why don't you go tell Zhao Wannian on me?"

Xiao Chi stamped her foot: "Come on. You promised me!"

"I didn't promise you anything. I don't care what they all say about you. I don't want to get involved."

"What did they say?" She took the handkerchief away from her mouth.

"Nothing."

The handkerchief went back up. "If you hadn't said you wanted to go to Tianle to join the production team, I wouldn't have signed up. I didn't have to go. I could have stayed here. My father could have sent a few kilos of meat to the right person, and I could have had a good job here."

"What does that have to do with me?"

"You can't just say you're going to go and then not go. I already signed up. I can't just desert now."

I put my hand over my mouth. "I'm sorry. I wasn't thinking when I said I wanted to go to Tianle."

"Now it's too late to even register."

"I don't really want to go."

She looked at me hard: "What if I order you to come?"

"Who are you to order me?"

Xiao Chi turned on her heel, tossed her handkerchief to the ground, and walked away. I couldn't figure it out. Why was she so upset? She seemed so helpful and was generally a good person—I'd never even seen her angry. Maybe it was political again. Maybe my thinking was backward. But still, I wasn't sure why that would make her angry. I kicked the handkerchief. I looked up to watch her walk away.

The warehouse, meanwhile, had been completely rebuilt. It was reborn as an assembly hall with a broad stage decorated with banners and flags. One of the banners bore a slogan exhorting school graduates to go down to the countryside to learn from poor peasants. I was overwhelmed by the beauty of the assembly hall. It wouldn't exactly be fashionable now, but it was definitely in keeping with the fashion of the time. With the exception of the black text on the banners, everything was decorated in red: red flags, red cloth, red paper. Even the microphone on the stage was sheathed in red. Onstage, the school graduates making ready to go down to the countryside were holding bouquets of red flowers. Their eyes were looking at the ceiling.

The assembly hall was full. All of the teachers and students from the Number Five Middle School were there, and some of their parents, and people who lived on the streets nearby. The cement benches in the hall were full, and many in the crowd were forced to stand. Outside the windows of the warehouse, the people looking in became piles of heads. I had never imagined that the warehouse could look like this.

Zhao Wannian took the stage and began his speech, breathing steam in the cold air of the hall. Zhao Wannian had risen quickly and was now the director of the Tiema District Revolutionary Committee. His voice rang out stronger than I'd ever heard it. He had been addressing crowds all over the city, and he was far more confident. But the PA system, designed by my father's factory, was one of their finest, most advanced works. The system was nearly perfect, from the microphone to the powerful speakers hung in the corners of the hall. His voice, once a modest creek, strengthened to a raging river. He was interrupted again and again by the applause and cheers of the audience. There was a big difference between an audience now and an audience then. They didn't just clap to clap, they smacked their hands together until they hurt and roared their approval. A speech barely ended before a revolutionary song began, and the song hadn't reached the end of the final chorus before the sound of drums and gongs echoed through the hall.

That night, I went back to the hall and looked in through a window. The benches were empty and the hall was dark. I thought I could hear the sounds of the songs and the speeches still echoing, I thought I could hear . . . I thought I could hear Uncle Zhao's cough. I thought I could smell my mother's perfume. I thought I could taste my dad's cooking. There was the smell of the soap in Ceng Fang's hair. When I closed my eyes, I could see time moving backward, the story of the warehouse told in reverse. When I opened my eyes again, I saw that Xiao Chi was standing beside me. "I knew you'd be here," she said.

"I saw you with your red flowers this afternoon."

"I'm leaving tomorrow, Guangxian. I wanted to say goodbye to you."

We were only seventeen years old. I didn't really know what to say at such a profound moment. I stared at her blankly. Xiao Chi climbed up on one of the benches: "Do you like my skirt?" I had never noticed her skirt. It was a warm winter skirt. Back then, nobody really wore a skirt, except actresses, maybe. It seemed very strange to me, especially in the winter. The skirt suddenly dropped from her hips, showing her thick, pale legs. I covered my eyes.

Xiao Chi took my shoulders. "Guangxian," she said, "we aren't students anymore. We can do whatever we want to do." I tried to breathe and found that my chest was tight. I felt pain where her hands rested on my shoulders.

"Let me go."

She held me even tighter. I shouted at her: "Pervert!" Her grip loosened, and her hands slipped from my shoulders. I took a deep breath. Xiao Chi pulled her skirt on again. She was crying. I slipped out one of the back windows of the warehouse and ran until I couldn't hear her crying. I turned back and shouted again: "Pervert!"

7

That night, she cried the whole way home. It was two kilometers from the warehouse to Xiao Chi's house. You can imagine how hurt she was. When she got home, she went straight to her room and unrolled the bedroll she had prepared for her trip. She took everything out of her bag. She stood over the unpacked toothpaste and clothes and snacks and cried. When her father came to ask why, she told him that she wasn't going to join a production team. She wanted to stay there. Her father shook his head and said it was too late to decide to quit. Xiao Chi cried until her father gave up and went to the kitchen, where he cut a few thick slices of smoked ham and went to find Zhao Wannian. He pleaded with Zhao Wannian to let his daughter quit or to find somebody to replace her. Zhao Wannian shook his head, too. He told Xiao Chi's father that children from good families should be tested, they should meet the wind and waves head on. He told Xiao Chi's father that all the ham in the world wouldn't save his daughter. Xiao Chi's father came home and set the bag of sliced ham on the kitchen table. He went to his daughter's room. He asked her why she'd signed up in the first place. He reminded her of all the grand talk about going out to see the world. She didn't stop crying, but the crying got quieter. She rolled the bedroll up again and repacked her things.

The next morning, I went to the train station along with our other classmates who were staying in the city. The students going to the countryside lined up and boarded the train to the drumming of a military band. They stuck their heads out the window and waved to us, tears on their cheeks. The red flowers that they had proudly carried onto the train were left to fall on the station platform. I hadn't seen Xiao Chi get on the train, but her parents were there. They were in the crowd, calling her name: "Chi Fengxian, Chi Fengxian." But she wasn't among the students at the windows. I wondered if she hadn't come. It was only after the train blew its whistle and the wheels started to turn that she suddenly appeared, leaning from one of the windows of the carriage, waving to her parents. Xiao Chi's mother and father ran along with the crowd, who followed the train to the end of the platform. We kept waving as the faces receded until they were as small as sesame seeds in the distance.

After the train disappeared, I went to the zoo. I had taken over my mother's position in her work unit, looking after the tiger, the lions, and the bears. I don't know if it had anything to do with it, but after I took the job and starting working with the animals, I grew five centimeters and started to grow hair where there wasn't hair before. When I went back to the dormitory, I'd get out a razor and shave everywhere I thought needed shaving, but it would grow back in a day or two. I stopped after a while. I couldn't keep up. I felt like working with the animals was some sort of fertilizer, speeding up my natural processes or something. I started to feel hot almost all the time. I'd have to drink a few jugs of cold water, and after that, I'd maybe even have to go out to the cistern and drench myself. Most days I'd do it at least five times, and sometimes three more times at night. See, when I went to bed, I knew I would toss and turn for at least a few hours. If I couldn't sleep and I felt the heat coming on, I'd sometimes sit in front of the iron bars of the animals' cages, just waiting for the heat to pass.

I was awake in the early morning, when the world was dark and silent except for the calls of the nocturnal animals in their cages and the sounds of the trains from Sanhe Road. I'd ride my bike to the railyard sometimes and watch the trains passing. I didn't just watch them—I stared at them, not even daring to blink. It felt like any of the trains could be sending some sort of message, or maybe like it was my duty to watch them. My heart always beat faster when I watched the trains leaving the station. I wasn't really sure why. It took a few nights to realize that the trains were sending me a message, but it wasn't in the way I expected. The message was about Xiao Chi. I was worried about Xiao Chi, but I hadn't been able to admit it.

The truth came to me just as a train pulled out of the station, blowing its whistle in the night. I felt a sudden chill come over me. I felt lightheaded and lowered myself to the ground, clutching at my bike. The bike tipped over beside me, its rear wheel spinning. I said: "No." Why should I care about her, some girl who had wiped my forehead with a handkerchief once? I wanted to wipe her from my thoughts. I pictured my mother and Ceng Fang. I thought about my mother and how tightly she had held me when we hugged. I thought about Ceng Fang pulling my hair straight with a handful of soap. I felt ashamed, having placed Xiao Chi before them. I should be thinking of my mother and my sister, I thought. I looked up, and there she was: Ceng Fang, walking between the steel tracks, stepping over a railway tie . . . but I looked closer, and I had been mistaken—it was Xiao Chi walking toward me. I blinked her away. I tried again, imagining my sister walking toward me. But it was always Xiao Chi. It was always Xiao Chi, her skirt stirred by a breeze in the night air. Maybe she had been more than just a comrade. Maybe she wasn't sick in the head when she put her hands on my shoulders that night in the warehouse. I told myself to think rationally. I tried to assure myself that there was nothing beyond friendship between us. I tried to tell myself that Xiao Chi wasn't in love with me. I sat in the railyard until it was light out, until the rails were revealed by the rising sun, track after track laid out across the yard.

I went back to the zoo and got to work with a shovel and bucket, cleaning out cages, shoveling shit. I started to think about Xiao Chi again. But this time I pictured her handkerchief, the way she had held it over her face. I remembered the day we'd brought my father to his factory. She'd wiped it across my forehead and I'd ducked away. But it must have been covered with my sweat. I wondered suddenly if maybe that was why she kept it over her face. Could it be that she wanted to smell me? I tossed down the shovel and ran over to the schoolyard. I remembered that that was where she had thrown the handkerchief to the ground. I hadn't picked it up. I'd only kicked it around a few times and left. It had been months since that day. I searched through the fallen leaves and garbage that had collected under the tree, but I couldn't find the handkerchief. I figured the street cleaners must have swept around the tree at least a hundred times with their brooms. If they hadn't swept the handkerchief up, then it was probably bleached out and ruined by all the time outside. I went around the entire yard, stepping in dog shit and sorting through fallen leaves. Maybe she hadn't been smelling me. But why was she holding it over her face all the time? Why did she have to throw it on the ground right in front of me?

As I thought about it more, I felt sick to my stomach. What an idiot I'd been. I wanted to blow my brains out. She'd given me the perfect opportunity. I'd messed it up. If there was any chance left, I had to take it. I went home and began to write:

Xiao Chi:
How are you? Are you having fun in Tianle? Did you climb up to that lake yet? What's it like working for the production brigade? Are you doing farm work? Have you cried yet? Are you homesick? Do you hate me? I finally understand. I shouldn't have called you a pervert. I apologize. Please forgive me.

I'd always thought that female and male relations were somehow unnatural. I'd been taught in school and by Zhao Wannian's lectures that the whole thing was sick. Don't forget how my mother had behaved, either. I was always calling people perverts. When I started working at the zoo, I used to take a stick and poke the male monkeys that got too close to the females. Director He finally took me aside and told me that if the monkeys didn't reproduce, his salary would be docked. So if monkeys were doing it, why couldn't humans? Right? Haven't you heard that line about humans being the highest class of animal? We might be the highest class, but we're still animals. We're not as crude as animals, though. Humans have ideals. We don't just jump on each other like monkeys. There's a process. You meet somebody, you see how they feel, then . . .

Anyways, I ripped up the letter. Reading it back, I wasn't even able to understand what I had written. I tried again and ended up ripping that one up, too. I had a general idea that I wanted to communicate: I'm sorry, I was wrong, and now I understand. By the fourth or fifth attempt, I started writing "Dear Xiao Chi" at the top of the letter. When I'd finally finished and the letter was ready to send, I went to a postal box, ready to drop in the envelope, but my hand paused over the slot. What if Xiao Chi got mad? What if she gave the letter to someone? What if I was being too bold? What if I wasn't being bold enough? Maybe she wouldn't even believe me. Here I was, the guy who had called her a pervert, writing her a letter like this. I eventually gave up and went home. I wrote another letter and went to send it the next morning. But I still couldn't do it. I took that letter home and wrote another. I repeated this process, writing a letter and not sending it, then rewriting and not sending it again.

The letters collected under the bamboo mat on my bed. As the pile got bigger, the letters became increasingly confessional. There was no mistaking the purpose of the letters I was writing now. I described her skirt and the shape of her legs. I began to dream about Xiao Chi. I dreamed that the skirt fell away and that I held her tight when she embraced me. I didn't move away. I made love to her. In the dream, her mouth was as sweet as sugar. Being with her was the most comfortable I'd ever been. I woke up with my shorts sticky. I'd never had a wet dream before. I got up and wrote a letter that told her: I miss you so much that I had a wet dream about you.

I realized what I'd been doing. I thought about my father drinking those jugs of cold water, not sleeping at night and calling Zhao Shanhe's name when he did, getting out of bed to go watch trains. Even worse, I was having wet dreams. One night I woke myself up, and I realized that I had been moaning "Chi Fengxian" and squeezing my pillow. Wasn't that exactly like my father? I'd learned from a master. It occurred to me that maybe hugging your pillow isn't really a sign of moral deficiency.

I decided to go to the factory to see my father. When I arrived, he was standing over the stove, stirring a pan of greens. I called out to him, but he didn't answer. I stood beside him and watched the greens darkening in the hot oil. He put them on a plate and took them into his room at the dormitory. He held the plate high, as if I were a beggar waiting for some scraps. Even when our arms brushed together, he didn't look at me. I heard him sit down at his table and begin to eat, chewing noisily. When I entered the room, he sat motionless. I said: "Dad, I wanted to tell you, I've been thinking about it, and there are some things I finally understand and . . ." He turned away from me and began to eat.

When he was done, he went to the kitchen and tossed his bowl and plate down. I washed the dishes and wiped everything down and swept the floor. When I went back to the room, my father stood and left. He came back with Liu Canghai. "Uncle Liu," I said.

Liu Canghai said: "I don't know if this is okay, Changfeng."

My father said: "Just say it."

Liu Canghai scratched his head and said: "Um, Guangxian, your father—your father says you should get back to work."

My father said, louder: "Did I tell you to say that?"

"You aren't speaking Russian. Why am I translating for you? Just say it yourself."

My father howled back: "I promise you, I will never speak to my son again."

Liu Canghai said: "You'd better go, Guangxian. Don't make your father angry."

I stood to go, and Liu Canghai followed. In a low voice he told me: "Your father came to get me. He wanted me to tell you to fuck off. He's not quite back to normal."

I wobbled off on my bike, wiping away tears until I reached the factory gates. I stopped and stood beside my bike. The world was a big place, and I was all alone in it. Auntie Lei saw me near the gate and came over. "Oh, Guangxian, what's wrong? Was somebody mean to you? I'll tell your father, and he'll take care of them." I cried even harder.

When I got back to my dormitory at the zoo, I wrote a letter to Xiao Chi. I told her that she was my only comfort in life. I told her that she was the reason I kept on living. I told her that I was willing to die for her. I loved her. I deeply, truly loved her. I wrote five pages, declaring my undying love for Xiao Chi. I dropped the letter in the postal box that same night. I counted on my fingers: the next morning, the post office would pick up the letter; in the afternoon, they'd sort it and put it in a mailbag; by the morning of the following day, the mailbag would be on the train to Tianle; by the morning of the third day, the mailbag would arrive at the post office in Tianle and get sorted and put into another mailbag headed to Bala; and by the next day, it would be on a bus to the post office in Bala and sorted to be sent to the Bala People's Commune. After that, it was harder to figure. If there was anyone heading from Bala to the village at Guli and the production brigade there, the letter might arrive in Xiao Chi's hands by nighttime on the fifth day. If there was nobody going to Guli, the letter might wait until the seventh day or maybe even the eighth day to get to her. When I thought about the path that the letter would take, I wished I could hand it to her personally—or even better: read it to her.

Six days after sending the letter, it came back to me. I had forgotten to put a stamp on the envelope. I took it back to the post office with two stamps on it. I was beyond picturing the path of the letter from one mailbag to another. I was picturing Xiao Chi's face when she opened my letter, the way her cheeks would flush red, how she'd be surprised at first by reading "Dear Xiao Chi," and then how a smile would play across her lips, how she'd press the letter to her chest after reading it very carefully, savoring each sentence. She'd write me a letter right away, whatever it was she had to say. The letter would pass through the same mailbags, going in the opposite direction. Five days or so later, it would be in my hands. If she didn't forget to put a stamp on her envelope, I'd get it in about five days and write a letter that same day. So in ten days, I would be able to answer her first reply.

Twenty days went by, and I hadn't received a letter back from Xiao Chi. I knew it didn't have anything to do with stamps. That night, I went to the train station and saw a group of people headed toward a train bound for Tianle. Not really thinking, I let myself be swept up with them and pulled across the platform. I stood for a while on the step leading up to the carriage, the wind in my hair, and then I stepped inside. I made the journey hiding in the bathroom and roaming the corridors, avoiding the ticket checkers. By noon the next day, I was in Tianle.

Stepping off the train, I saw that Tianle was hidden in mist. A soft rain was falling. From the muddy roads and the wet roofs, I could tell that it had been raining for a long time, maybe weeks. The moisture had permeated everything so thoroughly that it would take months to dry out. I went down to the lot where minibuses were waiting and asked about the trip to the Bala People's Commune. Everyone said the buses for Bala had already left. I decided I'd go ahead on foot.

I walked away from the train station and onto the road toward Xiao Chi. I immediately found myself in the hills. I walked past paddy fields and through forests rich with mist. Everything was wet. When I looked closer at the fields, I saw that the rice had ripened and then been beaten down by the rain. The fields were rotting. The road was muddy and cut with networks of troughs and gullies ripped out by runoff from the mountains. Clouds hung over the tops of the trees and in the mountain valleys like rags hanging out to dry on a line. Even the birds couldn't fly there. They took off from a branch and beat their wet wings a few times before landing again in the trees.

That was the walk to end all walks, I thought. It felt like if you strung together all the walking I had done in my life, it wouldn't be as long as that walk was. The rain was constant, soaking me through. Now that I've seen all those dramas where the hero arrives at his lover's window on a rainy night, I think back to that walk in the rain. But I doubt that any of those men at the window were ever as thoroughly soaked as I was.

It was nine o'clock at night when I arrived at the house where Xiao Chi was staying. I looked as drenched and wretched as I felt. There was a light in the window. A kerosene lamp was burning inside. I scraped my shoes off on the step, leaving a thick slab of mud behind, and then I knocked at the door. Xiao Chi said, shocked: "What are you doing here? I thought you were dead."

"I walked."

"No, I mean . . ."

"What's wrong?"

"You're too late. Your letter was too late."

"What happened?"

She paused and then said: "I hate you."

Xiao Chi bit her lip and looked at me for a long time, and then she led me into the house. She brought some wet firewood and put it in the stove. She dribbled some kerosene on the wood and lit it with a match. I stood in front of the stove and began to take off my coat. "No, leave it on. Just stay there and dry out. Get a bit closer to the stove." I felt my body steaming, and the steam began to rise from my coat, filling the room. It was already late, but Xiao Chi had left the door open. When the wind blew it shut, she stood up and opened it again, even wider, and propped it open with a wooden stick. She wasn't acting like herself, I thought. She stared down at her toes, as if hoping to find some sign there. All the things that I had said in the letter disappeared from my mind. All of Xiao Chi's bravery at the warehouse was gone, too. There was only the crackling of the stove to break the silence and comfort me. When I was nearly dry, Xiao Chi said: "You have to go to Captain Wang's house to sleep. Rong Guangming and Yu Baijia are staying there, too."

"I don't want to sleep," I said. "I just want to look at you. I have to go in the morning and get back to work."

8

"We're going to harvest rice tomorrow. I can't sit up with you all night."

"I came all this way to see you. I didn't even plan on it. I was just walking by the train station and got on. I barely made it here."

She looked up, studying me suddenly, as if looking for something she had lost. I said: "I was too stupid to understand before. I'm sorry."

"What's the use of saying sorry now?" She put a few roasted sweet potatoes in a plastic bag. "You should go. You might miss the bus back to town."

"You haven't told me what happened."

"Everything that was supposed to happen already happened. You can't change it now."

"If you don't tell me, I'll go ask Baijia and Guangming."

"What do you want from me?" She took a sheet of plastic and wrapped a flashlight in it. "It's time to go. Don't make trouble for me here. I'll tell you everything on the way."

We took the flashlight and the sweet potatoes and went out onto the muddy road. The clothes that had just roasted dry in front of the stove were soaked through within minutes. For a while before she spoke, there was no sound except for our shoes in the mud and the hiss of rain. She said she didn't know what had made her fall for me. She said that maybe it was my curly hair, which made me look a bit like a foreigner, or maybe it was something else. She thought for a while and said that maybe it was the way I smelled. We'd always been told that the capitalist class stunk . . . So maybe my body odor carried some trace of that scent. I must have been right about the handkerchief, I thought. She must have been smelling my sweat on it.

We went by the village of Niutangao and the tall sycamore that stood at its entrance. Xiao Chi asked me: "Do you remember the day I left?"

"Of course."

"Do you remember how I looked out the train window and waved?"

"You were waving to your mom and dad."

"I begged them to let me stay in the city. They couldn't help me. I was waving at you."

"I couldn't tell."

"Are you kidding me? I even called your name. I told you to write me. I could tell you didn't hear me, so I said it again and I saw you nod. I saw you wave back at me. Don't lie to me."

"I swear."

"Then why did you wave? Why did you nod your head?"

"I didn't."

"I saw you! If you won't admit it, that's fine. I'm not going to keep talking."

I hadn't nodded or waved at her, but I finally said: "Fine, fine, fine." She'd ended up in the countryside, waiting for her first letter to arrive. She had run out to check the mailbox every day to see if there was a letter from me. Baijia and Guangming got letters, but she received none. A single letter was all that she wanted. Even though food was sparse, she would have given up a meal in exchange for a letter. Baijia and Guangming waved their letters in front of her face, so she could see the names of their female classmates. While they read their letters, she went outside and looked at the trees on the ridge, imagining that I was somewhere out there. She finally gave up and took the bus down to town. She wrote a letter to herself and signed my name. She apologized, as me, and told herself she was beautiful. In the letter she wrote, I proposed to her. She wrote her name at the top of it, then went back and wrote "Dear" in front. If I had just sent the first letter I wrote, she probably would have gotten it around the time she wrote her own. But I never sent it. All those letters had piled up under the bamboo mat on my bed. If I hadn't been so stupid . . . She started riding the bus to town to send herself letters. Every trip, twisting on mountain roads and bumping over muddy roads, she got violently carsick. The scenery of the mountains was as beautiful as that essay in the newspaper had described it, but she could barely see it. Eventually she gave up. She held the letters she had written to herself and cried. Finally, she burned them. She told herself that she would stop missing me.

When she arrived in Guli, Guangming and Baijia had been taken to live in Captain Wang's home. Captain Wang sent Xiao Chi to live by herself in a concrete hut a short distance away. It was, he said, better for a girl to stay by herself. The hut was a simple concrete box, dark and cold inside. That first night, she had stayed awake under the mosquito net, shivering. She thought she heard footsteps outside and went to the window, but didn't dare to look out. She wished she had a man to sit with her, to hold her hand. She decided that she would marry the first man who came to save her. She didn't care how old he was or what he looked like. The sound of footsteps came again, nearer now. She was lightheaded with fear. She yanked the door open and ran out of the hut—straight into the footsteps. A voice said: "Settle down. I'm here to watch your door."

Everyone working on the production team was assigned a job. If they were digging, everyone had a patch of earth to dig. When they finished digging their own section, they sat down and watched the other workers dig their patches. On her first day, Xiao Chi had been handed a hoe and given a section to work. She had never held a hoe before. By the end of the first day, her hands were covered in blisters. The next day, she was given the same tool and another patch to work. The blisters ripped open on the shaft of the hoe, drenching her hands in blood. The pain was so horrible that she felt as if she were working with a knife that she was holding by the blade. She couldn't complain; she would be criticized by the other workers. The whole point of coming to the countryside was to experience the hardship of the poor farmer. At first, some of the other workers would give her a hand. She fell behind again and again. Finally, most of them stopped offering to help. But one person continued to help her, even when the other workers laughed at him. He was the same one who had come to her door that night and kept watch. She was thankful for him. She thought that Chairman Mao had sent a man to look after her on the production team.

One day he came into her hut and told her that he wanted to get serious with her. She shook her head. Even though he had helped her and protected her, she turned him down because she was still in love with me, and she didn't want to marry a man from the countryside and be stuck there forever. She always used me as an excuse, saying she was in love with a man in the city. She even showed him the letters that she had written to herself with my name on them. But he said: "If he really loves you, why doesn't he come here to see you? Why is he just sending these letters?" He wasn't discouraged by her refusal. He kept helping her. He carried water for her, chopped wood, and washed clothes. He went to the market in town and brought her back brown sugar.

Two days before my letter arrived, a heavy rain had begun to fall. When she went back to her room after work, tired and hungry, all of the firewood was soaked. She filled the stove and tried to light a fire. The stove belched white smoke, but the fire would not stay lit. Tears began to stream down her face. It was hard to separate the tears of pain from the tears caused by smoke in her eyes. Just as she was about to give up, the man came to her hut and helped her light the fire with a drop of kerosene from the lamp. She looked up at him with amazement, as if she had just seen the birth of fire itself. She stood up and fell into his arms. It wasn't that amazing, really: he had merely used kerosene to light some wet firewood. But she hadn't thought of it herself. From then on, she always used kerosene and a match. She'd once cried and sweated over the wet firewood. Learning this method was a blessing.

Maybe it was fate that my letter arrived right after that night. If it had come only a few days earlier, maybe she wouldn't have fallen into his arms so easily. If I hadn't forgotten to put a stamp on the envelope, if I had sent the first letters I'd written . . .

The sky was just lightening when we arrived at the Bala People's Commune. The minibuses outside the Revolutionary Committee office were waiting, driverless. From a PA above us, announcements intermittently echoed down the muddy roads. We sat down on the stairs outside the office. I asked: "Who is he?"

"I don't want to tell you yet."

"Is it Baijia? Guangming?"

She shook her head.

"He's a farmer?"

She shook her head.

"Do I still have a chance?"

"No, I've already . . ."

"Already what? Slept with him?"

She frowned. She said: "That is none of your business."

"I'm not going back. I'm going to stay here with you. I'll join the production team."

"Forget it. I told you to sign up. You said you didn't want to go to the countryside."

I felt a lump in my throat. My tears came freely, mixing with the rain on my cheeks. She said: "You're still a child. What are you crying about? It won't help. All my tears couldn't bring you here." That only made me cry harder. It made me feel better, though. She turned her back to me. "There are lots of girls in the city," she said. "I'm sure you can find someone better than me."

"I only want you."

"You can't have me. I can't just split myself in two. You have to go. I need to get to work." She left me there, holding the bag of sweet potatoes. I called after her, but she kept walking until she disappeared into the rain.

Are you getting tired of this story yet? Let's take a break. Sorry, I forgot to bring cigarettes. I didn't know you smoked. Order a pack, it's fine. As long as you're listening, I'll keep going. Order another plate of fruit.

When I got back to the city, I took all the unsent letters from under the bamboo mat on my bed. I put them in envelopes and put two stamps on each envelope. The way I did it, I put one on the back and one on the front. Even if one stamp fell off, the other one would still be there. I went out and mailed all the letters. A little over a week later, I got a parcel from Xiao Chi. When I opened it, I saw all of my letters, unopened. I fell asleep holding the letters that night and woke to the sound of myself calling her name. My heart was broken. I stood facing in the direction of Tianle. I saw a light on the horizon and imagined it was Xiao Chi's kerosene lamp and the fire in the stove. I imagined I could see the smoke rising from the chimney of her concrete hut.

I went to the warehouse and sat on a bench in the hall. I thought back to the night that Xiao Chi had climbed up on the bench and twirled off her skirt. I thought about her big, beautiful legs. If I had seized my chance, if I had taken her in my arms, I wouldn't be here now. I was filled with regret. Now the chance was gone and she hated me. I looked at the bench that she had stood on, and it seemed to glow as if illuminated by a spotlight. I saw her stepping up onto the bench. I called out: "Chi Fengxian." The only response was the bark of a dog. I turned on my flashlight and saw a stray dog, filthy and sick, cowering below one of the benches. I lifted the dog up and held her against my chest. I carried her back to my dormitory at the zoo and fed her sugar water and rice. The dog seemed to improve, and her breathing, which had been shallow and labored, began to strengthen. After a few hours, she had the energy to lick my hand. I brought medicine from the zoo's veterinarian and took some of the meat that was meant to be fed to the tiger and the bears. After a few weeks, the dog's coat was glossy again. After that, she followed me everywhere. When I went around the zoo, doing my chores, she was with me. I called her Xiao Hua, after my dog that had died and been hung from the tree. But this dog had appeared after I called Xiao Chi's name, so I started calling her Xiao Chi. Whenever I called her name, she ran to me. If I felt sad, I'd talk to Xiao Chi. When I missed Xiao Chi, I had the dog, at least. I scrubbed her clean every night and let her sleep in bed beside me. Now when I called Xiao Chi's name in my sleep, Xiao Chi was there. The dog healed my broken heart.

Autumn came, and the zoo was covered in fallen yellow leaves. Every day when I got off work, I was met by Director He's cousin, He Caixia, who'd been given a job as the zoo's accountant. If she was sure nobody else was looking, she'd steal over to my side. "That curly hair," she'd say, "is it Soviet revisionism or American imperialism? I'm guessing it was American imperialism your mother preferred. You aren't the child of landlords at all, are you? You're the son of American imperialism. You'd better listen to me, or I'll turn you over to the Red Guards." While she spoke, one hand would be in my hair and the other would be between my legs. She would grab me so hard that I felt sick to my stomach. I used to walk away completely shaken. The only things I had to look forward to after work were my dog and talking to Zhao Jingdong, another one of the workers at the zoo.

Zhao Jingdong didn't talk much, but he sure could listen. He was a great audience for a story: he'd laugh in the right places, slap his thigh when something was really funny, sigh sympathetically at the appropriate moment—all the things you'd expect of a good listener. He also knew how to keep a secret. I was always worried about that, since I'd gotten myself into so much trouble telling the wrong things to the wrong people. I told him the story of Director He and my mother, how I'd found them together, and the story never went beyond him. He was like a vault. He taught me something, too: if you wanted to be a good friend, you had to be a good listener. One night, I sat up and told him the story of the warehouse and Xiao Chi taking off her skirt. He responded: "A girl drops her skirt right in front of you and you reject her? Well, that's gotta hurt, right? She had to be disappointed. Maybe you've heard about the Widow He, who works at the zoo. I've heard lots of stories about her trying to seduce certain men who ended up turning her down. Nobody wants to be turned down, right? Even if what they're asking is unreasonable."

Zhao Jingdong kept telling me that I should go visit Xiao Chi: "Make some time. Go see her. At the least, you're comrades, right? It's because of what you said that she ended up all the way out there, so you should show some concern. You should show her you're still thinking about her." He kept saying it: go see her, go see her. It was like a buzz in my ear. Eventually I saved up the money to take the trip, and I planned to use my sick leave to get time off work. When I told Zhao Jingdong, he seemed even more excited than I was. He asked me over and over again how far Tianle was from the city. Finally, he came to my dormitory room and spread out a map marked with an arrow pointing from the city to Guli. The way he'd marked the map, it felt like Xiao Chi was a military objective. He went out again and came back with three jars of braised pork and five bundles of dried noodles for me to give her. He saw me off at the train station and went back home with Xiao Chi the dog.

A cold wind blew against the windows of the train as it left the city. After a few kilometers, the train passed into mist, which then covered the windows. Anyone looking at the train as it rumbled by would have seen its color darken and take on a hue like raw steel as the sunlight shrank down to a red ball on the horizon.

The next evening, I arrived at Guli. Everyone in the village seemed to be gathered under the lanterns at the commune hall. They were standing around a low stage. When I got closer, I could see two figures kneeling on the stage with old shoes hanging around their necks—it was Xiao Chi and Yu Baijia. Xiao Chi's hair was in disarray. Her face was cut, and there was blood on her lips. Yu Baijia had clearly been beaten, too. His left eye was swollen shut and ringed with a black bruise. I finally realized that it was Yu Baijia who had protected Xiao Chi. It was Yu Baijia who had played Prometheus in her cement hut.

‹ 9 ›

The crowd pressed forward, thronging around the stage. The commune members gave their testimony one after another. The basic story was that Xiao Chi and Yu Baijia had been caught in flagrante delicto, together in a haystack. The rice straw in which they had enjoyed their rendezvous was meant for the commune's cows. The cows needed the straw to survive over the winter. It wasn't the physical act between the two comrades that was offensive, the commune members said, but rather that they had sullied the cattle feed needed to support the commune. Someone speculated that perhaps it would be unsafe for the cattle to eat the straw now. There was agreement from another commune member, who wondered about birth defects when the calves came the next year.

I was frozen in place, watching the crowd. They circled the stage with their mouths wide in laughter, but all I could hear was a roar in my ears. The villagers looked like wild animals circling their prey. I shivered and felt my teeth chattering. A woman in the crowd grabbed a handful of rice straw and pushed it into Xiao Chi's face. "Eat it! They're nothing but animals; let them eat straw." Xiao Chi tried to twist away. Commune members straddled her and forced her face down toward the straw, chanting: "Eat it! Eat it! Eat it!" When the straw was forced on Yu Baijia, he opened his mouth and chewed placidly. The crowd applauded.

Xiao Chi struggled under the hands of the commune members. I could tell she was trying not to cry, but a few tears leaked from the corners of her eyes. Yu Baijia swallowed the straw and then retched onto the stage. Some of the commune members chanted for him to eat his vomitus. Rong Guangming held up a lantern, waving it over the heads of the audience: "Come on, we can't do that. We'll run out of ideas and have nothing to do tomorrow night. That's enough for today." The commune members began to leave the stage. They untied their captives and took their lanterns down. They seemed hesitant to leave, as if they hadn't had their fill.

I followed Xiao Chi back to her cement hut. I started: "I'm sorry. If I'd known it was so bad, I would have been here, I would have joined the production team. I wouldn't have been like Baijia, so irresponsible—." I heard the slap before I felt it. My cheek stung, and my ears were ringing. The net bag that I had brought from the city fell to the floor, and the three jars of braised pork shattered. She still thought she was on the stage, I thought. In a louder voice, I said: "Xiao Chi. It's Guangxian."

"Yeah, I know who I slapped. Don't think you can just rush in and rescue me now. I don't need rescuing, I don't need sympathy. I don't regret anything. It was my choice. Put me in prison, shoot me in the head—I'll never regret it. I just want you to leave me alone."

"I just came to see you. I didn't think . . ."

"You didn't think it would be this savage here? You didn't think I'd get myself in trouble? Why don't you get out of here and go tell everyone? Tell our classmates, our teachers, tell everyone in the city, put it in the newspaper. I don't care what you do. I'm not afraid. Do I look afraid? Have I ever been afraid?"

I thought she must be hysterical. I didn't say anything and bent down to pick up the broken jars. I salvaged what I could of the pork, heated it in a pot, and put it beside her bed. I left as quietly as I could.

On the train back to the city, I felt my heart beating in time to the click-clack of the rails. I took out a piece of paper and began to write, leaning on the windowsill.

Baijia:
How are you doing? I feel there's something deeply wrong with Xiao Chi. You two have been through so much, so I can understand how emotional she must be. But I worry that maybe it's been too much for her to handle. I hope that both of you will look after yourselves.

I wanted to tell you something I noticed while writing this letter. There's a woman sitting across from me on the train. You know, there might be some chance for me to talk to her. Maybe she'll ask me to help open a bottle of water. Maybe she'll start talking to me. We'll make eye contact. The thoughts that follow, there's no telling where they'll go. So I've made it into a game with myself. If I don't look at her, if I don't try to meet her eyes, then it means I haven't had impure thoughts. I think you should be careful with things like that. Don't go into any more haystacks. You were the one to snatch Xiao Chi away from me. You might say that you took my place. Please look after her just like I would. Take her into consideration before doing anything rash. If you really can't control yourself, try using your hand. My father taught me that. Might as well give it a shot.

May we share mutual encouragement.

May revolutionary friendship last forever.

Ceng Guangxian

Don't laugh at that. Those last two lines were just stock phrases that we put in all the letters we wrote each other back then, even if we didn't really share the sentiment behind them.

Oh, it wasn't that? What were you laughing at? The part where I told him to use his hand? It seems like a joke, but it was deadly serious. If he couldn't control himself, it could end in tragedy. Anyways, we're living in liberal times, but it was a lot different back then.

I thought I was friends with Zhao Jingdong, but he'd never told me about his cousin. The first two things I learned were that she was older than he was and very beautiful. She was more beautiful than you, even. No offense. She was just a very beautiful girl. So beautiful . . . that . . . It's sort of hard to describe. But anyways, she was beautiful. A few specifics come to mind, little things like the way her hair hung over her forehead, cut perfectly straight. And her nose and her eyes were amazing—I'm not just saying this as a man. I'm sure you'd say the same if you saw her. She didn't have big eyes, but there was something about them. She looked like she could play a spy in a TV series. Her eyes had a certain curve when she squinted. It always seemed like she was trying to tease you, the way she looked at you, like she was trying to seduce you. And she had long, long eyelashes, too. A small mouth, too, but perfect, red and round like a cherry. I'm saying that without lipstick, her lips were cherry red. Back then, the taste was for women with small mouths. Nowadays, all the women on TV have big mouths. The first time I saw her—no, wait, I should tell you about the second time I saw her. It was at Zhao Jingdong's funeral.

I'm getting off track again. I'd better tell you how Zhao Jingdong died, or this won't make any sense.

When I got back to the city, I went to get my dog and found that she and Zhao Jingdong were inseparable. I tried calling Xiao Chi over, but she only bent her head down to lick Zhao Jingdong's foot. He said, "Call her Noisy!" I called, and the dog looked up. Zhao Jingdong nudged her with his foot and said: "Go." The dog took a few steps toward me but then turned back and licked Zhao Jingdong's foot.

"You've been feeding her too well!"

"I went and bought some meat for her."

"I never thought I'd be betrayed by my own dog. Unbelievable."

"Hey, what about Xiao Chi? How is she?"

"She's great."

I didn't want to tell him about what I had seen in the countryside. I picked up a stick and waved it at the dog. She ran ahead of me into my dormitory room. I had made a hole in the bottom of the door so that she could get in and out. I blocked it up and went to lie on my bed. I was dead tired. I thought about getting up to wash my face, but I didn't have the energy.

In the morning, I saw that Xiao Chi was gone and the hole in the door had been unblocked. I figured that if the dog had wanted to get out badly enough to unblock the door, there must be some reason. I got out of bed and looked over at Zhao Jingdong's house. I noticed that his old window frame had been replaced with a new one, and the dirty glass had been replaced. The window had been covered by an old newspaper. I wondered what he was up to in there. When I tapped on his door, I heard the sound of the dog inside. When Zhao Jingdong came to the door, Xiao Chi was by his side.

I asked: "Why do you call that dog Noisy? What does that mean?"

"What do you mean what does that mean? She's noisy. Take her back."

"I'll tie her up so she can't get out again."

"That's too cruel. Why don't you let her stay here for a while?"

"Come on, Jingdong. You know that dog is all I have."

"I don't want to argue with you, but that dog isn't going to replace your mother or your sister."

"It's weird: that dog used to be so loyal."

"I don't get it, either."

From my room, I could hear Zhao Jingdong playing with Xiao Chi, getting her to bark and roll over. I heard it all. I paced around the room and sang a song to distract myself, a Party anthem that was popular at the time. I felt a bit better for a while, but the dark feelings came back to me. The next morning, I went to the animals' cages with a bucket of cow guts. I called out to the dog: "Noisy! You can have some of this, too. Just come on back to me." I didn't hear any sound from the dog, and she didn't come. I tried to pretend that I didn't really care about the dog betraying me. I went and fed the tiger and the lions and took some of the guts out of the bucket. It bothered me to be stealing from my job like that, but nobody was watching. I looked around one more time to check and saw that the tiger and the lions were watching. I shivered.

When I got home, I put some oil in a pot and dumped in the intestines. They browned nicely in the oil, and the smell of cooking meat filled my room. The smell had my mouth watering, but I didn't cut any for myself. I took the pot out to my front door, dumped the guts into the dog's bowl, and clanged the ladle a few times to call her. I called out: "Dinner!" The dog rushed out of Zhao Jingdong's door. She bent her head down to the bowl and swallowed all the guts in a few mouthfuls. I thought she'd thank me, maybe wag her tail, at least. But she only turned and went back to Zhao Jingdong's door with her tail down. The next day, when I went to feed the animals, there were a few thick beef bones left, and I took one back to my dormitory. I tied a string around one end and left the bone outside my door. I ran the string through the hole in the door and hid inside. When I heard the dog approach, I jerked the string and pulled the bone into my room. The dog followed. She stopped, halfway in and halfway out, looking at the bone. She refused to take another step. I couldn't believe it. A nice thick bone like that, and she wouldn't even come in to get it. Stubborn dog, right?

When the weekend came, I was left to shuffle around my room, bored and anxious. Zhao Jingdong seemed to be out, and there was a lock on his door. The dog—Xiao Chi or Noisy, whatever she wanted to be called—was nowhere to be seen. I sat outside for a while and watched insects buzzing up and down, going about their business. A few leaves fell, spinning through the air from somewhere. The dog finally appeared, walking toward Zhao Jingdong's door. I watched her walk by, and she turned to look at me. We both stood still, looking at each other. I guess she'd forgotten her time with me: all the time we'd spent together, and she seemed not to even remember me. I called to her: "Xiao Chi, Xiao Chi . . ." I kept calling, remembering how she used to respond to her name and rush over to me, jumping up on me. No matter how many times I called Xiao Chi, the dog would not answer to her name. She must have lost her memory! Maybe she didn't like the name. I tried out a few other names—whatever she answered to, I'd call her that: "Red Flower! Happy! Money! Fatty!" I went down the list, trying to find a name: "Commander! Well-Fed! Pretty Girl! Director He!" I ran out of names after a while, and the dog began to lick her lips. I don't think that had anything to do with the name.

Maybe the names were too informal, I thought. Maybe this dog was . . . —I hesitated for a moment and then called, "Mom." The dog didn't move. I tried "Grandpa," and "Grandma." My heart ached, calling those names. The dog didn't move, but I thought I saw her frown. I decided to take more extreme measures. This dog didn't care about being called a pretty name or eating a good meal. I went and grabbed her by the neck and dragged her into my room. I tied her up and blocked the hole in the door. She started whimpering and turning in circles. I thought that I would keep her there for a few days and she'd eventually come around, get back to normal.

That night, I slept comfortably. You might think it sounds silly, but I felt like I had dragged my runaway lover back home. That dog really upset me. It was about the only thing that could knock my life off track. Now, thinking back, it does sound silly. It's possible I'm exaggerating a bit, but you have to remember that the dog was the only company I really had. My family was broken up, and I'd even lost my friendship with Xiao Chi. I needed some warmth in my life, and the dog had provided it. If I lost my dog, my life would be colder than ever.

I really didn't expect to wake up the next morning to find a length of rope and the hole in the door gaping open. The dog was gone. I didn't even get out of bed. I lay there feeling hopeless. If even the rope hadn't held her, then what could I have done to keep her? If I had known she was so cruel, I wouldn't have brought her back from the warehouse in the first place.

Director He heard me talking about the dog. I'd been saying how ungrateful she was, how she'd betrayed me. He stopped me: "It's just a dog. Come on. You're talking like your wife ran out on you." If somebody is unsympathetic to you, that's bad enough, but if somebody is going to make fun of you, you might as well not bother telling them anything. I told the same story to Lu Xiaoyan, who took care of the birds at the zoo. I ran into her while walking through the aviary. She listened to the whole story, the betrayal, the sense of loss, and said absentmindedly: "Oh, really?" I realized she hadn't been listening at all. I went to feed the tiger and the lions. They were the only ones that seemed to listen sympathetically.

One day while I was cleaning up the walks in front of the cages, I saw He Caixia coming toward me. It seemed like she hadn't seen me, so I dropped my broom and tried to hide. It was instinct at that point to avoid her. I guess I wasn't quick enough, because she came right over, and her hands were down between my legs the next instant. "Auntie He," I croaked. "I want to tell you something."

She squinted at me. I started telling her about the lost dog. She laughed and looked around a few times: "You mean you haven't heard? Everyone knows about it. That Zhao Jingdong . . . was . . . well, he was having relations with the dog. Somebody found out, and he's going to be dragged into a struggle session. Some of the comrades have already prepared their speeches. You really didn't know?"

I was stunned. I couldn't move. He Caixia reached for one more handful and then skipped away, humming. I didn't want to think about it—or maybe I didn't even know what to think. How . . . ? A dog and a man?

How did they do it? It didn't make sense to me. They weren't even the same species. But it made sense when I thought about it. That's why the dog had betrayed me. That's why he had replaced his broken window frame and covered up the new glass with newspaper. It was a long time before I could even move. I was disgusted by Zhao Jingdong.

‹ 10 ›

I started ignoring Zhao Jingdong. When he knocked at my door, I pretended not to hear it. We worked together, so it was hard to avoid each other, but I made it clear to him that I didn't want to talk to him. After a while, he took the hint and started to lower his head when I came near. I went to Director He and told him that I wanted to move. I couldn't stand living next to Zhao Jingdong. Director He said: "We don't have any other place for you to go. Unless you want to live in a cage, you're stuck there."

He Caixia wouldn't stop repeating the story, always adding more details. Our comrades at the zoo loved to hear it, laughing until they cried. One day when everyone was in her office to pick up their wages, she said: "Do you know what he used to get it wet? Lard!" Everyone laughed.

"How do you know?"

"I saw him! I happened to look in his back window and I saw him. "

"You're sick, watching him like that."

"I'm sick? He was the one doing it." Everyone laughed again. Nobody could count the wages that the bookkeeper handed out to them, they were laughing too hard. Zhao Jingdong walked by the door, ready to collect his wages, but he turned and left, staggering away. I thought she was going too far.

That night, I went to his door and knocked. He came to the door. Blushing, he said: "Guangxian, I can't be your friend anymore."

"You know what Widow He is saying about you?"

"Yes." His hand was on top of Noisy's head, patting her lightly.

"Is it . . . true?"

Zhao Jingdong nodded his head. "I didn't want anyone to know. I was hiding in here. But she was too nosy. She came snooping around like she was going to rob the place."

"How could you do that?"

He avoided my gaze, looking down at his legs. "It was the only way. I couldn't take it anymore. You would have done the same."

"You think I've never been through the same thing?"

"You really think so? I'm in love, and it's not with a woman like He Caixia, some ugly old thing. I'm in love with a goddess."

"What goddess?" I looked around me.

"She lives at my grandmother's house. She's my cousin. She's a performer with the provincial propaganda team. Her body is amazing. She's shameless. Every time she goes to take a bath, she calls me in, saying she forgot the soap. She opens the curtain and lets me see everything. She'll do the same thing when I'm sleeping there, wandering around completely naked. I couldn't take it anymore. This dog was her replacement until the widow saw us."

I felt sympathy for him. I'd had no idea what he was going through. I told him: "You need to get ready. They're going to take you to a struggle session. The widow said that they're almost ready. It's going to be just like they did to my dad."

The color drained out of his face, and his body stiffened: "Really?"

"Anyways, that's what she said."

"Everyone is going to hear about what I did. How will I live with myself? Should I just run away?"

"Either get ready or run."

"Where would I even go?"

Zhao Jingdong wasn't at work the next day. From the monkey cage, where he made his first stop of the morning, there came a desolate chorus of howls. Director He went to the door of Zhao Jingdong's dormitory room and knocked and then pounded. Red in the face, he kicked at the door until it swung open.

Zhao Jingdong was lying stiff in his bed. There was blood at the corners of his mouth. When the coroner cut him open, his verdict was poisoning. Zhao Jingdong had drunk pesticide. A few of the comrades from the zoo went to the funeral. Lu Xiaoyan was there, and Fang Ziyu. They mixed with the members of the Zhao family who had come to see Zhao Jingdong off. I noticed a woman among the mourners, a particularly beautiful woman—a goddess. These actresses nowadays couldn't even stand next to her. Judging by those curves, she had to be the cousin that Zhao Jingdong was talking about. I stole a few glances, and my heart began beating faster. She came over, stretching out a hand to me: "You must be Ceng Guangxian. Jingdong mentioned you. I'm his cousin Zhang Nao." Noisy Zhang, in other words—no wonder! He had named the dog after his cousin. I was speechless. My hand stayed at my side. She turned to go.

I had the feeling that I'd seen her before. I guessed that it was Zhao Jingdong's stories about her; they probably had left an impression on me. I thought a lot about that missed handshake, the way her hand had hung in the air. It had seemed to glow in the dark. Sometimes I even shook my own hand, pretending that it was Zhang Nao's. I wished I hadn't let her go without reaching my hand out to her. I was left to shake my own hand. I played back what she had said to me: "You must be Ceng Guangxian. Jingdong mentioned you . . ." I prayed that she'd give me another chance to take her hand.

One morning I went to take a piss in the bushes near the dormitory and came across Noisy. The dog had already stiffened. There was blood on her muzzle. I guessed Zhao Jingdong had fed the pesticide to her before he drank it himself. She must have staggered out of the house before he died. But she hadn't made it very far. I wrapped her in a burlap sack and carried her to the warehouse. I had found her there, after all. I dug a pit behind the warehouse and laid her in it. I had mostly covered her with dirt, but her rear half was still hanging out of the ground. I'm going to tell you this, but I don't want you to laugh. I had a bizarre sensation—or rather I had two sensations. My body stiffened, and I felt a sense of deep disgust and retched. It felt like I was doing battle with myself. It was only when I had covered the body of the dog completely with dirt that I finally relaxed. I can't recall what I said, maybe "Rest well, Noisy" or "Rest in peace," something like that, but I don't really remember. Maybe I didn't say anything.

The dormitory room where Zhao Jingdong had lived was left empty. The door was left unlocked and rattled against the frame every time the wind blew through the zoo. Some people said that it must be Zhao Jingdong's ghost, still haunting the room. But I wasn't afraid. Sometimes I found myself going over there and standing quietly by myself. It felt like Zhao Jingdong could come back at any moment. It felt like I could still sit down and spend the afternoon chatting with him, his dog at his feet. Everyone else was scared to even approach the dormitory, but I didn't mind at all. I realized that a certain change had come over me. I wasn't scared of much anymore. One day when I heard He Caixia talking about Zhao Jingdong and the dog again, I heard myself say: "You killed him."

She covered her mouth with her hand and went quiet.

I kept going: "Every night, I heard him crying in his room. He told me that it was you who discovered him, and you who told everyone his secret. If it hadn't been for you going around telling everyone, the zoo's leaders wouldn't have found out. There wouldn't have been all that talk about struggle sessions. It was pathetic to hear him crying in the middle of the night."

He Caixia looked like a criminal under the lights of an interrogation room. I could see the fear on her face. She stammered: "You—you're spreading lies."

What's wrong? Anyways, this was thirty years ago. Don't shake like that. Oh, the cigarettes are here. Go ahead, have one. Let me light it for you.

The next day, He Caixia stood in front of everyone and said: "Ask anyone here. They'll tell you it was you that killed him."

I leaned in the doorway. I said: "Why would they say I killed him? Everyone knows it was you."

"Think about it. Who was it that told him about the struggle session?"

"You kept talking about it."

"I did keep talking about. I was talking about it for weeks. But he never killed himself. He didn't even know about it. It was only after you told him that he went and killed himself. It was you who brought him the dog in the first place. It's all your fault. You set the trap for him. Is it clear to you yet?"

I pointed toward Zhao Jingdong's room: "Then why don't you go in there? If you really didn't kill him . . ."

She walked toward the door but couldn't seem to bring herself to step inside. I walked around her and went in. I sat down on a dusty bench in the room. Her face darkened, and she turned as if to go but then turned back around and sat down beside the door. "Come in and sit down. Right on the bed. If you can sit on the bed, I'm willing to admit that you didn't kill him."

She stood and walked over to the bed and sat down on it. "I know you killed him." The bed creaked under her.

"You're sitting on his blood. Have a look for yourself."

"Anyways, if there's a ghost, it's not looking for me. He'll come back to get you. You told me if I would sit on the bed, you'd admit I didn't kill him."

"You just sat down. Stay awhile. That's how I'll know you're really innocent." The room was quiet enough to hear insects ticking off the light bulb. We made eye contact once and then looked around the room, as if examining the spider webs in the corners of the ceiling. "How about if I turn off the light?"

The bed creaked under her again. She said: "I'm innocent. There's nothing for me to be afraid of."

I stood up and switched off the light. The room was completely dark and silent except for the creak of the bed. I said: "You can almost hear him crying now, can't you?" I heard the bed creak one last time and saw a shadow moving toward the door. She was outside, panting. I called to her: "Guilty conscience?"

"I'm innocent and I proved it. I sat on the bed." She stalked off.

I sat in the dark alone. I thought about what He Caixia had said and felt myself trembling. If I hadn't told him about the gossip, if I hadn't told him about the struggle session, then maybe he wouldn't have killed himself.

The worst decision I'd made was letting him look after the dog in the first place. I could have asked Lu Xiaoyan or Fang Ziyu or even He Caixia, I thought, and none of this would have happened. My mind raced, and a shriek escaped from somewhere inside me.

The next day, as I was passing the hippo enclosure, I heard He Caixia's voice. She was helping one of the keepers dredge the hippo's pond. As she worked, she talked, loud enough for anyone to hear. I guessed she wanted everyone to hear.

She said: "Last night, I got into it over who killed Zhao Jingdong."

The keeper, Hu Kaihui asked: "So, who killed him?"

She said: "It had to be Ceng Guangxian. He told me that I had to prove it wasn't me. He got me to sit on Zhao Jingdong's bed. I went right inside and sat down for a while. I think that proves it, doesn't it? If I had a guilty conscience, I couldn't have sat there with all that blood still on the bed."

She knew how to tell a story. She'd taken a piece of rotten meat and doused it with sesame oil, added a bit of salt, and finished it with MSG. Each time she told it, it sounded even better. Hu Kaihui and Lu Xiaoyan both stopped to ask me if it was true, if she'd really sat on Zhao Jingdong's bloodstained bed. Even the deaf groundskeeper came over to ask me about it. It took me a while to figure out what he was getting at, waving his hands around, but he finally got down on all fours and rolled on the grass, his tongue sticking out. Think about that. Everyone wanted to know about it. There were a hundred workers at that zoo. It felt like every one of them came up to me and finally got around to asking: "Is it true that you killed Zhao Jingdong?"

How could I even answer a question like that? I'd learned my lesson, though: I didn't say a word. But He Caixia wanted to keep up the pressure. At a study meeting one afternoon, she took the stage and asked: "Did I sit on Zhao Jingdong's bed, Ceng Guangxian?" Everyone turned to look at me. I felt the weight of their stares in the middle of my forehead. I stood and looked over at the door. He Caixia grabbed my sleeve: "Tell the truth, or we'll get it out of you at a struggle session."

"Yes, you sat on the bed."

"And you said that proves I didn't have anything to do with Zhao Jingdong killing himself."

I nodded.

"Say it!"

"Yes, I said it means you had nothing to do with it."

"Louder!"

"Yes, I said it. I said it means you had nothing to do with Zhao Jing-dong's death."

She let go of my sleeve. "You all heard him. If anyone else goes around looking at me like they have been, they can go to hell."

I ran from the room. The instant I got out of there, standing under the tree in the yard, I shouted: "Then since when are you scared of the dark?"

I heard laughter from the room behind me and He Caixia's voice: "You son of a bitch. I'll rip your arms off, I'll . . ." She ran out of the room toward me and picked up a stone. She chased after me as I ran toward the dormitory.

‹ 11 ›

There's no way she could have caught me, even if she'd trained for a year. Every time she got close, I bolted away. She kept going, trying to chase me down. She'd clearly lost weight over the last few weeks, most likely from all the worrying about Zhao Jingdong, but it was probably still good for her to get a good jog in. But she wasn't going to catch me. She called after me: "Tell the truth, Guangxian—did I kill him or not?"

"I don't know. But it wasn't me."

She finally dropped the stone and bit her lip. She said: "You're cruel, Ceng Guangxian. You don't have a conscience."

That night, He Caixia surprised me by coming to my door with a gift of a bag of apples. I was overwhelmed by the unexpected gesture. I sort of wandered around my room, not sure whether to sit or stand. He Caixia looked around and then sat down. "We shouldn't be fighting over this, Guangxian. I'm not going to be chasing you around anymore. I don't need to lose weight. Anyways, if you don't believe me, I don't care. I'll tell you something: since Zhao Jingdong died, I haven't been able to sleep through the night. I wake up every night in a cold sweat. You didn't help when you started accusing me of killing the man. It's gotten even worse. I'm not sleeping at all. I can't rest. But you're right, I shouldn't have been going around telling everyone what he was up to. He hadn't even found a wife yet. But you . . . you won't take any responsibility. The way I see it, you pushed him to kill himself."

"If you came here to tell me that, you can get out."

"Now, hear me out. The way I see it, Zhao Jingdong had the predisposition. He didn't place much value on his own life. We can agree on that, I hope. Somebody who never thought about it doesn't just drink a jug of pesticide on a whim. He must have thought about it before. He was just waiting for something to push him over the edge."

That made sense to me. I felt a weight lift from my shoulders. But she went on: "What pushed him? You were the one who rushed to tell him that the work unit was planning a struggle session. If nobody had told him, he might not have killed himself right then. He was ready to do it all along. But he needed someone to strike the match and light the fuse. Whether you admit it or not, I don't really care. Facts are facts. All I want is for you to stop trying to persecute me. I told you already, I can't sleep at night!"

I picked up an apple and tossed it through the open door.

"To tell you the truth, the work unit wasn't even planning a struggle session. If you don't believe me, go ask Director He." She stood and walked out. It looked as if a great weight had been lifted from her—and dropped right on me.

Since that night when I'd sat on the bed, I had thought about asking Director He about the struggle session. If He Caixia was telling the truth, then Zhao Jingdong had killed himself for nothing. He Caixia was spreading rumors about a struggle session, but I was the one who had carried the rumors straight to Zhao Jingdong. I was trapped: should I have told him and let him know, or kept it to myself and maybe let him be dragged before the struggle session without any warning? She had pushed me into a corner. I woke up early the next morning and heard the cries of Zhao Jingdong. The sound of his sobs echoed down the street, rising and falling. I couldn't handle it. I ran to Director He's home.

Director He answered the door, startled by my pale face: "What's wrong with you? Are you sick or something?"

I shook my head. "Promise me you'll tell the truth."

"When did I lie to you?"

"Tell me the truth: Did you plan to take Zhao Jingdong to a struggle session? Were you thinking about it?"

"Bullshit. What are you bringing that up again for? I heard the rumors, but I never took them seriously. We've got bigger problems here. Half the animals are starving. Who has time for that crap, taking him in front of a struggle session?"

I was expecting the answer, but when I heard it from Director He, I was shaken. I felt a chill come over me, and my entire body shook violently. Director He wrapped a blanket around my shoulders and sent me back to my dormitory room. When I got inside, I bolted the door and shut the window tight and locked it. I hid under a heavy blanket, trying to block everything out. It had happened again. I couldn't keep my mouth shut, and it had cost someone his life.

After that, I always slept with the bolt on my door and a lock on my window. I shut out everything. I couldn't even hear the wind howling outside. But every time, as the night wore on, a fear stole over me. I shut my eyes, afraid that if I opened them I would see Zhao Jingdong. When I got up in the morning, I would find myself dozing off as I went about my daily chores. One morning, cleaning out the tiger's cage, I fell asleep against the bars. The bites of mosquitoes and my numb legs woke me up, but I could have slept there until dusk. My face was creased with new wrinkles. I was in rough shape. But my neighbor was a vengeful ghost, so . . . what can I say?

That Sunday, I brought one of the zoo's carts to the door of my dormitory and loaded all of my things into it. He Caixia happened to be walking by. She asked: "You moving, Guangxian?"

"I have to move or I'll go insane."

He Caixia could only laugh. She laughed harder than I'd ever seen her laugh, doubling over. "I thought I was the only one who was scared. That makes me feel a lot better. I guess I don't have anything to worry about. Come on, let me help you."

I tried to help her by pushing the wheelbarrow from behind, but she was pulling it so fast that I could barely catch up.

I went back to the warehouse. You know the warehouse, the same one that got converted to an auditorium for revolutionary speeches, the same warehouse where I was born and where Xiao Chi had stepped out of her skirt and, yes, where I had found that dog. I spread a mat on the dusty floor of the building's tiny loft and finally slept. It felt like weeks since I had really slept, instead of just tossing and turning on my dormitory bed. I simply wanted to find a place to sleep. I didn't really think too much about returning to the warehouse. It was merely a place that I wasn't afraid of. But I'd unknowingly stumbled out of the frying pan and into the fire. If only I'd stayed at the dormitory . . .

I managed to sleep until the early evening, when I was awoken by a sound from below. The loft of the warehouse was built of wooden beams, and a sort of curtain of old newspapers had been tacked in place along them. I ripped a hole in the newspaper so that I could look down. The attic was about where a projectionist would be in a theater, and the hole in the newspaper was about as big as the hole that the lens of the theater's projector would require. Below me, on the stage, the provincial propaganda team was rehearsing a performance of one of the Eight Model Operas, *Red Detachment of Women,* with Zhang Nao playing the role of Wu Qionghua. I watched Zhang Nao run through a routine of pliés and splits, playing the revolutionary peasant daughter Wu Qionghua with all the passion that she deserved.

The next day, I borrowed a pair of binoculars from Hu Kaihui. When I got home to the loft that night, I could see the stage as if I were sitting in the front row. I could see every detail: her pale white neck, the soft line between her breasts. I felt my temples throb. I ran to check the door and crept back to the hole in the newspaper. I hesitated. I thought that if I looked down and watched her, it would mean that I was sick, and if I could resist, it would mean that I was still innocent, pure. I felt like the two sides of me were doing battle, sin grappling with purity. Eventually there was a winner, and I went to the rip in the newspaper and pulled some paper back into the hole and covered it up. The lights from down below still shone through, and I thought that I could still see the silhouette of Zhang Nao on the stage. I'd made my decision. But my body was in disagreement. My dick was rock hard in my pants. I muttered toward my crotch: "You didn't get the message, I guess."

In the morning when I went to work, He Caixia asked me: "Did you sleep well?" I had never been asked that before. Most people asked, "Have you eaten yet?" That was the usual greeting. She looked like she had just had the best sleep of her life. It was like a butcher asking a beggar how his supper was. She said: "If I hadn't had to get up to come to work, I could have just kept hibernating." All the weight that had been on her shoulders had been dumped onto mine. She had looked frail and thin that day she had chased me, but I could tell she'd been eating well again. She took to greeting me like that: "How was your sleep?" At least she was sleeping well again, even if I wasn't.

I sat in the loft every night listening to the sounds below. When the girls took the stage, I looked forlornly at the ragged rip in the newspaper. I thought about going over to take a look, but I couldn't do it. I thought about my father being dumped in front of the warehouse, and Xiao Chi and Yu Baijia forced to eat straw on that stage in Guli. I forced myself not to go over to the hole in the newspaper. Finally, though, I couldn't hold myself back. I crept over and peeled it open again. I lay on the floor with my binoculars, watching the heroic lead, Zhang Nao, take the stage. She was wearing a white singlet tucked into a leather belt. The buttons at the top of her shirt had come undone, and I could see almost everything. My breath came ragged, and I felt lightheaded. I went to the loft's small window and gulped the night air until I had calmed down. I went back to the newspaper hole and watched for a while longer. But I wasn't completely committed: every day, I covered the hole up again with fresh scraps of newspaper and told myself I wouldn't look again. It was ridiculous, because I always went back. I made the same mistake and tried to wipe it out, but I couldn't stop myself. After a while, there was an inch-thick layer of newspaper on that side of the loft, and the light shone even brighter through the ragged tear that I made every night.

When I tried to sleep, she would come to me in my dreams. She would come floating across the ceiling, naked and descending until my nose settled between her breasts. I thought back to what Zhao Jingdong had told me, how she'd come to him at night, completely naked. I realized that I'd had no right to look down on Zhao Jingdong—a woman like this, I can see why he'd done those disgusting things with that dog. My throat felt dry. I wished there were somebody I could tell my secret to.

One night when the rehearsal was over, I was looking out the window of the loft and saw Zhang Nao getting on her bike. I raced down and got my own old bike from the side of the warehouse and followed her. The night was quiet, and I knew it was a risk, but I got as far as the Culture Bureau gate in Red Star Alley before she noticed my bike squeaking along behind her. I grabbed at the brake, but it was too late. I went coasting right up to her, gripping the brakes the entire time. She said: "Ceng . . . Ceng Guangxian? What are you doing here?"

"I . . . I . . . I was going to visit one of my classmates."

She stood a few feet away from me. She arched her back, her breasts standing up. I stammered and panted: "There's—there's something I want to tell you, but I'm not sure if I should."

"What is it?"

"It's about Jingdong."

"It's getting late. Can't we talk about that some other time?"

She got back on her bike and pedaled away. I stood for a long time, watching her go into the dark. I got on my bike and flew into the night, singing as I went: "Sailing the seas depends on the helmsman / Life and growth depends on the sun . . ." I don't know where that sudden burst of energy came from, but it bubbled up out of me and wouldn't stop.

I held out for a few days, but eventually I found myself in Red Star Alley again, stopping under a light post. I leaned on my bike and waited. To pass the time, I looked carefully at the wall that ran down one side of the alley. Moss had colonized the concrete, and the plaster along the top of the wall was crumbling, showing the brick skeleton. The insects that were flying against the streetlight whizzed around my head, and I could see their tiny wings before they swung back up to the light and became so many tiny black specks against the bulb. My legs had almost given out by the time she appeared. I called: "Zhang—Zhang Nao!"

She stopped: "Oh, it's you. What's wrong?"

"I wanted to tell you about Jingdong."

"Isn't there a better time?"

"I've been waiting five days. It has to be now."

She leaned back in her seat.

"I killed Jingdong. I heard about his secrets and told him that the work unit was planning a struggle session."

"What secrets?"

I told her all about how Zhao Jingdong had been obsessed with her, how he'd named the dog after her, what he'd done with the dog. Her face showed no emotion.

"If it hadn't been for all those crazy thoughts about you, he wouldn't have broken down and done those things."

"Bullshit. Why are you dragging me into this? You want to put the blame on me?"

"It wasn't all my fault. You and He Caixia should share some responsibility."

"Why are you doing this? Just let the man rest."

She pedaled away and disappeared again. After that, I came back to the alley to meet her as she came home, and she rode past me, turning her face and pretending not to see me. If I called her, she would pedal faster, rushing toward her dormitory. I realized something that day. Nobody wants to hear things that are unpleasant, especially pretty girls. If I had realized that sooner, I wouldn't have bothered with going to talk to her about Zhao Jingdong. I thought maybe she still cared about him in some way. I was wrong. All I had was that souvenir: "Bullshit." That's what she'd said. It came to my mind sometimes when I was shoveling the shit out of the cages at the zoo, and it made me laugh. How could such a pretty girl say something like that? I couldn't help but burst out laughing when I thought about it. It was just out of place, I guess, like seeing a revolutionary merit badge on a corrupt official. That was a long time ago, and it's like it was yesterday. I've forgotten so many important things, but I'll never forget that.

She wasn't a good actress, I decided. How could she play the heroic lead in *Red Detachment of Women* when she was so crude? Even after she'd heard the truth about her cousin, she was still so cold. She could never be an actress! I covered the hole with newspaper, and then I covered it with a sheet of wood. I would never, ever steal a look again. If I somehow happened to be at one of her performances, I would walk out. But I couldn't stop her from coming to me in my dreams. I still wasn't sleeping well. I drifted through the day, half awake. I eventually went to the doctor and got some sleeping pills, and that helped a bit. But I still felt something . . . something like that ring Sun Wukong had stuck on his head that cut into him whenever he got out of control. I decided to go to see Auntie Nine in Six Alley, off of Sanhe Road. When I told her what was happening, she told me that I was being haunted. I asked her if it was my mother, but she said it was too late, and what reason did she have to haunt me? It must be someone else. I knew it was Zhao Jingdong, coming for revenge.

On Tomb-Sweeping Day, I was going to go to the Beishan Cemetery to burn paper money at his grave. I got together all the other things you were supposed to bring, too, like incense and lard and rice and meat and salary slips and other things he liked while he was alive, rendered in paper. I got the paper and offerings ready. I wanted to ask him to leave me alone.

I thought there was something missing, though. I wasn't sure what it could possibly be, but I knew there was something I had forgotten. I went through my room, looking through drawers, searching under the mat on my bed, and turning my dormitory room upside down. I went outside and walked through the neighborhood, still looking for that missing item. As I was searching, I heard a familiar voice and looked over to see a group of girls pushing their bikes along the road. Zhang Nao was with them. I called to her. One of the girls in the group turned and said: "Hey, who's that calling you?"

Zhang Nao looked over and saw me. She said: "What do you want?"

‹ 12 ›

"The day after tomorrow is Tomb-Sweeping Day. I want to go to Jing-dong's grave. I was wondering if you were going to go."

"That's none of your business."

"I'm worried that if I don't, he'll keep haunting me. You aren't worried?"

Zhang Nao muttered: "You're crazy." She got on her bike and left. I realized that thing I was missing was her. I had to take her to the grave. Think about it. If you're supposed to bring things to the grave that the dead person loved when they were alive, it makes sense that I'd want to bring Zhang Nao, right? I chased after her. When I caught up, I grabbed her bike. She stared daggers at me. "What are you trying to do?"

I got in front of her bike. "I'm sorry, but Jingdong needs you. You have to burn paper at his grave. He loved you. Nothing would make him as happy as that. Please, promise me you'll go. I'm begging you."

She tried to twist the handlebars away from me.

"Are you crazy or something?"

"Promise me."

She glanced up, as if she were about to say something. She gulped and looked down.

"I've got everything ready to take to the grave. If you come, too, then he has everything he needs. He can finally rest."

Zhang Nao frowned and said: "I already promised my aunt I'd go. What are you going for? He's not even related to you."

I went back to the loft. I had added Zhang Nao to my list of offerings to bring to the grave.

After I got back from the Beishan Cemetery, I didn't see her for another two months. I never forgot about her, though. She appeared to me again and again. I could study her body, dancing in front of me. Finally I went to the dance studio at the Culture Bureau and stole up to the window. I watched her go through a routine, dropping to the floor, legs splayed, somersaulting back up. I figured she hadn't seen me. I didn't notice her glance at the window even once. But ten years later, she told me: "Of course I saw you! I saw your reflection in the mirror on the wall. You were wearing an old army jacket, right? The one with the worn-out elbows." How did she keep that secret for a decade? What a fucking actress!

Zhang Nao was all I was thinking about in those days. When Yu Baijia came back, it was a surprise. I wasn't expecting to see him hobble up to me with a crutch under his shoulder. His first words were: "I'm back!"

"You're done with the production team?"

"Leg's busted. What the hell am I going to do on a production team?"

"They broke your leg?"

He shook his head no.

"Did you get the letter I sent you?"

"I got it. You should have just looked at that girl."

"What girl?"

"The one on the train who you were trying not to look at. You were talking about turning over a new leaf or whatever, trying not to look at her."

I said: "Ah!" I remembered that girl on the train now. No wonder Zhang Nao had looked so familiar when I saw her at the funeral! It had been Zhang Nao sitting across from me on the train that day.

Yu Baijia started coming to the warehouse every night to sit with me up in the loft and talk. He was trying to run away from his lovesickness. There was nothing he could do but escape from the mountain village after the trouble with Xiao Chi. After they'd been discovered, he was scared to go to her, scared that somebody would find out. He was tired of life in the hills and the endless suffering at the hands of the villagers. He hated those hill people, their accents and their tobacco-stained teeth. He hated the smell of those hills. When he was in the struggle sessions, he tried to remember the taste of his mother's chaomian. She used to cook it for special occasions when we were kids.

I remember watching her at the stove. She would cook the noodles and then let them soak in cool water while she added chopped lean pork to the hot oil in another pot. On top of that, she'd add cabbage, wood ear, carrots, and celery, all chopped into thin strips.

No, no, no, I'm not off topic again. It's completely relevant. You'll see.

Anyways, apart from the chaomian, there was also the sound of cars on the road when he was a kid. It was the car horns, in particular. He'd hear them in his dreams when he was in the countryside. The car horns were calling him back to the city. After all the struggle sessions, he stopped talking. When he went to work in the paddy fields, he didn't speak to anyone. The whole time, he was planning his escape back to the city. The solution he came up with was: tuberculosis. He knew that if he was diagnosed, he'd be sent to a hospital in the city. One night at dinner, he went to the barefoot doctor who worked with the commune and traded a few bundles of dried noodles for a medical book. After he read the first chapter, "The Treatment and Prevention of Tuberculosis," he went straight to Auntie Wang. He started doing household chores for her, like splitting wood and carrying water. They'd sit together, chat about whatever, share bowls of thin rice porridge. During work, he'd be right beside her. During meetings, he'd always sit right across from her. Don't get the wrong idea. He wasn't sitting across from her to study her wrinkles and contemplate his own mortality or anything. He wanted her coughs and sneezes.

Auntie Wang coughed everywhere she went. When the weather changed, it got even worse. She'd cough loud enough to wake up the neighbors. Sometimes she would cough up chunks of phlegm, so big that you could hear them hit the ground when she'd spit. Basically, she was the perfect person to catch tuberculosis from. No matter what he did, though, he couldn't catch it. He started sharing her bowl, sharing her drinking gourd, but he still didn't get sick. It drove him crazy. He started going shirtless on cold days, sleeping without a blanket. But it seemed like he was only getting healthier. He started sleeping on the slab of stone outside the house.

It was early winter, and it was cold up in the hills. One night he could see frost forming around him on the smooth rock. The chill entered his spine and spread through his body. Finally, he coughed. He stayed there until he coughed again and again, until he couldn't stop coughing and his throat was raw. He went and washed with ice-cold water. The cough stayed with him. He coughed while he worked, still pulling down as many cigarettes as he could. It had taken a long time, but he was finally there.

The textbook had said that an X-ray was advised if the cough lasted three weeks and was accompanied by chest congestion and fever. When it reached the third week, he was sent down to town for an X-ray and examination. The doctor examined the images and took his temperature and told Yu Baijia that he was fine, just a sore throat. Yu Baijia protested that his head was on fire. The doctor took his temperature again and gave him a prescription for cough syrup. Yu Baijia refused to leave the office and demanded that the doctor try a different thermometer. When his temperature was still within a normal range, he asked for a second opinion. The doctor patted his chest and said: "You're sitting in front of the most famous tuberculosis specialist in the country. I'm down here in the countryside for a while, but in a few years you won't even be able to get an appointment with me."

"But I feel like I'm on fire. I'm lightheaded."

"It's all in your head. I've seen it before. Don't risk your health just because you want to go back to the city."

Yu Baijia went back up to the commune. The cough was gone. He was sure that the cough syrup hadn't helped—the doctor had scared the cough out of him. As long as that doctor was there, he said, he didn't dare try that method again. But if his hand or his leg was broken, there'd be no mistaking it. He considered it: if he broke his hand, it would heal pretty fast; if he broke his leg, he'd be out for a while. He decided to go for it. He'd make sure everybody saw him do it, too.

I'm serious. It was that hard to get back to the city once you had been sent to the countryside to join a production team. I know nowadays you could just go and buy a train ticket. But it wasn't that easy.

Hey, I forgot to ask. Where are you from? Let me guess. No . . . I don't know. I can tell you aren't from around here, though. Okay, okay. I didn't mean anything. I'll keep going with the story.

One night, Yu Baijia didn't feel like going home, so he stayed with me in the loft of the warehouse. In the middle of the night, I heard him suddenly call out "Xiao Chi!" I remembered when I had done the same. I patted his shoulder, and he sat up and lit a cigarette.

He took a slow drag and said: "I was dreaming about tofu."

"Really? I thought you were calling out somebody's name."

"You don't get it. She was just like tofu. You have no idea how soft she was, like she had no bones. That first bite I took was so wet. She grabbed me and pulled me in. It was like tofu that hasn't set, still soft, so you can't even hold it in your hand. Once we got into that haystack, I took it out and put it into her. It was just like a knife through a block of soft tofu. Once I was inside, she kept calling my name. I fucked her all night. Go for a while, take a rest. Take a rest, go for a while. I thought I had wrecked it. In the morning, I took a flashlight and shined it down there to check. It looked fine to me. She grabbed the flashlight and pulled me in again. She dragged me right in. I thought I was going to suffocate."

I felt my breath catch. I stood up and walked around the loft.

Yu Baijia said: "What the hell is wrong with you?"

I stammered but couldn't speak.

He reached up and flicked my crotch: "You can't take it, huh? You're rock hard. You a virgin? If you're a virgin, this is probably fucking you up. Why don't you go use your hand? Isn't that what you told me to do?"

"She—she hugged me, right down there, that night before she went to Tianle. Her hands felt strong. I thought she was going to suffocate me, too."

He ground out the cigarette. "That slut. You had her, too?"

"If I had, she wouldn't have ended up with you."

"I don't mean did you fuck her. She bled all over the haystack that night. It must have been her first time. That was why the production team brought us to that struggle session. I mean, did you feel her up? She's nice and soft up there, too, like cotton balls. Don't tell me you didn't get a feel."

"No way. I told her she was sick in the head. I ran away from her. If I'd known . . . I could have had a taste."

He tousled my hair. "I can't believe you didn't get a feel, you little perv."

"I swear. I didn't touch her. I've never touched anyone. One time I thought about touching Zhang Nao, but I couldn't do it."

"Too fucking bad." Yu Baijia lit another cigarette. "The type of girl I like, they've got some meat on their bones. I want to put my head between two pillows. But the thing about it is, you get addicted to it. One bite and you want another. Those bastards up there tried to stop me. That's what really hurt. It hurts so bad, I shouldn't even have bothered in the first place." He paused. "Who's this Zhang Nao you're talking about?" I described her and told him about Zhao Jingdong. He patted my shoulder. "Don't worry. I'll look after you. At the very worst, you'll end up marrying her."

"I don't want to marry her. I just want to talk to her."

That night, Yu Baijia gave me the second sex ed class of my life with Xiao Chi as his anatomical model. He told me all about how not to get a girl pregnant, what to do if you saw blood, stuff like that. His lecture was full of colorful descriptions of tofu and pillows and wailing and howling and bleeding like a stuck pig and swamps. As I watched his Adam's apple bob, I felt sick to my stomach. I hated myself. It could have been me instead of him. Now, when I wanted to reach out and touch her breasts, gently stroke her, I could only remember that I had run away. Two years ago, I had the chance and I let it pass me by. As the days went by, my thoughts turned to Zhang Nao with even more intensity. I used all my new metaphors learned from Yu Baijia to describe her. I felt like a butcher packing up fresh cuts. I knew I was guaranteed to hear some of the "wailing and howling" that Yu Baijia had described.

It was June 24th. I had Yu Baijia's father help me buy a cake. That night, Yu Baijia helped me comb my hair and iron my shirt. I took the cake to the Culture Bureau, Building Number Eight, the second floor. We had it planned out: Baijia would stay behind me, acting as my wingman. I knocked on the door three times. Zhang Nao opened the door and said: "Who are you looking for?"

I said: "I came to see you."

"What are you two doing?"

I held a finger to my mouth. "Let me in and I'll tell you."

She opened the door, and we went inside and sat down on a bench.

"This is Baijia. He was friends with Jingdong. He just got back from the countryside."

‹ 13 ›

She looked down at Baijia's leg and said: "You had to come back because of that?"

Baijia said: "I come back this time every year."

I took out the cake and set it on her desk. I put two candles in the cake.

Zhang Nao said: "It's not my birthday."

I took out Zhao Jingdong's memorial photo. "Baijia came back for Jingdong's birthday. He didn't know that he'd died."

Zhang Nao was suddenly serious: "You're true friends."

I said: "Even though he's gone, we wanted to celebrate his birthday, just like we used to. We didn't want you to mark the day by yourself, so we came over."

I lit the candles, and we sat in silence watching them. Zhang Nao was sitting beside the door, and she occasionally glanced out into the hallway and back at us. We sat together for a while, and then Baijia said: "We should get going. We've taken up enough of Zhang Nao's time."

I could tell that Zhang Nao was in a hurry to get us out of her room. I picked up the portrait of Jingdong, and we went to the door.

Baijia clasped Zhang Nao's hands, one shoulder propped up by the crutch. He said: "I'm sorry to have taken up your time, comrade. It's just, when I first saw you, it was like seeing my old friend. I hope we didn't cause you any trouble, but we just had to come to reminisce about Jingdong. Guangxian has his faults, but I must say he's been so loyal to Jingdong." He was still clasping her hand in his, far longer than seemed normal. When he finally let her go, she shook her hand as if she were in pain.

On the way back, Baijia smiled and said: "That's how you do it. Anyways, she clearly wasn't into it, but she didn't really say much. I can tell she didn't care much for her cousin, though." I stared straight ahead. I couldn't help but think about Zhao Jingdong. It had just been a cover story to get into the apartment, but once I took out the photo and lit the candles, I couldn't stop myself from actually remembering him. "Why did Zhang Nao have that look on her face the whole night?"

I said: "We shouldn't have done that. I shouldn't have lied to her. I shouldn't have used Jingdong to fool her."

My whole life, I will always regret introducing those two to each other. When he came to the loft a few days later, I heard him on the ladder and ran to switch off the light and lock the door. He stayed outside awhile, smoking a cigarette, and then left, cursing me.

The next day, he showed up at the zoo while I was working inside a cage. He hobbled back and forth on the other side of the bars. With his broken leg, he could still walk almost as fast as before. He said: "You have to strike while the iron is hot, Guangxian. You can't let her forget about you." I drove the shovel down into a mound of shit. He said: "I was at the big department store downtown and saw a blue dress that I know she'd love. Girls love that kind of thing, dressing up, looking good. I don't know if you noticed that night the two dresses that were hanging on her balcony. You could tell they were already pretty old. The color was all faded. What do you think? I'll lend you some money if you want. I can even go deliver it for you."

I shoveled the manure into my wheelbarrow and pushed it out of the cage. He hobbled along behind me as I dumped it into the cesspool. "If you don't think that sounds good, I've got another idea. You could write an essay and get it published in the newspaper, praising the propaganda team, the model ballet, and in particular the heroic lead, Comrade Zhang Nao, whose every movement is permeated with revolutionary fervor. If you can't come up with anything, just find another ballet review and change a few lines, make it about Zhang Nao's performance. Maybe more than one, too. Maybe write a couple. Maybe write a series, all about Zhang Nao. It has to work. Any girl would fall for that. What do you think, Guangxian?"

I knocked the last pieces of manure out of the wheelbarrow with the shovel and turned to go back toward the cages. He kept going: "Or how about this? You could go talk to Zhao Wannian. He's director of the Tiema District Revolutionary Committee, but he came from the same warehouse. He used to be your family's servant. You could go to him and get him to pull some strings, maybe even put her in charge of the propaganda team at the Culture Bureau. There aren't many men who could look after her like that. Let's go see him."

I wasn't listening. His last idea had been a disaster. He kept talking, but it was going in one ear and out the other. After a while, he realized I wasn't listening. We went to the canteen for lunch, and he didn't touch his food. When I was done, he hobbled to the bus stop and left. But he didn't give up. He kept showing up at the loft. His sense of urgency seemed to exceed my own. He told me: "If you don't go, I'll go by myself." Why didn't I listen to him? I guess maybe I was sick of his plans and was trying to discourage him. But I should have listened. Things might not have worked out with Zhang Nao, but it would have saved me a lot of trouble.

One night, Yu Baijia came up to my loft and wordlessly dropped two envelopes on my bed. The letters were stamped with the red seals of the production brigade, the People's Commune, and the county's Revolutionary Committee. The stamps seemed to glow red, every character branded clearly onto the white paper. The letters said, basically: even with a broken leg, you can still receive reeducation from poor peasants, so get back here immediately. Vague punishments were promised. He took a drag from his cigarette and buried his head in his hands: "Should I go back?"

"All these official seals . . . I'm worried if you don't go back, it will come back to bite you in the future."

"I don't have much hope for the future anyway. As far as I'm concerned, sitting in a prison cell in the city is better than going back to the countryside."

"What about Xiao Chi? You should feel some sense of responsibility after everything that happened."

He swore and went back to smoking, one cigarette after another, until the pack was empty and the mosquitoes in the loft were crawling on the floor. He said: "Do you know what it felt like when I held Zhang Nao's hand that night?"

I shook my head.

"It was like touching a high-voltage line. I know I felt some sort of energy between us. There was a spark."

"I never held her hand. She never let me."

"If I go back to the countryside again, I don't know if I'll ever come back. If I really have to go . . . I want to fuck Zhang Nao before I leave."

My eyes opened wide: "That was your plan all along! No wonder you were giving me all those dumb ideas."

"If I could sleep with a girl like that just one time, I'd die happy."

"Just go. Save your mother and Xiao Chi their tears. Save the government their bullets."

"I noticed something that night. The window of her room in the dormitory has eight bars. They're made of wood. One of the bars was loose. I got to thinking there must be a reason for that, and I figured she probably forgets the key to the dormitory and uses that window to get in. The bar isn't loose enough that she can slip through, but it's loose enough that she can reach inside. The window is close enough to the door that she can reach over and unlock it. I checked out the window, and I didn't see a lock, just a latch. The latch looks like it could be flipped open pretty easily. It's all rusty, so it can't be latched tight. So you flip that latch, open the window, squeeze over, and unlock the door . . . You fuck her once, and she'll be yours. You think all those women walking out there with their husbands married those guys—because of what? That's how women are. That's what you do. I'm just telling you the truth."

A shiver ran through me hard enough to shake the loft. He patted me on the head and said: "If you can't handle the truth, you'll never be a man."

He went back the next day. After he left, his words continued to ring painfully in my ears. I guess it's like the words of a great man—they only become famous after he dies. The longer he was gone, the louder his voice got, telling me the truth, as he understood it. I hesitated for a few days, and then I did it—I went and bought the blue dress from the department store.

I knew it was stupid. I knew I wouldn't actually give it to her. I pictured her throwing it on the floor, calling me a pervert, so I hung it in the loft of the warehouse, where I could admire it from different angles. When I wasn't working, I would go back to the warehouse and move the dress like a marionette, imitating Zhang Nao's routine from *Red Detachment of Women*. When there was a breeze, I would bring it out onto the roof of the warehouse and let it flap there, imagining it was her moving inside of it. One night when the wind picked up and was blowing stronger than it had in weeks, I brought the dress to the roof. I watched it move, dancing and twirling in the wind, leaping and tumbling. I couldn't believe the grace with which it moved. I couldn't believe it was just the wind spinning it back and forth. I looked again and saw two long white legs below the dress. Two arms glided from the sleeves. At the collar, there was suddenly the pale white of a woman's neck. Zhang Nao was there, in the dress, smirking down at me. I ran toward the line where the dress hung, and she was gone. I held it against my face. I thought I could smell, faintly, Zhang Nao's scent.

That Saturday, I wrapped up the dress, went to Zhang Nao's dormitory, and knocked on the door. She looked out and asked: "Are you alone?"

"Yu Baijia left."

She leaned against the doorway and said: "I could tell he wasn't a good person, just the way he looked at me. Don't bring him here again."

I took the dress from behind my back. I said: "This is for you." She slowly ripped open the package, and I saw her eyes light up.

"Wow, it's beautiful. You got this for me?" I nodded, and she stood up and held the dress against her chest. It was just the right size.

She laughed and said: "Why are you giving me this? You have to tell me or I can't accept it." I tried to speak, but my mouth wouldn't cooperate. As I stammered, she handed the dress back to me. "Thank you, but if you won't tell me why you're giving it to me, I won't accept it."

I said: "Jingdong was my friend. I feel like you're family. So I guess it's like, since he can't buy you anything, I wanted to get you something. He used to tell me that he wanted to get you something, but he never had the money. He wanted to buy you a dress."

I saw her expression darken, and she pulled the dress back and tossed it into the corridor. "Always with Jingdong this, Jingdong that. You think about him that much? He was my own cousin, and I already forgot about him. What are you dragging him around for? I don't think even you care that much about him. I wish you'd stop using him as your cover. If you want to say something to me, just say it. Please, for my sake." At that moment, anyone else would have simply told her the truth. That was the perfect time to tell her that I liked her, no matter what happened next. Even if she called me a pervert or went around and told all her friends, there was no better time to finally tell her. But I guess I was too stupid. I mumbled an apology, turned, and left, while she stood in the doorway watching. She kicked the dress down the corridor.

I figured I was the dumbest person on earth, the world champion of idiots. I decided she'd probably ripped up the dress, and she'd go to her grave cursing my name. I had no idea that women get angry strategically, that she'd been pushing me to tell her that I liked her. If I'd simply told her, I probably would have ended up marrying her, I thought. I could have eaten tofu whenever I wanted. But I was too stupid to say anything. Later, when I saw her wearing the dress, I realized that I could have just said something, said anything. But I had lost my chance.

The rejection hurt me. Nice guys finish last, I thought. I stamped around the loft, smacking myself. I went and sat beside the river and thought about Yu Baijia's instructions, all that stuff about the window latch and the bars.

Those instructions played in my head so clearly that it felt like I was listening to a recording. I couldn't hear anything but "The window is close enough to the door that she can reach over and unlock it. I checked out the window, and I didn't see a lock, just a latch. The latch looks like it could be flipped open pretty easily. It's all rusty, so it can't be latched tight. So you flip that latch, open the window, squeeze over, and unlock the door . . ." I couldn't ignore it.

One night when I couldn't sleep, I got out of bed. I paced around the loft, then tried to lie down again, but I felt like I was lying on a bed of nails. I slipped down from the loft and walked toward Red Star Alley. There was nobody on the street. I walked on the shadows cast by trees in the streetlight. As I entered the alley, I pinched myself hard. It hurt, so I couldn't be dreaming. At the mouth of the alley, I heard a voice: "What the hell are you doing?" I wasn't sure whose voice it was. It wasn't Yu Baijia's. It wasn't my father's, either. I stood and looked up at the streetlights. The night breeze was cool and fresh through the leaves of the trees. I had never really paid attention to what the city looked like at night, but now it felt empty. It felt like it was mine. The voice came again: "Go back!" I tried to walk forward into the alley, but I was frozen. I stood there a little bit longer, and then I left.

I felt better for a while, but the feeling came back. It was almost like a woman's cycle, I think. About a month later, all I could think about was Zhang Nao.

No, that's not quite right. It wasn't *just* Zhang Nao, it was every part of her, floating in isolation: her face, her arms, and then her breasts and her legs, her pale neck. All the parts of her forced themselves into my head, pushing out anything else I was thinking about. There was nothing I could do about it. I went back to the alley.

That night, I didn't stop at the entrance. I went on down the alley. I raised my left hand and said: "What you're considering doing is a crime. You know that, right? If this goes the wrong way, you're going to be marched down the road with a sign around your neck, and then they're going to shoot you in the head."

I raised my right hand: "If I could sleep with a girl like that just one time, I'd die happy." I'm sure you remember that was exactly what Yu Baijia had told me.

My left hand came up again: "Even if you don't do it, if you're discovered in the dormitory, they'll beat you until you'll wish you were dead. They'll beat you the same way they beat your father that first time."

Right hand: "Everything has a price. My father was willing to pay the price. So was Yu Baijia. They both got through it."

Left hand: "But they have nothing to hope for now. They ruined their lives. If you turn back now, you can do anything you want—maybe not anything, but what about director of the zoo? There's still hope."

Right hand: "Who says I can't still have a future? If this works out the way Baijia said it would, maybe I'll end up marrying Zhang Nao. She'll accept her fate, like he said, and have to marry me. 'You think all those women walking out there with their husbands married those guys—because of what? That's how women are. That's what you do. I'm just telling you the truth.'"

Left hand: "You took that seriously? He doesn't even take it seriously himself. Look how he ran back to the countryside when he saw those seals on the letter."

Right hand: "I can't take it anymore. This is exactly what happened to Jingdong. She's a goddess."

Left hand: "No, Guangxian. Didn't your father teach you that there was nothing you couldn't take? He told you to just use your hand. Think about her while you do it. It's better than a bullet in the head, which is what you're going to get, doing this. Go over to that faucet. Run some cold water over your head."

I hadn't noticed the faucet. I went over and twisted it on and waited until it ran ice-cold. I put my head under it and soaked myself. I had been too close. It was getting dangerous. I'd been almost to the gate of the Culture Bureau. I stood up and shook my hair dry and pulled my curls straight. I turned around and left.

‹ 14 ›

A few days after that trip to the alley, I got a letter from Yu Baijia. He had more instructions for me: when I went to the window, I should blindfold myself. His idea was that my sense of hearing would be even better, and I'd be able to hear any potential hazards before I was caught. But, he said, he was just bullshitting anyway, and I shouldn't take him seriously. He told me that if I was dumb enough to do it, he wouldn't even bother to come see the police shoot me. I shivered. I finally realized that he hadn't meant for me to actually do it. I didn't want to end up with a bullet in my head. I didn't want to end up like that tiger at the zoo, pacing behind iron bars.

But that time of the month came again. One night the moon was full, and it filled the window of the loft and fell across the bed. Me, that moron, that stupid motherfucker, that maniac, that idiot . . . my legs carried me out of the loft and into the alley behind the Culture Bureau and toward Zhang Nao's dormitory.

It felt like I was sleepwalking. My body moved by itself. I took the strip of black cloth out of my pocket, tied it around my head, and covered my eyes. I went to the window of her dormitory room. I flicked open the latch and got my fingers into the crack between the window and the frame. I made no sound as I slowly lifted the window. I took off the blindfold and stuck my head inside. I reached across to the door and flipped the lock. Everything was working out just as I had planned, as if the rusty latch and the silent window and the cooperative door and I were all working toward the same goal. If it hadn't been for the blindfold, maybe it wouldn't have been so flawless. Maybe if the window had creaked, maybe if the lock hadn't opened so easily . . . I could have just run away and nothing would have happened.

As I walked into her room through the unlocked door, I saw her, fast asleep. I studied her long eyelashes, her small, perfect mouth and her snow-white neck, and then I saw it—she was wearing the blue dress that I had given her. That proved it: she didn't hate me; there was still some hope. I staggered back. I had to get out of there. Turning to rush out, I knocked over the chair beside the door. I heard her voice in the dark: "Who's there?" She sat up in bed. "Help!" I thought for a moment about running, but instead I pounced on her and muffled her cries for help. She tore at me with her nails and tried to push me off. Her voice cried out from between my fingers.

I said: "It's me. It's Guangxian. I just came here to see you. That's it. Please don't scream." But she only cried out louder. I tried to hold her mouth tighter. She kicked her legs on the bed and tried to wrestle my hand from her mouth. I was on top of her, using my legs on her legs, pressing my chest against her chest, and pressing down on her face with both of my hands. She could barely move and she couldn't cry out, but I heard it already: the sound of footsteps coming down the corridor. At that moment, I could have let her go and gone for the window. I could have slipped right out and run away. But the thought didn't occur to me. It was like I was holding in the pin of a grenade. All I wanted was for her to be quiet, not to cry out.

The door was kicked open. One of the men from the propaganda team was on me, pinning my arms back and throwing me to the ground. A few more followed him in, and I felt their fists and elbows and feet smashing into my body and head while they held my arms behind my back. Fucking idiot that I was, my first thought was to sympathize with them. It made sense, I thought, as they beat me. At the Culture Bureau, Zhang Nao was like a grape that had hung just out of their reach. They all wanted to snatch her. For someone like me to come in and try to uproot the grapevine by force, it was too much for them to take. They took out all their frustration and anger on me. But they didn't know what I had gone through. They grew tired and began to beat me with the chair and the bench, smacking me in the face, beating my legs with their belts. I slipped in and out of consciousness. I woke up once to the sound of Zhang Nao crying. What the hell was she crying about? I hadn't done anything to her, but she was crying like I'd raped her. I passed out again.

When I woke up, I was in the detention center on the north side of the city. My whole body was tight and swollen. It felt like my internal organs had swelled to twice their normal size. Another of the prisoners in the room, a man awaiting trial for rape, told me that the doctor had already come and put salve on my cuts and bruises and then listened with a stethoscope to check my breathing. That afternoon, the doctor came back. As applied the medication again, he said genially: "Just some cuts and bruises, Guangxian. You'll be fine in a few days." The doctor spoke kindly, and his hands on my body were gentle. As he worked, he asked me if it hurt. I had never been waited on like that. I moaned: "Mom." My mouth was too swollen to speak. At that moment, the doctor could have gotten me to confess to anything. I was still so naive.

As I lay in my cell looking up at the ceiling, I asked myself why I hadn't just jumped out the window. By the time I had gotten away and Zhang Nao had come to her senses, she might have merely thought she was having a bad dream. I could even have gone to see her after I gave her the dress. I didn't have to talk to her, but I could have at least hung around, and I would have seen that she was wearing the blue dress I had given her. Why did I have to sneak into her dormitory? And why did I listen to Yu Baijia? It felt like all of his instructions were stuck in my head. And that talk about tofu. What if he hadn't said all that stuff? What if he hadn't sent me that letter? Would I still have done it?

Baijia bore some responsibility, but he'd also warned me not to do it. I was the one who had actually crept in her window. And I was the one who had made him go back to the countryside. I was the one who had waved those letters and the gleaming red seals under his nose, trying to scare him. I was the one who had told him that he should remember his responsibility to Xiao Chi. If he had stayed in the city, I never would have done it. I should never have told him about Zhang Nao in the first place. If I hadn't told him about Zhang Nao, he would never have told me about the rusty latch and the bars on her window. All the fault came back to me, me and my big mouth. I raised my hand to my mouth, tearing at the freshly scabbed-over cuts until my chin was covered in new blood.

The two cops who came to question me brought me in twice to the interrogation room, but I couldn't answer any of their questions. My mouth was too swollen still, and all that came out when I tried to speak was something like a hiss. I thought it might be better if I couldn't speak at all for the rest of my life. Let them come to whatever decision they were going to come to. I'd go to the execution grounds without protest, maybe a nod of my head. I wouldn't have to answer a single question. I didn't want to talk about those sorts of things with the police, sexual things. It was different talking to Yu Baijia or Zhao Jingdong. I really couldn't face the questions from those stone-faced men in uniform. I began to tear at my mouth again, opening the cuts. When they dragged me into the interrogation room again, I shook my head to all of their questions. "What's your name?" I shook my head. I opened my mouth and showed them the pus leaking from the corners of my mouth, my tongue that I had bit until it was bloody and swollen, the scraped skin that looked like a peeled grape. My mouth was a mess. Even when the other prisoners called me a monster, I knew it was worth it. The stone-faced men in uniform realized they wouldn't get anything out of me. They threw up their hands in frustration and dragged me back to the cell.

The doctor came to see me again. As he applied the medicine and changed my bandages, he said: "I've seen this before, people like you. They want to hang themselves or overdose on pills or bite their tongues off, but they end up coming out all right in the end. They'll tell you that failure to confess will bring you harsher punishment, all that stuff. But I think it's true. You have to tell the truth." I was still conflicted. It was when I saw the man accused of rape being led out of the cell for the final time that I changed my mind. The man had answered all of the questions put to him and had been truthful. I followed the doctor's orders.

It took a few weeks for my mouth to heal, but it was already too late. The men who were guarding me were distracted with the chaos in the streets, the putting up and tearing down of Red Guard posters, the fight against reactionaries, the struggle sessions. I shouted at the window, calling for someone to question me again. But the policemen didn't return. A month went by, a year went by, and then two years went by, and the 1960s became the 1970s, and nobody came to question me. If I had just answered their questions, if I had cooperated, I could have been set free in the first few days. It was my fault that I ended up locked up so long in that cell.

When I finally went before a judge, I answered all of the questions put to me with complete honesty. The judge stopped me. He said that my account of the incident differed in every respect from that offered by Zhang Nao. He read Zhang Nao's testimony aloud: I had broken into her dormitory, torn her clothes off, and raped her. He held up the ripped blue dress. The skirt was torn into four ragged strips.

I said: "What about her panties? I didn't rip those." Some of the people in the courtroom laughed.

The judge said: "Zhang Nao testified that she was not wearing panties." There was another peal of laughter from the observers. Why did the judge believe her but not me? Yu Baijia had told me that she'd accept her fate, for the sake of preserving her dignity. What the hell was wrong with this woman? I felt like someone had hit me in the side of the head. I felt as if Zhang Nao had stolen up behind me and smacked me as hard as she could. I couldn't believe what I was hearing. My vision blurred.

The next thing I heard was the judge reading testimony from a medical professional, stating that Zhang Nao's virginity had been compromised. Fuck, how was that my fault? Did I stick it in through two layers of cloth? I told the judge it had been over two years since that night. How could he suddenly say she wasn't a virgin when I entered the room? The judge said that the examination was made directly following the incident. Someone brought the doctor's testimony over to me to read. I put the paper down. I had nothing to say.

The judged asked: "When is your birthday?"

I said: "September 26th."

The judge said: "What day was it when you entered her dormitory room?"

I said: "September 29th."

The judge asked: "Are you sure?"

I said: "I'm sure."

I was sentenced to eight years without the possibility of parole.

Why are you so surprised? It was a different time, like I keep saying. Rape was a very serious issue. If things had turned out differently, I could have faced the death penalty. I would have been shot in the head. If the charge had been attempted rape, I still could have gotten five or six years. Things are different now. Our society is far more lenient. Look at your necklace. Look at those clothes you're wearing, all that skin you're showing. Society has moved forward. I'm envious.

Are you getting tired? Have something to drink. All right, well, I'll keep going if you're enjoying it.

I took the eight-year sentence. I didn't argue with the judge. I didn't blame Zhang Nao. I knew that I hadn't raped her. I didn't even get anywhere near her inner thigh. I held her down, but the dress was still between us. But I'd definitely had the intention, and there was no mistaking what I'd had in mind when I broke into her dormitory room. There was a crime committed, I was willing to admit. My naiveté had led me there that night. There were so many things I didn't understand. Like the thing about Zhang Nao being a virgin. I knew there was something called a hymen that got torn when a girl lost her virginity, but I didn't really understand how it worked. I thought it could be torn by some violent act. But she could have torn it doing the splits in her dance class. I wish I had known that when I was pounding my head on the walls of my cell.

I was dumb, but not so dumb that I didn't figure a few things out. When I got sent to the Beishan "Reform through Labor" Tractor Plant, I figured out how to defer. You know what I mean by that? It means that instead of just saying whatever, you defer it. I mean, you think about what you're going to say, wait a few seconds or a few minutes, sleep on it, and when you're absolutely sure of yourself, then you say it. Some things you don't have to think about for very long. Like if somebody asks how you're doing, then you don't have to think about that for very long—but still think about it. Most people know about this already. I'm sure it's not surprising to you. But it was a revelation to me.

I'll give you an example. When I played chess with Hou Zhi and Li Dapao in the prison house, they would lose their patience with me. I would ponder every single move. We played with cigarette butts as chess pieces. I'd pick up my piece and start to move it, then look at the board again and put it back, trying to come up with a new move. That's how I tried to talk. But they weren't having it. I remember one of them said: "Ceng Malai! Quit wasting our time." Oh, "Malai" was just some local dialect. It means somebody who goes back on his word, basically. Come on, don't laugh. They all knew me as that in there. It was because of those chess games. I took forever to make a move, and when I did, I tried to take it back. Even the guards and the cadres there used to call me Ceng Malai. They used to take roll in the morning, and some of the cadres wouldn't even remember my real name. They'd say my name, then look down at their clipboard again and look back at the line of men. Everyone would look down the line at me, waiting for me to call, "Present!"

When nobody would play chess with me, I would lie on my bed and write letters. I wrote to Zhao Wannian, Yu Baijia, Xiao Chi, Director He, Uncle Zhao, Yu Fare, He Caixia, Lu Xiaoyan, Hu Kaihui . . . The letters were all about the same, just different names at the top. In them I told everyone that I hadn't raped Zhang Nao. I told them that my intention was to rape her and that I'd broken into her dormitory, but once she screamed "Help," I had covered her mouth, but that was it. I said it looked bad, but I told them that you couldn't judge someone by how something looked. In the prison house, everybody looked bad.

I stuck a few stamps on every letter. I didn't want the letters to get lost. I couldn't imagine getting out in eight years and running into those people if I hadn't gotten the chance to explain myself. Always two stamps. I'd learned my lesson. You remember that, right? It was the letter to Xiao Chi. If that first letter hadn't been returned to me, she would have been my girlfriend, and I never would have gotten involved with Zhang Nao, and I wouldn't have ended up there.

I kept writing letters, but I never wrote one to my dad. Sometimes I'd get as far as putting "Dad" at the top of a letter, but I'd always crumple it up. My father wasn't willing to talk to me, and the letters wouldn't help. What man wants to know that his son is a rapist? Even if I didn't put anything about it in the letter, there would still be the return address stamped on the envelope. I was worried that it wouldn't be good for his health, either, having to read that kind of news. I decided to wipe my dad out of my life. I thought maybe it would help him to wipe me out of his life, too. I thought it might give him a degree of comfort if he could whitewash that part of his life.

I never got any letters back. Every day, there would be a big pile of letters that would come up from the mailroom and be distributed to the prisoners. When Hou Zhi or Li Dapao got a letter, I would always try to read over their shoulders. I was only curious and a bit jealous. They turned their backs, worried that I'd learn something about their personal life that they would rather keep private. All I wanted was for some encouragement to come, someone whose letter would wish me a fresh start in life. The letters were like an investment that never brought me any returns. It was like I was marked. You know the grease that floats on the top of diesel fuel? Once you get it on you, you always have that stain on your hands. During my free time, I didn't do anything but write letters. Nobody wanted to play chess with me, anyway. So I wrote. Even if I was tired or in pain, I wrote letters. Every day when I walked by the mailroom, I'd rub my aching right hand and regret having written all those letters and wasted all those stamps without getting anything back. A little while later, my poor right hand received even worse news.

One night, I was called into the office of Warden Jia. He gestured down at his desk, and I saw a pile of letters. He said: "All this writing, Ceng Malai, and all these stamps. And I can't send a single one out."

I looked at the letters on the desk, dumbfounded. He had every letter I had written. I said: "Why?"

Warden Jia patted the pile: "You think you're not a rapist, huh? You burst into a girl's dormitory room—break into it, in fact—and you're found on top of her. What you're writing in these letters, it makes us look like we're locking up an innocent man, not a man who stole the virginity of a young woman through force."

I lowered my head. I didn't want to say something that would make things worse.

"You want people to think this place is full of innocent people?"

"I'm sorry. I didn't know the rules."

"Get rid of these. Don't waste the stamps you bought. I respect your rights, or I wouldn't even have informed you that they weren't sent."

"I won't do it again."

I took the stamps off the envelopes and stuck them onto new envelopes. I rewrote the letters to my friends, careful not to argue for my innocence. I told them what kind of place I was in, that I had broken the law, what law I had broken, and that I was going to work hard to reform myself and become a new person. I sent the letters out and started getting replies. They followed a pattern that I eventually got sick of reading. One night, I stood on my bed and read one of those letters: "Guangxian, I know you are a good man and that your crime was an impulsive act. I hope that you take this chance to examine yourself in a frank and honest way. Stick with the program of reform through labor; you may be able to have your sentence reduced. Keep making progress. Zhao Wannian."

The twenty or so men in the prison house looked up at me. I laughed and ripped the letter into shreds and tossed it at the ceiling. "They all say the same thing. I'm starting to feel like I'm really a rapist. Fuck Hu Kaihui, fuck Lu Xiaoyan, fuck them all." As I counted off the names, I held up their letters and tore them to pieces, one by one, throwing the paper down from my bed.

Li Dapao pulled me down from the bed and gave me two hard slaps to the face. He said: "Just fucking deal with it."

As soon as he dragged me down, I felt like I'd been plunged into an icy lake. It was my fault, I realized. It was my fault that they were calling me a rapist. I was the one who had told them I was convicted of rape. I wasn't allowed to say that I was innocent, but I didn't want to write to people to tell them I was a rapist, either. What was I going to write to them about, the weather? If I wasted stamps writing from lockup to talk about the weather, that would be stupid, wouldn't it? I patted my right hand with my left, my poor right hand that had worked itself until it ached writing those goddamn letters.

Baijia was the first one to come visit me. We met in the visiting room. His leg was healed. His head was shaved, and the skin showed through even brighter than mine. He said: "Didn't I tell you not to do it?"

"I just went into the room."

"What did you go into her room for? You might be able to fool other people, but don't try lying to me."

I lowered my head. I said: "I don't care if you don't believe me."

He lit a cigarette and passed it to me. I took a drag and coughed. The guard looked over. We were both silent for a while, and then he asked me: "Did you do it or not?"

"If you don't believe me, who will? As soon as I went into the room, she started screaming. There's no way I could have done it."

"Look at me, Guangxian." I raised my head and looked him in the eye. "You really didn't do it?"

"I swear, if I'm lying to you, may a tractor grind my guts."

He dumped his cigarette on the floor and stamped it out. He said: "I won't let my brother suffer like this. I'm going to deal with that bitch."

As he went to the door, he rubbed my shaved head; I rubbed his bare head, too. We grinned at each other. All of the awkwardness was finally gone. I said: "Baijia, I want you to do something for me. Go back and look at the window of her dormitory room. I want to know if I could have jumped out if I'd had to. I'll always regret that I didn't just go out the window."

"Don't worry. I'll have a real close look."

At the factory where the reform through labor prisoners worked, there was a natural camaraderie between men accused of the same crimes. Like, the political prisoners would hang out together, the murderers would hang out together, almost like a family. My family in the reform through labor factory was Li Dapao and Hou Zhi, two other men accused of the same crime as me. I had no idea before I went in that the rapists were the most popular guys in the prison. Everybody wanted to hear their stories. Convicts find that their desires get stronger while they're locked up. Quite a few of the convicts had never had any sexual experiences before they went in. Those stories, about taking women at knifepoint, that kind of thing—that's what they want to hear. Nowadays, I hear it's different. The popular guys in prison now are the white-collar criminals, the corrupt officials. Convicts want to know how to make money. Times change, I guess.

But back then, the rapists were celebrities on the cell block. Every night, Hou Zhi would tell his stories. He'd tap his chest and say: "Me, back when I was in the government, I could get away with anything. If I wanted a woman, I would have her. I raped four women: one was a journalist, one was my boss's wife, one was my wife's little sister, one was my secretary—and none of them squealed on me. Eventually someone caught me doing it. After that, they all testified against me. But I had my fun. I had my fair share. Four is enough. They weren't bad to look at, those four, either."

Li Dapao countered: "I bet you never raped a girl as pretty as Xiaoyun." He launched into a filthy, poetic recounting of her charms, which mostly consisted of comparing her body to various items of produce: eyes as black as grapes, tits like grapefruit, cheeks like tomatoes . . ."The first time I had her," he said, "was July 20th. She used to go down to the well to draw water. I waited until she'd sent the bucket down the well. She was bending over. I went right up behind her and jerked down her pants. I fucked her from behind—what did you say? Unlucky? I think she wanted it. The way I was fucking her, she could have just stood up, and I wouldn't have been able to get it in her. She bent over for me and let me give it to her, just moaning the whole time. I thought, well, that's it, I fucked her, so what? I didn't think she was going to accuse me of raping her, trying to pretend she was a good girl. Can you believe that?"

Hou Zhi had quantity and Li Dapao had quality, but both of them were basically full of shit. There was sort of a competition between them to try to win over the audience, get a few more cigarettes passed to them. Pitted against each other, their stories became distorted, exaggerated. It was never the same version that you'd heard before. If the judges who heard their cases had been given these stories as evidence, the two men would be locked up for life. I don't even want to consider what the women they hurt would think if they heard them holding court in the prison house.

Anyways, the stories became increasingly ridiculous the more times they were told. Hou Zhi was constantly interrupted by people asking for specifics and giving their own input. When he got to the part about grabbing his secretary's tits, they'd ask: "What was it really like?" "Kind of like a big sponge." Somebody interrupted to say that wasn't right, it must have been like grabbing a balloon. And so on, with people trying to find a good comparison, until it became ridiculous. Finally, Li Dapao would just agree with everyone saying: "Yeah, you're right, it was like grabbing water, sorta. I grabbed them and they just kind of flowed away from me, right through my fingers. Cotton? Yeah, sure, cotton. It was like cotton. Nice and soft."

Li Dapao was less patient. One night he was telling his story again, and when he got to the part where he jerked her pants down, an argument began about the right object to compare Xiaoyun's ass to. Li Dapao listened for a while and then broke in: "What the fuck are you guys talking about, it was like a wash bucket, it was like a tire—it was like an ass. Her ass was like an ass." Someone smacked him, and the rest joined in, beating him until he had a fat lip and a black eye the next morning. After that, he started letting them suggest possible comparisons, and he'd nod and say: "Yep, you got it, she had an ass like a swamp. Muddy as an old swamp, uh-huh."

Finally it was my turn. One night the prisoners turned to me: "Your turn, Ceng Malai."

I stammered: "I never actually did it. Maybe I could sing something for you instead." That didn't satisfy them. I was threatened with a hard slap if I didn't tell the truth. So I told them the truth: going into her dormitory room, the scream, covering her mouth, how I'd been beaten up and arrested. They wouldn't believe me. They told me they'd get the truth out of me one way or another.

I tried to explain to them again how I'd been honest, how nothing had happened. But there were murmurs, and then a few of the men jumped down from their beds. One of them grabbed me and jerked down my pants: "Let's have a look at it. I can't believe we've got a rapist claiming to be a virgin." I pulled my pants back up quickly, and more men circled me. I felt my scalp burning and my legs going weak. I couldn't take it anymore. I shouted: "Okay! I'll tell you."

The men fell back. Li Dapao said: "You saw what happened to me, right? You'd better make it good." I told the men how I sneaked into the room, how I tore her dress off, grabbed her tits, ripped open her panties . . .

I gained some degree of celebrity as one of the rapists on the cell block, but eventually, one night as I told the story again, I found that I could no longer bear to repeat the lie. I stopped midsentence with all the prisoners staring at me. One of them said: "Why'd you stop?"

Another said: "He wants a kick in the ass."

"No, he wants his teeth knocked out."

I shouted back at them: "It's all fake. Every word is a lie. This is how you get off, hearing this shit. Hou Zhi, Li Dapao, they're both lying most of the time, too. At least they actually might have done some of that stuff, but what about me? I never even held hands with a girl. All of it's a lie. I don't care if you believe it, but I don't want to keep lying." I started to hit myself with both hands, smacking the sides of my head. I knew that I shouldn't be there. Hou Zhi and Li Dapao, they were both genuine rapists, but I was nothing but a fake.

The next day, I got a letter from Yu Baijia. He told me that he had checked out the dormitory. If I had jumped that night, he said, I would have landed on the lawn of the dormitory, no problem. Even if I'd been standing on the windowsill when I jumped, I would have been fine. I could have run away, I realized again. I regretted that missed opportunity, but I wouldn't let it happen again. This time, I planned to escape.

I got the idea when I was washing up. A dozen or so men at a time were led in to wash up in a sort of bathhouse in the prison yard. We got bars of lye soap to wash with, and with all the men scrubbing up in the bathhouse, the whole place would be covered in suds as clean and white as fresh snow. The sudsy water went through a drain in the corner of the room and was gone. If the water can get out, I thought, why can't I?

I started paying attention to where the water went. If I could flow out of prison like the water did, if I could find some crack to seep into, I'd be free. There was a lot of water, I realized, once I started paying attention: the water we pissed down the drain, the water the janitors sloshed onto the floor, the water the wardens used to wash their clothes, the water from the kitchen—it had to be going somewhere. Some of it was absorbed by the floor, or it evaporated, but most of it went down a drain, which had to be connected to a sewer, which had to be accessible by a grate or a manhole. Over the next few months, I checked every inch of the prison that I could. Out in the prison yard, everything was cement, except where the roots of the big tree in the middle of the yard met the ground.

‹ 16 ›

I used to look out the window of one of the factory's workshops, trying to catch a glimpse of the outside world. At first, all I could see was a wall of green. But when I looked closer, I could see that the wall of green in the distance was a line of pine trees, which only partially concealed the prison's tall metal fence. When I had the chance to look for a while longer, I realized that there were gaps in the pine trees and that I could see through the fence and catch sight of the back side of Beishan and the spindly trees that grew in the hillside brush. If I looked long enough, my eyes blurred, and when I looked again, I could see the pine trees parting and the gate swinging open—I could walk right out! But the noise of hammers on iron sheets brought me back to reality: there was no way to get out through that fence. I gave up hope, until one afternoon that winter, looking out the window again, trying not to fall for the same fantasy, I looked closely at the pine trees along the fence. The cement ran up to the edge of the yard, but below the trees there was wet dirt. And below the trees closest to the building was a patch of earth that seemed to sit higher than the ground around it. That patch was dry, even though the dirt around it was wet. I knew that it had to be there—the entrance to the sewer. It made sense based on the location of the drains in the two buildings closest to the trees, too. The distance from the building was also about right.

But there was no way for me to get to the trees. The only exit that I had access to was the metal door at the back of our canteen, and it was locked tight. Some of the prisoners worked in the yard, but I never got the chance. I kept an eye on the pine trees, watching the yard around them change with the seasons, even if the trees never changed. Three years went by before I had my chance. The summer of my third year locked up, one of our wardens came to our dorms and told us that we were headed out to the yard to clean up: some Party officials were going to be coming for an inspection.

The prisoners were lined up, given shovels and shears, and sent out into the yard to start weeding and tidying up the lawn, pruning trees, and whitewashing the outbuildings under the watchful eye of two armed guards. I counted down the line of pine trees and headed for the tenth one from the left. I had taken one of the shovels, and as I made my way down the line of trees, I cut up the soil beneath them, turning over the weeds and grass that were growing there. When I got to the sixteenth tree in the line, where I guessed that the sewer entrance was, I slid my shovel into the dirt and heard the sound of metal on metal. I went to work, scraping away dirt and grass until I'd uncovered a manhole cover.

We were led back inside through the door at the back of the canteen. The door was slammed shut, and three bars were slapped across it and padlocks slid through them. There was no way I could get out that door, I thought. I kept an eye on the pine trees. The yard was hit with a heavy rain the next day and then warmed by the summer sun. The yard was once again covered in weeds and rough grass. .

That should have been the end of my plan to escape, right? But the problem stimulated my intelligence somehow.

No, come on. I'm exaggerating a bit, too. I shouldn't even say "intelligence"—you're the intelligent one. I could never do what you do, the way you can react to every part of the story. I'm almost fifty, and there aren't many people like you who do that: rolling your eyes, opening your mouth just a bit, frowning, letting tears form in the corners of your eyes but not drop, all at the right moments in my story. That's why I'm telling it to you. Sorry. You don't mind, do you? Oh, okay, I'll keep going.

I didn't lose all hope, as I said. One day, in the bathroom of our workshop, I started looking at the small window set high on one wall. If I had something to stand on, I could probably get out. The guards were not going to let me drag anything into the bathroom. But looking around the room, I saw a possibility: a brick in the wall on one side and a brick in the post on the other side, which, if I could stand on them, I could use to get up to the window. The problem was that the bricks were so far apart that I'd have to be in a position like Zhang Nao when she dropped down into the splits.

I started practicing on my bed at night, stretching, pushing myself down from standing to a full split. It took months, but eventually I was just about there and could drop down with my legs stretched almost flat on both sides. If Zhang Nao could do it, why couldn't I? I knew that with enough practice, I'd be able to drop as flat as she did. The other prisoners would do things like kick me in the balls as I was dropping down onto the bed. They'd say: "This fucking guy wants to be a ballerina." I was using the ballet thing as a cover. It was their idea, anyway. I started rehearsing the jumps and spins that I'd seen Zhang Nao do. It made an impression on my fellow prisoners. While I did my routine, they'd watch me hungrily. When I took my bow, they'd whistle and clap. Some of the prisoners wanted to take it further. They gave me gifts of candies and snacks. They had no idea what I was planning.

And I had no idea what Lu Xiaoyan was planning. When I was called into the visiting room, I never imagined that I would see her sitting there. You might remember that we had worked together at the zoo and I'd written her a letter. Lu Xiaoyan wasn't anything like Zhang Nao—she looked okay, don't get me wrong, but nothing like Zhang Nao. If I were comparing her to Xiao Chi, I'd say she was a bit better-looking. But if we brought intangible elements like education and personality into the equation, she'd come in dead last. One thing she had going for her was the half-smile that she almost constantly wore, no matter what was going on around her. That January afternoon, though, the smile disappeared, and she began crying as soon as she saw me. I said: "Thank you, Xiaoyan. I know you sympathize with me and everything, but this isn't necessary. Don't cry for me, Xiaoyan. You don't want to go back into the cold all teary-eyed."

She rubbed her eyes with her hands and said: "I'm not crying for you, Ceng Guangxian. I'm crying for myself." I had no idea what to say. I let her cry. After a long time, she fished a handkerchief out of her pocket and wiped at her eyes. She said: "What's wrong with me? I bought him clothes, fixed his shoes, knitted long underwear for him, cleaned his ears, clipped his nose hair, popped his zits, and I even bought a hat for his dad and knee warmers for his mom. But they told him not to see me because I smelled like an animal. Whenever I came close to them, they'd hold their hands over their face like I stunk. Smell me! Do you smell it? Maybe I don't smell like a princess, but it can't be as bad as they say."

"Who are you talking about?"

"That snob!"

"You came here to tell me *this*? I thought you wanted to show me that you still had some sympathy for me."

From the basket at her feet, she produced the long underwear that she had knitted for the man. She passed them to me: "These were for him, but I didn't even get the chance to give them to him. He broke up with me because of what his parents told him. I was going to rip them apart, but I suddenly thought about you. I made them a bit longer so they'd fit you instead. I don't even know what made me think about you. They'll keep you warm, though, I thought."

"I don't know if I can take them from you. They were supposed to be for him."

"You're really turning them down? I came here to see you, to see a rapist, and you're going to turn down a gift?"

"Just that word, it makes me sick. I didn't rape anyone. Zhang Nao is lying."

"I don't care if you raped someone or not. I came to tell you I will wait for you."

"Are you joking? I've got five years left. You're going to sit around waiting for me to get out?"

"I've already thought about all that. I didn't just rush over here. I've been thinking about this for months."

"I don't think you want that. Imagine what people would say."

"I don't care what they'll say. I know you won't tell me that I smell like an animal."

"Don't be so impulsive. Just cool off, wait a few years, then come and see me again."

"Cool off?" She grabbed my hand and put it to her forehead. "I'm as cold as ice."

I pulled my hand back. "If you really want to help me, Xiaoyan, I need something: a pair of shoes."

"Cloth shoes?"

"I need you to get me a pair of canvas army shoes. Get the biggest size you can find. Once you get them, I need you to put new soles on them, thick soles, rubber, stitched on with thick thread."

"What are you going to do with shoes like that?"

"Ballet."

She said: "Oh."

I looked at her, and she put her head down. I said: "I forgot how beautiful you are."

"Oh, come on."

"Really! Since I've been locked up, I haven't seen any women as beautiful as you."

"You've been locked up too long."

"It's not that. It's . . . just . . . you have a beautiful soul."

"So you don't think I'm beautiful?"

I smacked myself in the mouth. "No, I mean, um . . . sorry . . ."

A few days later, practicing my splits, my dick hit the ground. I knew that I'd gone as far as I could. I marked the distance between my feet, and when I went to work in the factory the next day, I went into the bathroom and compared the distance. I knew I wasn't there yet, but a couple centimeters more and I'd be able to stand between the two bricks. I thought about Lu Xiaoyan and the shoes. If I had the shoes, I could get the hell out of that place.

Lu Xiaoyan arrived soon after, as if she had somehow heard me in the bathroom of the factory wondering about her. As soon as she saw me, she asked: "What do you want these shoes for?"

"I already told you."

"I'm not an idiot. You'd break your foot if you tried doing ballet in these."

"What does it matter what I do with them? Let me see them."

She took the shoes out of her basket: "I wanted to embroider the inside of them, so it took a bit longer."

I looked over the shoes. The insoles of both had been embroidered with overlapping hearts. I felt a feeling of intermingled excitement and gratitude. It seemed like she knew what the shoes were meant for. The embroidered insoles hid the work she had done on the shoes. I asked her: "You know?"

"You're going to use them to escape, right?"

"Keep it down!"

"I figured it out while I was working on them. I knew they must be for something illegal."

In a low voice, I said: "I'm getting out of here, sister. A couple more days and I'm gone."

She frowned suddenly and said: "Please don't. If you want to get out of here the right way and be my husband, don't do it. You know what will happen to you? I've heard about guys who tried to escape. They ended up getting killed."

"I didn't rape anybody. What gives them the right to lock me up for eight years? They let me sit for two years before this, too, so that's ten years. A decade! Two Five-Year Plans. "

"You're lucky they didn't put you in front of a firing squad. Don't blame them. Really, it was Zhang Nao's fault. She's the reason you're sitting here."

I lowered my head. The events of that night played again behind my eyes. I said: "It was my fault, really. If I hadn't gone there that night, none of this would have happened."

"Just think, it's only five years. I'll be waiting."

"All right, fine. Five years to wait. Thank you for the shoes."

She put the shoes back into her basket: "If I take them back, you won't have any chance to regret what you might do."

I thought about grabbing the shoes back, but I thought one of the guards would notice the scene. She took the shoes out again and reached in to peel out the insoles: "You can take these, though. When you start to miss me, just look at them."

"If you aren't going to give them to me, why did you do all that work on them?"

"At first I wasn't sure what they were for. I thought you might actually do ballet in them."

"How do you know I won't?"

"You already told me you were going to escape!"

It wasn't her fault, I realized when she'd left. All that talk about deferring. Remember that? I said I'd learned to think before speaking. It was all for nothing. I'd told her exactly what I was going to do. I couldn't believe it. And even after all the spy movies I'd seen, I had still fallen for telling all my secrets to the first pretty girl that I ran across.

When I got back to my cell, I stuffed the insoles into my old shoes and wore them every day as I tramped back and forth and hammered sheets of iron in the workshop. When the insoles were wet with my sweat, I pulled them out and let them dry out on the windowsill for a while before putting them right back in again. Pretty soon, the beautifully embroidered insoles were reduced to thin slivers of unidentifiable black material.

My life became a never-ending cycle of eat, work, sleep. Even the letters I got from Lu Xiaoyan blurred together. They all said about the same thing. One read: "You're not even thirty yet. You have to be realistic about your future. You can't take risks now. The only way to get out of there is to truly reform your thinking. Once you get out, a new man, we can be married. Our future happiness relies on you. If I didn't love you, I wouldn't care, but I do, I love you. Be a good boy, and maybe I'll give you a kiss. If you won't listen, I'm going to pinch your ear."

Who was asking for a kiss? I tossed the letter on my bed. Hou Zhi picked it up, and a few others stood reading it over his shoulder. He said: "Come on, Malai. You've got a girl who loves you. What are you so pissed off about?" The men circled me, slapping my head, laughing. Reading the letter over Hou Zhi's shoulder made them happier than receiving the letter in the first place had made me. I went back to my rehearsal. I was at the point that I could leap into the air, spread my legs, and land on my bed in full splits. I practiced the move over and over again until my face was drenched with sweat. There was scattered applause. I guess they thought I was in a good mood or something. They stopped harassing me about Lu Xiaoyan's letter. I had already forgotten about it. But I couldn't let myself forget the escape plan.

‹ 17 ›

The letters from Lu Xiaoyan were very popular in the prison and began to be circulated among the men in the cell block. They eventually ended up in the hands of Warden Jia. He was inspired to read one of them during one of our political studies classes. After he read it, he said: "I hope that all of you have someone like Lu Xiaoyan in your life, someone who offers you the encouragement to reform yourselves and to work hard, to build more tractors to repay the Motherland for the crimes you have committed. A woman like Lu Xiaoyan is the reward that you can expect if you truly reform your thinking." The speech was met with applause that rang loud and long through the hall. The men turned to look at me. I was caught up in the excitement and joined in the applause, too.

After the meeting, a sort of press conference was held in the corridors, with men asking me about Lu Xiaoyan: "What does she look like?" "Where did you meet her?" "Have you ever kissed her?" "How did you find a girl like that?"

In a loud voice, I proclaimed: "She's as beautiful as a goddess." The crowd let out a simultaneous gasp and looked up at me with undisguised admiration before the applause and questions began again.

My fellow prisoners took a strange interest in my life, an interest that approached worship. Wherever I went, someone was there to give me a hand. After work, when I retreated to my bed, the men would rub my sore muscles and take my shoes to clean and dry in the sun. The grimy insoles were washed clean, and one of the men discovered the hearts embroidered on them: "Look at this! She embroidered his insoles. Two hearts on both of them." The insoles were circulated through the cell block, a relic of true love that they rubbed and stroked and examined and then passed to the next man. It was weeks before the insoles were put back in my shoes.

The long underwear that I wore to work were just long underwear until I let it slip one day that Lu Xiaoyan had knitted them. The prisoners reached out to touch them. One of them exclaimed: "They look so warm!" Anything that Lu Xiaoyan brought me became a symbol of true love, even the bar of soap that she brought me one day. If I happened to be out of the cell for some reason, the men would scrape pieces of soap off the bar or even try on the long underwear. At night they'd press me to tell them about Lu Xiaoyan. I indulged them, telling them how sweet her mouth was, how her tongue was as soft as tofu. One night, one of the men asked me: "You ever felt her up?"

"She asked me to, of course, but I couldn't do it."

One of the men said: "Hey, dumbfuck, you scared you'll get a rash?"

"You're talking about my wife. Anyways, the way I see it, if you really love somebody, you can wait. I know that if I wait until my wedding night, it will be even better."

Somebody said: "Don't forget to invite us to the wedding!"

I patted my chest: "Me, I won't forget. I'll invite every one of you. We'll have ten tables with big dishes of kourou, roasted pork, plenty of liquor. Enough of everything to kill you—at the very least, you won't be able to walk out of there."

"I'd be happy to eat myself to death, Malai."

Hou Zhi said: "It's too bad."

I said: "What?"

Hou Zhi said: "A great girl like that, and you're sitting in here. If it was me, I'd bust out of here and marry her before my dick shriveled up."

I said: "That's not funny."

It wasn't funny, but it made me think. I couldn't sleep that night. I tossed and turned, listening to the snores of the prisoners. Hou Zhi's joke was like a match tossed into a puddle of gasoline. The urge to escape flared up again. I wasn't thinking about busting out and sleeping with Lu Xiaoyan. That wasn't important to me. It was the sense of injustice: I was an innocent man, locked up for eight years. If there was any justice in the world, I'd be allowed to walk out of that place—that would prove that there was justice in the world. You know the saying "You reap what you sow"? There was no reason for me to still be sitting in that prison.

Lu Xiaoyan had tried to get me to forget about the fact that I was unjustly imprisoned. One Sunday when she came again to see me, I said: "If you really love me, you'll give me those shoes."

She said: "You have to push those thoughts out of your head. You're going down the right road now. Don't rush down a dead end. How can I sit here and watch you ruin your life?"

"It's my choice. It has nothing to do with you."

"I haven't told anybody about me and you. My parents, Director He, our old comrades at the zoo—none of them know. How am I supposed to tell them that my boyfriend is serving a sentence of reform through labor? If it turns out that I can't even make a relationship with a convict work, what would I tell them then?"

"I don't care about them. How can you tell me you love me if you won't give me those shoes?"

"You won't ever take responsibility, will you? If you're going to keep pushing me on this, I'll go straight to Warden Jia and tell him what's going on."

Her threat made my words catch in my throat. I thought back to my father. I had done the exact same thing to him. Was Lu Xiaoyan serving me with some kind of karmic retribution? Even this woman who had embroidered my insoles and brought me gifts of soap—even she was so quick to betray me. Who could I talk to? I slapped my hand over my mouth. She asked me what I was doing. I said: "There was a mosquito."

The letters from Lu Xiaoyan kept coming. Apart from a different date at the top of each, the letters were nearly identical. She used the same trite phrases over and over again: "Wake up to the dangers of your lifestyle before it's too late," "Do your best to reform your thinking and reenter society," "The hard part is not just facing your sense of injustice, but rather using that sense of injustice as a catalyst to better yourself." When I'd first gone inside, I was waiting for that kind of encouragement, but it was lost on me now. The letters read like bureaucratic proclamations, the kind that are just a series of slogans. The sentiment behind those letters may have been noble, but they read like a mechanical recitation of platitudes.

When I heard mail call, I'd drag myself out of bed and take the latest letter and open it. As soon as I read the greetings and she got to the key "But . . . ," I knew the truisms about personal growth were soon to follow, and I'd toss the letter onto my bed. When the letters began to pile up, some of the men noticed, and I knew they would sneak looks at them when I wasn't in the dormitory. Eventually, the pile of letters was left undisturbed. I'm not saying that it wasn't nice of her to write those letters. But that's not what someone who's locked up wants to read. Me, I wanted to hear about chaomian and kourou! I wanted to know how my animals were doing. I wanted to hear the gossip from back at the zoo, what He Caixia was up to, how Hu Kaihui was doing. After a while, I realized that, except for the fact that my name was at the top of them, the letters could have been intended for any of the prisoners. There was nothing particularly personal in them, nothing that showed an attachment to me in particular. They seemed to be simply a hobby, an exercise. She just as well could have sent them to that guy whose parents had made him break up with her. "Wake up to the dangers of your lifestyle before it's too late" isn't bad advice just in general, even if you're not in prison.

One day when Lu Xiaoyan came to see me, I said: "Those letters you write, they're almost word for word what we get in Warden Jia's speeches. Did you two go to the same school or something?"

She said: "I just want to try to lead you down the right road."

"You could write me about other stuff, too."

"What am I going to write about? Our lives don't exactly intersect. We can't go out for a walk or go to a movie together. All I can do is try to encourage you to stay in here and reform yourself." As she spoke, tears came to her eyes. "I've even gone to the temple to burn incense and pray for you."

I reached out and wiped the tears from her eyes. I said: "I have no idea how you spend your time. And you don't have any idea what it's like in here. We can't possibly ever understand each other. I read an article in the paper talking about how to make a relationship work. It said that a couple need to both work toward a common emotional goal. When I look at us, I don't see how that's possible. Our relationship has no foundation. Maybe it's not a real relationship at all."

"You don't understand. I'm always thinking about you. Even if you can't go out for a walk with me, when I'm by myself I'll pick out a shirt I think you'll like, or when I make myself dinner or eat something good, I'll think about saving some for you—but I can't. I know you're headed to a bad place. But . . . look, I brought these for you." She took the shoes from her basket.

I felt my eyes tearing up. "Lu Xiaoyan, apart from my mother, nobody has ever treated me as well as you."

She wiped tears away. "Think before you act. In the future, don't . . . don't blame me. Promise me."

"Thank you! I don't care where I end up, I will always be thankful to you."

Tears soaked her face, no matter how much she wiped with her handkerchief. She sobbed. I blinked away tears. With a heavy heart, I told her: "You should go."

She stood up and began walking slowly toward the door. I called to her: "Xiaoyan, really . . . there's nothing between us. Never was." She cried out and fell to the ground. I turned and walked away, out of the visiting room and back to my cell. I waited until I was in the bathroom and let out a cry of joy.

The shoes were a few sizes too big and had thick rubber soles. It took a few days before I was able to comfortably walk in them and perform the same acrobatics. It was a few days after that when I saw that I had been assigned to the late shift. My first day would be August 12th. As I prepared to go, I wanted to tie up one final loose end. I took out my flashlight and wrote:

Dear Zhao Shanhe,

How are you? Busy at work lately? All these years, I've never forgotten life at the warehouse. Remember how you used to bring me empty shells to play with? I was too young and too stupid to understand a lot of what went on in those days. I lied to my mother, and then I ended up exposing your relationship with my father. I brought shame to you and broke up my own family. I still regret what I did. I am writing to ask for your forgiveness.

I don't know when I can get out of here. I don't know if I'll ever get out of here. So I would also like to ask you to please check on my father for me. I've heard that his blood pressure is higher than it should be and his heart isn't great. If you could help me with this, I would be forever thankful. My father is alone in the world. Please help him.

Hoping for all the best for you and your family!

Sincerely,
Ceng Guangxian.

I waited a few days and then thought better of the letter. I ran to the mailroom to ask: "Did you send that letter to Zhao Shanhe yet?"

The mail clerk said: "Look at all these letters. How am I supposed to keep track of a single letter?"

"It's a white envelope. It's for Zhao Shanhe. If you happen to see it, please don't send it out. Bring it back to Ceng Guangxian in the workshop."

"Why are you coming back for it now?"

"I made a mistake."

"What kind of mistake? If you've got a good reason why it shouldn't be sent out, maybe I can keep an eye out."

"I wrote to apologize to her, but I ended up making myself look bad. I went on about how I was too stupid to understand things. But what did I really do wrong? Why did I have to help her hide what she was doing? Why did I lie to my own mother to cover it up?"

He laughed and said: "All right, come back in the afternoon."

I went back that afternoon, and the mail clerk said: "Usually we're pretty slow to get the letters out, but the past few days . . . I guess it's just bad luck for you. The letter is already gone." I went back to the cell block, cursing my bad luck. The big day was coming. If I made a stupid mistake like that on August 12th, I would pay for it with my life. That night I lay in bed in a cold sweat. I played over and over again in my mind what the escape would look like. In my mind, I had already escaped a thousand times.

The night of my first late shift, August 12th, I made ready for my escape. I checked all of my clothes and I checked the shoes. I worked in the workshop until 9:45 and then went to the bathroom. There was still fifteen minutes until the end of the shift. I shut my eyes. I had learned that night when I went into Zhang Nao's dormitory that the best way to be silent was to cover your eyes and listen even closer to the sounds around you. I jumped up and landed on the bricks just as I had practiced so many times on my bed in the cell block. I reached up to the window and slid myself out. When my feet hit the ground, I made my way to the sixteenth pine tree from the left. I scraped away the mud on top of the manhole cover and slid it back to reveal the sewer below. I slid into the darkness. Inside I could hear the sound of running water and smell the stink of sewage. I shut my eyes and felt my way along the wall, letting the flow of sewage and water guide me.

Eventually I heard the sound of water getting louder, and I knew I must be near the exit of the pipe. I opened my eyes, but I was still in complete darkness. As I felt along the walls of the sewer, I eventually came to a grate that blocked my way. The bars of the grate were about as thick as my thumb, five in total, too close together to squeeze between and too strong to bend. I had escaped from the prison only to be blocked into a sewer. These bars could have been here ten years, even twenty years, long before I ever even thought of escaping. All this time, they'd been waiting for me. My plan had been doomed before I'd even come up with it. I crouched in front of the bars and thought to myself: Do I go back? Do I wait here to be caught? Would anyone even come down to catch me?

I went back to the walls of the sewer and began to feel around again. I knew there was no way I could go back, and there was no way I could get through the grate, so I had to keep looking. I found a small tunnel leading off from the main sewer and crawled along it on my hands and knees. From somewhere ahead of or above me, I heard the wail of an alarm. Eventually I saw two shafts of light ahead of me. When I was underneath the light, I looked up and saw that it was coming down through a manhole cover from a streetlamp. I let out a cry of delight. I was out! With my heart thudding in my chest, I stood and pushed the manhole cover with all my strength. When I'd moved the iron cover back onto the asphalt above, I grabbed the edge of the manhole and pulled myself from the sewer. I came face to face with three rifle barrels. The handcuffs and shackles were on me in seconds, and I collapsed in the road. The soldiers dragged me back toward the cell block and tossed me in solitary confinement.

The warden and Li Dapao both told me later that the night I escaped, someone sounded the alarm and all the lights in the place were turned on. Even the mosquitoes in the cells were scared to fly. Some of the guards ran out the back of the canteen and saw the manhole cover and guessed where I'd gone. They weren't willing to follow me into the sewer. They set up chairs there, waiting over the hole with their rifle barrels pointed into the darkness.

‹ 18 ›

The guards in the watchtower had swung their searchlight around to light up the yard. It wasn't long before guards were stationed over the only other manhole cover in the yard, which was almost directly under the watchtower. Another group of guards were stationed inside the tower. Both groups kept watch over the sewer entrances without speaking. The commander of the guards reassured them that there were only two exits; the rest of the sewer had been blocked off. The guards stood over the manhole, peering down through the two holes in the cover. There wasn't much else to do but wait. Another thing I found out later was that the commander of the troops who served as guards at the prison had advised the warden that he was giving me three hours—if I returned from the original hole, I would be granted clemency, and if I came up out of the second hole, I would be charged with attempting to escape. The commander's name was Mai Langyong. You know, it's hard to imagine, especially in those days, that sort of romantic idea, letting me decide my own fate. But Mai Langyong was a Renaissance man who enjoyed dabbling in gutishi, a practically ancient form of poetry. It didn't look to me or to the men with machine guns that what was taking place that night was simply an examination, an elegantly devised test administered by Mai Langyong. From above me, the commander was watching like a child watches a bug. I was unaware. I didn't hear the footsteps of fate behind me.

Three years were added to my sentence. For a long time thereafter, whenever I saw Warden Jia in the yard, I would stand at attention and slap myself in the side of the head in a kind of salute and shout: "I'm sorry!" I told him: "I shouldn't have come up from that hole. I thought about going back, but I couldn't. I don't know why. I will regret it until the day I die."

Warden Jia said: "I told you to sincerely repent and earnestly reform yourself. The thing you should be sorry for is trying to escape in the first place." Warden Jia would give me my lecture and then turn on his heel and walk away, leaving me still standing at attention in the yard.

He was right: I never should have tried. Lu Xiaoyan had wasted all her time, all her tears. She had told me countless times that it wasn't worth it. I began to think about her again. She really cared about me, I realized. If that's not love, what is?

When the weekend's visiting hours were close, I asked to work overtime.

I had already been transferred from my job assembling parts in the workshop to a job in the foundry shop. Working in the foundry shop was considered the toughest, most tiring job in the entire factory. The foundry workers poured molten iron to cast the gearboxes and engine blocks for the tractors. Every day, I put on a new uniform of canvas gloves, a face mask, heavy-duty blue coveralls, and thick-soled leather shoes—thinking back, if I'd gotten a pair of those shoes, I never would have had to ask Lu Xiaoyan to bring me the ones I'd used to escape. I started out at the bottom again, shoveling coke into the furnace. Somebody would yell: "Malai, why are you just standing around? We need heat!" I'd shovel even faster. Somebody else would yell: "Malai! Time to pour!" I'd run over to where Li Dapao was working and help him maneuver the bucket of molten iron into position to pour into the mold. But somebody else would be yelling at me to check the ingots that were going to be melted down for the next load. So I'd rush over to break them up and load them.

When I first started working there, I had no idea what I was doing. I would wait for somebody to yell at me and then move as fast as I could. If they'd shouted, "Climb into the furnace," I would have jumped inside without a second thought.

The announcement came over the PA, barely audible over the roar of the furnace: "Ceng Guangxian, Ceng Guangxian, please proceed to the visiting room." I ignored it and kept rushing between stations in the foundry. The PA crackled again, clear now over the roar: "Ceng Guangxian, Ceng Guangxian, Lu Xiaoyan is here to see you. Please proceed to the visiting room." I kept working. In my mind, I was like one of the miscast engine blocks that got tossed back into the furnace. Lu Xiaoyan had said she'd wait five years for me, and I had added three years to that time. How could I face her?

It was a few weekends before a new announcement came: "Ceng Guangxian, Ceng Guangxian, your father is here to see you. Please proceed to the visiting room." I was loading iron ingots into the furnace when I heard it. My hand slipped, and a lump of raw iron sliced through my glove and into the index finger of my left hand. I took my finger out of the glove and held it in my right hand. I ran toward the visiting room with my left hand drenched in blood. I couldn't believe it! The man I had betrayed, the man who had refused to speak to me, the only blood I had left in the world, was there to see me. I went into the visiting room with my head lowered. When I dared to look up, my father was not there. Lu Xiaoyan looked up at me. She said: "Why won't you see me?"

I said: "Three . . . three more years."

"I know. Eight years, right? I'll wait for you!"

"Please, no. You'll get old waiting for me."

"Look at me. Am I getting old? Fang Ziyu said I look younger than ever. That's the power of love."

"You'll be in your thirties by then. It's a bit . . ."

"A bit what? Maybe it's you who isn't willing to wait."

"I don't deserve you. Before you came along, I was losing hope. I thought there was no justice in the world. You treat me so well. You give me hope again. I figure you must have been sent from heaven to look after me. That's the only way I can understand it."

She took my hand. She blew softly on the cut. We didn't speak, but our hands communicated something to each other. When our time together was nearly done, she said: "We've both been hurt, Guangxian. If we hadn't found each other, we'd both be alone."

"I can't make you happy."

"Let me decide for myself. Actually, I always liked you, even at the zoo. I just couldn't say anything then. I was too young, maybe. I never got the courage to actually tell you."

"You should have! If you had said something, we wouldn't have turned out like this."

"If I'd known it would end this way, I would have worked up the nerve to write you a letter."

With Lu Xiaoyan's encouragement, I wrote a letter to my father and asked her to take it to him. When she handed it to him, he asked why I had never written a letter before. She said: "He didn't think it was right. He heard that your heart wasn't good. And he knew it would look bad for you if anyone here saw that the return address was a reform through labor factory."

"He already made me look bad!"

In the letter, I told him how I'd been caught, the sentence I'd received, and the extra years added onto the sentence. I asked for his forgiveness and told him that I didn't want to bring shame to him or his father or the Ceng family ancestors. I didn't want him to look at me like a common criminal. At the end of the letter, I wrote: "Dad, if you don't believe me, nobody will believe me. Please, just once, have some faith in your son. Even if everybody else thinks I'm a criminal, your belief that I'm innocent would mean so much to me. I swear on my mother's grave that I am telling the truth. I ask for your forgiveness." My father finished reading and stood up. His hand went slack, and the letter floated to the ground. He gripped the doorway with one hand, and the other one went to his chest. Sweat beaded on his forehead. Lu Xiaoyan went pale and called for help.

Liu Canghai and Xie Jinchuan took my father to the hospital.

Lu Xiaoyan went home and made a pot of chicken soup. She brought it to my father's hospital room. For the most part, he had recovered. As he drank from the cup of soup, he said: "You brought my appetite back."

Lu Xiaoyan said: "I should come every day, then."

My dad lifted his arm over his head and said: "This tall?"

"What do you mean?"

"Is he this tall?"

"Oh, Guangxian? He's five foot eight, 154 pounds, his blood type is B, his hair is curly when it's short, but . . . I should let you rest. Too much excitement could be bad for your heart."

"I can handle it."

"He . . . looks like you, but more handsome."

My dad smiled and barely kept from laughing. He turned serious: "I guess you know him better than me."

When it was time for her to leave, my father reached under his pillow: "This is a letter for him." Lu Xiaoyan reached out to take it, but my father pulled it back. "Forget it. I said I never wanted to talk to him again."

"He would be so happy to hear from you."

My father stuffed the letter back under his pillow. "Just forget it. I said I'd never talk to him again. I won't go back on my word."

My dad stayed in the hospital for a week or so and then went back to his dormitory and his job at the factory. Lu Xiaoyan went to see him once a week and helped him out, cleaning his dormitory room and washing and mending his clothes. At first she called him "Uncle," and then it was shortened to "Dad." It seemed natural to both of them, though. They grew closer over the months. When it was time for her to leave the factory, my father would see her off. Lu Xiaoyan remembered that his lips would quiver. She said it looked like he had Parkinson's disease. Each time, she expected him to say something more than his usual goodbye: "Well, that's it. Goodbye." My father seemed to Lu Xiaoyan to always be on the verge of saying something important. He would look as if he were about to speak, and then he would blush and turn away. But she kept visiting him and tried to look after him as best she could, and one day it finally came spilling out: "I want to see him, Xiaoyan. Let's go see that bastard."

My father rode the bus to Beishan with Lu Xiaoyan, carrying the cans of sardines he was bringing as a gift. Before they'd left the dormitory, he had carefully combed and oiled his hair. He'd had Lu Xiaoyan fix the broken button at the cuff of his sleeve. He wore a freshly ironed undershirt and starched black pants. His shoes were shined, and the laces were carefully tied so that they looked neat. I had never seen him in that pair of black leather shoes. It turned out that he'd borrowed them from Liu Canghai's brother-in-law. From every angle, he looked like a once-privileged scion of the landlord class, which is precisely what he was.

Before he went inside the grounds of the prison factory, my father paced back and forth in front of the gate. He said: "I don't even have anything to say to him."

Lu Xiaoyan said: "Then just listen! Guangxian has a way with words." She went inside to register and fill out the required visitation paperwork, but when she went back outside to get my father, the cans of sardines were stacked beside the gate, but my dad was nowhere to be found. She ran back toward the bus stop. When she caught up with him, she said: "You're right here. You're finally here, and you're not even going to go inside. He really misses you."

"Take the sardines. I think it's better if I don't go in." My father turned and got onto the bus. Lu Xiaoyan watched as it rumbled away.

My father was a hard man. Even when Zhao Wannian handed him over to the Red Guards, he didn't give in. They beat him until his dick was a bloody red ball. They beat him until tears ran down his face. But he never cried out. He never went crawling to Zhao Wannian to ask for mercy.

That day when he returned home to the factory, he had finally resolved to give up being a hard man. He bought two packs of Peony-brand cigarettes and went out to catch the bus to the warehouse. He made it as far as Tiema Road and then stopped, pacing back and forth. The wind was blowing hard. A yellow leaf fell and landed on his head. He went home. He stood at the bus stop for a while and watched the buses bound for the warehouse picking up passengers. But he didn't get on. A few days later, he tried again. That time he got on the bus. He looked out the window as the bus rolled past the warehouse. The building was covered in slogans now, and many of the roof tiles were broken or missing. Moss and grass sprouted from the roof and walls. At the front of the warehouse hung a banner: "Tiema District Revolutionary Committee."

Oh, did I forget to mention that? The warehouse had been renovated again, to house the Tiema District Revolutionary Committee. Their old offices were replaced by a Clothes for Cuba factory, which produced clothes for our Cuban comrades. That was the first time I heard about people wearing Made in China clothes.

But anyways, he didn't get off the bus at the factory. The ticket taker called out his stop: "Comrade, this is your station."

"Next stop," he called, and paid the fare to the next stop.

It was a week before he tried again. He got on the bus, carrying the two packs of Peony cigarettes. He got off in front of the warehouse and paced for a while, looking at his watch, slicking down his oiled hair, and patting the dust off his clothes. It was a bit like me with Zhang Nao, and just like me, he finally made it all the way. He found Zhao Wannian in his office. "I bought these for your father. How are your parents doing?" He handed the packs of cigarettes to Zhao Wannian.

Zhao Wannian said: "Sitting at home all day, worrying. They got some clothes together to give him, but when they went up to Beishan, they couldn't figure out how to register. They haven't even managed to visit him after all this time."

"That's actually why I came to see you. Guangxian didn't rape that girl. I've heard there's been some directives recently about 'unjust, falsified, and mistaken cases'—that sounds exactly like what happened to Guangxian. I was wondering if you could try reaching out to your contacts."

"I mean . . . you know what kind of person I am, don't you? If I interceded on behalf of a rapist, how would that look?"

‹ 19 ›

"He's not a rapist."

"Forget it. Like father, like son, I guess."

My father's face flushed red. He grunted and began to walk away. Zhao Wannian chased after him, waving the packs of cigarettes: "I can't accept these. Take them with you."

My father threw himself onto the bed in his dormitory room and ripped open one of the packs of cigarettes that had been meant for Uncle Zhao. He stuck one in his mouth and struck a match, and then another and another, but his hands were shaking with rage, and he couldn't get the cigarette to stay lit. He looked up to see Lu Xiaoyan coming into his dormitory room. She helped him light the cigarette. He took a long drag and coughed the smoke out again.

Lu Xiaoyan said: "Dad, you shouldn't be smoking. It's not good for your heart."

"These were expensive. If nobody else is going to smoke them, I might as well. Here, have one."

"What? I'm not that kind of girl."

My father forced one of the cigarettes into her hand and said: "Smoke. Listen to your dad."

Lu Xiaoyan had never heard my father call himself "dad" like that. She liked it. She took the cigarette and lit it. She took a hesitant drag and coughed. If anybody had walked by the room then, they would have seen the two of them sitting in a haze of cigarette smoke, both of them coughing.

My father sighed and said: "I can't believe I went to see that piece of shit. Forget being ashamed of Guangxian, I feel ashamed of myself."

My father was the first way that Lu Xiaoyan and I really connected. We talked about him all the time when she visited and in our letters. It felt like she was my wife. One day when she visited, I asked her about the zits on her forehead. She said she had her period. Can you believe that? She didn't even blush, either. She just told me, like it was natural. It was like we were married! I realized for the first time that I wanted to live with her like husband and wife. I wanted a normal life.

I began to ask her for things: "Get those cigarettes from my father and bring them the next time you visit." "Go to the newspaper and put a notice in the missing-persons column about my sister." "Clean up the loft of the warehouse so that the mice don't take over." "I need you to go ask Zhang Nao why she lied." "Can you find out if any of your relatives have any political connections that could help me?"

I thought I was beginning to understand how a husband felt. I looked forward to seeing her every weekend. We sat across from each other and placed our hands on the table. Our hands moved toward each other. I don't think either of us thought about it. Our hands wrapped around each other. Until I looked down, I could I forget which fingers were mine and which were hers, but our hands were very different: mine were rough and dark, pitted with scars, and hers were soft and pale. Sometimes I pressed my palms against her palms and we rubbed our hands together until they were warm. I dug my nails into her hand, gently, and she did the same. Our hands stayed tangled together until visiting time came to an end. It reminded me of the snakes I had seen mating at the zoo. When our hands were together, we were married, in my mind. You can laugh if you want, but if you've experienced anything like it, you'll know exactly what I mean. I remember the way her face looked when our hands met. Her cheeks flushed deep red and her lips pressed together, and she hummed a tune that I didn't recognize. I felt my entire body tingle. It felt like I was floating. It felt like I could float away with her. You know the feeling when you can't even remember your own name? You can say everything that needs to be said just by holding hands—I still think that's true.

My hands were the connection between myself and Xiaoyan, so I wanted to take care of them. I made sure to wear gloves when I was working, and I rubbed facial cream into my hands every night before bed—I had her bring me a jar. They slowly grew less dark, less twisted by my work in the foundry. One night I went into the toilet and crouched beside Li Dapao and saw that he was masturbating. After he finished, he said: "Your turn, Guangxian."

"Gross!"

He stood up and pressed my face against the wall with his hand: "What the fuck do you mean it's gross? I know you do it, too."

"I have a wife now. It would be an insult to her."

"You aren't even fucking her, you dumb son of a bitch."

"Xiaoyan is my wife."

"She can be whatever you want her to be, but you aren't fucking her. You might be able to hold out for a while, but . . . three, four years?"

"I'll tell you a secret."

He relaxed the pressure on my head: "About how you got into the sewer?"

"I know it's hard to believe, but when I touch her hand, I get the same feeling as when I do it myself. It's better than beating off, just touching her hand."

He grabbed my hand and forced it down into the filthy latrine pit, wiping it back and forth over the slimy wall. I ripped it away and ran to the faucet, letting the water run over my hands.

In the foundry shop, I made a habit of holding on to things, like an old iron pot that I saved from being melted down. Li Dapao asked me: "Why are you keeping that?"

"It's still good! I can use it when I get out of here." When I saved a wrecked steel board that we used in the shop, he asked me the same thing. I said: "I could use this as a bench." When the men in the shop were given new gloves, I collected the old gloves that they'd tossed on the floor. I cut them into strips and made them into a mop head. Li Dapao told me that by the time I got out, they'd be no good. But I wasn't listening anymore. I wanted to get ready for life after reform through labor. When I looked at the mop heads and the iron pot and the other items I'd saved in a corner of the workshop, I could imagine my new life. I could imagine Xiaoyan mopping the floor of our new home with the mop I'd made, or bending over the iron pot, the room full of the smell of huiguorou. Even though the men in the workshop laughed at me, they began to use the things I'd saved. They used the steel plate bench and scrubbed the floors with my glove mops. I didn't really mind. I kept collecting things for my next life.

That day, we finished our work early. The furnace was allowed to go cold. Li Dapao sat down on a bench and took a long drag on a cigarette. He looked over at the items I'd saved in the corner and said suddenly: "Xiaoyun! Xiaoyun!" We looked over at the corner where Li Dapao was staring. Li Dapao rubbed his eyes. He said: "Malai, it's strange. I saw her over there just now. Down in front of the stove."

Somebody asked: "Who's Xiaoyun?"

Li Dapao said: "You don't remember? I've told the story a thousand times. She's the girl I raped. She wrote me a letter."

I said: "She regrets going to the police?"

Li Dapao took a drag from his cigarette and exhaled. He said: "I can't fucking believe it. Back then, she wanted me dead. But now . . . what do you think she said to me? She said that her reputation is ruined. She still isn't married. She says that her only option is somebody like me. She wants me to marry her. If she'd only realized back then how things would turn out, she wouldn't have run to the police. All this time, and she suddenly wants me to marry her."

After the day he saw Xiaoyun in the corner, Li Dapao told me: "When I see all those things you keep over there, I get homesick." He started to recycle the tools and leftover items in the workshop. He made his own pile of repurposed items for his new life, and when our work was done, we'd sit in the corner and imagine that we weren't in the factory anymore, but in our own homes.

One day Li Dapao said: "I want to do what you did."

"Come on. That's not a good idea."

"I dream about her every night. I dream that I'm kissing her. I can't handle it."

"It's a long road. You have to keep going."

"I don't want to keep going. I want to get out of here."

"Don't do it, Dapao. I promise you, it won't turn out well. When I got the same advice, I ignored it. Three more years in here, that's what I got."

"I have to."

"Think about it. I tried it. It's impossible. Even these flies are stuck in here."

"Don't worry about that. I have an idea."

Over the weeks that followed, Li Dapao grew gaunt. The only time I saw him talking was late at night, when he'd sit up with Hou Zhi and the two of them would talk in whispers. When I went near them, they'd fall silent and drift away, snickering. I said: "Do you know what regret feels like?"

"I've never regretted anything. Save your breath."

"You will regret this. You know what it feels like? It's a feeling like . . . you're walking home, and you know the way and you know you should be there already, but the road just keeps going, and you can never make it home. You might as well be walking to Cuba. You feel like everything you ever did was wiped away. Even if you try to rebuild your life, there's always a piece missing. If I could do it again, I'd rather go to the firing squad than try to escape. I don't know why I didn't just listen to her . . ."

He said: "Don't bother telling me all this."

"I'm telling you this as a friend, Dapao. Don't do it. Please listen to me, or you're going to make a very stupid mistake."

His eyes opened wide, and he grabbed me by the hair and tossed me to the ground. As I lay on the ground, he kicked me and shouted: "What stupid mistake? Motherfucker, what did you say?" I cried for mercy, and he let me up. His fingers were full of my hair. He held it up and blew my own hair across my face. He said: "Next time I'll cut your tongue out."

A few months later, Li Dapao somehow got himself transferred to the warehouse where the tractors were stored between inspection and shipping. Nowadays the tractors would just be loaded on a truck, but back then they were driven out of the factory, one by one. Li Dapao took an interest in the men who arrived to drive the tractors out. He told us about the men, who wore clean, pressed undershirts and warm jackets. Li Dapao noticed that their lips were always oily, as if they had just eaten a dish of fatty kourou.

Li Dapao told us that Xiaoyun had written him a few times and had come to see him and brought him a warm jacket. One night he came into our cell block and gave the jacket to Hou Zhi, saying: "It doesn't fit me. You might as well have it." Hou Zhi took the jacket and slipped it on. It didn't fit him, either. It hung down to his knees. He gave me a pair of gloves. He said: "You're always looking after those hands. Next time Xiaoyan comes to visit you, remember me when you're holding hands with her." He laughed, and I didn't say anything.

The next day, while waiting for iron to set in a mold, I sat and smoked a cigarette. I looked down at the new gloves. I tore them off and tossed them toward the corner. I looked at where they had fallen and saw the stove that Li Dapao had built from scraps of iron. Something came over me, and I walked across the workshop and kicked over the stove. I paced for a while and then went and kicked over the pile of items that I had collected for my new life. I went toward the door but stopped. Should I stay or should I go? I sympathized with Li Dapao. Both of us were men in love. I could sit here for another seven years. I was willing to do it, for Xiaoyan and our new life together. But seven years! No, I couldn't wait that long. If Li Dapao missed his girl, I was missing Xiaoyan even more.

The guard in the foundry dragged me to the warden's office. Warden Jia asked me: "What's wrong?" I told him that I wanted to confess something. When he pressed me for details, I asked about getting some time taken off my sentence. I wanted those three years that had been added for escaping reduced. He said: "We can discuss that. But in this kind of situation, reducing time for good behavior depends on what you have to tell me."

I said: "What I'm going to tell you, it can't come back on me."

Warden Jia said: "That goes without saying."

My eyes darted to the door of the office. "Li Dapao is planning to escape."

"When?"

"In the next couple of days. Last night, he gave Hou Zhi his jacket. He gave me a pair of gloves. That must mean he's close to ready. He told me that he wants to escape to see Xiaoyun. He's been planning for it a long time."

"How is he going to do it?"

"I'm not sure. But I think it has something to do with the drivers who take the tractors out of the warehouse. Maybe he plans to disguise himself as a driver, something like . . ." The warden stood, mashed his hat onto his head, and stormed out of the office.

As soon as I said those words—"Li Dapao is planning to escape"—my palms began to sweat. When the warden was gone, I shuddered, and my legs seemed to give out under me. The guard shouted: "Get up." I tried to stand, but I couldn't. I had no strength left.

The prison alarms began to wail. I heard the martial footsteps of the guards marching in the hallways. I thought: I wish that none of this were real. But it had to be. I wished that Li Dapao hadn't told me his stupid idea. I wished that Li Dapao had come to me a few days after he'd told me he wanted to escape and chuckled and slapped me on the back and said he was just joking. I wished that Li Dapao were already gone, already up in the hills.

‹20›

The warden ran down to the gates, where five tractors were moving in a convoy out of the factory, each of them towing a trailer behind it. The drivers came down from the tractors. None of the men looked like Li Dapao: they were well fed, their hair was combed and shiny, and their teeth were white and straight. The guards and soldiers surrounded the prison and began a careful search for Li Dapao. There was no sign of him. I wondered how he could have disappeared. Did he simply vanish? Did he turn himself into a fly and buzz off into the hills? The warden, though, was looking for a more realistic solution. He went back to the drivers. He checked them very closely. Was that a wig on one of them? Were those false teeth? They seemed to be the real deal. He paced in front of them, his eyes on his shiny black shoes. He turned back to the drivers again. The men all looked innocent enough. But the warden knew that this was the way Li Dapao would escape—it had to be! Finally, someone searched the tractors again, and Li Dapao was found under the trailer being towed by the last tractor in the convoy, hanging from four hooks that were welded on the underside. The warden said: "Welcome back, Li Dapao." Li Dapao was dragged from under the tractor. As he was pulled to his feet, he farted.

Li Dapao was tossed into solitary confinement. When he was brought in for interrogation, he revealed that Hou Zhi had welded the hooks under the trailer. Hou Zhi had done the job in exchange for a promise by Li Dapao to take a gift to the secretary Hou Zhi had raped. He was still in love with the secretary. I remember he told us how beautiful she was, how her mouth had tasted, her soft voice—it wasn't her fault, he said! She'd been forced to confess that he had raped her.

The other women had been unwilling to confess for fear of harming their reputations, but the secretary had been forced. After all their years working together, Hou Zhi had a good relationship with the secretary, and he wanted to give her a gift. The gift that he had in mind was sunflower seeds. He knew she loved them. He imagined her face lighting up when she got the basket of sunflower seeds. She used to eat them all the time. She ate them on the bus to work, and she ate them in the office. There always seemed to be a pile of cracked shells under her.

You're laughing. It's weird, right? But it was a different time. Even rapists were romantics. It's different now. These days people will just name their price. They walk in and say: "Five hundred." What's wrong now? Everything has a price today. I don't mean you. But if you took a few dollars . . . Okay, okay. Fine. Yeah, have a drink.

Li Dapao had three years added to his sentence. Hou Zhi got an additional two years and was moved from the welding shop to the foundry. My sentence was reduced by two years, but I wasn't allowed to tell anyone. I was in the foundry when Li Dapao came back. I heard a voice from outside the workshop, calling my name. I looked up to see Li Dapao coming in, more emaciated than when he had left. He collapsed against my chest, sobbing. Li Dapao was weakened by his interrogation and time in solitary confinement, but he put all his strength into the arms that he wrapped around me. It reminded me of the time that Xiao Chi had hugged me. I stood stiffly in his embrace, and his tears fell on my shoulders. I felt a lump in my throat. My eyes were moist. He said: "I finally realize now, Guangxian. You were my only friend. If I had only listened to you, I wouldn't have ended up like this." Li Dapao's gratitude was like a finger in my wound. Tears finally dropped from my eyes. He shook my shoulders and sobbed: "Why didn't you stop me? You should have tied me up. Why did you let me go?"

He took his hands from my shoulders and began to slap himself in the face. The blows fell wetly on his cheeks, which were soaked with snot and tears. "I will always regret not listening to you." The slaps hurt him as much as they hurt me. Hou Zhi walked past and said: "Fucking coward." If it hadn't been for Hou Zhi, I probably would have said something. I was so close to letting it slip out.

I don't know what I was going to say. I think it might have been "I'm sorry." I noticed that he hadn't called me Malai. I was Guangxian again after that.

Things began to change in the workshop. The work was still tough. The men who worked in the foundry were filthy. They breathed black dust every day. Before, I'd been the one who had usually done the hard work in the foundry. But now Li Dapao started rushing to clean the spattered iron that fell around the mold. When it was time to clean out the blast furnace, Li Dapao went first. I heard him inside, the sound of metal on metal. When I ducked my head in, he shouted at me: "Fuck off. I don't want anything to happen to those hands. Give her hands a couple of squeezes for me." I felt even worse. I squeezed into the blast furnace, and he pushed me back out, as if the furnace were his lair.

Once a week, the prison canteen gave the foundry workers a bowl of pork blood. They said it was good for our lungs. We inhaled so much dust. I tried to slide my bowl across the table to Li Dapao. He tried to slide his bowl over to me. Both bowls ended up being spilled onto the floor.

I said: "I don't care if the dust kills me."

Li Dapao patted my cheek: "Hey, how old are you? You've got a long way to go. Look after yourself. Somebody's waiting for you out there."

"Dapao, I . . . I . . ." I couldn't bring myself to complete the sentence with "I'm sorry."

Li Dapao looked at me closely: "Just get it out. I was holding one in, hanging under that tractor. I let it go as soon as I got out from under there."

I looked away from him. "It's . . . nothing."

I told Xiaoyan about the two years being taken off my sentence, and she came that weekend with two cartons of cigarettes. I ripped open one of the cartons as I left the visiting room and held it under my nose. I went to the foundry the next day with a pack in my pocket. When I walked in, I saw that Li Dapao had a butt in his mouth, already burned down. I took a cigarette out of the pack, handed it to him, and struck two matches. My hands were shaking too much. The matches scratched down the pad but didn't light. He took the pack of matches from me and struck one. He lit his cigarette and then held the match for me. He saw that I didn't have a cigarette and said: "You aren't smoking?"

I put the pack back in my pocket: "I quit." Hou Zhi and the others gathered around me, and somebody tried to take the pack out of my pocket. I put my hand over my pocket, and they called me a cheap bastard. I patted my pocket again: "I can't smoke these."

When I went to work, I carried a pack in my pocket and made sure Li Dapao always had a cigarette. I couldn't look him in the eye. But when I struck the matches to light his cigarettes, my hands didn't shake anymore. His eyes were the same as they'd always been. But whenever we locked eyes, I felt a chill run through my body. If he looked deep into my eyes, I thought, he would know my secret. His eyes were like an X-ray that would reveal that I had told the warden about his plans. One day as he sat in the corner surveying his recycled benches and stoves and kitchen tools made from iron scraps, he said: "You're like a brother to me, Guangxian."

I said: "Actually . . . you don't get it. I . . ."

He said: "Don't do that. 'I . . . I . . . I . . . '—just say what you want to say. Stop holding it in."

"I . . ."

One night I woke up with a start and saw a blood-red light in the corner of the room. Li Dapao was crouched there, smoking a cigarette. I slipped out of my bed and went over and knelt beside him. He slapped me hard on the back: "You're a sleepwalker? Go back to bed."

I said: "I'm . . ."

He said: "I used to talk in my sleep, too, when I was a kid. When my mom heard me, she'd slap me on the back a few times. Did it work for you?"

"I'm . . . I'm fine."

He sighed: "Guangxian, I lied to you. Xiaoyun never wrote any letters to me. That jacket was from my mother. My mother is the only one who came to visit me. I don't care about Xiaoyun, but I wanted to see my mother. You might not know it from looking at me, but I'm just a scared little boy who misses his mom." He began to cry.

I said: "You're not the only one who misses your mother. I . . . I'm sorry . . . to my mother."

That weekend, I told Xiaoyan how I had betrayed Li Dapao. She went pale: "How could you do that to your friend?"

"Right, so I need you to help me with something."

"What is it?"

"I need you to go find somebody. She's on the Taoli Production Team at the Changlong People's Commune in Nanguan County. Her name is Luo Xiaoyun. I want you to bring her here to see Li Dapao. Tell her that he loves her very much. Whatever you have to do, get her here. I don't care how you do it, even if you have to pay her."

Xiaoyan wrote a few letters to Xiaoyun, but there was no reply. Eventually she decided she would have to go there herself. When Xiaoyan finally found her, Xiaoyun was not willing to go anywhere, let alone to the prison factory. She said: "Who the hell do you think you are? Are you one of his relatives or something? You think you can march in here like Party Secretary Yang and order me to go there? Bitches like you marry Party members, and you want me to marry a rapist?"

Xiaoyan said: "I married a rapist. The man I'm married to is a good friend of Li Dapao."

"Who gives a shit? You want me to suffer, too?"

Xiaoyan wasn't happy, but she turned and left. She went back to the city. She told me to give up on Xiaoyun, but I told her it was impossible. There had to be a way, I thought, to get Xiaoyun to come to the prison. It was the only way to cleanse myself. I lost my temper. I told her that she had to do it, no matter what.

She said: "I tried. I don't know how to bring her here. If you want Xiaoyun to visit Li Dapao, you'd better come up with something. I'm not your servant. I don't have time to run your errands. I have to feed myself. You know what happened when I went there? And now you're yelling at me, too." Her voice was stronger and clearer than mine had been when I shouted at her. She stood and walked out of the visiting room.

That was really the first time I had a falling-out with Xiaoyan. I had always managed to maintain things as they were, even if I had to work at it. But now, even though I realized I'd gone too far, I didn't know when I'd have the chance to explain things to her, or even when I'd have the chance to see her again. I felt like a light bulb waiting for someone to come in and flick the switch.

I went back to work in the foundry. From then on, I didn't bother wearing gloves. I didn't care about my hands. When I was shoveling coke into the stove of the blast furnace, my hands were bare. I felt my arms going numb from the baking heat. When it was time to carry the buckets of molten iron to dump into the molds, I took over from Li Dapao. During one shift, as I was walking to the mold for the last time, I felt my foot slip, and the weight of the bucket dragged me down. The bucket hit the floor, and a glowing red pool of molten iron began to spread across the surface. I bounced back up and leapt back, but I wasn't fast enough to save my right foot from the spreading puddle. Li Dapao and the other men rushed to my side and began to pull off my burned pants and the scorched shoe, but it was too late.

After the doctor saw my burned foot, I was left to recover in the cell block. I lay in bed. The doctor came to see me once a day and applied medicine and gave me injections, but Li Dapao was my nurse. The warden had excused him from his duties in the foundry, and he attended to me in the cell block. He was at my side all day, helping me clean myself and change my clothes. When it was hot, he sat beside my bed and fanned me with a palm-leaf fan. I pissed and shit in a basin, and he dumped it for me in the prison toilet. When the work was done, he'd put a cigarette in his mouth, light it, and then transfer it to my mouth before lighting another one for himself. He said: "This is the life, huh? Like we're Party members now. We don't have to bust our asses in the foundry. It's all thanks to you burning up your foot, too."

"You know how much that hurt? Next time we'll switch places. I will wait on you."

"It's still better than carrying buckets of iron."

"Dump a bucket of molten iron on your foot, and I'll see if you say that again."

One day we were both in the cell block when the PA crackled to life above us: "Li Dapao, Li Dapao, please report to the visiting room."

Wait.

Sorry. They would have called his actual name. What was it again? Let me think. I can't believe I don't remember. Such a good friend, and I can't even remember his name. It's completely slipped my mind. Anyways, I'll just keep going. It's not important now.

So he heard the announcement and ran right out of there. He was halfway through helping me with my pants, and he left me on the bed with my pants around my ankles.

When he got to the visiting room, Xiaoyun was waiting for him. She was wearing a red-checked shirt and black pants with a black belt. She had two long braids and pink cheeks. He couldn't tell if it was a sign of good mountain air or if she was blushing. Dapao awkwardly moved around the room before sitting down across from her, his hands moving from the table to his lap and back again. His arms looked like they belonged to another person. Xiaoyun looked down at the table and played with the tip of a braid. She said: "I can't believe you bought these clothes for me."

Dapao laughed awkwardly and stammered: "Don't . . . don't mention it. They fit okay?"

"Did you go blind in here or something?"

Dapao studied the clothes for a moment: "They look good on you."

"If you had treated me this well before, I wouldn't have told on you."

Dapao's hands finally found a place to rest as he cradled his head in his hands. He said: "You really mean that?"

"Did I ever lie to you before?"

"Why didn't you just tell me that? I would have bought whatever you wanted, even if I'd had to sell my house."

"You don't understand women. How could I just tell you?"

"These . . . clothes . . . How did you come—I mean, how did you get them?"

"Lu Xiaoyan brought them for me. Are you friends with her or something? She really looks after you. When she first came, I was too hard on her. Turns out she's a really good person."

"A great person!"

When Li Dapao was back in the cell block, he sat down beside me, and I called him to bring the basin. As I pissed, he said: "I could have just bought her some clothes. Why didn't I think of that?"

"That's the way it is sometimes. You look back on what you should have done, but it's too late to change anything. Dapao, I . . ."

"Again with the 'I . . . I . . . I . . . '? What the hell do you want to say?"

"I'm sorry."

"It's nothing. I can't let you piss on yourself, can I? It's nothing compared to what Lu Xiaoyan did for me."

"It's not that. There's something else I need to tell you. I know you won't like it."

"I've been through a lot. It'd be tough to piss me off now."

"That day when you tried to escape, I went to the warden. If not for me, you probably would have gotten away. I'm sorry."

His eyes opened wide: "You sold out your brother. You have no fucking soul."

"Please forgive me."

"Fuck your mother—'forgive me.' You know I'm sitting here for another three years because of you?" He lifted the basin and dumped the piss over my burned foot. He stood up, tossed the basin to the floor, and walked out. A sharp pain spread upward from my burns to my chest. I curled my body into the fetal position, the pain ripping through me. If I'd known this kind of pain existed, I never would have ratted on Dapao. I was wracked by pain and by regret. I screamed.

‹ 21 ›

After an hour or so, the pain was gone, but the regret was still there. It felt like there was a rock pressing down on my chest. I understood how Li Dapao felt, but I thought it would pass soon enough. A couple hours at the most and he'd be back.

That night, he came back and knelt beside my bed. Hou Zhi crouched beside him. They asked me what I got out of it. They asked how many years I'd had reduced from my sentence. I said: "Two years."

They spat in my face. Li Dapao stood and made a proclamation to the other prisoners: "Ceng Malai is a rat. He's a traitor. He's a collaborator. Deal with him at your own risk." He held up a fist.

I wiped the spit off my face. I felt humiliated. I said: "I thought we were brothers. Who got Xiaoyun to visit you? Who told you not to escape? I gave you cigarettes. You don't remember?"

"This is mild compared to what should happen to a rat like you. You added five years to our sentences."

I put my hand over my mouth: "I shouldn't have told you. I should have known you'd react like this."

"You got what's coming to you. I thought they heard me let a fart go. I thought that's how they caught me. I didn't ever suspect somebody ratted. I thought I'd fucked up. I hated myself. All along, it was you." He grabbed my bandaged burns hard. I cried out in pain.

With Li Dapao having threatened the other prisoners, I was left without anyone to look after me. The warden transferred me to another cell block, where I was tended to by a man named Sun Nan, a thief. After the burns healed, I was sent back to my original workshop, and another year was reduced from my sentence.

The years that had been added to my sentence for the escape had been dropped. I had gone through all that trouble for nothing. After all my pain, I had only broken even. But Li Dapao and Hou Zhi weren't ready to leave things as they were.

One day, Li Dapao and Hou Zhi set a basin of shit above the door of the bathroom that was shared by three of the workshops in the factory, including the assembly shop, where I worked. Whoever opened the door would be showered with shit. Li Dapao made sure the information about the door spread through the group of forty workers who used that bathroom. I thought there was something strange happening when I saw that nobody was using the toilets. I noticed Sun Nan wink at me, too. But I had no idea what he was trying to tell me. Toward the end of my shift, when I ran for the bathroom, I heard laughter from the three workshops, but it was too late—I was covered in shit.

After that, I knew that I had no friends in the prison factory. I had been marked. I was a rat. If I hadn't told the warden about Li Dapao's escape and if I hadn't told Li Dapao about telling the warden, none of this would have happened.

Later, when the men in the three workshops collaborated on a plan to escape en masse, I was the only one left in the workshop. I was driving a screw into a plate when I heard the sound of gunshots coming from outside. I didn't even blink. I'm serious. Reality is the best teacher, as they say. I'd learned a lot. If you regret everything you've ever done, you stop wanting to do anything at all. All I wanted to do was get through the next two years and marry Xiaoyan.

I began to count down the days I had left. The day that winter when Xiaoyan brought me a warm jacket: one year, two hundred and thirty days. The day my father fell while working at the factory: one year, one hundred and eighty-seven days. The day I held Xiaoyan's hand and rubbed her ring finger: one year, one hundred and thirty-seven days. The day Baijia and Xiao Chi came to visit me: one year, sixty five days.

I remember how they looked that day. They were so happy to be back in the city, especially Xiao Chi. She looked happier than I'd ever seen her. She'd gotten her paintings into an exhibition and taken a job at the Culture Bureau. Baijia had gone to his father and gotten a job at the department store, where he worked as an accountant. When she showed me the award she had received for the exhibition, I had a bittersweet feeling. I said: "I should have gone down to the countryside, too. It should have been us three. I doubt I'd have become an artist. But anything would be better than being locked up in here."

Xiao Chi said: "You deserve it. I told you to come."

I turned to Baijia: "Did you tell her?"

Baijia said: "Tell her what?"

I said: "You didn't tell her Zhang Nao lied?"

Baijia said: "You've been in here for nine years. It doesn't matter what I say. People will think what they want."

I said: "You don't have to go around telling people I'm innocent, but couldn't you, you know, mention something to your own wife? It feels like you're doing it on purpose."

"If you didn't rape her, why did you sneak in there?"

Can you believe that? Does that seem like something a friend would say? I felt like I'd been smacked in the back of the head. The veins in my neck stood out. My eyes stung. I lifted my hand and slapped Yu Baijia across the face. He stood and raised his hands. Xiao Chi held him back. She pushed him back into the reception area and came back alone into the visiting room. She sat across from me: "You never learned to control yourself, Guangxian."

"After all these years, I thought Baijia understood more than anyone what happened that night. I thought my father was the only one who thought I really did it. I never thought . . ."

"You didn't rape her?"

"You don't believe me, either?"

"Are you going to hit me, too?"

"He got off easy. You know he's the one who told me how to do it? He wrote me a letter, telling me exactly how to get into her dormitory. It was all his idea."

"It's his fault you raped her?"

"I didn't rape her."

"You sat in here for nine years for a crime you didn't commit. Are you stupid or what?"

"That's right, I'm stupid. There's nobody dumber than me."

"I mean, you didn't ever think of getting a lawyer? That doesn't look good to me."

"It's useless. Unless Zhang Nao retracts her testimony, there's not much I can do. When I get out, that bitch had better run."

That night, I went back to the cell block and sat alone. I smoked one cigarette after another. Things were changing outside, I realized. Kids were coming back from the countryside. A girl like Xiao Chi could make a living as a painter. Maybe there would be some hope if my case went in front of a judge again. I went to Warden Jia and asked his opinion. He told me that it wasn't worth it. He told me not to waste my money on a lawyer. It wasn't a question of money. It wasn't even about getting out early. He looked down at his desk and told me that I had one year, sixty-four days to go. It was up to me, he said.

I wrote a ten-page letter to Xiaoyan. I told her to find me a lawyer as quickly as she could. She came to see me before the letter arrived. Her cheeks were rouged, and she was wearing greasy red lipstick. She smelled of perfume. I wrinkled my nose: "Aren't you worried about the Red Guards, going out like that?"

She took the bottle of perfume out of her pocket and spritzed me with it. "All the girls are wearing red dresses and lipstick. This is normal."

"What happened?"

"People are even listening to pop songs from Taiwan now."

"Get me a lawyer."

Her eyes widened: "A lawyer? You only have a year and sixty days left."

"Even if I were getting out tomorrow! It's about clearing my name. You want to marry a rapist?"

"Who cares? Everybody knows I'm marrying a rapist."

I howled at her: "You're the rapist!" Her mouth clamped shut.

I never thought it would happen. The day I got the letter from Zhang Nao, I had one hundred and seven days left on my sentence. I can still remember every word:

Ceng Guangxian:

How are you? It's Zhang Nao from the provincial propaganda team. Do you remember me?

As your release date approaches, I can't stop thinking about what I've done. I've walked by the court building so many times, but I can't bring myself to go inside. I want to retract my testimony, but it's humiliating. I feel so stupid. I let you sit in there for so many years. You must hate me.

I want the chance to discuss things with you. If you need me to, I can go to the judge again and let them know that what happened nine years ago was simply a misunderstanding. I will tell them that you didn't rape me. I've never done anything as shameful as what I did to you. I am very sorry.

Waiting for your reply.

With best wishes,
Zhang Nao

I held the letter up to my face and began to cry. After all these years, there was no way this was the final chapter. But the tears came as if a valve inside me had finally been opened. The letter was quickly soaked with my tears. I wiped my eyes with it as if it were a handkerchief. The prisoners on my cell block gathered around me. They watched me with curiosity. Sun Nan plucked the letter from my fingers. He puzzled over it for a moment and then turned to me: "What does this say?" I looked at the letter, and my tears immediately stopped. The ink was running, and the paper threatened to tear at the slightest touch.

I scrambled for my matches. I struck one and held it below the letter. "Hold it for me, Sun Nan. We have to dry it out. This letter proves I'm innocent." The other prisoners gathered around. I handed out cigarettes, and as they smoked them to butts, I motioned for them to hold the smoking ends under the letter. When the butts finally went out, I made sure they had another cigarette already burning. The letter was bathed in smoke. But it wasn't enough. I ripped one of my shirts in half and lit it on fire.

Sun Nan said: "That was a nice shirt! What's this letter?"

I patted it: "Have a look. See what this says?"

Sun Nan bent over the letter: "Oh, it just says you're a rapist. I thought it was going to be good news."

I looked up with surprise. I searched the letter and saw that my tears and the cigarette smoke had smudged "you didn't rape me," so that it looked more like "you did rape me." I pointed down: "Look closer. It says 'didn't.'"

Sun Nan said: "I really can't tell."

"'Didn't'! It says 'didn't.'"

"That's not what it looks like to me."

I looked over the letter again. There were a few places where the words had been completely blotted out by ink smudges. If you read it in the state it was in now, you could still get the gist of it, but only if you squinted through the ink blots. I crumpled it and tossed it on the floor. I said: "If I hadn't cried, the letter wouldn't be wet. If the letter hadn't gotten wet, I wouldn't have ripped my shirt. Fuck me." I slapped myself hard across the face. Sun Nan picked up the letter and smoothed it. I took it back and ripped it in half. Maybe I shouldn't have done that. Even if you read it when it was all smudged, you could still figure out that it was a letter of redress from Zhang Nao. It was the strongest piece of evidence I had that I was innocent. I stuffed the two halves of the smudged letter in my pocket. During lunch the next day, I used a mouthful of rice, chewed to paste, to stick the two halves to a blank sheet.

When I took the repaired letter back to the cell block, I let all of the men on the block read it, taking pains to point out that it was "didn't," not "did rape me." The prisoners asked: "What are you doing here?" Their words were like a kick in the ass. I wrote a letter to Zhang Nao, asking her to come to discuss the case with me. I took the letter to Warden Jia and stood over his shoulder while he read it. He said: "I'll send a message to my superiors. If this turns out to be what it looks like it is, you'll be free to go." I bowed deeply to the warden.

‹ 22 ›

Every morning when I woke up, I made sure that my clothes were tidy and my hair was combed. I expected Zhang Nao to come at any moment. There were a hundred days left in my sentence. As those days counted down to ninety-nine, ninety-eight, ninety-seven . . . she had not yet appeared. I had no way of knowing what had happened. Maybe she'd reconsidered. Maybe my letter had never arrived. I wrote her two more letters, each with two stamps on the front and back. As the days went by and my release date approached, the urgency eased. But I kept wondering: Why didn't she come? Why would she write the letter and then not come? Is she afraid of me? I thought about it until my head hurt. I mean, I had spent almost a decade in prison for a crime that I didn't commit, so I kept things in perspective. It was minor, after all that I'd gone through, for Zhang Nao to go back on her word now. But I couldn't stop thinking about it. For the first time, I started to hate her. The other prisoners heard me muttering, "That fucking whore."

Xiaoyan caught me, too. She asked: "Who are you calling that?"

I looked up to see that I had fallen into a daze. I had been staring at the slogan on the wall: "Tell the truth and receive a lighter sentence."

She took my hand and asked: "Who were you talking about?"

"That fucking whore."

"Who are you talking about?"

"She kicked a hornet's nest. Why did she write that letter? Did you get a lawyer for me yet?"

"I got you a lawyer. He told me he was going to see Zhang Nao."

"I want you to go ask that whore why she wrote me a letter and now won't come see me."

"Forget it. I don't even want to see her. If I had to talk to her, I'm worried that whatever's wrong with her is contagious."

"Listen to me, Xiaoyan. I'm going to put it simply: if you really care about me, you'll go ask that whore why she didn't come."

"That's how I show you that I care about you?"

"This is about my future, my reputation. This is more important than love."

"If that's the way you feel, then you've wasted my time. All these years, you've wasted them." Xiaoyan staggered to her feet and went to the door, her eyes red.

"I have to clear my name. I can't let that whore . . ."

Sorry. It's a bit tough to hear, isn't it? But I want to tell you exactly what happened. The only reason I called her that is because I couldn't think of a stronger word. Lots of good words hadn't even been invented yet back then. "Scumbag." People say that now, right? But we hadn't heard that one yet.

So with sixty-one days left in my sentence, I received very important news.

What? Are you looking at the clock? I was watching the time, too. We've got ten more minutes, right? If you don't mind, let's go for a bit longer. Two hours should be good. It's just that I haven't come across an audience this good in a while. Here, you make the call. Let them know, two more hours. Thank you!

So with sixty-one days left in my sentence, I received very important news. Warden Jia arrived in the assembly shop with an embossed document. He held it up and said: "Ceng Guangxian, you are free to go." It felt like I had grabbed a live wire. Jia Wenping said: "Take this. It proves you're innocent." I took the document and looked it over carefully. It was all there: Due to false testimony from Zhang Nao, I had been falsely charged with rape. The judge had ordered my release. At the bottom right corner of the letter was a big red seal with the date stamped under it.

The other men in the workshop began to crowd around, realizing what the order in my hands meant. They celebrated around me like I'd just kicked a goal, picking me up, hugging me, smacking me on the back, as I stood staring blankly down at the document. Jia Wenping led me out of the workshop and across the yard. I looked up and saw faces pressed against the windows of the workshops and men in doorways waving and calling my name. More men came to doorways and opened windows and called to me. The birds in the trees in the yard took flight. Jia Wenping wiped at his eyes as we walked. But I didn't wave back and I didn't cry. I didn't realize until later how emotional that day was, for everybody but me. It's not that I'm immune to emotion, but that day came without any preparation. It felt like I was sleepwalking out of the prison.

I went through the gates of the prison factory. I walked around a jeep that was parked beside the gate. At that moment, I thought I heard somebody calling my name. But when I turned to look, nobody was there except the soldiers guarding the gate. I thought I must be hearing things. I heard it again, though. And I turned to see that it was coming from the jeep. The door was pushed open, and a woman stepped out. I said: "Are you calling me?"

She said: "Who else would be calling you?"

I squinted at her. She was beautiful.

She walked closer to me: "You don't remember me?"

"Zhang . . . Zhang Nao?"

"So your memory is fine. Come on. Get in."

This woman's testimony had caused me to be locked up for a decade, and instead of choking her to death with my bare hands—or at least giving her a hard slap—I was supposed to jump in that jeep with her? I gritted my teeth and stared at her, clenching my fists at my side. I have to tell you, too: she was still beautiful. She still had the same sharp expression that looked even more shrewd when she smiled. She had the same perfect nose and tiny mouth. Her skin was still soft and pale. I think that's what stopped me from smacking her.

She said: "I came to pick you up. I'm sorry, Guangxian." My hands relaxed. "I didn't have time to come see you. I went right to the court and tried to change my testimony. It took more than a month, but we got the sentence overturned." She had been working on the case the whole time, I realized. I finally had the document that cleared my name. I stopped gritting my teeth. My face relaxed. "I've been waiting for hours. Get in!" Every word from her mouth brought waves of relief to my body. I got into the jeep.

The driver pulled away before I had even shut the door. My head smacked back against a steel pillar. I watched the back of Zhang Nao's head. I studied the fine hairs on the back of her pale neck. The smell of her perfume wafted back to me. For a moment, I wondered why I hadn't done it. I had sat in prison for a decade. I might as well have actually raped her.

"Why did it take so long? Why didn't you go to the judge sooner?"

She pretended not to hear.

The jeep rattled onto a side road and stopped beside the river. Zhang Nao said: "Go down and wash up. There're some clothes for you in that bag." At that point I noticed the bag on the seat beside me, and I noticed the tangy odor of sweat coming from my body. I had sweated through the clothes I was wearing when I walked out through the prison factory gates. "Don't go in too far unless you can swim. The water is pretty deep here."

I said: "I'm sure I've been in deeper."

I took the bag and went down to the bank. I set the bag under a stand of bamboo and found a bar of soap set on top of the clothes. I waded in and stripped off my old clothes. I stood naked in the river and washed myself with the soap, scraping at the grease stains and grimy sweat until my body tingled and glowed bright red. I waded in again, letting the water wash away the soap. I went back onto the bank and went to the bag and took out the clothes that had been prepared for me. She had thought of everything: there was even a belt already run through the pants, and a bottle of cologne, and a pair of sandals, sunglasses, a mirror . . . I took the mirror and moved it up and down, checking every part of myself. There were no traces of my old life. I was no longer a prisoner serving a sentence of hard labor—I looked more like one of the overseas Chinese coming to the Mainland to visit their ancestral village. I took the sunglasses on and off, checking the mirror, trying to decide which way looked best. I figured that Zhang Nao knew best and left the sunglasses on. I went back to the bag and shook it to make sure it was empty. A pack of cigarettes and a lighter fell out. Like I said, she'd been thorough.

I pulled a cigarette out of the pack, lit it, and took a slow drag. I turned back when I heard Zhang Nao calling to me: "Can we get out of here?" Of course. Of course we can get out of here. I looked up, and she was waving me over: "Hurry up!" If I'd seen a stopwatch in her hand, I wouldn't have been surprised.

The jeep dropped us off at the Guijiang Restaurant. Zhang Nao picked a table near the window and ordered chaomian, fenzhengrou, and egg-drop soup—my favorites. I said: "How did you know?"

"You think it was easy? I thought about you every day for ten years."

"You waited nine years and ten months to withdraw your testimony. Why didn't you go to the judge sooner?"

"I'll tell you, but you can't laugh."

"Just tell me."

"You know the thing about my virginity being examined? Well, a couple of months ago, I was reading an article in a magazine that said a girl's hymen could be broken without sex. I assume it was because of my dancing. You know . . ."

My hand gripped the tablecloth: "You don't even understand your own body?"

"Yes, but ten years ago I didn't. Nobody ever told me about that stuff. Like, my parents, my teacher, whoever—they never told me. So when I got taken to the doctor and he said that it looked like I wasn't a virgin because of that . . . Well, I didn't know. I thought it must be because of something horrible. I didn't know what to say. I just said it must be because of you. It was the only thing I could think to do. If you hadn't done it, there had to be some other excuse, and I didn't have one. I knew it would hurt my chances to become a dancer. I was just a girl. I was worried about what everyone would think of me."

"So you lied. You ripped your dress. You made me sit in there for ten years."

She wiped away tears: "I had to make them believe you did it. I had to rip the dress."

"You bitch!" I clenched the tablecloth harder and ripped it off the table.

The chaomian fell in her lap. There were pieces of fenzhengrou stuck to the front of her shirt. Her pants were soaked with soup. She stared at me, her heart pounding and her lips trembling. I stood up and rushed out of the dining room.

I got onto the first bus that came along. I pressed through the passengers, smelling everyone's musky sweat. I stood in the back of the bus. That's where the ticket taker found me. I told her I didn't have any money. She said: "Where'd you get those fancy sunglasses, then? Come on." The other passengers watched with curiosity. I made a show of feeling my pockets. Then suddenly I felt something in the back pocket of the pants. There was a ten-yuan note on top. I counted at least a hundred yuan. I couldn't believe she had been so thorough. I hadn't expected that she'd even put money in my pocket. The ticket taker took the money and handed back my change: "Trying to ride without a ticket, and you've got a pocket full of cash."

I got off in front of the warehouse but started walking back toward the Guijiang Restaurant. I wanted to apologize to Zhang Nao, help her clean the food off her clothes, pick up the broken dishes. But after walking for a while, I stopped. Was a hundred yuan worth ten years in prison? Did she think she could buy me off with a hundred yuan? I wasn't going to be fucked over again. I felt my chest and throat tighten. I walked back toward the warehouse.

When I reached the warehouse, I saw a middle-aged man coming through the main door carrying a cardboard box. His head was down, and he walked right into me. Office supplies and paper fell from the box. I heard him mutter an apology. I bent down to help him collect his things. I looked at him more closely. I said: "Zhao . . ."

"Not Director Zhao anymore. They gave me the boot. I'm going to be working at the Clothes for Cuba factory now, watching the door. You're looking for Director Liang. Actually, I don't even want the job. I don't care. If being a director is carrying out the revolution, then being a gate guard at a factory—that has to be carrying out the revolution, too. I'll still be contributing, right? You young people don't seem to understand that." Zhao Wannian never looked up at me. He was cramming pens and pencils into the box, picking his desk calendar up out of the dirt and stacking it on top of his old books.

I took off my sunglasses: "It's Guangxian."

Zhao Wannian slowly rose to his feet and looked me up and down. He shook my hand: "You're finally free, my boy. It's too bad you didn't get out two months earlier. I could have gotten you a job as my assistant. Bad luck."

Who can you blame? If Zhang Nao had read that magazine two months earlier, she would have gone to the judge sooner. I would have gotten out of prison in time for Zhao Wannian to give me a job. I would have been happy working in the mailroom or even going back to my old job at the zoo. Actually, that thing with the hymen, Hou Zhi had told me about it. It was shortly after I met him, so maybe three years after I was locked up. I could have written her a letter and told her to look into it. With all the time I had, I could have researched and written an entire series of books on female sexual health, but I didn't send her a single letter until it was too late. Maybe I could have been out after three or four years.

I went up the ladder to the warehouse loft. My climb was unsteady, and I almost slipped a few times. There was a new lock on the door. I tried to pull it off but eventually had to kick in the door. The room was clean. There was no dust on the wooden chest. There was a mirror with no trace of dust on it. There were two photographs pasted to the back of the mirror. One photo was of me; the other was of Lu Xiaoyan. I opened the chest and found my old clothes, carefully folded. I took out a shirt and held it to my nose. The smell took me back to my old life, ten years before. I stripped off the new clothes that Zhang Nao had brought for me and put on my old clothes. One of the buttons fell off and rolled toward the door and down the ladder. They had been sitting for so long that the thread that held the buttons on was brittle and easy to snap.

‹ 23 ›

By the time I got to Lu Xiaoyan's dormitory, it was already dark. From the doorway I could see her sitting in front of a basin, washing clothes in soapy water. I called to her, and she fell backward off the bench. She landed on the floor and looked up at me: "You're . . . you're out?"

She stood and came to me. We held each other tight. I felt like I was being suffocated. She kissed me, and we fell together onto the bed. To tell you the truth, that was my first kiss. Her mouth was as sweet as sugar. I had been waiting five years for that moment. Now that I was in her arms, everything had been worth it. I would have waited another ten years for her. As we rolled on the bed, she unbuttoned my shirt and pulled her own shirt off. But I couldn't do it. I pulled my shirt tighter around me. I made sure my hands stayed above her shoulders. We lay, tangled together, kissing, waiting for something to happen—but nothing did. You don't believe me, do you? You expect since I just got out of prison, I should have been going for it. Like I keep saying, things were different back then. Nowadays, you fall into bed and rip your clothes off. I promise you—wait, no, I swear to the Chairman. Nothing happened. The time in prison had something to do with it. Actually, I'd sworn to myself that nothing would happen. There was no chance I was going to go back in there.

Lu Xiaoyan suddenly asked me: "How did you get out early?"

"Zhang Nao retracted her testimony."

"Retracted her testimony? The lawyer told me it was impossible."

"I have the court order right here."

"Go get it. I want to see."

I rolled off the bed and felt in my pockets. I said: "Shit. I must have lost it in the river." She came down and looked through the pockets, too. They were empty, except for the money that Zhang Nao had given me.

"How could you lose it?"

"I got undressed by the river. I just tossed my old clothes in. That was the only thing I brought out of the prison. That's the only thing that proves I'm innocent."

"You couldn't have taken better care of it? It's like you want to go through life with everyone thinking you're a rapist."

I stood up and went to the door. When Xiaoyan asked where I was going, I said: "I have to find Zhang Nao. She got the document in the first place; she must have some idea of what to do."

"You're going back to her? Hasn't she done enough? You're better off going into the tiger cage to ask for help."

"She apologized to me."

"Why did it take so long? She had ten years to retract her testimony. Now, when you're already out, she apologizes? She's just scared that you'll do something to her."

"She's not like that, Xiaoyan. If it weren't for her, I wouldn't even be out now. I wouldn't have been able to clear my name. If she'd wanted to, she could have just let me sit in there and come out without clearing my name. When I came out, she could have just ignored me."

"Fine, fine, fine. How long have you been out? A few hours? Fine. Go find your dream girl." She pushed me out of the dormitory room and slammed the door behind me.

I still didn't understand women. I didn't know that after she slammed the door she waited behind it, listening and hoping that I would come back inside. I raised my hand to knock. I thought she must be angry. I turned and left. On the way, I thought about where I might have left the document. Maybe it wasn't in the river at all. Maybe I had put it back in the bag that Zhang Nao had given me. Maybe I had stuffed it in one of the pockets of the clothes she'd brought. As I'd walked out of the gates of the prison, I'd still had it. I was sure of that. I couldn't have just lost it. I had waited ten years to get that piece of paper.

When I got back to the warehouse loft, I looked through the clothes. The paper was not there. I thought to myself: If I hadn't gotten in the jeep with Zhang Nao, none of this would have happened. I could have taken the bus here, shown Zhao Wannian and Lu Xiaoyan, let them see that I was innocent, finally. I probably would have even had time to go to a photo studio and get a nice frame for the document. If I hadn't gotten in the jeep, I could be in bed right now, with the frame hanging above me, so it would be the last thing I saw before falling asleep on my first day of freedom.

I spent the next two days in a haze of cigarette smoke, with butts collecting on the floor under the bench. I sat in the same spot where I had watched Zhang Nao dancing ten years before. Every now and then, I'd look down toward the spot where I first saw her. I don't know if you know what it's like to suddenly not have a job. It was like I was fired. I felt empty, bored. When I was in the prison factory, I had work every day. I was either in the assembly shop, screwing together plates, or in the foundry, pouring iron. It was tiring, but it gave me something to occupy my time. Now I had absolutely nothing. Smoking cigarettes and looking down into the warehouse watching people work were the only comforts I had.

I've told you how the warehouse was laid out, with the loft up in the back, about where a projectionist would be in a theater. But now the interior had been carved up again, as it was when we lived there. Down the middle there was a long dividing wall, with five offices on both sides. I numbered the offices 1 to 10. The offices on the left side were 1 to 5, and the offices on the right side were 6 to 10. The stage was still there, which might help you picture the layout. The offices farthest from me and closest to the stage were 1 and 2 on the left and 6 and 7 on the right. In those offices closest to the stage, there were three men and one woman. In the rest of the offices, different numbers, were men and women reading newspapers, talking on the phone, typing at typewriters, stamping documents . . . The fat woman in office 1 must have been Director Liang. Every time she finished her mug of tea, she would clear her throat, and almost before the mug had hit the desk, the young man in office 2 would be on his feet, rushing in to pour hot water for her.

The bald man in office 6 often went to office 10 to see the female typist there. When nobody else was around, he rubbed her shoulders and ran his hands through her hair and down over her breasts. When they heard someone approaching, they would move apart from each other, looking as innocent and chaste as me and Xiaoyan. I could barely stand to watch them. I felt certain urges rising within me. Sometimes when I watched the bald man and the typist, I felt my hand sliding down between my legs.

Every afternoon, I went down to the row of food stalls near the Culture Bureau and walked around the grounds, trying to catch sight of Zhang Nao. The dormitory looked about the same, except for a fresh coat of paint and a row of flower pots under the windows. I finally found Zhang Nao in the old practice space, where I had watched her through the window. She had her leg on a rail, stretching. Her peaceful expression hardened when she saw me. I said: "Don't worry. I'm not going to rape you."

"What do you mean?"

"I need you to help me get another copy of that document."

"Of course, of course. Don't just stand there. Come up for a cup of tea."

She led me up to her dormitory room. I hesitated for a moment and looked inside. The room had been decorated since I'd last been inside and was furnished with a mahogany desk and a dressing table, which was under the window. I could have left then, but something made me step inside and go to the window. There were curtains over it now, a layer of pink and a layer of indigo fabric. I pulled the curtains back and looked down. Yes, it was about nine feet down, but the lawn below would have made a nice landing pad.

"Why didn't I just jump? I could have jumped. Nobody would have caught me." I climbed onto the windowsill. I wanted to try it. "I was an idiot. I could have just gone right out."

She pulled me down from the windowsill: "It would have been better for both of us. You're not the only one who suffered. Do you know how I was treated after the story came out? I was spat on! I was called a slut. People said I must have been asking for it. They came and wrote on my door. You know what they wrote? They wrote . . .—I can't even say it."

"Who did it? What did they write?"

"My door was like a bathroom stall. They wrote that I was a whore. They told me to leave the door unlocked for them. They . . . all the things people write on a bathroom stall, that was on my door for everyone to see. Every night when I came home, I'd have to scrub it off, crying the whole time. That wasn't even the worst part. The worst part was, they wouldn't let me play Wu Qionghua. I was forced to work backstage, doing makeup, pulling the curtain, sweeping up . . . I was the best dancer in the company, but my talent was wasted. Sometimes I'd dance by myself, alone in my room. When I went out to buy vegetables, one of the women always used to tell me that even when I was carrying cabbage, I still looked like a ballerina. How could I take it? I didn't even want to live. A few times, I had a bottle of sleeping pills in my hand. I was ready to swallow the whole bottle. But my hands shook too much. I ended up dumping most of them on the floor. If I'd known what was going to happen, I wouldn't have screamed. I'd rather you had just raped me. It would have been easier. You care about clearing your name, but who's going to clear mine? People avoided me. They held their noses when they had to walk by me. I had nobody. I never had a boyfriend. I'm still single. There was no one to talk to. Nobody would have believed me, anyway. Imagine if I'd started telling people that you hadn't raped me—you were just breaking into my dormitory to see me—who would believe me? It's not like I suddenly came up with the story about you raping me—it was after you broke into my room!"

As Zhang Nao told her story, tears fell from her eyes. I got down on my hands and knees in front of her and hit my head on the floor where the tears were falling. I hit my head on the floor until blood mixed with the tears. Zhang Nao knelt beside me: "Don't do that, Guangxian. Please don't. We're the same now, Guangxian. We're both stained. If I'd known what we were going to go through, I would never have screamed."

That night I went back to my loft and bandaged my head with a strip of gauze. I went to Xiaoyan's dormitory. She asked me: "Where have you been?" I sat on the bed and lit a cigarette. She suddenly shrieked: "Your head! What happened? Did you get in a fight?" I sat silently, taking drags from the cigarette. She put her hand on my forehead: "Is it a deep cut? Does it hurt?" She bent down so that her face was level with mine. I wiped the sweat from her face with the sleeve of my shirt. She took an envelope from her bedside and held it out to me: "Do you know what this is?" I opened the envelope and took out the formal document inside. When I saw the red seal at the bottom right corner, I thought it must be a copy of my letter of redress. I looked closer and saw that it was a letter from Xiaoyan's work unit, giving permission for her to marry.

"I've been waiting five years for this day." She sat beside me on the bed and took my hands in her hands. It was like we were in the visiting room again.

"Are you ever worried I won't treat you right?"

"I'm not worried about it."

"If I'd known I would be here with you someday, I never would have tried to escape. I never should have gone to her dormitory. Why do you think I did it?"

"You were a young man who couldn't control yourself. You wanted to rape her."

"Then you realize it was my fault. See, when I was locked up, I didn't get it. I wanted to spit in her face. I wanted to beat her to death. But now I realize: it was my fault."

Xiaoyan stood up: "Can't you shut up about that slut for a minute? After all this, you can just forgive her?"

"She's not a slut. I cleared my name, but what about her? Don't call her that again. She's had it tough. If I hadn't gone to her dormitory, she wouldn't have had all those people talking about her, saying she was asking for it, calling her a slut . . . If she had gotten the role of Wu Qionghua, she could have gone on to big things. She could have been a star. She could have married a Party member. She wouldn't be sitting in that same dormitory, still single, ten years later."

"She can marry an ex-convict."

"I think if I weren't with you, I'd go to her. I owe her that."

She shot a glance at me: "There's something wrong with you, Guangxian. You think you're the savior here? You're the one that I'm saving. If it weren't for me, you'd be alone. I don't think Zhang Nao is dumb enough to marry a loser like you."

"Whether she's willing to marry me or not is her decision, but I was talking about wanting to repay my debt to her."

"You're getting full of yourself. If Zhang Nao agreed to marry you, I'd be the first in line to bring you a wedding gift."

"That's how you see me? You think that without you, I wouldn't find somebody else?"

"Go see for yourself. You'll find out exactly what you're worth on the open market. I sympathize with you. You haven't realized it yet." She tossed the letter on the floor.

As she turned to go, I grabbed her arm: "Come on. I was just letting off steam. I'm going to get a permission letter tomorrow so I can marry you."

She pulled her arm out of my grip: "Go ahead. And then you can marry Zhang Nao. I'm finished with you."

"You're going to regret it."

"I don't even know what that word means."

After she walked out, I sat down and went over the argument, word by word. She was exactly right, I realized. In my mind, I was rehabilitated. My name had been cleared. I was like the revolutionaries who had gone through hell to build a new nation or an artist who had suffered for his work. In actual fact, my name might have been cleared, but I was still marked: I had spent ten years behind bars. I had no job and no future. In the eyes of most people, I was a piece of human garbage. If Xiaoyan hadn't reminded me, I might have mistaken myself for a member of the human race.

I waited a while to go see Xiaoyan. I went home and tried to sleep, then went back to her dormitory early in the morning. I went to the door and raised my hand, about to knock—but I guess I was just like my father: I had my pride. I would live to regret that decision. The decision was like a fork in the road. If I let myself knock, I would take one road; if I didn't knock, I was going down another road. I would torture myself with that decision. That's how fate works: you come to a fork in the road and make a choice, without knowing where the road leads.

Now, at that moment, what I was thinking about was love. I was seriously considering the question of love. I thought about Xiaoyan: if she really loved me, why did she look down on me the way she did? Maybe it was no different from Xiao Chi. Xiao Chi had said she loved me for my curly hair. Xiaoyan might merely have found in me a captive audience. She knew that I couldn't reject her. I wouldn't complain about her smelling like an animal or worry about my parents' opinion. That wasn't the kind of love I'd seen in movies and books. I stared for a long time at the closed door with its layer of new paint. Finally, I turned and walked away.

I'll tell you something. It's not something you can think about. Just . . . don't think about it. When you sit down and think about love, you'll quickly realize that it doesn't really exist. I'm telling you this so that hopefully you won't suffer like I did.

‹24›

That weekend, I found a note from Xiaoyan on my door: "Your father wants you to come for dinner tonight."

Since I'd come back from Beishan, I hadn't gone to see my father. I didn't want to upset him. His doctor had ordered him to keep an eye on his blood pressure, and getting overstimulated would be very harmful. I knew that my visit would definitely stimulate my father. I had decided to wait until my life was more stable before visiting him. I didn't have any good news. Going to see him would be like going to a wedding without any cash for a gift.

I wanted to get the letter of redress, at least. I went to the address Zhang Nao had given me for the shop that she'd opened on Dongfang Road. The shop sold ceramic tiles, but also other things like toilets and sinks, the kinds of things you'd need to renovate your house. When I got there, she was negotiating with a middle-aged man.

She said: "I'm asking for two fen extra per tile. I can't give it to you at the price you want. I'd be taking food out of my own mouth. You really want to push me on two fen? Whatever, if you can't come up, let's settle it: come tomorrow morning and take them away."

The man said: "Listen, I know you're not losing money here."

Zhang Nao said: "Don't worry, the price is good. Bring the money, and I'll take you out for lunch. I'll get you a bowl of mifen. I'm doing fine: if I want to treat somebody to a bowl of mifen, I can."

The man asked: "How much is a bowl of mifen?"

"Three mao!"

"I'm giving you all this money, and you're taking me out to eat a three-mao bowl of mifen?"

Zhang Nao smiled innocently: "What did you have in mind?"

After the customer left, Zhang Nao told me: "That's the way it is. Since the Culture Bureau reformed the team as a song-and-dance ensemble, there's just not as many performances. If I didn't have this shop, I wouldn't be able to pay for the extras, like some new clothes every now and then."

Zhang Nao was called to the front of the shop, and I helped her load an order into a truck and then sat outside smoking a cigarette. She called me back into the office and handed me an envelope. My new letter of redress was inside. She was already at work at her desk, making notes in an account book and pressing the keys of a calculator. The calculator emitted digital beeps, and I looked up to watch her work. I called her name and she looked up, but I told her: "Nothing. Um . . . go back to work." She bent down again. She brushed back the hair that kept falling across her face. I smoked two more cigarettes, and then I called her name again.

We went through the same procedure again: I called her name and she looked up, and I shook my head and told her to go back to work. I looked at the clock on the wall. My time was running out. Finally, when I'd called her name four times, she turned to me and said: "Something you want to say?"

"Nothing. Go back to work."

She set down the calculator: "If there's something you want to say, just say it."

"I don't want to bother you." I stood and walked toward the front of the shop.

She put a hand on my arm: "You want to borrow money, don't you?"

I shook my head. "Then what do you want?"

I felt my face go hot, and I told her, stammering out each word.

"It's not that bad, really. Why did your face go all red?"

"I've never lied to anyone before. This will be the first time. I just want to make my father happy. I'd like you to fill out this letter of employment."

"Go get it printed out. There's a shop across the road."

Five minutes later, I was back in the office with the sheet of paper. Zhang Nao reached over and stamped the bottom right corner of the paper: "Dongfang Construction Materials Corporation." I put the stamped paper in my bag, along with the letter of redress. Zhang Nao looked me over and said: "With that paper, you can't go around dressed like that." She took me to the department store downtown on the back of her motorcycle. We went to the men's department, and she picked out the most expensive outfit in the place: a new shirt, a tie, suit pants, and dress shoes. We went back to her dormitory room, and she helped me change into it.

I said: "I'm not going to meet a girl. What do I need all this for?"

She said: "Nobody should look down on you."

I had never tied a tie before. Zhang Nao stood in front of me, showing me the steps and guiding my hands. As the slogan on the prison walls said, "Tell the truth and receive a lighter sentence. Refusing to confess brings harsher punishment"—I was on the verge of committing the crime that I had been sentenced to in the first place. I wanted to grab the hands that were holding the tie at my neck and throw Zhang Nao onto the bed. No other woman brought up those feelings in me. I felt like something in me was about to explode. I felt the same way I had that night ten years before.

I turned my back to her, suddenly short of breath. She said: "What are you doing? It's not even tied."

"I'll tie it myself." I worked at the tie, trying to figure out what those feelings were. I wanted to throw her on the bed and hold her down. Had ten years in prison not been enough to extinguish those thoughts? Maybe it was simply her physical beauty. It seemed to be irresistible. Maybe that idea I'd had ten years before was buried so deep inside me that I couldn't stop it from bubbling up again now.

That night, I went to my father's factory. My dad had been transferred from the old dormitory to a flat-roofed house inside the compound. He was waiting for me with Zhao Shanhe. I called: "Dad." He looked at me but didn't say anything. "Auntie Zhao! I didn't expect you."

"I got a call from your father yesterday. He told me he was having guests. I asked who it was, but he wanted me to guess. It took me a while, but I finally figured it out."

I knew this dinner must be important to my father. But he kept silent, and when I met his gaze, he looked away. I took the letter of redress out of my bag and handed it to him. His face darkened, and his hands seemed to shake.

Zhao Shanhe said: "Don't get worked up, Changfeng." She took the paper from his hands.

"This is good! At least one of you has cleared your name. You should get copies made of this. Anyone who looks down on you, you can show it to them. I knew you couldn't have done something like what they were saying you did. Just as I expected, you were framed. You have to be careful who you associate with, Guangxian. My mother used to say that women are far more cruel than men, especially when it comes to things like this."

My father said: "Fucking cunt." I couldn't tell who he was talking about. I looked at his face for clues. Maybe it was directed at Zhang Nao, but it could just as well have been directed at all of humanity. At least it didn't seem to be directed at me specifically.

Zhao Shanhe shot a glance at me. I picked up my chopsticks and put a piece of tofu in my father's bowl. I said: "I do have to take some of the blame . . ." I felt Zhao Shanhe's foot under the table and stopped talking.

Zhao Shanhe reached over and fingered my tie: "I remember seeing men wearing these when I was young. Even your father and grandfather, they used to wear them. But after Liberation, you never saw them. Now they're coming back again. I guess it's like they say, 'the more things change . . . ' It's hard to even keep up."

"It feels like I've got a noose around my neck, actually. But I have to wear it at work."

"Oh, that's right, your dad went to Director Pang a few days back, asking about a job for you. Sounds like you already found something by yourself."

I took the other piece of paper from my bag and set it on the table.

She read aloud: "'This letter confirms the appointment of Ceng Guangxian as purchasing agent for the Dongfang Construction Materials Corporation.' Wow! Changfeng, your boy has a future." She passed the letter to my father.

My father took the letter and looked it over, his face seeming to soften. I even noticed a half-smile that formed and faded almost imperceptibly.

Zhao Shanhe turned back to me: "How is everything?"

"Everything's great. I haven't eaten like this in ten years."

"I made everything, but your father told me exactly what he wanted. Did you notice? All of the dishes have heart! Your father wanted to remind you that the thing a person needs most is heart."

I looked down at the table, trying to figure out what she was talking about. Then I saw it: the tofu was stuffed with leeks, the bitter melon was filled with lean pork, the ground pork was wrapped with eggplant, the fish maw had chopped peppers and tomato inside . . . I saw what she meant: all of the dishes had heart.

"You know, while you were at Beishan all those years, Xiaoyan really looked after your father. She brought him chicken soup, mended his clothes, fixed that old lock on the door. You and your father are both spoiled, can't even use a screwdriver. Your father needs a daughter-in-law like Xiaoyan."

"Can't use a screwdriver? That's what I did every single day at the tractor factory."

"I think you'll still need her around. Just because you get a new shirt, you don't throw away the old one. If it weren't for Xiaoyan, your father wouldn't have had anyone to mend those old shirts, anyway."

"I never said I don't need her. She's the one who told me she doesn't want to get married now."

Zhao Shanhe said: "I bet you're talking to that slut Zhang Nao again. Hasn't she put you through enough?"

"You should know better than anyone, Auntie Zhao. You can't just call her a slut. She was a good girl. It was all my fault, anyway. She was the one who helped me clear my name."

"I'm not going to argue with you, but I'm going to give you a piece of advice: If you want to get married, you want a woman like Xiaoyan. Remember this: beauty fades. You want a girl who can steal you from another woman? That's fine until she finds another guy to steal. You'll regret this."

My father coughed, and Zhao Shanhe fell silent. We stared at our food. There was no sound except for the sound of chewing. Everyone heard the creak outside, but only Zhao Shanhe's ears were sharp enough to know exactly what it was: "Sounds like my husband's bike out there."

She was exactly right: it was Lao Dong, Zhao Shanhe's husband. You might remember him from the first part of the story. He was the railway engineer who drove her away from the warehouse in his big truck covered in banners.

I heard him yelling from outside: "You're working overtime, are you? That's what you said, overtime. And then I find you here?" He came through the door, rolling up his sleeves. He grabbed Zhao Shanhe's arm and jerked her to her feet. Her knees hit the table, knocking over the bowls and spilling the soup.

My father said: "Come on now, Comrade Dong. This isn't the right way to handle the situation. I invited her here today to see my boy. It's been ten years!"

Lao Dong said: "What about all the other days she ended up over here? What was that for? She was here for something else."

My fathered stammered and clutched at his chest. I went to his side and patted his back.

While my father slowly recovered, Lao Dong was already dragging Zhao Shanhe toward the door. Zhao Shanhe pulled back with all her strength, her feet dragging on the floor. Lao Dong let her go, and she fell backward. My father moved faster than I'd ever seen him move. He grabbed Zhao Shanhe's shoulders before she could hit the floor. It looked like a scene from one of those Hong Kong action movies, where the actors are on wires. But it was even more impressive if you remember that my father was already over fifty and had a bad heart. Zhao Shanhe got back to her feet and brushed herself off. She shouted toward her husband: "One more time! Touch me one more time and I'm leaving you."

Lao Dong went for his wife again. I moved behind him and held his arms. He bucked and kicked and tried to get away from me, but strength and youth were on my side: eventually the will to fight went out of him, and I felt his ribs heaving against my arms as his breath came heavy. I settled him on a bench. I said: "Let's talk it out, Uncle Dong. Don't come in here and start dragging people around."

A few of the other workers who lived in the compound had arrived at the door, attracted by the commotion. Zhao Shanhe slammed the door shut in their faces. Lao Dong turned to me: "There's nothing to talk about. You've seen it with your own eyes. This slut wants to be your stepmother."

Zhao Shanhe pulled up her shirt to show the bruises across her stomach: "Look at this. Look at this. Tell me: can I go back to him? It's been like this since the day we got married. Every time things don't go his way, he takes it out on me. It's my fault that I never got pregnant, he says. Can you believe that? You know the Zhao family, Guangxian. That doesn't run in our family. I still went to Doctor Mei, just to confirm it. He still has some pride left—or I would have already left him. But I can't bring myself to do it."

"He knows very well what you're up to. I know what went on in that warehouse. You were filthy. You're going to stand here and try to tell him that you never cheated on me?"

"Watch your mouth. If I'd been cheating on you, Guangxian would have a little brother."

I looked over at my father. He had turned red. His face looked like it was painted in the same red ink as the stamps on my letter of redress. He looked up and saw me looking at him. He bent his head and walked out.

Lao Dong said: "You aren't cheating. Did I get that right? Why the hell are you never home, then? Over here every damn day . . ."

Zhao Shanhe said: "I needed somebody to talk to. If I sat at home all day, I'd suffocate."

As their argument grew louder, I turned to go. Zhao Shanhe grabbed my arm: "Don't go. You're my witness, Guangxian: I want to divorce him."

Zhao Shanhe went over to my father's desk and found a paper and pen. She gave the pen to her husband and told him to write out a contract agreeing to the divorce. Lao Dong took the pen and handed the finished document to me.

Zhao Shanhe said: "You know why I married you, don't you? My boss took me aside for some 'ideological work.' There weren't many other choices after that. Let me tell you: since the day—since that very first night—that we were married, I have wanted to get as far away from you as possible."

"You have to write a contract, too."

Zhao Shanhe wrote her own contract and handed it to Lao Dong. He stood and said abruptly: "Buh-bye!" Zhao Shanhe told me later that it was something he'd learned while working for the railway. There had been some sort of push for the workers to learn a few phrases in some foreign languages. The whole situation, though—I wanted to laugh! But I realized it was kind of a serious moment. Once the door had shut and Lao Dong was gone, I almost let a giggle slip out. But I could tell that Zhao Shanhe wouldn't have appreciated it.

It wasn't just the jaunty "Buh-bye" on the way out. Look at these two: my father and Zhao Shanhe had just been lecturing me about how to live my life, and then their own real lives had come knocking. She had just called Zhang Nao a slut a few minutes before, and then her own husband had called her a slut! Zhao Shanhe was talking about Zhang Nao stealing men or whatever, and then her own husband stormed in to accuse her of adultery. I didn't laugh, though. I waited until I was out of the factory gates, and then I howled. But the laughter tasted bitter in my mouth. I asked myself why I wasn't more sympathetic. It surprised me to find delight in their suffering.

What I really regretted, though, was leaving behind my fake letter of employment—the one about being a purchasing agent for the Dongfang Construction Materials Corporation—in my rush to leave. It was the next day, when Xiaoyan visited my father to ask about me, that she found it.

‹ 24 ›

A few days after she came across the letter of employment, Xiaoyan was in the aviary, finishing feeding the birds, when she decided to pay a visit to the retail operation of the Dongfang Construction Materials Corporation. Walking into the shop, she was met by Zhang Nao. Xiaoyan asked: "Is Ceng Guangxian here?"

Zhang Nao said: "I'm afraid he's in Guangdong on a buying trip."

Xiaoyan said: "Thank you." She turned and left.

As soon as Xiaoyan had walked out, Zhang Nao went out the back door, climbed on her motorcycle, and sped toward the warehouse. Xiaoyan hadn't expected Zhang Nao to recognize her, but Zhang Nao had realized almost immediately who the woman asking after me must be. Now both women were headed toward the warehouse. Zhang Nao got there first. She rushed up the ladder to my loft and told me: "Your dad sent someone to come looking for you. I told them that you were away on business. If you want to keep going with this, you've got to get out of here. They'll be coming here next."

I followed her back down to her idling motorcycle and jumped on the back. As we pulled onto the main road, I looked back to see Xiaoyan getting off the bus. I had expected to see my dad!

To keep up the ruse that I was out of town, Zhang Nao booked me a room at the Laodong Mansion Business Hotel. I figured that after three days I'd simply reappear, and nobody would suspect anything. The most important thing to me was my father's health, and I didn't want to disappoint him again, especially in his current condition. The room was small but clean, with two single beds each covered by a bamboo summer sleeping mat and a pillow. Zhang Nao sat on one of the beds and I sat on the other, facing each other. Our knees were almost touching. I read something once about how geography can influence how we think. Like if you grow up in a place with lots of wide open spaces, your mind develops to match—so what kind of thoughts come to you in a cramped business hotel room? That's a good place to have dark thoughts, in my experience. After all those years locked up, I still had the same thoughts in my head as I'd had ten years before, standing in the alley below Zhang Nao's dormitory. I dug my fingernails into my hand, trying to shake the thoughts.

With my fingernails dug into my palm, I managed to focus enough to push down the dark thoughts and have a conversation with her. I noticed her own hands going to her stomach. When I saw her wince slightly, I asked her if she was okay.

"Just a once-a-month thing."

"Shouldn't you see a doctor?"

"It's fine. I get through it."

I poured her a cup of water. She drank a few sips. I could see now that she had broken into a sweat. I handed her a towel, and she wiped the sweat away and then lay down on the bed, groaning. I asked: "So . . . what is it?"

"Period pain, I guess."

"Why don't you go see a doctor?"

"This kind of thing isn't exactly easy to fix. It's the sort of thing a husband can fix, if you know what I mean."

"Why don't you get married, then?"

"Nobody wants me."

"No way. How is that even possible? A girl like you . . .—you've got to be kidding me."

"You see anybody lining up for me? Even you gave up."

"Are you serious? Xiaoyan kept telling me there's no way you'd ever even consider somebody like me."

"You can't shut up about her, can you? If you love her so much, why are you here with me now?"

I had no idea how to answer. I sort of wrung my hands, trying to come up with something. I looked down at my hands, and when I looked over at where Zhang Nao was lying on the bed, I saw that her eyes were closed. Like I said, I was clueless: I didn't know that she wanted me to kiss her—I thought she was in pain or something. I stared down at her and said nothing. Her breathing started to come heavy and even. She was asleep, and I was left to sit and watch her. Her shirt was unbuttoned to the second button. I could see an expanse of pale flesh, white and wide as a high mountain pass. I could have reached out and plucked the next button down. I could have . . .—but I couldn't do it! I had been unusually brave or desperate that night ten years earlier. I knew now how much I would regret any action. I didn't want to hurt Zhang Nao again. I didn't want to take advantage of her, either. I didn't want to end up behind bars again. I sat and watched her sleep. When her eyes opened again, I asked her if it still hurt, and she shook her head. She sat up and buttoned up her shirt. She asked how long she had slept. I told her: "An hour and three minutes."

She ran her fingers through her hair: "What's wrong with you?"

The next day, she came to my room with a dress on that I'd never seen before. We went out and got something to eat and then went back to the room. She lay on her back on one of the beds. She said: "Come here, Guangxian."

I shook my head: "Don't lead me on. I don't want to go down the same road I went down ten years ago."

"I want it. I owe you for all that time."

I felt a lump in my throat. I was about to cry. I said: "Why does it have to be now? Why not ten years ago? I don't want to take the risk now. You know, Xiaoyan is so good to me."

She sat up on the bed: "Xiaoyan's ugly."

"She's kind. When I was in there, she came up to Beishan to see me, brought me clothes and soap, and she held my hands in the visiting room, looked after my dad, and even if we aren't married, she still ran all over doing stuff for me, like bringing Xiaoyun to see Li Dapao. That first time I tried to escape, she brought the shoes I used. She wasted so much time. She took so much shit. I wouldn't have put her through everything if I'd known you were interested in me. I had no way of knowing. You didn't write to me. You didn't try to let me know."

"You owe me more than you owe her. Think about it. A hundred times more."

We sat in silence. Even the sound of traffic outside seemed to have momentarily ceased. I wished there were a way to split myself in two: one half for Xiaoyan and one half for Zhang Nao.

Zhang Nao put her arms around me: "Think about what we've been through, Guangxian. Ten years. Everyone wanted us to be ashamed of what was natural. It's been ten years—you're still going through it." I moved away from her and shook my head. She rolled off the bed and stomped a heel down on the floor: "They used to beg me! They used to beg me, and I ignored them. What makes you so special?" She turned and walked out of the room, slamming the door behind her.

I mean, why wouldn't I pursue Zhang Nao? She was beautiful. I suppose I did owe her something. Marrying Zhang Nao would be like washing myself clean of the last ten years, all those sick thoughts, the time behind bars . . . But what about Xiaoyan? I wondered what might have happened if things had started earlier between us. I don't know how things would have gone. Maybe Zhang Nao would have been simply another one of my fantasies. But who knows?

After my exile in the hotel, I went back home and collapsed in my bed. I spent the next few days in bed. Sometimes I thought about

Zhang Nao and sometimes I thought about Xiaoyan, but mostly I wasn't thinking about anything. One afternoon, I ripped a strip of paper in half and wrote "Zhang Nao" on one piece and "Xiaoyan" on the other. I crumpled them up into balls, shook them in my hand, and threw them on the floor. Before I could pick up either one, Xiaoyan burst into the room, saying: "Why didn't you tell me you found a job? I went to Director He with a bottle and everything, asking him to take you back."

"They sent me to Guangdong right after I got hired. I didn't even have time to let you know."

"Who told you about the job?"

"It was . . . Yu Baijia." As soon as I said it, I knew I'd made a mistake. "I mean, not him. I mostly found it myself." Xiaoyan didn't know that it wasn't a real job yet, but both of us knew Zhang Nao was involved. There was no point in lying.

Xiaoyan laughed: "You think I'm dumb or something?"

"I didn't want to upset you by mentioning her."

"I waited five years for you. You think I'm going to let her just step in now and take you? I'm not going to let all my time be wasted. Oh, you think those five years were easy? All of my free time, I was either looking after you or your father. Everyone said I was stupid. They said I was crazy. They . . ."

As she spoke, tears began to run down her cheeks. I took her hands. It was just like those days in the visiting room. I said: "I can't imagine what everyone would say if I didn't marry you. I owe you so much, but I also owe Zhang Nao something. I owe you five years, but I owe her one night. Ten years ago I put a mark on her, and now I have to wipe it clean. I have to take responsibility for that."

"Then who's going to take responsibility for me?"

"I'm resigned to my fate. Watch. Each of your names is on one of those pieces of paper."

Xiaoyan looked at the balls of paper. I heard her breathing. She said: "I don't think God would be cruel enough to let you choose her . . ."

"Then I'll choose."

She watched, holding her breath. I reached out and then stopped: "Whichever name I choose, that's it. And you can't blame me."

Xiaoyan did not speak. I closed my eyes and felt around until I reached one of the balls of paper. I unwrapped the crumpled sheet: "Zhang Nao." I passed the paper to Xiaoyan. She started to cry. She said: "I don't think that slut will treat you better than I treated you."

I shouted back at her: "Why didn't you stop me? Why didn't you pick up both of the pieces of paper and throw them away? You didn't have to let me do it."

Later, Zhao Shanhe told me that Xiaoyan had gone to see my father to tell him about how I'd chosen Zhang Nao. She said: "Guangxian doesn't need me anymore."

All of the blood drained out of my father's face. He said to her: "I knew he'd end up turning his back on you. That's just what he's like, ever since he was a kid."

She pleaded with my father: "How can he just throw me away, like a piece of garbage?" She pounded her chest. "You have to help me. I deserve better."

My father's hands went to his throat. He looked as if he were about to be sick.

"Try to reason with him. How could he choose her over me? If it were somebody else . . . but it has to be that horrible woman who's already hurt him! I waited five years, and . . ."

My father tried to speak, but his lips only quivered, and bubbles of saliva formed at the corners of his mouth. Zhao Shanhe shouted at Xiaoyan: "That's enough! You know he's not well." As the women shouted and cried, my father slowly leaned over and then fell from his chair, landing on the floor. They rushed to his side and managed to get him to his feet. They helped him to the factory gates and bundled him into a taxi and took him to the hospital.

That night, with my father somewhat recovered and sleeping in a hospital bed, Zhao Shanhe said to Xiaoyan: "You can't do that to him. He can't handle the stress." Xiaoyan cried and worried the crumpled balls of paper in her hands. She tossed them onto the floor, just as I had, and picked one, and then she did it again. She thought to herself: I had as good a chance as Zhang Nao. She asked Zhao Shanhe: "What if I got him to choose again? He might pick me this time."

"Girl, it's fate. It's been decided already. If I had married somebody else and we'd had a son . . . I'd hope he'd choose a woman like you."

"You know, I thought it was in God's hands. I mean, I didn't think there was any chance he'd pick her."

"Even God blinks sometimes."

One day shortly after that, Director He came to visit the warehouse. I'd tidied up the loft and made sure everything was spotless. When he came in, I politely offered him a cigarette and welcomed him. We discussed my time since I'd left Beishan and how much I wanted to get back to the zoo.

He told me that Xiaoyan had also spoken to him, and he recognized my previous hard work looking after the tiger and lions.

"But with all this stuff with Xiaoyan, you're not going to receive a warm welcome. They'd like to drag you out and shoot you, to be frank. I don't know if you're aware, but Hu Kaihui was also pursuing Xiaoyan for a time. She was faithful to you, but there's a certain atmosphere in the workplace now. If you aren't with Xiaoyan, I would have a hard time hiring you back."

"What does all that have to do with my work? As for my time in prison, I was falsely accused. I was innocent. Look." I produced the letter of redress.

He looked over the document and said: "Who said you did it?"

"Zhang Nao."

"Then what the hell are you doing going after her now? You must know that Xiaoyan is not the type of woman who stays single. You could spend your whole life looking for a girl as good as that one. All I have to be proud of, this work I've done over the years, is looking after good people like Xiaoyan. You know, this loft, she used to come here once a week to tidy it up. What do you think people thought of her? They thought she'd lost it. I wish your mother were still alive to push you in the right direction."

"I realize what I'm missing out on. But I put it in God's hands."

"Who chooses a wife based on some bullshit superstitious game like that, balls of paper?"

‹ 26 ›

After Director He left, I put a cigarette between my lips and reached for the box of matches on my bed. I struck a match and let it burn down to my fingers. I struck another one, the cigarette still unlit, and let it burn down. I watched the flame peel down the match head, turning red and then green, the fire burning in a column and then shrinking down into a ball. I started to play a game with the matches, saying to myself: "If this match burns, I will marry Zhang Nao. If this match doesn't light, I will marry Xiaoyan." I don't know what I hoped to accomplish. It was more like a quality assurance inspection than divination. After a while, I switched the order of the names: if it burned, I would marry Xiaoyan. Of course, most of the matches lit, so there wasn't much chance, and I had already made my choice with the balls of paper. As I swept up the burned-down matches from the floor, I knew that I had to stand by my decision, however I had made it—or I had to make my own decision.

Who was it going to be? I went and asked just about everyone I knew for advice: Zhao Wannian, Uncle Zhao, Chen Baixiu, Fang Haitang, Yu Fare, Rong Guangming, Fang Ziyu . . . When I went to Uncle Zhao, he came up close to me and looked me over and said: "The only thing wrong with you is you don't have a heart." The results were unanimous: everyone told me to run back to Xiaoyan. But I wasn't ready to just go along with popular opinion like that. They had no idea what I had gone through. I finally decided to go to Yu Baijia and Xiao Chi. They knew the situation the best.

A few days later, I went to their apartment in the evening. They had been given an apartment in the dormitory compound of the department store where Yu Baijia worked. Their new place was tidy and spacious. On one wall hung a banner with a red double happiness character, which newlyweds traditionally displayed. The edges of the banner had begun to peel from the wall. Above the sofa hung an oil painting of a placid blue lake. On the wall beside it were a few movie posters featuring most of the famous actresses around that time, so there was Joan Chen and Zhang Yu and Liu Xiaoqing and whoever else was popular back then. The couple still looked about the same as they always had, except Xiao Chi had maybe put on a bit of weight. I got right to the point.

Xiao Chi seemed surprised: "How is that even a question? Lu Xiaoyan is the only choice."

Baijia said: "If it were me, it'd be Zhang Nao for sure."

Xiao Chi said: "Why?"

Baijia said: "Just look at her!"

Xiao Chi said: "Who cares about looks? You want a wife who will look after you, who when you're sick is even more worried than you are—that's the kind of woman you can grow old with."

Baijia said: "Yeah, but as a man . . . you don't want to marry some hideous freak. You can't go through life like that. I read something recently about how looking at beautiful things can extend your life."

"Bullshit. Did it say anything about all the men who went broke married to some witch? You think being a cuck is going to add years to your life?"

Baijia: "A perfect peach is better than a basket of rotten pears."

Xiao Chi was cutting her nails at the living room table. She looked up at her husband.

Baijia stammered: "I wasn't talking about you! I meant . . ."

Xiao Chi said: "So who's your perfect peach?"

Baijia looked at the floor: "I never had one."

Xiao Chi said: "You got stuck with the basket of rotten pears, is that what you're saying?"

Baijia said: "That's not what I meant."

Xiao Chi said: "Don't worry. I know exactly what you meant."

Baijia said: "Fine, fine. I'm not going to argue with you." He turned to me: "Marry Lu Xiaoyan. I guess some people don't want to hear the truth."

Xiao Chi picked up a broomstick from beside the sofa: "You can't shut up, can you?"

"Whatever, it's Guangxian's problem. Don't drag me into it."

"I'm not talking about him now. You're a snake. Every night when you should be looking me in the eyes, you're looking over my shoulder at these . . ." She slashed at the posters with the broomstick, knocking the actresses with their perfect hair and gleaming eyes and expensive clothes to the floor.

By the time I walked out through the gates of the dormitory compound, I had made up my mind to go back to Lu Xiaoyan. But how was I going to tell Zhang Nao? If I didn't handle the situation correctly, everything could blow up in my face. I had to come up with a reason to turn her down. I decided to make a special trip to Beishan to ask Jia Wenping for his advice. Warden Jia was a warden, after all, so I figured he'd be able to come up with something to help me. Just as I thought, his advice was sound: "Put the ball in her court. It's very simple."

I wasn't sure exactly how to put the ball in her court, though. As Warden Jia dragged on the cigarette I lit for him, he said: "You ask her why she loves you. After that, you'll be able to see the situation a lot more clearly." That was it! Why, in fact, did she love me? I had spent the last decade behind bars, and my future prospects weren't exactly dazzlingly bright. What was there to love about me? I had wanted to ask her before, actually. But when it had come time to ask, I couldn't get it out. The situation with Lu Xiaoyan was clearer, I thought. For her to marry a man like me was easier to explain, even if only from a socioeconomic perspective. Zhang Nao's future looked promising. She even had her own business now. If we got married, Zhang Nao would be the one marrying down. So why did she still want to get married?

Since that night many years ago, I had never seen Zhang Nao dance. But that night when I went to her room, I found the door open and heard the score from *Red Detachment of Women* playing inside. She was dancing: the room was small, and her motions were small but graceful, her body bending as easily as a length of rope. I don't really know what to compare it to—she bent as easily as a rope, but her body was as straight as an iron rod, projecting the indomitable spirit of the heroine. The tips of her soft white ballet shoes swept the floor. In her black leotard, I could see her body perfectly, her breasts swaying with her movements. I could see the taut muscles in her calves and thighs under the close-fitting fabric. The leotard was stretched tight over her round ass, and through it I could see a hint of the pale white skin beneath. Maybe I had looked before, but now I could see everything, how round and tight her ass was. She wasn't wearing panties. Maybe she never wore them, even when she was onstage. For the first time in my life—and I was almost thirty then—I realized the beauty of the human body. Zhang Nao's perfect body was the equal of all the Motherland's natural vistas. I know that kind of statement is hard to take seriously, but that's how I felt.

She spun in the air and landed in front of me. She kicked up her right leg and laid her ankle on my left shoulder. I smelled her body. I couldn't take it anymore. I pulled her close and we fell to the floor. I kissed her mouth and pulled at her clothes. All those thoughts about why she loved me were gone. I wanted her mouth and her body. I peeled her leotard down over her shoulders, and her body was laid out before me. I pressed her soft white breasts together and buried my face between them. I fumbled down her body and tried to peel the leotard down the rest of the way. It was tight, and I struggled to pull it down over her ass. As I fought with the fabric, I heard a voice cry: "Help!" I wasn't sure if it was Zhang

Nao or—maybe it was Lu Xiaoyan? My body froze, and I rolled off of her and lay on my back on the floor. Zhang Nao straddled me and kissed my mouth. I lay absolutely still.

"What's wrong?"

"I want to wait until we're married."

She started to unbutton my shirt: "We'll go get the marriage certificate tomorrow."

I pulled my shirt closed: "I want to wait."

She picked her leotard up from the floor. She said: "Whatever. Don't do that to me again—don't stop halfway."

You think I didn't want to do it? Of course I did! But I had just spent ten years locked up. Once bitten, twice shy, as they say. I watched her get dressed. I know, I know. If I'd just slept with her, it's not like anything would have changed; the world would have kept turning. But I was still a bit nervous. And back then, you know, I still kind of had the idea that you had to marry a girl before you slept with her. I mean, things had changed already. But I was out of the loop, I guess. You know about birth control and all that, right? Now they've even got a "morning after pill." They should call it the "regret pill"! You know what that's for, right? I wish they made a "life after pill," so you could erase all the other bad decisions you've made, just in general.

The next day, I went to the Huanqiu Photo Studio and had a portrait taken. I paid the extra fee to have the photo developed right away, and the photographer rushed off to the darkroom. I sat for a while, looking out the window and flipping through old newspapers, but finally I dragged a chair over to the curtain over the darkroom door and called inside: "Is it ready yet?"

"It'll be ready when it's ready," the photographer called back. "Patience, please." Her assistant came over and brought me an album of her work to look through. On the first page of the album was a picture of Zhang Nao.

I said: "This is why I'm in such a hurry. I'm going to marry her." The assistant laughed.

I rushed over to Zhang Nao's shop and showed her the picture. She looked it over and said: "It's too late now, anyway. They're probably off for lunch already."

"When are we going to do it, then?"

"We'll go over in the afternoon."

I took her hand and flipped over her wrist: "They won't be going to lunch for an hour yet. Let's take your motorcycle."

"You want to go over there looking like that? They'll laugh at you."

"You said you know somebody over there. Talk to her. I probably don't even have to go."

She thought for a moment and said: "That's right. I just need the stamp from her. You go back to my place and wait for me."

I went to the dormitory and let myself in with the key that Zhang Nao had given me. I sat for a while, looking over the room, and then a thought came to me—you know my story well enough to know that's not a good sign! What would I change in the room after I moved in? I thought the bed would probably have to be replaced. But what else? What did the apartment of newlyweds need? I thought back to the red double happiness banner in Baijia and Xiao Chi's apartment. There had to be a few banners in here, too. I could get gold hooks. A banner with red tassels would look nice. Maybe some streamers coming down from the ceiling, too. I could see it clearly, how I'd put the whole thing together.

I started to go through the drawers and cupboards of Zhang Nao's wardrobe. I found a pen and paper, but there was no ink. I found another pen, but it was dry, too. I went to her dressing table and found a tube of lipstick. I ripped the paper into strips and used the lipstick to write the character xi on each of them. I stuck one on the door and another on the window. As I was standing on a chair to hang one of the strips of paper on the wall, I heard a voice behind me: "Are you crazy?" I fell backward off the chair.

Zhang Nao tore down the strips and stared at me. I said: "I was just trying to, you know, improve the atmosphere."

"How? By hanging up all this paper? It looks tacky."

I had thought she'd be happy. I picked up the strips of paper she'd torn down and began to scratch the glue from the walls.

"If you're really worried about it, I can renovate."

"I'm not worried. It's just, if we could hang a banner, I think it would be nice . . ."

"All right, give me a couple days. We'll make ourselves at home. Now, is the groom going to come see his bride?"

She tossed the marriage certificate onto her dressing table. I picked it up and ran a finger over the stamp at the bottom, which still glowed a wet red. I felt my body begin to shake. I had thought that day would never come.

I had decided to wait until we were married, but even now, with the marriage certificate right there in front of me, I still wasn't ready. I asked myself why I wasn't ready yet. Legally, there was no problem. But I wanted to set the mood. I wanted to follow procedures. Part of it was vanity, too. As I said before, one of the reasons I had wanted to marry Zhang Nao was to scrub off the mark that ten years in prison had left on me.

Every morning when I woke up, I went straight to the marriage certificate. I would sometimes sit in front of it for more than an hour, wiping it clean with a dry rag. I carried it around with me, keeping it safe in an inside pocket, where I could pat it and reassure myself. One day, I went to find Zhao Shanhe at the railway office. When I showed her the certificate, she gasped: "You can't tell your father about this. His heart can't take it."

"That's why I came to see you. I need to borrow some money. I want to do something for Zhang Nao, but I'm broke."

She reached into one of her desk drawers: "You can't tell Lao Dong about this. This is from my savings."

"I'll pay you back as soon as I can."

‹27›

I took the money that Zhao Shanhe had lent me and bought new blankets, a rice cooker, an electric kettle, and double happiness banners. I loaded everything onto my bicycle and rode over to the Culture Bureau and Zhang Nao's dormitory. I went up the stairs with my arms full and scraped my foot against the door. When there was no answer, I called out: "Zhang Nao!" Silence.

I took the blanket off my shoulder and set it down so that I could knock. I heard a crashing sound inside the room. I wondered if maybe someone had broken in. The door suddenly opened a crack, and I saw Zhang Nao putting her hair up and looking out at me: "You aren't a cat. What are you scratching at the door for?" Over her shoulder, I saw a shadow moving, dropping down from the open window. I rushed past her and looked down. I knew immediately who it was. I had chased the same shadow all around the warehouse when I was a kid: it was Yu Baijia. It made sense, I guess, since he'd given me the idea to go in through the window in the first place. I had even sent him to Zhang Nao's dormitory when I was up at Beishan. He had written back to say that there was no problem, I should have jumped. He'd gone a step further than just doing reconnaissance: he had actually taken the jump himself.

I looked around the room. The blanket on the bed was new, and there were new pink sheets and a new mosquito net. Double happiness banners with red tassels hung on gold hooks. It was exactly like I had imagined it. It was as if she knew what I had dreamed about and she was making it come true. But in my dreams, I hadn't imagined that the sheets and blankets would be heaped on the bed, leaving no doubt in my mind what I had just interrupted.

Zhang Nao shut the door and pretended as if nothing had happened.

"I thought all of this was for me. What's going on here?"

"You saw. What do you want me to explain?"

"Then why are you marrying me?"

"I've told you a thousand times. I owe you a debt."

"You're saying you don't love me?"

She sat on the bed: "What do you think? If I don't love you, why would I go get a marriage certificate?"

"Then what are you doing with him?"

"I don't really know, either. But as I see it, there's nothing wrong with loving more than one person. The love is still real."

She stood up, as if she were about to launch into a speech.

I took the marriage certificate out of my pocket and waved it in front of her: "I'm divorcing you!"

"Sure, if that's what you want."

I went to the drawer of her desk and found a sheet of paper. It was just like that day with Zhao Shanhe and her husband. I started to write out a divorce agreement. I passed it to her so she could sign it.

"Give me some time, at least. Think about what people will say. Don't worry, I'll let you go. But give me some time." She took the paper, ripped it up, and mashed it into my face.

The humiliation was unbearable: I was a cuck. This woman had slept with another man in our matrimonial bed, and now she was literally rubbing our sham marriage in my face. I raised a fist, and she took a step closer: "Hit me! If you even touch me, I'll never sign that stupid paper." I put my hand down. "That was the right decision."

I shouted at her: "When? When are you going to sign it?"

"Six months. I don't want you to think I was just marrying you to repay a debt."

It's kind of funny, right? There I was, about to go ask her if she really loved me, and I ended up marrying her two days later, and by the end of the week I was asking for a divorce. I thought I was fast. But Yu Baijia had been even faster. He was always faster than me, though. I remember one time back in school, our homeroom teacher—we used to call him Mr. Clueless, a play on his real name—devised a contest where the first student to arrive would get a picture book as a prize. I recall the day he set was August 15th. So on that day I got up at about three in the morning. I rushed to the school, sure that I'd get the prize. But when I got there, Yu Baijia was seated right in front of Clueless's desk. I should have known, though. I mean, the thing with Zhang Nao and him. There had been clues all along, but—just a while before, actually, he'd been talking about how beautiful she was, how a perfect peach was better than a basket of rotten pears. I hadn't really paid attention.

Why hadn't I been more careful? Why had I told her I wanted to wait?

I took Zhang Nao at her word. I agreed to give her six months. I packed up the rice cooker and the electric kettle and the new blanket and took them back to the warehouse. That first day back, I dropped everything at the bottom of the ladder and went up and sat, staring at the walls. I don't know how many days I spent like that, sitting alone in the loft.

One day, I happened to notice the pictures that Xiaoyan had brought, the one of her and the one of me, pasted to the back of the mirror. Something inside me snapped, and I stood and rushed over to them. The bamboo mat I had been sitting on was stuck to my ass. I had been sitting for so long that the mat was glued to me. As I ran through the door, it caught and I fell backward. I ripped the mat off and went down the ladder.

I loaded the things I'd brought from Zhang Nao's dormitory back onto my bike and headed toward East Tiema Road. I couldn't believe that nobody had taken my stuff. It was a miracle. I reached the zoo and went to find Xiaoyan in her dormitory room. Her door was open, and I went inside. She pushed me back out and slammed the door. A second later, it flew open again, and she kicked out the rice cooker. The door slammed shut again. I gathered up the rice cooker and the electric kettle and the banners and put them at her doorstep. I shouted inside: "Take these. Take these, and in six months, after I divorce her, we'll get married." There was a sound of breaking glass from inside the room. I stood outside until my legs felt as if they'd give out. I sat until I couldn't keep my eyes open any longer. I spread out the blanket and slept in the hallway of the dormitory. I don't know how long I slept there, but it must have been a while, because when I woke up, it was light outside and my face felt hot in the sunshine. Beside my head was a bowl with two mantou inside. I took a bite and began to cry. Xiaoyan loved me so much, and I'd been so ungrateful. I had run after a bad girl, and my revenge had been as swift as it was painful.

I ate the mantou and rushed to the aviary. I stood behind a tree and watched as Xiaoyan fed the pigeons. They flocked around her feet, scrambling for the feed that she poured out for them in handfuls. She was careful, though, making sure that even the birds on the fringes were given enough to eat. One of the pigeons even rested on her shoulder as she spread the food. I watched as she turned to go. As she walked away, I watched her back. I shuddered and grabbed the tree to steady myself. What I felt wasn't regret, but something far more severe.

For the next few days, I followed Xiaoyan everywhere she went. I walked a few steps behind her, like her shadow. I didn't say anything. She went about her business without speaking to me, either. Sometimes when people stopped to talk to her, they would cast a glance back at me, maybe wondering what I was doing following her around. I followed her into the feed room one day and watched her empty two bags of seeds into a bucket to mix them. I rushed over with a shovel and began churning the seeds together, until they were evenly mixed. She turned to me, then asked: "What are you doing this for? You're already married. Why can't you just leave me alone?"

"Give me another chance."

"You're getting what you deserve. I tried to tell you . . ."

"One more chance. I'll do anything you want."

"Get down on your knees."

I knelt on the ground in front of her.

"Slap yourself. Show me how you feel."

I slapped myself hard across the mouth. I grabbed her hand and hit myself in the face with it. She pulled her hand back. She said: "I don't want to touch you. I'll have to scrub my hands." I slapped myself again, harder.

"What took you so long to realize I was the right choice? I don't want to see you feeling sorry for yourself now. Go get a divorce. I'm giving you a month. If it takes longer than that, forget about it."

I got to my feet and raced to my bike.

I pedaled furiously, cutting across town, nearly hitting a few people on the way. I rushed into Zhang Nao's shop and found here there. I was panting and dripping with sweat. I said to her: "Let's do it right now. That's all I need from you, this one mercy: let's go to the Bureau of Civil Affairs right now."

"What's your hurry? You said six months."

"Xiaoyan won't wait six months." As soon as I spoke, I knew I had made a mistake.

She sneered and said: "You haven't even divorced me and you're looking for another wife, huh? How many do you need?"

"You're the one who already found someone else while you were still married to me. I'm done with you."

"Not according to our marriage certificate. It's got your name on it, doesn't it? That's your picture on it." She waved her copy of the certificate in my face. I grabbed it from her and was about to tear it up.

"Go ahead. But the Bureau of Civil Affairs has its own records. You can't get married again without a divorce certificate. That would be a crime, wouldn't it? You might get sent up to Beishan again."

I held the marriage certificate crumpled in my fist. She knew exactly what to say to set me off. She stepped back and said: "You'd better relax, or it won't be six months—you'll be waiting another ten years. By the time you get divorced, Xiaoyan's kids will be starting middle school."

I slammed my fist down on the desk. "You never loved me. Why are you doing this now?"

"You still don't get it, do you? I got everything ready for you. I gave you your moment—you missed out. Why are you blaming me?"

"Got everything ready for me? I wish I knew how many men there were before me. Slut."

"'Slut'? You think I've never heard that before? Do you know why everyone calls me that?" She picked up a bottle of ink from the desk and threw it at me. A blotch of ink spread across my shirt. "I got that name because of you!" She picked a calculator up off the desk and threw it. It hit me in the face and fell to the floor, breaking open. I put my hand to my cheek and felt blood. I rushed at her, grabbing her by the collar. "You want to divorce me? Six months—how about a year?" Just as I was about to hit her, she shouted: "You idiot! You don't get it, do you? You still don't get it. I love you. I can't divorce you." Suddenly it all made sense to me. That had to be why she wouldn't divorce me. She must love me. My fist unclenched. My hand fell to my side.

Maybe I should have hit her. Maybe I regret it. Since I left Beishan, she'd been working on me. That first day when she picked me up, she was softening me up. That night when I discovered Yu Baijia jumping out the window, I agreed to postpone the divorce. Now she was playing me again: suddenly declaring her love for me.

That same day, I went to a print shop and had them print me a divorce contract. I bought a red ink pad and a fountain pen, too. I went to Zhang Nao's shop to look for her, but her assistant, Xiaoxia, told me that she was away on business. I went to Zhang Nao's dormitory room. I knocked on her door, but there was no answer. I waited, and eventually one of the actors who lived in the dormitory asked me if I'd forgotten my key. I nodded and he walked away. As he left, I thought to myself: why not be honest? I had nothing to hide. I called after him: "I didn't forget my key. I don't even have one. Zhang Nao changed the locks." He brought me a stool to sit on and walked away again.

At around ten o'clock that night, I heard the sound of a motorcycle and rushed to the hallway window to look down. I saw Yu Baijia pulling up on his motorcycle, Zhang Nao jumping down from the back, and the two of them kissing goodbye. I had held back my anger until I couldn't hold it in any longer. My anger was like a reservoir, and I had planned to open the dam that night. But what I felt at that moment was something far more powerful, a nuclear detonation of anger. I picked up one of the flower pots that hung below the balcony window and threw it down. The pot exploded at their feet, and Yu Baijia turned his motorcycle and roared toward the gates of the compound. Zhang Nao rushed up the stairs, shouting: "Are you trying to kill someone?"

I followed her into her dormitory room. She sat down and began to fix her hair in the mirror, watching me the entire time. I tapped my finger on the desk. She pretended not to hear. I grabbed her arm and dragged her toward the desk. With my other hand, I grabbed her index finger and pulled it toward the red ink pad. She jerked away and ran toward the bed. I grabbed her again, pulling and pushing her toward the desk. I jammed her inked finger down onto the divorce contract, then put the pen in her hand and wrote her name in crude handwriting over the red fingerprint. She spun away from me, grabbing the divorce contract and tearing it to pieces while I watched. I couldn't hold back any longer: I slapped her. She looked up at me and said: "That's one year." I slapped her again. "Another year. Keep hitting me. I'll add a year every time. We'll grow old together if that's what you want." I grabbed her by the wrist and pulled her down to the floor, kicking her in the back. She wailed and pounded the floor with her fists, pretending to cry. It was as if she were acting out a scene from one of the model ballets she loved, crying under the blows of the wicked landlord. She cried out: "Help! Ceng Guangxian is trying to kill me."

I knew that I had to start being more careful. I needed a plan. I made up my mind to go see Xiao Chi. I'd thought about going to see her in the days after I discovered Yu Baijia and Zhang Nao's relationship, but I didn't want to drag her into the mess that my life had become. But now that Zhang Nao was scheming to postpone the divorce and Yu Baijia was shamelessly going around town with her, I decided that it was finally time to go see Xiao Chi.

When I got to Xiao Chi's studio that day, she was chatting with Rong Guangming. You remember Rong Guangming, right? Our class monitor in our school days, who went to the countryside with Yu Baijia and Xiao Chi. He had come back from the countryside and entered the foreign languages department of the university and was doing quite well. But anyways, they were talking, and I was stuck listening to a deep conversation about French Impressionists. The studio walls were hung with Xiao Chi's paintings, and I thought that I recognized some of them from the newspaper. I sat through their conversation until I couldn't take it any longer and interrupted: "Xiao Chi, I need to talk to you." She looked up at me. I said: "In private." When Rong Guangming had left, Xiao Chi glared at me. I said: "Zhang Nao and Yu Baijia . . ."

Before I finished, she said: "Impossible! There's no way."

"I've never lied to you before. There's no doubt—I mean, I caught them."

She stamped across the room, knocking over a bottle of paint. She left red footprints across the floor. "We went through so much together. All those struggle sessions. I can't handle this. We went through all that, and now he can just run around like nothing matters. Back then, he wouldn't have even tried it. You saw what happened to us. Things were more strict." She sighed and fell against the wall, knocking down a painting.

"I know where they go. There's a hotel they use. We could catch them in the act."

She gestured at the paintings on the wall: "This is what I want to see. I want to see beauty. I don't want to see something so ugly."

"Are you just going to let them keep doing it? He's your husband; she's my wife."

"No. I don't even want to hear about it." She put her hands over her ears.

See, I had been planning on telling her the whole story, how'd I'd first discovered Yu Baijia jumping from the window of Zhang Nao's dormitory room. When I saw the look on her face, though, I knew it wasn't the right time. I ended up walking out. As soon as I left and got back on my bike, I felt like the weight of the world was off my shoulders. I rode back toward the warehouse with my coat flapping behind me. I knew there was nothing else to do. I had told Xiao Chi what was happening. What else was there? I just wanted to get back to my loft and see how everything played out.

One night Xiaoxia arrived at the loft, calling through the door that Zhang Nao wanted me to meet her at the Guijiang Hotel. The hotel's restaurant was the first place Zhang Nao had taken me after she picked me up at Beishan. I grabbed the divorce contract, the red ink pad, and the pen and rushed over. When I got there and went into the lobby, I saw about twenty people being herded around by Public Security Bureau officers. Yu Baijia and Zhang Nao had been swept up in a raid targeting people who were violating the laws against unlawful cohabitation and solicitation of prostitution. I saw Zhang Nao standing in the middle of a small group of women. Some of them were seated on the floor; others squatted, their faces buried in their hands. The raid seemed to have swept up some important people. Many of the men wore glasses and brandished expensive cigarettes.

As soon as Zhang Nao saw me, she said to the officer beside her: "My husband has come. He can take custody of me."

The big cop squinted at me: "You her husband? What's your name? What work unit are you with?" I looked up and pretended not to hear. "Hey, I'm talking to you. You, looking up at the ceiling!"

"What? Oh, no, she's got the wrong guy."

She tried to step around the PSB officer, but he stuck out an arm to hold her. She shouted over him: "Ceng Guangxian, I'm going to cut your lips off!" I took out the divorce agreement and waved it under her nose.

"I'll get you out of here. But I need your signature and your fingerprint." She reached for the paper and I pulled it away. I knew what was coming! She'd already ripped it up a few times before.

"Then fuck off. So what? They'll make me join some study sessions. That's it."

That's loyalty, isn't it? Even with a gun to her head, the woman would have refused to divorce me. If that isn't loyalty, tell me what is! I mean, she could have just been a shameless bitch, but it was impressive either way. I got out of there fast. Zhang Nao was still cursing me as I walked down the front steps of the hotel.

I saw Xiao Chi leaning against a pillar in the lobby. Her face was lit orange by the cigarette she was taking angry drags from.

I said: "They deserve it."

Xiao Chi said: "I couldn't take it. I've been following them for a few weeks. I called the PSB."

"I knew you'd come up with something."

She had a camera with her. She went inside and began to snap photos of Yu Baijia and Zhang Nao. When the flash went off, Zhang Nao and the other people rounded up in the raid covered their faces. Only Yu Baijia remained motionless, as if he were posing for her.

I thought that was going to be the end of it, but my troubles were only beginning.

Yu Baijia went home, where Xiao Chi was waiting for him. After the arguments gave way to silence, Baijia tried a new tactic: he replaced all of the movie posters he had hung on the walls earlier with playbills from Zhang Nao's *Red Detachment of Women*. The posters highlighted the special pants that had been created to show off her muscular legs and flexibility. Xiao Chi came home and tore down the posters.

Yu Baijia put the posters of Zhang Nao up again. Xiao Chi ripped them down. Now, as you can imagine, there wasn't an infinite supply of posters from a local performance of a model ballet, so Yu Baijia eventually had to go to enlargements of pictures he'd taken of Zhang Nao. These were quite revealing photographs, too, for the time. He put them up on nearly every inch of flat space in the apartment and secured them with a thick layer of glue. Xiao Chi tore her fingernails scratching the photos off the walls and ceiling of the apartment.

After Xiao Chi fell while scraping pictures off the ceiling, she packed a bag and moved into her studio. Yu Baijia showed up there, too. He said: "If we can't live together, then why not just divorce me?"

She said: "You think it's going to be that easy? I want them to throw both of you in jail again." Yu Baijia picked up a bottle of ink and splashed a slash of black across one of Xiao Chi's paintings. The two fought, and more ink was thrown, and eventually Xiao Chi jumped on her husband and bit his head hard. It was like—imagine biting into a baozi; that's what it was like. He ran out the door, and she chased him. They fought like that off and on for a few days. Can you imagine? She'd chase him around, shouting stuff like "Go see your whore, Yu Baijia!"

It hurt my heart to see Xiao Chi treated that way. Sometimes I went over to their apartment and saw them arguing. I thought about grabbing Yu Baijia, holding him so that Xiao Chi could beat him with her shoe, but I never did. I thought about going to see her at the studio, but I got only as far as the door and never knocked. There were a bunch of editorials in the papers back then about "non-interference in the affairs of other countries." I guess I was trying to adopt the same stance.

One night, Xiao Chi wrote a suicide letter and climbed the stairs to the top floor of the Guijiang Hotel. A crowd formed around the hotel. Traffic police arrived to keep order. Peeking out of the doorway to the roof were Yu Baijia, Xiao Chi's parents, and two PSB officers. She told them that if they took a step, she would jump. Yu Baijia sent someone to bring me to the hotel. When I arrived, they'd already been up on the roof for more than an hour. Yu Baijia said: "Just talk to her. Make sure she doesn't jump. Basically, distract her long enough for us to grab her." I couldn't believe that he was getting me mixed up in something like that. I mean, if she jumped, I'd be the one to blame. I turned to walk back down the stairs. Xiao Chi's mother knelt on the floor, looking up at me with her eyes moist: "Please try, Guangxian. You're our only hope." I had a policy of non-interference. But the pleas of Xiao Chi's mother changed my mind.

When the door to the rooftop swung open, I could see the crowd below and the leafy trees just budding in late spring. Xiao Chi was wearing white pajamas. In her hand she held a framed painting. She was balanced on the outside of the railing around the building. I called to her, and she turned and said: "Don't come any closer."

"It's Guangxian."

"Don't come any closer."

I stood for a while and then glanced back at the door. Yu Baijia was motioning for me not to keep going. I was about eight feet away from her.

"I know what that painting is, Xiao Chi."

I immediately regretted saying that. I told you she was holding a painting, but there was no way to see what it was. I had only said it as something to say, something to take her mind off jumping. She looked down at the painting in her arms. I said: "I'm going to say what it is: if I'm right, you come back inside; if I guess wrong, you can jump or not jump, whatever you want to do." My mind raced. I thought back to the paintings in her studio. I ran through images in my head: water, mountains, a tractor, a hoe, money, grassy plains, the ocean, a farmer, a worker, an intellectual, a tiger, an orangutan, a pigeon . . . my brain had never worked so fast. It felt like the entire world flashed through my mind. Finally, I said: "It's a lake."

I saw her move toward me, ever so slightly. "It's Tianle, isn't it? Xiangya Mountain, Wuse Lake. You said you wanted to climb it. I never thought you would. But I guess you did climb it." She let the painting drop to the floor, smashing the frame and the glass inside it. I was right: it was an oil painting of Wuse Lake, looking down from Xiangya Mountain in Tianle. I couldn't believe I'd been right. What were the chances of that?

"It's all your fault! You said you were going to come with me. You ran away." I took a few steps closer to her. She was gripping the railing, sobbing. "Don't come any closer."

"I'm sorry. If I had gone with you, I wouldn't have gone through everything I went through. I was wrong."

"You said I was sick. You called me a pervert."

"I was wrong."

"Why did you have to tell me about those two? Why? You thought I wanted to hear about it? Why couldn't you just shut up and let me live my life? It's all your fault."

"I just can't shut my mouth." I slapped myself hard across the face. The sound echoed down from the building, so even the people below could hear it.

"Why did you come here?"

"I love you." I knew it was the wrong thing to say. I slapped myself hard again.

"Would you marry me?"

"I would." Slap.

Xiao Chi took off her pajamas. She threw them over the edge of the building. She climbed back over the railing, so she was back to relative safety. She was completely naked. "If you love me, take off your clothes. I want to let Yu Baijia see us." My cheeks glowed red. I took a few steps back. She said: "Are you coming over here or not? Come on. Do what I say or I'll jump."

"I'm coming."

"Take your clothes off."

I started to undress, slowly unbuttoning my shirt. Why had I come there? Why hadn't I just walked away when Yu Baijia told me to go out onto the roof? Why hadn't I just kept my mouth shut? I didn't want to be there, undressing on a rooftop. Each time my hand slowed, I felt her eyes on me. I took off my shirt and dropped it on the floor.

"Now your pants."

I opened my belt and began to slowly take off my pants. I was moving in slow motion. I had never really undressed in front of anyone but my mother. Suddenly, the thought of the hole in my underwear almost stopped me. It was bad enough getting naked, but that hole seemed even worse somehow. I looked back at the door. The small crowd in the doorway seemed to have grown. Everyone was motioning for me to go ahead, get my clothes off. I said: "Maybe we could do this somewhere else, Xiao Chi. It's a bit cold here, and it kind of feels wrong to do it out in the open like this."

"This feels wrong? What those two did wasn't wrong?" She put her right leg up over the railing. "Hurry up. Hurry up or I'll jump."

"I'm doing it."

I took off my pants. The hole in my underwear was out there for everyone to see. Xiao Chi shouted: "Your underwear, too!" I wished I could float away. I wished I could have turned to steam, floated away. There's nothing I wanted more than to be back in my loft. I ripped down my underwear and stepped out of them. I ran over to Xiao Chi and took her in my arms. I moved with my eyes shut tight. I used my ears instead of my eyes, just as I had that night when I'd slipped into Zhang Nao's dormitory room, and during my escape through the window of the factory's bathroom. As soon as she was in my arms and I heard her crying, I motioned behind my back, and some of the men watching from the doorway rushed over. I held Xiao Chi as tight as I could. She tried to pull herself free, biting and scratching at my arms and face. I held her and wouldn't let go. I opened my eyes and let go of her only when someone pulled me away and tossed a shirt around my shoulders. I heard Xiao Chi's mother crying in the stairwell as her daughter was bundled down the stairs. Finally, I was alone on the roof with her father. I pulled on my clothes. He said: "You should have married my daughter. If you were my son-in-law, I would give you everything I have to repay you."

He went downstairs, leaving me alone on the roof. I went over to the railing where Xiao Chi had been poised to jump. When I looked down, I saw what had been visible only to her: the terrace of the neighboring building was about two feet away and six feet down. If she had jumped, the fall would have been about as far as Yu Baijia's fall from Zhang Nao's window. Why the fuck did I even bother?

‹ 29 ›

Embarrassment kept me in bed for a few days. But eventually I left my bed and the loft again and went to the big department store downtown, carrying a wooden bat. It was five forty in the afternoon when I saw Yu Baijia coming out of an employee exit, pushing a bicycle. I smashed the bat down on the handlebars. He dropped the bike and took a step back: "What are you trying to do?"

"Nothing. I want you to go through the same thing I did—drop your pants."

He glanced around: "You're crazy."

"You're the crazy one. I'm not even talking about sleeping with Zhang Nao. You brought me up to that rooftop, and you saw what happened. So let's make it even."

"This is between you and me. Don't show up here and make a scene where I work."

I raised the bat and tried to decide where I would hit him. In my moment of hesitation, Yu Baijia jumped toward me, grabbed my arm, and pushed me up against the wall of the department store. I slipped out of his grip and fell backward on him, twisting around so that I was straddling his chest, holding the bat over my head. Yu Baijia covered his face with his hands. He said: "Why did you have to tell her? She wouldn't have been up on that roof if you hadn't told her about me and Zhang Nao. If she hadn't been up on the roof, you would never have had to walk around naked in front of everyone. I'm not going to make it even. It's your fault. You're the one who owes me."

"Stop giving me excuses."

"I never told you to take off your clothes. If you want to get even, go talk to Xiao Chi."

"Why did you get me to go up there, then?"

"You didn't have to go. You went out there yourself. You took your clothes off. Nobody put a gun to your head. Why are you blaming me?"

I tossed the bat on the ground and got up off Yu Baijia. I looked back at the crowd that had formed around us. I walked away. I realized I had never really wanted to make a scene in the first place.

Zhao Wannian helped me get a job at the Clothes for Cuba factory. My job was packing up clothes according to order forms and stamping the boxes with MADE IN CHINA.

One day when I left work, I saw that Xiao Chi was waiting for me. She was sitting on the sidewalk with her legs crossed. I had always thought of her as very ladylike, sort of refined—I told you about her background, how she always seemed different from us back when we were in school together—so it was surprising to see her on the dusty sidewalk like that. I flicked my bike's bell and she looked up, but she didn't seem to recognize me for a moment. She finally smiled and stood, and we walked together. She told me that she had finally ended things with Yu Baijia. She said: "I used to be a famous young painter, but now I'm the famous once-divorced young painter." If Yu Baijia and Xiao Chi had split up, then why was Zhang Nao still torturing me? Why was she going to so much trouble to hold on to me? Without saying anything, I got on my bike and started to pedal away. Xiao Chi grabbed my coat and pulled me hard enough that I almost fell down. She said: "You promised me. You promised you'd marry me."

"When did I say that?"

"On the rooftop. You told me you loved me. You said you'd marry me."

"I did? I can't even remember. I was worried you'd jump."

"You're just like Yu Baijia. Maybe I should have jumped." She was still holding my coat.

"I can't marry you, anyway. I haven't divorced Zhang Nao."

She let go of my coat and gave me a push: "Then what are you waiting for? Go get a divorce."

I pedaled away, my bike creaking up the sidewalk. When I looked back, Xiao Chi was still walking along the sidewalk—no, not walking, but skipping! I thought about turning back, saying something to her. I knew I couldn't comfort her, though, and I didn't want to become too deeply involved with her. In my opinion, she was about eighty percent insane. I'm no psychiatrist, but I could see it in her eyes. There was a slackness in her face. And the way she'd been sitting on the sidewalk, too. Not to mention threatening to jump off the Guijiang Hotel.

I rode my bike to Zhang Nao's dormitory. After she let me in, I laid out the divorce agreement on her desk and asked: "Are you finally going to sign it?"

She was standing over her ironing board. She looked up, brandishing the iron: "You think I'm going to just sign it? You called me a slut: that's one year. You hit me: two years. You told Xiao Chi about me and Yu Baijia: three years. You wouldn't tell them you were my husband at the hotel: five years. That adds up to eleven years."

"I thought you were waiting for Yu Baijia. He's already divorced his wife."

"You underestimate me, Ceng Guangxian. You think I want to marry Yu Baijia?"

"Then why did you sleep with him?"

"Two different things. Who says I have to marry everyone I sleep with? I only have one husband—that's you."

"I've never even slept with you. How can you call me your husband?"

"What's stopping you? You have the right to sleep with me, don't you? Come on." She lifted up her shirt.

"I wouldn't so much as touch you."

"If you won't even sleep with me, don't blame me."

"What's the real reason you won't divorce me? You don't love me. Why not put an end to this?"

"Go ask the Women's Federation. Go ask the United Nations. Ask them why I won't let you go."

I had no idea what the hell she was talking about. I decided to go find Zhao Wannian at the factory and ask him. He said: "I'd have an easier time with Goldbach's conjecture. Might as well go ask Chen Jingrun." That wasn't much help, either. I knew I'd have to take matters into my own hands.

That night, July 15th, I went out and had a few drinks and then went to Zhang Nao's dormitory. Stinking of liquor and cigarettes, I kicked off my shoes in her doorway and sat down on her bed. I said: "From now on, I'm sleeping here."

Zhang Nao got undressed and got into bed. "Get under the covers. Come over here. Show me how much you want to divorce me." I turned away, and she stretched out a leg. She moved under the covers. I looked over at her. I was her lawful husband, wasn't I? There was nothing wrong with looking. I slowly lowered myself to the bed, moving like a sick animal. Why didn't I just do it? I didn't want to be a cuck. I didn't want to grow old with a woman like Zhang Nao. Zhao Shanhe had told me that marrying a woman like Zhang Nao would be an insult to my ancestors, and more importantly, she had told me that if a couple didn't consummate their marriage within two years, there was a good chance that a court would allow a divorce even if one party didn't sign an agreement. I was four months away from that two-year anniversary. I knew I'd regret it if I slept with her.

I wanted to torture Zhang Nao. I slipped down to the floor and lay there. I smoked two pack of cigarettes, letting the ashes fall around me.

She was unexpectedly tranquil in the morning: she got up and cooked a bowl of noodles for me and swept up the ashes.

I tossed my clothes on the floor, and she picked them up, cleaned them, and hung them up to dry. After breakfast, I began drinking beer, rolling the bottles across the floor. She got a cardboard box and began to collect them. I said: "I don't want to sleep on the floor tonight."

"You don't have to. Take the bed. I'm going away on business for a couple weeks. I'll leave a key for you."

I went to bed that night wearing my work clothes. Her smell was still on everything, though. I finally tossed the pillow to the floor and found a floral dress on the bed. I rubbed the dress on my balls and then jerked off on it. No matter how patient she was, that would have to upset her.

One day I got word that Director Pang wanted to see me. Remember him? He was the boss at my father's factory. I thought he was going to offer me a job. Before I went into his office, I checked that my fly was up and reminded myself not to mention my temporary job packing orders.

Director Pang was a big man, with a jiggling double chin and a bald head. Behind him, on a shelf, were the products made by the factory, ranging from early tabletop radio receivers to modern wireless sets. I said: "You might have heard about that letter of employment I showed my father, but it was only to comfort him. I'm unemployed. I would never do anything like that again."

Director Pang looked at me closely. It felt like I was being X-rayed. He held out a cigarette: "You smoke?" My throat felt dry and I was frozen in place, so I only shook my head, and he put the cigarette to his lips and lit it. "I didn't call you here to offer you a job. I have some news for you."

"What is it?"

"Something very important has come up. But I'm worried that your father couldn't take it. I thought I should let you know first."

"You know about my dad and Zhao Shanhe?"

Director Pang squinted: "What about them?"

"Nothing, nothing."

Director Pang blew a cloud of smoke. It seemed like he wasn't willing to tell me. Maybe he wanted to stall. The office was quiet. I could hear a clock ticking somewhere behind me.

"You wore those shoes to my office? I want you to go get a new pair tomorrow, something leather."

"How am I going to afford that?"

"You'll afford it. I never thought I'd see someone like you, the son of a filthy capitalist family, a scion of the landlord class, get everything back."

He was trying hard to display no emotion, but cracks were showing. I studied his face. There was almost a smile. "Tiema District got me on the phone yesterday. They want your father to go down to their offices."

"For the study sessions? What did he do this time?"

"This time, nothing. In the future, it's hard to say. It seems they want him to come fill out some paperwork."

"What kind of paperwork?"

He coughed. He wanted to draw it out as long as he could. He said: "The government wants to 'rectify mistaken judgments.' One of those judgments involves confiscated property. To put it in simpler terms, your family is getting the warehouse back. I went there about ten years ago for a struggle session. Good location. I'd guess it's worth about two million yuan now, probably more. That's not even counting the building itself. The lumber alone is worth a fortune. So there you go. You can go back to being capitalists. Don't worry about affording a new pair of shoes. You can buy enough to last two lifetimes."

"Are you serious?"

"Do you think I have the time to jerk you around?"

I felt my body go slack. It felt like my insides were slowly thawing. I stood up and smacked my head on a bare bulb hanging in the center of the office. The bulb swung and then fell to the floor.

"Look at you. You spent all that time locked up, so I assume you have a bit of ice in your veins. Your father, though, this might kill him."

I went out of the office, not forgetting to call out, "Thank you!" as I left. I felt like I was walking on air. I wasn't walking; I was floating over the pavement. I went to the bus stop, and the bus came and went and I didn't get on. I decided to walk over to Zhao Shanhe's place. I wanted a chance to think on the way there. A few people said hello to me on the street or waved to me. I mumbled back and waved, but it was almost like I hadn't seen them. One of them was Liu Canghai, and then I saw Zhao Shanhe. Right, that's who I was going to see. But I walked right by her. I had to jog back to find her.

Listen, get another bottle of something. Whatever you want, order it. I just told you: I inherited a warehouse worth two million yuan. What do I care about a bottle? How about cigarettes? Order another couple packs. You're enjoying the story? Good, good. As long as you're enjoying it, I'll keep going. You're an excellent audience. I've said it before, but it's true. I've tried to tell these stories before, and usually I get about halfway through and they already have their phones out. They never want to hear the ending. They come up with an excuse to leave. You know what they want to do? Go out and gamble, find a girl. I never thought I'd find someone like you, especially at Shakespeare's Sauna. No offense meant— you're a diamond in the rough.

Zhao Shanhe and I walked together to the warehouse. We went up to the loft, and she lay on the floor, looking down into the warehouse. I told her that it was coming back to the Ceng family. I smoked three cigarettes, and she lay without moving. After a while, she stood and wiped her eyes. "I never thought it could happen. After so long, we'll be back in the warehouse. If I can get Lao Dong to finally agree . . . I got him to sign the agreement, but he tore it up. I've argued with him about it so many times. He still won't sign. But I know I can get him to agree. I will marry your father, so everything will be legal. We'll move back in here. We'll all live here. One bedroom for you, and one for us. We'll have the kitchen over there. A living room, too. We'll have the biggest house in town."

"I don't want to have to walk a block to use the bathroom."

"Don't be silly. Every bedroom will have a bathroom attached."

"Why not just rent it out? We can collect a couple thousand a month. We can live in hotel suites, just live off the rent. If we get hungry, some- one will cook for us. When our clothes are dirty, we'll buy new ones. Someone will clean the place every day. Dad can retire. I can take over."

"Take over? With the money we're going to make, you'll never have to work. Even if we just sold the building and the land, we'd have enough for the rest of our lives. We couldn't spend it all."

"Let's buy a house."

‹ 30 ›

"You could buy a whole building."

Back then it was different, I keep telling you. Coming up with something to spend two million yuan on wasn't easy. Nowadays you'd spend it on cars, a villa, but back then, just getting a phone line installed was a luxury. Two million went a lot further, too. We wanted to fly to Beijing, go to Tibet, pay Zhao Shanhe's parents as housekeepers again, help out Lu Xiaoyan, hire a xiangsheng performer for my father . . . We still weren't anywhere close to two million.

Zhao Shanhe told me to set aside a hundred thousand yuan to pay for a mistress. We argued over that for a while, and then a thought came to me: "We can't spend it all. We have to save my sister's share."

"Poor Ceng Fang. I wish I knew where she was. We might never know what happened to her."

"I know she's still out there. I know she'll be back."

"We'll hold on to her share. The only way we'll ever spend this money is if you give your father some grandkids. Maybe your kids' kids will be able to spend it someday."

I reminded Zhao Shanhe: "What about the money for Zhang Nao?"

"Money for Zhang Nao? Why?"

"That's the law. The husband and wife have to divide their property."

"No wonder she married you. This must have been her plan all along. We have to be careful. I need to treat my issue with Lao Dong with care, too."

I had finally figured it out: she wanted a piece of the warehouse. My mind went blank. Zhao Shanhe patted my cheek: "You still there?" She finally slapped me. I collapsed onto my bed.

When I'd recovered, I went straight to Zhang Nao's dormitory and packed up my things. I made sure there wasn't a single cigarette butt left. I started to wonder, though, if maybe I was wrong for suspecting her of using me for my money. I mean, I didn't have any money yet, and how could she know that the warehouse was going to come back to my family? But as I said before: once bitten . . . I didn't want to take any chances. I packed my bags and ran, scattering socks and cigarette lighters as I went.

The next day, I went down to the office of Director Liang. She looked up at me: "So, you're Ceng Guangxian?" I nodded.

"Do you know my name?"

"Director Liang."

"Call me Auntie."

I rubbed my head.

"Zhang Nao didn't tell you? I'm her aunt!"

I said: "Oh," and my mouth stayed open in that shape for a long time. I had wondered if I was wrong to suspect Zhang Nao, but she had beaten me again. The entire time we were together, her aunt had been sitting below me in her office at the warehouse.

"As you may know, other jurisdictions returned expropriated property years ago. We've taken a little longer. But that's neither here nor there. Your possessions will be returned to you in due time. I told Naonao that when you two are spending all that money, don't forget your Auntie." Director Liang launched into a long lecture about the formalities of the handover, and I was given two forms to fill out.

I took the forms back up to the loft, where Zhao Shanhe was waiting. We agreed that we had to have my father's name on all the documents. If my name was mentioned anywhere, Zhang Nao would have the legal right to take a share. But how would we tell my father? I didn't want to risk his health over a piece of paper. Zhao Shanhe and I paced the floor of the loft. Finally, she said: "I've got it. Give me some time. Don't worry about his heart. He'll be singing Russian folk songs after I tell him."

Zhao Shanhe decided that my father needed to be in the best mood possible before hearing any news. She arranged to meet him at the factory dormitory, but their date was disrupted by the arrival of Lao Dong. They moved to the warehouse loft instead. I was ordered to stay outside, ostensibly to watch for Lao Dong, but really just so I'd be out of the way. I heard the floor creaking inside and the muffled moans of Zhao Shanhe—it wasn't hard to figure out what was going on. When I went back in, their clothes were disheveled. Their hair, though, was slicked down as if it had been combed. I mean, I don't know exactly what they were doing in there, but it was more than a casual talk.

Things went on like that for a while, with me watching the door while Zhao Shanhe and my father went into the loft together. When they were done, I could never look them in the eye. I watched Zhao Shanhe's purse, which she kept under her arm. One time when I walked her out, she reached into her purse and tried to slip me a few bills. It was like a mom rewarding her spoiled kid for being good. I slapped the bills out of her hand. She thought I had to be bought off, I guess. She thought she owed me something. I knew she was trying her best to break the news about the warehouse to my father. But part of why I was willing to stand guard was that I wanted to make it up to the two of them for telling Zhao Wannian that they were sleeping together when we were all living in the warehouse.

Altogether, I stood guard nine times. So she had at least nine occasions on which she could have told my father about the factory. That's not including the other times they met without telling me. After about six months, she still hadn't told him. I don't know, maybe she didn't actually care about all that money we'd talked about spending. I heard a lot of moaning through the loft door, but I didn't hear any frank conversations about the return of expropriated properties. The tenth time they met, I let my father go down the ladder first and asked Zhao Shanhe: "Why not just tell him already?"

"You want to kill him? Look at him. You see his red cheeks? That's a sign of heart disease. Have you ever heard of cerebral hemorrhage? His health is only getting worse. I've tried to tell him. I've been this close to saying it, but I can't do it. You know, even good news could shake him."

"What about the warehouse?"

"I want him to live." She took the forms out of her purse and handed them to me. "Put your own name on them. I don't even want him to know about it."

"You want Zhang Nao to take half of it?"

"It's been two years, hasn't it? Go get the divorce."

I smacked myself: "That's right!"

I waited outside Dormitory 5 at Lingnan University for two nights before I managed to catch Zhang Du, the famous professor and attorney. After I told him my story, he tapped his chest: "Lots of these lawsuits, once they hear I'm involved, their lawyers will go for a settlement without even meeting me. This Zhang Nao doesn't sound like she stands much of a chance." He led me into his dormitory.

"I just need you to get her to agree to a divorce. Cost is not an issue." His gaze went down my body and settled on my filthy sneakers. I knew what he was thinking. I shifted on the sofa.

"I assume Rong Guangming told you what I charge." He held up five fingers: "That's what I need. If not, I'm afraid I can't waste my time."

"Five thousand? If you take care of it like you say you can, I'll give you ten."

He raised an eyebrow and looked me over again. He wasn't convinced. I took out the forms and explained the return of the warehouse to my family. I told him that money wasn't a concern. He blinked twice and said: "I didn't know I was dealing with a landlord. I guess you can't judge a book by its cover. But rules are rules: I need a deposit. Let's say two thousand." I shifted back and forth on the sofa, as if I could squirm out a solution to the two thousand. But he hadn't become a famous lawyer by not noticing these kinds of things. He said: "That's fine. Let's sign a contract. I won't take a deposit, but the final price will be a bit higher than usual."

"As long as the warehouse comes back to me, price isn't an issue. If you can get me a divorce, I'll give you twenty thousand."

He took little sips of tea, about fifteen in all. From his briefcase, he took a sheet of paper and jotted down a contract, specifying time and payment. I took the pen he offered and added a sentence: "Payment depends on securing a divorce."

He chuckled and took a newspaper from his briefcase: "Have a look at this. My last lawsuit, the complainant was dead for ten years. I still won the case for her." I took the paper and scanned the article. I turned back to the contract and signed my name. I took my copy of the contract and went back home. I kept my hand on the paper the whole way. I didn't want to lose it like I'd lost my letter of redress.

I locked the contract in a box. Every night when I came home from work, the first thing I would do is take it out of the box and read it aloud, passionately, as if it were Gorky's "The Song of the Stormy Petrel."

Ten days later, Zhang Du arrived at my loft with his copy of the contract. He handed it to me and said: "Things are more complicated than you let on. I want to strangle this Zhang Nao."

"What do you mean?"

"Tell me the truth: did you sleep with her?"

"I swear I didn't."

"She presented your pubic hair as evidence. I challenged her on that, but then she came out with a dress that appears to have your semen all over it. I might be a famous lawyer, but I can't really argue against physical evidence like that."

I was about to slap myself. I let my hands fall to my side. You know how many times I had slapped myself? Enough times that I should have smacked some sense into myself. You probably remember that night in her dormitory room. I slept in her bed, hoping she'd get sick of me. I wanted to disgust her. I never thought I'd end up talking to a lawyer about it. I slapped myself hard on the cheek and walked out of the loft. Zhang Du called after me: "Where are you going? You don't even have to pay me. Don't run away."

I got on my bike and rode over to Zhang Nao's dormitory. I used my key to open the door and began searching the room. I tossed all of her expensive dresses on the floor and dug through the back of her closet. I found nothing but a stack of bills. I tossed the money on her dressing table and began looking through the drawers. A slip of paper tumbled onto the floor, and I bent to pick it up. In Zhang Nao's handwriting it read: "I thought you might come looking for my evidence. You're too late. I've put the evidence in the safest place possible." I jumped onto the bed and began kicking and stamping, tearing down the mosquito net and trampling it. I ripped through the apartment until I was sweating. I went out of the dormitory room cursing Zhang Nao's name.

I went straight to my father's house. It was early in the morning, and the sound of my knock echoed loud in my ears. After a long time, my father opened the door and stuck his head out. He didn't say anything but simply stared at me. I pushed past him. Zhao Shanhe was in bed, buttoning up her shirt. She said: "I was worried about him. I thought I should spend the night." I knew they must be living together. Why wasn't she worried about Lao Dong? They had probably already divorced. I turned my back and waited for her to get dressed.

"We have to tell him. There's no time. Zhang Nao has a plan. My name can't be on the documents."

Zhao Shanhe blinked and then glanced at my father: "Are you okay, Changfeng?"

My father sat down on the bed: "Why wouldn't I be?"

Zhao Shanhe said: "I think we should step outside for a moment, Guangxian."

I looked over at my father. There was so much I wanted to say. Zhao Shanhe was pulling at my arm. I said: "Dad . . ." She pulled hard on my arm.

I said: "He's fine. Just look at him."

My father said: "Shanhe, let him talk. What's with all this sneaking around?"

I shook off her hand: "He said he's fine. Let me say it."

"It's nothing, Changfeng. Don't worry about it." Zhao Shanhe dug her fingernails into my arm and pulled me toward the door again.

My father said: "Stop that. This is worse than anything you could say."

Zhao Shanhe let me go. I said: "It's actually good news. I'm going to tell you, but if you start to feel unwell, just hold up your hand and I'll stop." He nodded. I coughed and started to tell him about the warehouse being returned to the family. He never held up his hand. He actually seemed to brighten somewhat.

My father said: "They're finally giving me justice, Shanhe."

My father slapped his thigh and stood. I took out the forms. He found a pen and spread the documents out on his desk. "Shanhe, this is good news. Why didn't you tell me? Let's go deal with this tomorrow."

She and I looked at each other and nodded.

Zhao Shanhe told me later that the day he signed the documents, he pulled her into bed and didn't stop until dawn. He was like an eighteen-year-old kid again, not a man in his fifties.

The next morning, my father rushed to the warehouse before the sun had risen. There was still a lock on the door. He walked around the yard, looking up at the trees growing around the building. There was no traffic on the road. The only sound was the scrape of a branch broom on pavement. My father pointed at one of the trees: "Shanhe, you see that tree? We hung those dogs up there. Remember that?" Zhao Shanhe shook her head.

"How could you forget that? They were mating in the yard. Your brother came along and wanted to have a struggle session for them."

"I remember now. You used one of the bamboo mats. Got it all covered in dog hair."

"You wanted me to buy you a new mat. You ended up ripping my sleeve."

Zhao Shanhe giggled. "That night I went to go to the bathroom, and you were waiting at the door. I don't know how you worked up the nerve. You put your arms around me and . . ."

"It was those two dogs. They got me thinking. That's what I was doing sitting out there."

"I slapped you. Remember that?"

Zhao Shanhe playfully slapped my father's cheek. He turned and sat down on the ground. It was like watching an actor slipping back into a favorite role. Zhao Shanhe reached down to tickle him, but he didn't react. She said: "Come on, get up. You'll get your pants dirty." My father seemed not to hear. He slumped to lie on the ground. Zhao Shanhe called over to me: "Something's wrong with him, Guangxian."

When we got my father to the hospital, the doctors and nurses surrounded him, sticking tubes in him and pulling open his clothes. In the quiet of the hospital room, Zhao Shanhe said: "I told you not to tell him. You wouldn't listen. Now look what you did."

"He was fine last night."

"The doctor said the symptoms might take a day or two to show up."

"I won't talk about it again."

"You can't take it back now. Your mouth got you in trouble again."

"Just staple it shut."

Zhao Shanhe sighed: "I just hope it's nothing too serious with your father."

One night, Lao Dong came to the hospital. He hadn't just rushed over there; he had carefully considered the visit. But I didn't know that then. He sat beside Zhao Shanhe. He looked at the floor and said: "Shanhe, I didn't want to let you go. I realized that I was being cruel." He gestured toward my father: "Do you really want to marry him?"

Zhao Shanhe turned to Lao Dong: "Of course I do."

"You really love him?"

"What are you talking about? You think I still love you?"

"Then I want to help you." He took out the divorce agreement, which was already signed.

Zhao Shanhe and Lao Dong went to the Bureau of Civil Affairs to complete the divorce. That night, she went back to the hospital and laid the divorce certificate on my father's pillow: "Changfeng, I finally got it. I wish he'd come to his senses sooner—Guangxian would already have a brother. I gave that man the best years of my life. I was beautiful. I was young. Twenty years I gave him. Changfeng, can you hear me? If you can hear me, nod your head. When you get out of here, we can get married."

Zhao Shanhe wiped her tears away and wiped her wet hands on the bed sheets. My father didn't nod his head. Whether he could hear her or not, I don't know. After ten days, the doctor called us into his office and told us that my dad would probably never wake up. The doctor said that he couldn't breathe on his own anymore. He would never move. The speech and language centers in his brain were dead. There was no conclusion to my father's story that could have shocked me more. Zhao Shanhe and I didn't cry. The doctor left the room, and we sat in silence for a while, then walked back to my father's bedside. As soon as she saw him lying in the bed, Zhao Shanhe turned away. From another bed, she grabbed a pillow and began to hit me with it, over and over again, until the cotton stuffing floated around the room.

"It's all your fault: if you hadn't told your mother about the two of us, I wouldn't have married that man, and if I hadn't married that man, I wouldn't have had to be kicked and punched every day, and I would have a kid now. I told you not to tell your father about the warehouse. You wouldn't listen. You turned him into this! Are you happy? Huh?"

She swung the pillow until it was empty, screaming at me the whole time: "You don't want to talk now? I went through so much to get here—and this is how it's going to end?" She finally collapsed beside the bed. I brought her a hand towel to wipe her face, but she knocked it out of my hand. I wiped my own face and bent down to sweep up the cotton stuffing. I worked at cramming it back through the holes in the pillow.

Zhao Shanhe left the room, and I went to my father. I held his head in my hands: "Wake up, Dad. Please wake up. You can't sleep in. You always told me that. Dad, there's going to be a big meeting at work today! That used to—remember? When you heard there was a big meeting, you'd jump out of bed, even when it was the middle of winter. Please, please wake up." My father didn't respond. His face was frozen, as if cast in rubber. I shook him. I dug my nails hard into his ear. I bent down and bit his arm. He didn't cry out. He was motionless. "If I'd known this was going to happen, I never would have told you about the warehouse. I should have listened to her. I know it's my fault. If you don't wake up, I don't think I could take that, the responsibility for leaving you like this. Please . . ."

I slapped myself hard across the face with my right hand and then with my left. The sound was clear and loud. I felt Zhao Shanhe's hand on my arm then: "Stop it! You're going to end up like him, hitting yourself like that."

I shook her off and hit myself hard again. I wanted her to see, even if my father couldn't. I wanted her to know how much I regretted everything. She reached for me again, but her hand froze halfway. She stood still for a moment and then slapped her own cheek: "You think you're the only one who feels that way?" She turned away from me. She said: "You know why Lao Dong suddenly came to grant me the mercy of signing that divorce paper? He came a few times before that and went to the doctors to find out your father's condition. He planned it. He only agreed to the divorce when he knew that your father would never leave the hospital. If I'd known that, I never would have let him go. I would have been like an anchor around his neck."

While my father was in the hospital, Director Pang took me to the factory and let me work in my dad's place. My job was to sit beside the assembly line and take the half-finished radios off the line. After I installed the speaker component, the radio was moved to the next station. I could do the job, but sitting on my father's stool would never be comfortable. I switched stools with the person next to me and felt a bit better. The feeling of regret was too strong for me to sit on my father's stool. It was my fault that he was in the hospital. It was my fault that the three of us would never live in the warehouse.

The factory assigned new housing that could accommodate my father and me, but the bedroom was always damp, which wasn't good for someone confined to a bed. After I moved in, I went out and bought a roast duck, some pig's-head meat, and two bottles of erguotou and brought them to Lao Yang, the man who stood guard over the construction site beside the warehouse. After a big meal and a few drinks, I asked about maybe borrowing some steel from the worksite, and he waved me over to a pile of reinforcement bars. I dragged them back to the new house. I set about fabricating a bed for my father with the steel bars and a welder borrowed from the factory. The bed could be raised and lowered, and there were hooks to hang an IV bag and spaces to put a bedpan and a heater and a radio. The bed could be stripped and used when we bathed him, too. It was quite impressive. I should have applied for a patent on it. But I was only thinking about making my father as comfortable as possible. The more comfortable he was, the less regret I felt over causing him to be in that condition.

After the bed was finished, my father could have come back, but Zhao Shanhe wanted to wait. She took me to the bank one afternoon. She said: "There's no reason to keep all of our old stuff. A new house needs new furniture." She clutched the bank book tightly, crumpling it. "We're going to be coming into some money. We don't have to live like poor people anymore. Two million yuan—that's what's coming, right?" I protested, but she was set on the plan. She smoothed out the bank book and went into the bank.

Once the house was finished and everything had been moved in, Uncle Zhao helped us bring my father home from the hospital. My dad would sleep on his bed, and Zhao Shanhe would sleep on a bed beside him. My bedroom had a double bed and was decorated in bright red, like the bedroom of a just-married couple—there was something missing from the scene, though.

I thought about Zhang Nao. Wrapped in that red blanket, my head on a red pillow, I thought about the way she had decorated the dormitory room after we'd gotten married. I couldn't help but wonder about her. Maybe I'd been wrong all along, I thought. Maybe she wasn't as bad as I imagined. If I'd married Xiao Chi or Lu Xiaoyan, I could have ended up in the same situation. My wife was entitled to a share of my money. Zhang Nao liked designer dresses and shoes, she bought expensive makeup, so it made sense that she'd want a cut of the money, but it would be unnatural to not want anything, right? Anyways, if I was so rich, if I was sitting on property worth two million, what was the point of trying to keep her from getting a share? I had already decided that there was no way I'd ever spend that much money in my lifetime. Another way of looking at it was: no matter how much money I had, would my life really change for the better? Money couldn't change what had happened to my father. Money wasn't what I needed—I needed a woman to share that double bed with me. I didn't want to sleep alone in a big bed. Things had changed. It was the 1980s. Even old Wang Zhiqi at the factory had started buying his girls popsicles and lipstick. There's no such thing as pure love, is there? If I could trade half of the warehouse for a life with Zhang Nao, growing old together—wouldn't it be worth it?

Late that night, when I heard Zhao Shanhe dumping my father's bedpan, I got out of bed and went to her. I told her everything I'd been thinking. She pointed at me: "In your thirties and still acting like a little kid. You know why I decorated the room like that? I want you to hurry up and get a divorce, bring Xiaoyan back, give your father some grandkids. You're talking about that bitch again. You're a disgrace."

If Zhao Shanhe hadn't reminded me, I would have forgotten all about Xiaoyan. That's the way people are, I guess: if someone wrongs you, you will never forget them, but if they help you, it's easy to forget about them. On the twelfth of the month, I went to the bank and took out three months' salary. I went to the department store and bought a pair of designer shoes like Zhang Nao wore and a mohair sweater with a cowl neck. I took the shoes and the sweater to Xiaoyan, along with a bag of apples. It was a lot of money, but I was counting on the profits from the warehouse coming to me soon. It was tough to work up the nerve to see her, since she'd given me one month to divorce Zhang Nao, and two years had already gone by. Would she be upset? Would she act like Xiao Chi and threaten to kill herself? On the way I bought two packets of tissue, just in case she cried. I was ready, I thought. I got on my bike and pedaled even faster.

Before I arrived at her dormitory, I heard the sound of music, some-one—clearly not a professional—playing an accordion. When I got to her door, I looked in and saw that Hu Kaihui was the player. He had an accordion strapped across his belly. He was squeezing out the melody to "My Chinese Heart," while Xiaoyan watched and hummed along. They looked up at me but didn't miss a beat. When the song ended, Xiaoyan said: "Kaihui is learning to play this thing. We want our child to learn music. English, too. Kaihui and I have learned a few phrases." I'd had no idea. They were already married. Xiaoyan was already pregnant. I gave her the gifts, and she slipped on the shoes and put on the sweater. She did a few spins and asked us how she looked. Kaihui nodded. I nodded. She said: "Thank you."

"Why didn't you tell me? I should have been at your wedding."

"There was no time. Once I found out she was pregnant, we went and got married right away. Under the circumstances, it would have been a bit strange to have a wedding."

Hu Kaihui tried to pretend that nothing was unusual about this meeting. He excused himself to go to the kitchen and came back with a plate of steamed eggs and another of fried peanuts. He set the dishes on the table, along with two bottles of erguotou. Hu Kaihui and I began to drink, talk-ing about the old days, our old comrades like He Caixia and Zhao Jingdong and Director He, and then about politics. Xiaoyan sat beside us, not say-ing anything. She finally interrupted to say: "What about Zhang Nao? She must be pregnant, too?" She looked awfully pleased with herself.

I said: "Sure is. Probably going to be a boy. The doctor said since both the parents are so good-looking, the kid will probably end up being a model."

Xiaoyan said: "Really? Have you heard about prenatal education? That's what we've been doing, playing music, the English phrases . . . That's how you get them into a good school."

I managed to fake a smile, but I felt sick to my stomach. If I had slept with her that night after coming back from Beishan, if I hadn't chosen Zhang Nao instead of her, the baby would be mine, not Kaihui's. I'd be the one sitting here playing "My Chinese Heart" for her. I drank to wipe out the sting of regret. I drank until my head was spinning and I felt my heart beating hard. I raised my glass: "Xiaoyan, Kaihui, you're just in time, you know that? Ten years ago, the two of you wouldn't have been able to do this. She gets pregnant before you're married . . . well, it didn't happen like that back then. We're in a new age. If things had been this liberal back then, your old friend Ceng Guangxian wouldn't have spent a decade locked up. I wouldn't have been afraid to fuck my own girlfriend . . ."

The last thing I remember was them muttering: "He's drunk, he's drunk." Everything went black after that. I woke up the next day on the floor of Zhang Nao's dormitory room. The key was still in my hand. There was a fresh pot of tea on the desk, and the calendar had been flipped over to the thirteenth of the month. It looked like Zhang Nao must have just left. Nothing looked out of place except the covers on the bed and the mosquito net, which she hadn't replaced. You remember, right? I tore up the place. I stamped all over the blanket. My footprints were still there. I tried to wipe them off, but it was no use. Eventually I took everything down to the cistern in the dormitory yard and washed it and hung it up to dry in her room. Before I left, I wrote a note for her: "I hope we can talk." I mean, Japan and China were finally negotiating, so why couldn't we?

The last person I expected to run into was Xiao Chi. Right as I was about to go, I heard a knock at the door. When I opened it, there she was. She said: "Do you know where Yu Baijia and Zhang Nao are?" I shook my head. "I do." She pulled me along behind her. I tried to check for signs of—I don't know, mental illness? But she looked okay. She was wearing a leather jacket zipped up to her chin and tight jeans. She looked fine.

She took me to the Guijiang Hotel, and as we rode the elevator up to the seventh floor, she said: "This is where they come. The four of us are going to sit down and work this out." I thought that was a pretty good idea. We marched out of the elevator toward room 703.

She banged on the door, and I heard the shriek of a woman from inside. Xiao Chi banged on the door again, and it opened a crack. A hand emerged and pushed her back into the hallway. I kicked the door and shouted inside: "What are you doing?"

The door opened a bit wider, and I saw a middle-aged man. He spoke with a Guangdong accent: "I could ask you the same thing, coming here, violating my privacy. That crazy bitch was here yesterday, too, banging on the door, scaring my girl."

Xiao Chi stood in the hallway, shivering. I finally realized that she was not well. I muttered an apology to the man in the room and pulled Xiao Chi toward the stairwell. She said: "They must have switched rooms! They were here before. Very strange." I knew what was happening. Remember the day that Zhang Nao and Yu Baijia were caught in the raid? They were in room 703 that day. That had been two years earlier. But it had stuck in her head that they were in that room. I should have realized it sooner. I could have saved us both the trouble.

‹32›

One weekend that spring, three trucks pulled up in front of the warehouse. Director Liang and the other office workers started packing up their desks. Workers came in and began to load up the desks and tables, and then they took down the wooden partitions between the offices and ripped out the telephone lines. There was a carpet of paper and ink bottles and cardboard leading to the trucks.

The workers climbed aboard the trucks. Director Liang and the bald man went last, pausing to take the sign off the warehouse door. Director Liang came over with a handful of keys and passed them to me: "The warehouse has been returned to you."

I said: "Thank you."

The trucks pulled away. As they drove into traffic, a gust of wind blew a trail of papers behind them and stirred the papers that had been dropped in the yard. I pocketed the keys and went into the warehouse. I found a fire smoldering in a corner and stamped it out. Scraps of paper still fluttered in the empty space. I saw my mother again and I saw Ceng Fang again, floating like the scraps of paper. I saw the dog that I named Xiao Chi fluttering among them. I cried and let my tears drop to the floor. I couldn't believe it: a man of my age, finally on the edge of a new life, crying like a lost child.

For the next few nights, I couldn't sleep. I felt hot, but when I opened the window, the sound of the traffic was too loud. When I threw off the blankets, I felt too cold. I tossed and turned. There was no shortage of reasons for my insomnia. I didn't want to sleep in that big bed all by myself. After work, I started going to the warehouse, sweeping up, tossing out the garbage that had collected there over the years. I took some tools and began tearing out the window frames and replacing them. I put new glass in the windows. I went around oiling hinges. The creaking doors and windows were now silent. The new window frames looked out of place in the warehouse now. I took some money out of my father's bank account and bought some green paint. I painted the door and window frames green. Everything finally looked about right.

The work in the warehouse had let me sleep at night, but now that it was over, I went back to tossing and turning. One night when I couldn't sleep, I decided to walk over to the warehouse. I unlocked the door and switched on the light. In a corner I saw a man and a woman, half naked and wrapped around each other. I covered my eyes and backed out. I switched off the light and waited beside the front door. After I had smoked three cigarettes and the couple still hadn't come out, I decided to go in and check on them. The warehouse was empty. At the back of the building, near the old stage, a window had been smashed out. They must have come in through the window—or at least they went out that way, without so much as a thank you. I had to clean up broken glass, too, and replace the pane. The next day, after I fixed the window, I set up a bed on the stage and slept there in the warehouse. I hadn't fallen asleep that quickly in years. I slept soundly.

When I woke up that morning, I saw that the window was broken again. On the windowsill was a zongzi, a parcel of sticky rice wrapped in reed leaves. There was a note on it that read: "Li San and Chuntao offer their sincerest apologies." I took the zongzi and turned, dancing across the stage, freezing and leaping, dropping down into splits—it wasn't great dancing, but I was full of joy: I had slept through the night for the first time in a long time. I hadn't even heard the window break. In the days before I rented out the warehouse, I slept on the stage every night.

One night Zhang Nao came to see me. She looked better than she ever had before—or at least different than before: her makeup was thicker, and her eyebrows were penciled in as thin lines; her clothes looked more expensive, her shoes were pointier, and she carried a new handbag in soft brown leather. She looked like one of the young capitalist ladies of the years before Liberation. She sat on a chair beside my bed. She crossed her legs. The foot that hung down swung back and forth. She looked over at the stage and then at me: "You said you wanted to talk. So let's talk." I walked around the warehouse, flicking on lights. I sat on the bed across from her. I didn't know how to start. She said: "Do you want to live with me, or do you want to give me half of this?"

"Can we not get a divorce?"

"You're the one who kept telling me to sign. Did you change your mind?"

"I want to be a father! I want someone to share my bed with. Look at this place. What am I going to do with it if it's just me alone?" I stood up and began to pace the stage. "If you decided to come back to me, we could forget about everything. Can you stop seeing Yu Baijia? If you can stop seeing him, I'll give you the key to the warehouse."

"Why not? If you had been this generous before, we could have already had kids by now."

She stood up and walked toward me. I met her. I stretched out my hand to take her hand, but I stopped. You might be thinking, she was my wife, so why couldn't I take her hand? I never felt like she was my wife. We had a marriage certificate—that was about it. I know nowadays you can sleep with a woman a hundred times and never get a marriage certificate. So what's the problem, right? But a marriage certificate was more important back then. But don't let me get off track here. We're getting there.

Zhang Nao said: "You can't bear to give me half, can you?"

I handed her the key: "You can't be with him anymore."

She laughed grimly: "Don't bother. You can't buy me off. What are you going to do? Change the locks tomorrow?"

I patted my chest: "You can trust me. I'll write up a contract. But you have to promise me that you won't be with him anymore."

"Write the contract. I swear, it's over with him."

I looked around for a sheet of paper and a pen but couldn't find one. I said: "Come over to our new house, and I'll write it for you. I want to show you the place, too. Zhao Shanhe got my room all set up for me. But it's empty. That first night when I slept there, I thought about you."

She laughed: "Are we in a play right now, Guangxian?"

"What do you mean?"

"We're standing on a stage!"

I jumped down from the stage and told her again: "Let's sign the contract. I missed you."

She pinched my cheek: "I never saw this side of you. I will move tomorrow. We'll start living together tomorrow. But don't forget our deal: half the warehouse."

I nodded. She turned and walked out the door. For an instant I pictured a snake wriggling down a hole.

The next day she came to the new house just as she'd promised. She came in and saw my father lying on the bed I'd made for him. She went into my bedroom without saying anything. She sat down on a chair in the room and took out a gold-plated lighter. Her thumb flicked open the cover of the lighter and flicked it back down. The sound of the lighter flicking open and shut filled the silent house. I looked at her hands as they worked the cover. I wondered about a ring, but I suddenly noticed a band of gold already on her left ring finger. It was bright gold. I laid out a sheet of paper on the bed and wrote out the contract. The contract basically said that she was entitled to half of the warehouse as long as she lived with me as my wife. I took out the red ink pad and put my fingerprint at the bottom and signed my name over it. She took the contract from me and said: "Your father's really sick, huh? It must be hard for you to give up half the warehouse."

"You're my last hope. Xiao Chi's out of her mind. Xiaoyan is already married, about to have a kid. What do I need with a warehouse if I don't even have a wife?" I took off my clothes and got into bed. "What are you waiting for? I'm sure our kid will be better-looking than Xiaoyan's."

She took out a long, thin cigarette, put it to her lips, and lit it. She sat and smoked, playing with the lighter. It was like she was testing my patience. I thought: after so many years, what's a little while longer? It had been so long already. The cigarette burned down, and the ash still hung from the tip. I thought maybe she was embarrassed. I reached over and switched off the light. I watched the glow of her cigarette in the dark until it finally disappeared. The sound of the lighter opening and closing was the only thing that broke the silence. Maybe she was on her period? I tried to think of some reason why she wasn't getting into bed.

Her voice filled the silence: "You know how much this lighter cost?"

"I'd guess at least fifty."

"Fifty? Try twenty times that."

"Twenty times that? That's almost what I make in a whole year."

"It's normal. This bag was two thousand. A friend brought it back to me from Hong Kong."

"So you're doing okay?"

"Have you ever seen Zhu Jianhua, the high jumper? That's what my life's been like the past couple years: I've cleared the bar. So the warehouse, I'm not saying it's meaningless, but I finally realized there's more to live for than money. I need to move on."

I reached up to turn on the light again. I wanted to see who was in the room with me—it couldn't be the woman who had lied to me all those years about a divorce, who had played a long con in order to get half of the warehouse. Before the light came on, the room was already lit up by Zhang Nao's lighter. She held the contract over the flame and ignited it. The paper was reduced to ash.

"I don't want the warehouse. I'm not a thief. I'm asking for a hundred thousand yuan. Whenever you're ready to divorce, let me know. That way, neither of us owes anything to the other."

Why had she waited until the very moment that I didn't want to divorce her? Why had she waited until I was naked, waiting for her in my bed? Why was she only asking for a hundred thousand? I rolled out of bed and grabbed my pants. They weren't even all the way up before she was out the door. I got back into bed and stared at the ceiling. Half of the warehouse would have been worth at least a million yuan, and yet she turned it down. She said she wanted to move on, but I guess getting back with me wouldn't have been a move in the right direction. I wondered what would have happened if I hadn't seen Yu Baijia going out the window—or maybe if I hadn't argued with her about it, if I had just gone right to the messy bed with her. Years later, when she'd already had my child, would we have found ourselves in this same situation? I regretted not being able to find out. I regretted giving her another opportunity to humiliate me. In the end, I had been nothing but proof. Burning the contract had been her way of proving to herself that she didn't care about money. She was proving to herself that she was better than me. She had made it over the bar, like she'd said. I lay in bed until early morning and didn't bother going to work. Zhao Shanhe finally came into my room and ordered me out. I sat up and dragged myself to the door.

I went straight to Zhang Nao's dormitory room and found her giving herself a facial. I pushed open the door and dragged her onto the bed. I tore at her clothes and yanked down her pants. I wanted to take what was rightfully mine. She screamed. She bit me and kicked my arms. I kept tearing at her clothes. She suddenly stuck out her tongue. It was shocking, that bright red tongue and her face covered in white cream. I staggered back, and she twisted away from me. She ran and picked up a kitchen knife: "Stay away from me!"

"It's not fair. Your own husband can't have you, but all these other men can."

"You could have. Now you're here attacking me. But you could have had me a long time ago."

"What do I have to do? I married you. Now you're asking me for a hundred thousand."

"If I hadn't burned that contract, it would be a lot more than a hundred thousand."

"I'm not giving you anything."

"That's fine—be a cuck all your life, die without ever having a son, go ahead. I'm going to move on with my life."

"Back when Xiaoyan told me that I had one month, you wouldn't give me a divorce. Now she's about to have a kid. It could have been my son. You make no fucking sense." I picked up the dressing table stool and smashed it down on the dressing table. The mirror shattered.

"If you wanted her so bad, why didn't you marry her as soon as you got out of Beishan?"

One Monday I was cleaning the windows of the warehouse when Yu Baijia arrived carrying a leather briefcase. I tossed the rag in the bucket, splashing the case with grimy water. He shook a few drops off it and set it down. It flew open, and I saw that it was full of bills. I looked up at him: "Did you rob a bank or something?" I had never seen that much money in one place in my whole life.

He said: "I want to rent the warehouse. There's fifty thousand here. At the end of the year, I'll give you another fifty."

"You stole my wife. I'm not doing business with you."

"I didn't know she was your wife. I mean, back then I had no idea. If I had, I never would have done it."

"Cut the bullshit. You found out she was my wife and kept going. You knew it when you went to that hotel together."

"If you hadn't run to Chi Fengxian to tell her about me and Zhang Nao, she would still be okay. You know what she does all day? Chases me all around the city—chases ghosts, knocking on hotel doors. She spends her days looking for someone who isn't there. That's your fault."

"You had a part in it."

"If you hadn't told her, she never would have known. You don't think couples have problems? They get through them by keeping their mouths shut, suppressing things."

"Then why did you do it?"

"She's fucking that lawyer now. Why don't you go tell everyone about that?"

"Wait, who?"

"That son of a bitch you hired to get you a divorce, Zhang Du."

"I set the two of them up, I guess." I slapped myself across the face. "No wonder she didn't care when I told her to swear she wouldn't get back together with you—she was already fucking a new guy."

‹ 33 ›

"It's nothing to her. That's how it works these days." He pointed down at the briefcase. "Take this and buy ten new Zhang Naos. It's that easy. Sit down and count it if you don't believe it's all there. This stuff is addictive, though. Be careful."

I counted the bills in the briefcase. All those bills and not a single one missing, not a single one extra: fifty thousand yuan. I shut the case, but I didn't want to give it back. I told him to show me the contract. I put a fingerprint and a signature on it. We agreed to a rental period of five years, a hundred thousand a year, to be paid twice a year. I'd stand to make five hundred thousand over the next five years. I took the briefcase home and slept with it under my bed for a week. I didn't want to take it to the bank.

Yu Baijia took over the warehouse and completely renovated it, adding a new tile floor and a drop ceiling, and dividing the large space into rooms. He installed the plumbing for showers and steam rooms. Out front, he hung a bright sign that read Baijia Massage. I'm not sure "bright" is the right word. The lights he installed in the sign were enough to blind you. The massage girls he hired were the best I've ever seen. Every afternoon around five o'clock, he'd have them lined up out front. Their boss, a girl just a bit older than them, would deliver a daily lecture, and then they'd march with military precision into the warehouse. That was the first massage place in the city. Shakespeare's Sauna wasn't around back then. Every night there was a line of cars waiting out front. The two big doormen would be out front directing traffic. You could tell from the cars and the license plates that these were important men. You can guess what kind of guys were coming.

I used to go up to the loft, but the new ceiling blocked my view. I could guess what was happening, though, based on the sounds from below. I heard the sound of bodies being smacked and kneaded, men grunting, women moaning . . . When I went home at night, I'd tell Zhao Shanhe what I'd heard. She said: "When we get the money together, you should go get a massage, too. Maybe your dad, too? That might bring him around."

We already had the money, actually. That first year, Yu Baijia brought me another fifty thousand. I had a hundred thousand in the bank. The next spring, I had a hundred fifty thousand. By the end of the year, there was two hundred thousand in the account. The money felt like a pistol on my hip. There was nothing I couldn't do. I liked going to watch the supervisor lead the girls in their afternoon formation. The only comparison was to a sergeant surveying troops. She was always deadly serious, pacing the ranks. She was fond of slogans, which she repeated until I knew them by heart. "Prudery is the enemy of our business" was one I was particularly fond of. But there was also "The return customer is the best customer." If you were measuring Zhang Nao against her, there was no competition. She had a certain bearing, a certain refinement. One look and you could tell. Her hair was shiny black and always combed back and tied in a single braid held fast with a white pin. She wore a black jacket and a crisp white shirt. Around her neck, she tied a red scarf. Her skirt came to her knees—not too long and not too short—and below it she wore flesh-colored stockings and black pumps. Her appearance was always flawless. I fell completely in love with her, starting with that carefully tied-back hair and perfect outfit. I made sure I was there to hear her deliver her lectures.

One day I asked Yu Baijia what her name was. He gaped: "All those beautiful girls down there, and you fall in love with the ugly one!"

"She's got class. She's the right age for me, too."

"You want to fuck her or you want to marry her?"

"What are you talking about? I want a wife. I want to start a family. I owe it to my father."

"In that case, I'll do what I can."

Around that time, I stopped sleeping again. I had two hundred thousand in the bank. But instead of a pistol on my hip, it started to feel like I was sitting on a pile of stolen bills. I couldn't wrap my head around the fact that the money was mine. I jumped at every noise. When the house creaked, I thought it must be someone kicking in the door to drag me away. My thoughts were hazy for weeks. I couldn't relax. I couldn't focus on anything. There was something hovering there, though, somewhere in the haze, but I couldn't bring myself to face it. Finally, one day, crossing the street without looking, I was hit by a van. I was fine, but I banged up my arm pretty bad. I finally asked myself: money or life?

On March 25th, I met Zhang Nao at the bank closest to the warehouse. I said: "I couldn't shake the feeling that if I didn't give you the hundred thousand, I'd end up getting killed off somehow."

She laughed: "I knew you couldn't stand it." I gave her the divorce agreement, and she signed it and put her fingerprint on it. "I don't need a hundred thousand. Give me eighty. The other twenty, call that your commission."

"This is just business to you? I'm giving you a hundred thousand. You think I care about twenty thousand? That's an insult."

She stuck her tongue out at me: "Sorry. That twenty thousand is for your dad. I owe it to him. Consider it filial piety."

I hadn't expected that kindness. My eyes teared up, but I bent my shaky hand to the agreement and signed my name. I filled out a check for eighty thousand. I wouldn't have to be scared anymore. I wouldn't jump every time the house creaked. We took a taxi to the Bureau of Civil Affairs. On the way, neither of us spoke. When we were pulling up out front, Zhang Nao leaned over and kissed me on the cheek. It wasn't the first time she'd kissed me, but that day her lips felt hot. My cheeks burned. If only I had known this side of her! I would have overlooked her mistakes. If I'd been able to get past those things, instead of the two of us sitting in the back of the taxi, we could have had a son sitting between us.

We got out of the taxi and went into the Tiema District offices. I went to the Bureau of Civil Affairs, and Zhang Nao went to the washroom. I sat and waited. After about half an hour, I knew something was wrong. The phone on the desk in front of me rang, and the man at the desk picked it up. He listened for a moment and then looked up at me: "Are you Ceng Guangxian?" I went over and took the phone.

I heard Zhang Nao's voice: "That eighty thousand is for the rape, compensation for psychological trauma. We're even now."

"Then where the hell are you? Let's do the paperwork."

"We don't need to. The marriage certificate was fake. If you don't believe me, ask at the desk. There won't be a record of our marriage."

I dropped the phone. I told the man at the desk to check his records. He looked up the date: November 20, 1980. He shook his head. I grabbed the file and looked at the list of names of people married that day. Neither of our names was on the list. I ran out of the office and jumped into the first taxi and sped toward Zhang Nao's dormitory. When I arrived, the room was empty. I asked someone passing by, and they told me that she had moved out a year earlier. I went over to the offices of the drama company and found a lock on the door. The guard in the hallway told me that the troupe had disbanded. I went to Zhang Nao's shop, but it was gone, too, replaced by a coffee shop. I fell to my knees. It was like a hallucination. I sat there, cradling my head in my hands. Night fell. The streetlights came on.

When I finally got to my feet, I promised myself that no matter when or where I met Zhang Nao again, I would cut her throat. She had wasted years of my life. She had kept me from marrying Xiaoyan. She had stolen my money. You tell me, did she deserve anything better than being cut into little pieces? I turned and slammed my fist against the trunk of a tree beside the road. I didn't feel any pain. As I walked up the road, I looked down and saw that the skin on the top of my hand had been torn off. Blood was running down my fingers. If I had run into Zhang Nao right then, I might actually have killed her.

The fire burning inside me cooled, but I still felt a pain somewhere deep within. One night I went down to the warehouse to look for Yu Baijia. I told him the story, and he patted me on the cheek: "Are you stupid or something? You think you can just send someone to get a marriage certificate for you? You have to be there. What the fuck were you thinking?" I asked myself the same question. What the fuck had I been thinking? You remember what happened that day? She told me that I couldn't go get the marriage certificate in the clothes I was wearing, and my hair was messy, whatever, but she said it'd be okay because she knew somebody at the office, so she'd go and get the stamp, nothing to worry about. I slapped myself hard enough to dislocate my jaw.

Yu Baijia said: "Look at all these girls here. I'll give you one on the house, your choice."

"The supervisor."

"All right. Go wait in there."

I was led up to room 11. I took off my clothes and waited in a recliner. A few minutes later, the supervisor entered and began to undress. She peeled off her shirt and her skirt. Her body was pale and fleshy. She lay down on the massage table, and I moved toward her. I suddenly noticed a mole on her hand. The hair stood up on my neck. I said: "What's your name?"

"Who cares? You can call me Mimi."

"Let me see your hand."

On her palm was a black mole. It was exactly the same as my sister's mole. I said: "Your name isn't Ceng Fang, is it?"

She pulled back her hand: "Are you crazy or something?"

We both put our clothes back on. She split a seam on her shirt driving her arm through the sleeve as fast as she could. I said: "I'm sorry. Can you just tell me . . . where are you from?"

"Are you taking a census or something? Why should I tell you?"

"Twenty years ago, the day my mother killed herself, my little sister was at the zoo. Nobody ever saw her again. She had a mole on her palm, just like you."

"Look again. Do you see a mole?" She held out her hand for me to examine. There was no mole.

"I'm sorry, the right hand."

"This is my right hand."

It was her right hand. But I'd seen the mole only a second ago! How could it have just disappeared?

Hey, you want to order something else? Are you sick of this story yet? No? Let me keep going.

After that, I refused to go back for a massage. I wasn't, you know, trying to be decent or anything. But something stopped me. It's hard to say what it was, exactly. I couldn't do it, though.

Hey! No, no, no, stop that. Keep your hands to yourself. I just came here to talk—nothing else.

Hands off. Hey, that's my belt. Can you just listen to the story? I'm almost there. After this, I'll make sure I take care of you. It'll be worth your time, even if we just talk.

Let me see your hand. Hey, look. Look at that mole.

What? Yeah, I guess my eyes are playing tricks on me.

I don't know what my problem is, but I can't stop seeing them, those moles. I always check a girl's hands. I know you can't be my sister, but you could be her daughter. If she had a daughter, she'd be about your age. I'm almost fifty, but I still won't do it. I'm always worried that I could be laying my hands on my own flesh and blood.

Hold on. I think that's my phone. What did you say? Don't pay you? Come on. Sympathy is one thing, but—wait a minute, I have to get this.

That was Zhao Shanhe. She said there's something wrong with my father. He's not breathing right. I have to go.

Hold on, here's the money. Thanks for listening.

‹ 34 ›

Dad, Zhao Shanhe is gone. I locked the door. We're alone. I wanted to talk to you, just the two of us. I know you don't want to talk to me. You told me you wouldn't. I still remember that day. It was thirty years ago, but you kept your word. I have something to say, though.

If I hadn't seen that mole, I might have ended up marrying the supervisor of the massage girls. I still see her sometimes. She ended up putting on a lot of weight. That's not a problem for me, really. I've always felt that fat girls were better partners. They're better mothers, at least, I think. She got over what happened in the room that day. We put that incident behind us. When I see her, she'll usually give me a nod. Sometimes we'll talk for a while. She likes to tell me about her childhood. She was a tough kid, always getting into something. After she left her job at Baijia's place, she opened up a clothing shop on Beipu Road. Whenever she gets anything in that she thinks I might like, she'll give me a call. Zhao Shanhe and I, everything we wear is from that shop. She gives us fifty percent off, too. She makes a pretty good living. For a while, I thought there was still a chance that she was my sister. I finally got her to show me her shenfenzheng, and it turns out she's four years younger than Ceng Fang. Her name is Fan Laidi. Born somewhere in Dongbei. Nowhere close to here. You'd have to fly there. So I'm pretty sure. If it hadn't been for that day in the massage room, I probably would have married her ten years ago. Just looking at her, I know that our kids would have been good-looking. Imagine if I brought a fat white grandson home to you. You'd get out of that bed, I know you would.

I wish I'd figured out that the marriage certificate was fake. Even a few days earlier, I would never have given her the money. You know, eighty thousand back then was worth about eight hundred thousand now. You could buy a big piece of land outside town with that or an apartment in the city. I would rather have donated it to charity than given it to her. From what I can tell, she'd almost forgotten about me by that time. She had already moved out of her dormitory room without telling me. She was living with a new guy. I would have eventually figured out that the marriage certificate was fake. I suppose she probably would have married the new guy. If I had met Zhang Du a bit earlier and sent him to her . . . Anyways, the money ended up in her bank account. What would I have done with it? I guess I could have built an addition on the house. I'd have made sure the milk you drink was even fancier—the most expensive milk in the world.

I ended up running into the lawyer about three years after that day at the Bureau of Civil Affairs. He turned up at the donation ceremony. He took me aside and told me that he'd broken up with Zhang Nao a while before. She had gotten together with a bureaucrat, who had bought them an apartment. They ended up having a son. But after a while, she broke up with the bureaucrat. She refused to move out of the apartment, and the bureaucrat ended up moving out. The kid's name was Chunhai: "chun" as in "spring" and "hai" as in "ocean." Zhang Nao gave the kid her last name, so it's Zhang Chunhai. I told you before, I promised myself revenge. I've been boxing, and I used to fantasize about using these hands to tear her apart. But the strange thing is, the kid looks like me. Can you imagine that? She slept with so many men, but the kid looks like me. How is that possible? I never slept with her. God's got a sense of humor, I guess. When I found out where she was living, I went over there. I still wanted revenge. But the kid answered the door. He was about four years old. He called me uncle. The kid looked just like I did when I was a kid: curly hair, high nose, long eyelashes. Dad, you should see that kid. I wouldn't be surprised if you called him by my name. He looks just like me. After I saw him, there was no way I could hurt his mother. My heart started beating faster. I bent down and scooped the kid up and hugged him for a long time.

Zhang Nao couldn't believe it, either. She said that after everything, she'd had my kid. I told her that unless it was artificial insemination, I wasn't responsible. She said she'd forgotten that we never slept together. How could she forget that! If it weren't for that, I probably would have tried to work things out with her. I'd finally be able to give you a grandson.

Dad, you heard about the warehouse, right? Yu Baijia paid his rent on time for a while, but eventually he stopped. I had to go to his office to demand it. He'd been renting it for a few years, so I was surprised. He kept telling me that he'd pay me tomorrow. But tomorrow never came. Eventually I confronted him, and he wrote me a check. I went to the bank, and they told me that Yu Baijia's account was already overdrawn. I went back to him. I treated him to dinner, looked after him for a few days, and then asked for the money again. He said to me: "Brother, I'll get the money to you right away. Give me two days." Two days, he said.

That winter, when it was time for him to pay his rent again—and he still hadn't paid me for the last time—I went to his father's house to look for him. He wasn't there. I went to the warehouse and found that the neon sign out front had been switched off. The place was abandoned. As I was waiting out front, a few PSB cars rolled up and started sealing up the doors and windows. There was a line of police tape around the warehouse. Yu Baijia was in big trouble. There was a warrant out for him. He was accused of violating decency laws, misappropriation of public funds, and tax evasion. There were posters of him all over town. They even put his picture in the newspaper. His parents went out in disguise. When they went to the park to walk in the morning, they wore surgical masks and sunglasses. They didn't want anyone to recognize them. Their son was infamous.

I took the rental contract to a lawyer to have a look. Just as I'd feared, the PSB came looking for me. Detective Huang was in charge of the case for the Public Security Bureau. He said they weren't interested in me for the misappropriation of public funds charges, but the contract seemed to suggest that my relationship with Yu Baijia wasn't merely a rental agreement but rather a profit-sharing agreement, so I was on the hook for violating decency laws and tax evasion. I read the contract closely for the first time. Unfortunately, it looked like Detective Huang was right. I should have been more careful. If I had added a line to the contract about my lack of involvement in the day-to-day running of the business or put in a clause that I was not to be held responsible for any criminal activities that Yu Baijia took part in, I would have been safe. If I had rented the warehouse to someone else, I'd still be collecting rent. We'd be taking a BMW to our villa in the mountains.

You have no idea what I went through with this rental contract. Every morning when I got up, I'd go out and couldn't help but notice the men tailing me. I'd see them posted on buildings, watching me with binoculars. I remember one time I was buying toilet paper, and the guy who had been following me all day got in the line behind me, holding the exact same package of toilet paper. They didn't want to grab me right away. I guess they thought I'd lead them to Yu Baijia. I didn't want to go near the warehouse. The police tape was still around it. I went to Zhao Shanhe, and we checked our bank account. There was a hundred thousand left. We make about a hundred yuan a month between us, so that money would have been more than we'd ever need. I decided that I was sick of having legal issues hanging over my head. I went to the Tiema District offices and told them that I wanted to donate the warehouse. They held a banquet for me at the Guijiang Hotel. There were articles in the paper about it. You probably heard them talking about it on the radio. I was even more famous than Yu Baijia. If you could open your eyes, the first thing you'd see is the plaque they gave me. I hung it on the wall. It's got a gold seal on it. The frame is hand-carved. Actually, the frame is probably worth a lot. It's pretty impressive.

Yu Baijia ended up being caught. He had gone back to the village he'd been sent to when they went down to the countryside to join a production brigade. He took responsibility for everything. He could have pulled me into it, but he didn't. The judge sentenced him to thirteen years. If I'd known he was going to be caught and take full responsibility, I would have held on to the warehouse. We could still be collecting rent. I didn't realize what I was doing when I sold the warehouse. After buying this house from the factory, there wasn't much money left. The economy isn't what it was. That money I had in the bank didn't last very long. If I'd held on to the warehouse until now, I could sell it for about ten million.

If I had known the warehouse was going to end up going back to the government, I never would have told you about it in the first place. You'd still be up and walking. You know how long you've been lying there? Thirteen years. I could have kept the news to myself. You could have married Zhao Shanhe. I could have paid for your honeymoon. I can picture it, the two of you going for a walk in the afternoon, coming back to cook together, arguing over stupid things. Zhao Shanhe wouldn't have to suffer, either. She wouldn't have to work her fingers to the bone. She wouldn't have all those white hairs. She'd be looking after a kid instead. She could forget about Lao Dong. She could walk down the street, leading her son by his hand, hold her head high for once. I could have stopped you and Zhao Shanhe from meeting in the loft. I knew it was wrong, but I didn't stop you. I could have handled the business with the warehouse and then given you the wedding banquet you deserved.

If I hadn't gone to Xiaoyan's dormitory that day and seen Hu Kaihui playing the accordion, Xiaoyan wouldn't have asked me about Zhang Nao, and I wouldn't have gotten drunk and slept on her floor and left that note. After Zhao Shanhe decorated my bedroom at the new house and I started thinking about bringing a wife back there, I shouldn't have run to Zhang Nao and written that agreement. I should never have given her the chance to humiliate me again.

You know what she said to me? She said I had no class. She said she needed to move up in the world. We were the people who were attacked for having class. Did she realize that? We were the ones who were attacked because of our class. She wanted to imitate us! You can't imagine what the world looks like now. The things everyone is imitating are exactly what we were attacked for. It's a poor copy, though. They buy expensive clothes with the wrong label, the baijiu is counterfeit, their diplomas are fake . . . They want to live a cosmopolitan lifestyle and hold themselves apart from the crowd.

To tell you the truth, that kid could have been mine. I mean Zhang Nao's kid. I could have had a kid with her. I had so many chances—in the hotel, in her room—but I never seized the opportunity. We wouldn't have had a son, actually. I'm sure it would have been a girl. Why a girl? I read somewhere that when a man and woman are really passionate, it's more likely they'll have a girl. I was passionate then. I had just gotten back from Beishan. I'd been waiting years for that moment. We would have had a beautiful daughter. She would have been an actor or a singer. Zhang Nao and I could have sat home. We wouldn't have had to work for a living.

I remember one night when she was waiting for me in bed, I turned out the light and slept on the floor instead. I could have gotten into bed and really given it to her. You know what I mean? I could have made her forget about Yu Baijia. He's not half the man I am. She'd have given him up. If I'd slept with her once, I know she would have stuck with me. When I went away on business, she would have come along with me. She would have worried about losing me to somebody else. She wouldn't have ended up with Zhang Du.

Zhang Du was the lawyer I hired to handle my divorce from Zhang Nao. I knew he was a good lawyer. He had a way with words. He charged a lot. But he met his match in Zhang Nao. He met her twice and ended up giving her the idea of using my pubic hair and the stained dress. I was so fucking stupid. I didn't even need a lawyer. If I'd just gone to the Bureau of Civil Affairs myself, I would have found out that there was no record of our marriage. I could have gotten rid of Zhang Nao and gotten somebody better. I'm serious. It would have been easy. I could have put an ad in the paper, said that I had property worth two million yuan. I know I could have found a woman younger, more beautiful, nicer. I know there must have been a better woman waiting for me.

I could have just forced her to sign the agreement. I was a strong man back then. I was boxing. I had worked in the foundry. I could have grabbed her and jammed her hand down on the paper. I could have forced her to sign it. I could have gotten her drunk. I could have begged her. I could have gotten down on my hands and knees and cried. I didn't even try. Why didn't I even try? I could have rushed to Lu Xiaoyan and married her. She told me she'd wait a month. But she gave me more time. It was years before she married Hu Kaihui.

I could have gone to Xiaoyan and lied to her. I could have told her that I never married Zhang Nao. I could have said I was tricked. I know she would have forgiven me. We could have gotten back together. I could have lived with her. There's nothing Zhang Nao could have done. The marriage certificate was fake, after all. After Xiaoyan married Hu Kaihui and had the kid, I know she brought him here. When he called you Grandpa, it was like a knife in my heart. Zhao Shanhe described the way that Xiaoyan looked at Hu Kaihui. She could have been looking at me that way. Hu Kaihui ended up as the vice-director of the zoo. He rose in the ranks to the People's Congress. Now, even if the Public Security Bureau wanted to, they couldn't arrest him. That could have been me! I could be where he is.

After Yu Baijia went to prison, Xiao Chi started coming around. She'd wait for me at the factory gate. If she caught me, she'd walk beside me, asking when I was going to marry her. I started hiding out in the bathroom until she left. I should have told her the truth. Even on the rooftop, I should have told her the truth. All I can do now is bring her a bag of fruit every now and then. If I hadn't lied to her, she probably would have become China's Picasso or Van Gogh. I didn't even know who Picasso was a few years ago, but his paintings are worth millions. Xiao Chi could have sold her paintings, and Yu Baijia wouldn't have had to embezzle money or not pay his taxes.

I realize now that society runs on lies. If I told the truth to everyone, there's no way I could get through a single day. I should have just told her: Baijia loves you, and there's no way there's anything between him and Zhang Nao.

If I'd gone to the countryside with her, things would have been different. But I made so many mistakes in those years. I told Zhao Wannian about you and Zhao Shanhe. I spat in my mother's face. When Xiao Chi came to me in the warehouse, I called her a pervert and told her she was sick. I thought I was the only clean one. I thought everyone around me was filthy. A person like that finds it hard to fall in love. I would never have climbed into that haystack with Xiao Chi like Baijia did. If I hadn't cared about being clean, I could have saved Xiao Chi from what she became, a desolate wretch being fed pills in a hospital. If I had accepted her that day in the warehouse, if I had taken her in my arms, I could have saved her. I know I would have treated her right. We would have had a son. We'd be married, and she would go to her studio every day and do her work. I'd stay at home, look after the kid, clean the house, do the laundry. There's no way things would have worked out like they did.

‹ 35 ›

I thought about Xiao Chi a lot. If I hadn't brought Yu Baijia to Zhang Nao's apartment, he never would have known about her. He would have stayed with Xiao Chi. He would have been committed to his wife. Humans are easily tempted. As soon as they see something they want, they'll give up everything to get it. If I hadn't gone to get those stupid things for Zhang Nao's dormitory room, Yu Baijia wouldn't have had the chance to sneak into the room. I ended up pushing him into her arms. I wrecked Xiao Chi's life. If I'd been a bit more careful, I wouldn't have introduced Yu Baijia to Zhang Nao again until after she was already pregnant. There was no shortage of other women for him to go after, right? Even if he'd been out with a different woman every night, I wouldn't have said a word to Xiao Chi. The only problem I had with him was that he slept with my wife. If it had been another woman, I wouldn't have minded at all. I would even have covered for him.

That night when Yu Baijia told me about tofu, I should have run out. I wouldn't have told him I was a virgin. He wouldn't have cooked up that plan for me to meet Zhang Nao. He wouldn't have told me to rape her. If I hadn't brought him to her dormitory room, he wouldn't have told me about her window. I wouldn't have shut my eyes and slid open the window. I wouldn't have sneaked into her dormitory room. Zhang Nao would have slept soundly through the night. If she had slept through the night, I wouldn't have been arrested. I wouldn't have spent a decade locked up at Beishan. If I had cooperated with the PSB, I wouldn't have spent those extra two years in prison. If I hadn't bought that dress for Zhang Nao, the judge couldn't have brought it up at my trial. She tore the dress and let the judges use it to convict me.

If I hadn't been so vain, I would have gone to the Bureau of Civil Affairs with her. Why did I care how my hair looked? Why did I care about my shoes? There's no law against getting a marriage certificate with messy hair. How can a piece of paper tie two people together like that, anyways? Look at Zhao Shanhe. She's here for you every day, dumping your bedpan, massaging you, making sure you get turned. She crawls into bed and holds you and falls asleep beside you. You don't have a piece of paper, but who would say you're not man and wife?

I should never have gotten that letter of employment from Zhang Nao. I was only trying to make you happy. If I hadn't lied to you, Xiaoyan wouldn't have gone to Zhang Nao's shop to ask after me. If she hadn't gone to the shop to ask after me, Zhang Nao wouldn't have taken me to the hotel. If Xiaoyan had arrived before Zhang Nao, things would have turned out differently. It all came down to speed. If I had sold the warehouse, I could have bought a sports car. You know, if you go out now, everyone is driving. It wasn't like that before. Nobody owned a car. You know why everyone wants to drive? It's the same thing: speed. They want to get where they're going as fast as possible because they're worried somebody else will get there faster. I worry that the fake letter of employment gave Zhang Nao the idea to get a fake marriage certificate. If I hadn't given her the idea, she might never have come up with it on her own. I was the victim of my own vanity again.

If I hadn't lost the letter of redress, I wouldn't have gone to her to help me get another one. Zhang Nao couldn't have told me what happened after the rape. I wouldn't have heard about how she was called a slut and how people wrote those things on her door. I wouldn't have apologized to her. If I hadn't heard all that, that seed of sympathy wouldn't have been planted.

That night when I went to ask Zhang Nao why she loved me, I had hardened my heart. I wanted to spend the rest of my life with Xiaoyan. I gave her the chance to seduce me. She put her leg on my shoulder, and I grabbed her. When we were rolling around on the floor, I forgot what Xiao Chi had said about finding a wife who would be more worried about me than I was. If I had listened to what everyone told me, I would have married Xiaoyan. If I had married Xiaoyan, my bed wouldn't be empty. I have nobody to talk to. If I'd married Xiaoyan, I wouldn't be at a sauna telling my life story to some massage girl. You know, it isn't cheap. I wouldn't have to pay seventy yuan an hour to find somebody to talk to.

If I hadn't sold out Li Dapao, I wouldn't have lent him five thousand yuan. He was getting married to Luo Xiaoyun, so I agreed. When he first came to me, I could tell that he knew I was getting rich. When I asked how much he needed, he held up a finger, and I thought he meant one thousand. But it turned out that he was asking for ten thousand. I didn't agree, but I told him I'd take care of him. I tossed and turned all night and finally went to the bank. I told myself that it was my fault that he had spent an extra three years in prison.

He took the money and turned his back, like I owed him or something. I should have expected it. You know, I got Xiaoyan to go to the countryside to talk to Luo Xiaoyun. He not only never thanked me, he dumped a bucket of piss on my burned leg and a bucket of shit on my head. I feel like my whole life, I've been digging a pit. I've been digging my own grave. What have I done with my life? I . . .

It's like when I was at Beishan. Xiaoyan told me not to, but I still tried to escape. Even when I was down in that sewer and I ran into an iron grate, I wouldn't turn back. I never knew when to turn back and save myself. I never learned. If I hadn't sat around with the prisoners, telling them those filthy stories, I wouldn't have had all those thoughts . . . If I hadn't tried to escape, I wouldn't have gotten the extra years on my sentence. I wouldn't have ratted on Li Dapao. I wouldn't have written to Zhang Nao. I could have gotten out and married Xiaoyan. If I had never run into Zhang Nao, maybe something would have happened, but nothing as bad as her trying to take half the warehouse.

If I hadn't told Zhao Jingdong about the struggle session, he wouldn't have killed himself. I wouldn't have been run off to the warehouse loft. If I hadn't moved to the loft, I wouldn't have seen Zhang Nao on the stage. I would have stayed at the zoo and found a wife. It might have been Xiaoyan. If I hadn't borrowed the binoculars from Hu Kaihui, I wouldn't have become obsessed with Zhang Nao. I sometimes wonder if Hu Kaihui knew what he was doing. Maybe he thought I would steal Xiaoyan from him, so he wanted to throw me off her trail. He pointed me toward the most dangerous woman in the world.

If I hadn't gone to the countryside to visit Xiao Chi, I wouldn't have given that dog to Zhao Jingdong to look after. If I hadn't given the dog to Zhao Jingdong, he would never have done those things with it. I ended up hurting a good friend. Mom used to tell me that the friends you have say a lot about you. I think you used to say it, too. More advice I never listened to.

If I hadn't spat in Mom's face, she wouldn't have gone to feed herself to the tiger, and Ceng Fang wouldn't have disappeared. If I hadn't climbed up to catch that sparrow, I wouldn't have seen you and Zhao Shanhe. If I hadn't told Zhao Wannian about what I saw, you wouldn't have been dragged away to those struggle sessions, and we wouldn't have been kicked out of the warehouse. If I had never spoken again after my mother took me to the old woman who sealed my mouth, my life would have been smooth and I wouldn't be alone. If I had seen those dogs out in front of the warehouse and shooed them away, you wouldn't be in a coma. You wouldn't have gone to Uncle Fang's and asked to sleep with his wife. You wouldn't have gone to Zhao Shanhe. If I hadn't brought that stick to Zhao Wannian, he wouldn't have chased the dogs into the street. If he hadn't chased the dogs into the street, they wouldn't have been hit by the bus. If the dogs hadn't been hit by the bus, none of this would have happened.

I've told you everything, I think. You know what I regret the most? I've never told anyone before. But I know you won't laugh. You know what it is? I'm still a virgin. That day when Xiao Chi dropped her skirt, I called her a pervert. When I broke into Zhang Nao's dormitory room, she screamed before I did anything. Xiaoyan tried to take my belt off that day, and I stopped her. I had the chance again with Zhang Nao, but I wanted to get a marriage certificate and fix up the room. After I found out that Yu Baijia had slept with her, I couldn't do it. After that, when it came time to do it, I felt like there was a wall in front of me.

I don't know why I told you all this. You can't even hear me. Maybe I just wanted to say it, even if nobody can hear me. Are—are you crying? Dad? No, after thirteen years, it couldn't be. Can you hear me?

Are you awake? Are you really awake?

I want to tell you, I never did anything with Zhao Shanhe. She came into my room a few times. I never laid a finger on her.

Still, I can't look you in the eyes.

Zhao Shanhe! Come quick! Dad's awake.